Though An Army Come Against Us

Rick Levine

For My Children and Grandchildren
by blood and by choice:
You know who you are

Though an army should encamp against me
My heart shall not fear.

Tehillim 27:3

One

The spy awoke with a start as the train slowed just outside Vinita. He felt a momentary impulse to check for his badge and gun – could someone have taken them while he was napping? – but restrained himself. Somebody might see him. Who knew who his fellow passengers were? This trip would be wasted if he revealed his identity before even arriving.

In the heat and the dust of Oklahoma in late May, Special Agent James Amos had fallen asleep on the hardwood train seat: body twisted, mouth wide open. He turned his head from side to side to get the crick out of his neck and swallowed a few times to moisten his dry throat.

The front half of this Jim Crow "combination" rail car was filled with shipping crates, trunks, and suitcases. Here in the back half, every Negro on the entire train was packed into the bench seats along with him. While they were boarding in St. Louis, Amos glanced through the windows of the coach car behind them, where all the whites and Indians were sitting in padded comfort. He wondered, *Why did Indians get to ride with white people out here?*

Outside the train the oak trees and limestone cuts of the Ozarks had given way to the grass and flat prairie of eastern Oklahoma. He saw miles and miles of recently tilled fields, delicate green sprouts already visible, but still difficult to identify as cotton plants. The oil rigs, though, were unmistakable. There were hundreds of them, as far as he could see. There were more millionaires here than on Wall Street! Or so they said. 27¢ cotton and $2-a-barrel oil? Either way it was a bonanza and this was surely the Promised Land.

Three days earlier, Special Agent Amos, the sole full-time Negro employee at the Bureau of Investigation, had been polishing Director Hoover's shoes at Hoover's mother's home on Seward Square. Other agents of the Bureau – white agents – mowed the lawn, washed the windows and painted the fence, but John Hoover often said, "You, James, are the only one I trust with my wardrobe." Amos knew that the Director's trust extended far beyond shoes, suits and ties. Amos, like Hoover, came from a long-time Washington, D.C. family and Amos knew that John Hoover had "a little something in him." Hoover knew that Amos knew and was confident that he would keep it quiet. And that was not young John Hoover's only secret.

That day Hoover, wearing a bathrobe and slippers, walked quietly into the dressing room where Special Agent Amos was applying a final buffing to a pair of wing-tip oxfords. "Excellent work, as always, James," complimented the Director.

"Thank you, Mr. Hoover."

"As soon as you are finished I have a job for you in Oklahoma."

"The lynching?"

"No," frowned Hoover. "You won't be able to help investigate there. That ignorant class of Negroes in the country towns will only speak to white agents."

Amos kept his mouth shut and his expression flat. John Hoover was a brilliant man; his appointment to head the Bureau of Investigation at such a young age was proof. But he had a habit of strongly expressing some very stupid ideas, and this was among the stupidest. Did he even believe it himself? It really didn't matter, because the Director had no interest in making arrests or preparing prosecutions in lynchings anyway. The all-white teams of agents never asked, "Did you see any members of the lynch mob? Did you recognize any of them?" Their only question was always the same: "Which Negroes fired guns?" So the Director's actual assignment for Special Agent James Amos came as no surprise to him.

"We have reports from Tulsa that militants styling themselves an African Blood Brotherhood are arming themselves to launch attacks on white people. We want you to go in and find them. And remember, no arrests until we find the actual troublemakers. It might be Jamaicans from New York City, but we suspect white radicals. Look for evidence of anarchists or IWWs. We don't think it's likely that these country Negroes came up with this idea on their own. And by all means, look for explosive devices."

Anarchists. IWWs. The Justice Department, the Bureau of Investigation, Director Hoover… none of them could imagine Negroes organizing themselves. That had been the problem with Special Agent Amos's reports from New York on Marcus Garvey. He spied on Garvey and his associates for months, pretending to be a militant himself and worming his way into the upper ranks of the organization. He filed pages and pages of reports – both stolen internal documents and records of his own surveillance – but the Bureau wasn't satisfied because the only Reds who Amos discovered were Hubert Harrison and Cyril Briggs... and they were Negroes, too, not the white agitators that John Hoover was looking for.

And why did it have to be launching attacks on white people? Since the end of the World War, white attacks on colored people had grown in size and frequency. In the summer of 1919, thousands of white people invaded Chicago's South Side, burning homes and businesses, beating the colored people they caught, and killing twenty-five. That fall, white mobs rampaged through the Arkansas Delta and murdered over two hundred colored people. Then they held jury trials for another hundred and sentenced many of them to hang, apparently for the crime of surviving the initial pogrom. In central Florida, a white mob burned out an entire Black community. That crowd killed over fifty people, and mutilated their bodies, too. Could it be that this "Blood Brotherhood" was arming in self-defense?

James Amos shared none of these thoughts with the Director. He showed no sign of them on his face, either. If Hoover directed him to shine shoes, he would shine shoes. If Hoover directed him to look for white radicals, he would. He was an agent. In all his years working for Theodore Roosevelt, Amos kept his opinions to himself, and did what he was asked: carrying confidential messages abroad, being a personal bodyguard, entertaining the President's children, sitting by Roosevelt's bedside as he took his last breath. He served because he trusted Roosevelt the man. John Hoover was not Mr. Roosevelt. He did not have Teddy's common touch, his spontaneity, or his instinct for fun. But John Hoover was devoted to his work and Amos respected that. So when he received these new instructions he didn't question them. He only asked, "Files at the office?"

Now the train was rolling into Tulsa. Agent Amos took his satchel from the overhead rack and walked through the small depot of the Frisco Railroad – white waiting room on one side, colored on the other – and out to the street. A line of hacks waited for the passengers. Many were transferring to the Katy or the Atchison, Topeka and Santa Fe. In this city, each railroad had its own station.

He spotted a Negro cabbie and said, "Greenwood. Stradford Hotel." It was the only colored lodging he knew by name. Six blocks later they stopped in front of a surprisingly grand three-story brick building with a second-story portico over the colonnade in front of the entrance. A block away was an equally impressive edifice labeled Red Wing Hotel with elaborate carved stonework over the large, ground floor display windows. Across the street, the Carter House, with New Orleans-style wrought-iron grillwork. Every person on this busy street – every one! – was a well-dressed colored man or woman. Amos had heard Booker T. Washington refer to Tulsa as the Black Wall Street; now he reflected that this might even be an understatement.

A liveried bellman reached for his satchel, but with practiced grace Amos pretended not to see the man and, keeping a firm grip on his bag, went to the main desk to register.

"Name, please?" asked the desk clerk.

"Henry Washington," answered Amos.

"And how long will you be with us, Mr. Washington?"

It was an indefinite stay. As long as it took to get the job done. As soon as he figured out an approach to the people here he would probably have to switch to a less conspicuous place, probably a boarding house. "Two nights. Can I store some things in your safe?"

"Of course, sir. And may I have the bellman show you to your room, Mr. Washington?"

"Safe first," said Special Agent Amos.

The desk clerk signaled for the concierge who took Amos downstairs and handed him a lock box. Amos waited until he was alone, then opened his bag and transferred his federal government identification card, ten $10 bills and an M1911 Colt automatic into the box, along with two boxes of ammunition. He took the Bureau of Investigation badge from his vest pocket and put that in, too. The snub-nosed .32 revolver on his belt remained where it was. That was a personal gift from Mr. Roosevelt. It was also concealable and easy to handle. Agent Amos took no extra rounds. If the five in the chambers weren't sufficient, he was probably dead anyway. Then he called the concierge back.

"Could you please have my bag dropped in my room and leave the key at the desk?"

"Certainly, sir. Will there be anything else?"

"No, thank you." Amos wanted a shave. He also wanted to visit a barbershop immediately to begin gathering intelligence. But he did not necessarily want to go to any shop that this high-end hotel would recommend. Nor did he want this concierge knowing his business. Over the years Special Agent Amos had found hotel employees to be a rich source of intelligence. He had paid dozens of them for information during his investigations. That's why he trusted none of them with his own comings and goings.

Back outside on Greenwood Avenue, Amos marveled again at the prosperity of colored Tulsa. Givens Hotel. Buster's Waffle House. B.C. Franklin, Attorney at Law. O.W. Gurley, Real Estate. Freedom Bank. D.W. Hutchens, Attorney at Law. Hughes Dry Goods. P.A.Chappelle, Attorney at Law. The bonanza in oil and cotton must be benefiting Negroes, too. And, he thought, they must enjoy suing each other a lot.

March 24, 1908
101 Ranch, Oklahoma

Mitákuye!

I do not know whether you know my name or reputation, but yours are known up and down the reservations of North and South Dakota. Even if they haven't read your books and articles, even if they don't speak English, all Lakota people know of our Dakota sister, Zitkala-Ša. I read about your conflicts with the administration at Carlisle School. The principal, Colonel Pratt, is like a second father to me, but I share your doubts about his insistence that we have to "wash the Indian" out of us. He has now officially warned every one of us graduates that you are an enemy. He says that we are not to speak or correspond with you, but, in truth, I don't know who else to confide my concerns in. I am far from home now, and in any case, most of my family does not have the same experience I do, trying to live in two worlds at once. You are a teacher. You taught at Standing Rock with my *Húŋkpapha* cousins. You know what it means to make our language and religion illegal.

My name is Luther Standing Bear. I am *Sičháŋǧu* Lakota, son of Standing Bear and Pretty Face. I was a boy when Custer's bluecoats fell into our camp at *Pȟežísla Wakpá*. I was a man when they butchered our people in the snow at *Čhaŋkpé Ópi Wakpála*. I attended Carlisle Indian School in Pennsylvania because my father said we could never survive without learning to communicate with the *wašíču*. I found, though, that I could no longer live at home – even as the owner of my own business – under the control of Indian Agents who treated me as a child.

That is my reason for this letter to you. I pray you can understand the questions I am wrestling with and that you can share with me your own thoughts on these matters.

When I first graduated from Carlisle Indian School I worked as an assistant teacher on the Rosebud reservation, where much of my family lives. I was a new and inexperienced teacher so I followed the same monkey-see-monkey-do approach they used with me when I was in school. Like me, my students would repeat all these words and phrases in English, but their actual meanings were obscure, and often referred to a world the children didn't even know. You know all those memorized dialogues about ordering a meal in a restaurant and asking directions to the opera? I see this clearly now, and I don't know whether to laugh or cry, but I didn't understand any of it back then.

Back then I truly believed that once we mastered the white people's learning we would be welcome to enter into their world. I thought I had personal evidence of this: when I was a student at Carlisle I worked summers at Wanamaker's Department Store in Philadelphia. Every summer my hard work earned me a promotion. Returning home to Rosebud, I immediately got what seemed to be a great job as a teaching assistant. I thought opportunities were opening to me. I believed that I could provide even better opportunities for my pupils.

Then the agent at the Pine Ridge Reservation asked me to transfer from Rosebud to the Allen school near *Wagmíza Wakpála:* as head teacher, not assistant! I thought everything was going perfectly, and I was confident that I could be a better teacher than the *wašíčus* from the moment I took over my own classroom. After all, I am Lakota, just like my students; that would be an immediate bond between us. I speak their language; I wouldn't have to waste time pantomiming to make myself understood. But it did not work out that way. Not at all. Being head teacher turned out to be more of a test than I ever imagined. I was doing no better at reaching the children than the white teachers.

At first I thought the problem was my suit and my short hair. But thinking about those things didn't help me make any progress in the classroom. And, truly, I failed to see just how accurately my white man's clothes and white man's haircut represented my inner state at the time.

Don't you find that the best moments in a teacher's day begin with digressions and misunderstandings? That's how it happened with me, anyway. One day I was reciting a dialogue in English – with appropriate gestures, of course – about doffing one's cap when being introduced to a stranger. One of the big boys, a kind of class clown, always pretended to mishear and misunderstand what I said. I still remember his name, Isaac Iron Cloud, and in my mind I can see his laughing face. It occurs to me now that his ability to joke may have shown that he understood the words better than any of his more cooperative classmates! They were all, as I said, simply repeating everything I said, like a flock of parrots.

Anyway, there I was, bowing from the waist and taking off my imaginary cap. Suddenly Isaac asked, in *Lakȟótiyapi,* "Why do you have a beaver on your head?" He was punning on the Lakota word for "beaver", which, as you know, sounds a little like "cap."

I'm sure that Corn Creek, like all those creeks in South Dakota, used to have lots of beavers. But by the time I was a teacher they were pretty much trapped out for their furs. So I asked, in *Lakȟótiyapi,* "How many of you here have ever seen

7

a beaver?" A couple of the boys surprised me by raising their hands. And that made me wonder to myself, *What do I really know about any of these children other than what I observe in the classroom?* Then, just when I thought we were as far away from the lesson plan as possible, a quiet girl, Esther Big Owl, took us even farther. She said, also in *Lakȟótiyapi*, "I know the story of how *Iktómi* captured Beaver."

I had a moment of clarity. Why were we performing dialogues about taking off caps, and serving tea with biscuits, and asking for directions to the nearest train station? I said, "Esther, tell us that story." Most of the class already knew how *Iktómi*, the spider, tricked the beaver into thinking there was something dangerous in the water, and how he clubbed Beaver when he got near the shore. They had heard it from their own grandparents. But they all listened with great attention to Esther's account.

Then I told them, "Open your notebooks. Everybody write the story of *Čhápa* and *Iktómi* in English." Jaws dropped. Loud protests erupted. This was unheard of. English was for school and the agent's office. *Lakȟótiyapi* was for home and for the fields. Were there even words in English to tell this story? But I insisted, "In your notebooks!" So they picked up their pencils and began – laboriously, and with a lot of hushed conversation – to struggle through this task. I had *never* seen them so engaged. I had never seen them learning so much.

Next day, as soon as class began, Amos Yellow Thunder raised his hand and asked if he could tell the story about why we hunt the buffalo instead of the buffalo hunting us. Now remember, like the beaver, the buffalo herds were long gone by then. Nobody was actually hunting buffalo. But Amos knew the story of the Great Race between the two-leggeds and the four-leggeds that was run on *Khíiŋyaŋka Očháŋku* and how Magpie beat Buffalo. Again I asked them all to write the story in their notebooks in English. Again they all set to work with great intensity. This time I asked who would read their English version aloud. Amos did, haltingly, to both laughter and applause from his classmates.

Isaac Iron Cloud, the class clown, raised his hand and I groaned inwardly. What now? But he wasn't making jokes. He said, "The Great Race is a good story. But I heard that the reason *ptéhčaka* give us their meat is because of a cow buffalo who married a man."

I had him save that *very* strange story for the next day. We still had to fit in our required lessons, especially arithmetic. And I had Isaac tell that story to the class in English too, but, again, only after everybody had written it out in English.

8

I did not yet understand why this was going so well. I only knew that I felt like a much better teacher when all my students were working so hard. I remembered an experience from my student years. It seemed to be related, although at the time I wasn't sure why. One day an astronomer came to visit us at Carlisle. During an assembly he informed the entire student body that there would be an eclipse of the moon the very next week. In the auditorium, under the eyes of our teachers, we all listened to this preposterous statement in respectful silence. Later, back in the dorms, we mocked him mercilessly.

All the boys knew stories of *haŋwí*, the light of the night, crossing *áŋpawí*, the light of the day, and causing darkness in the daytime. In fact, there had been a solar eclipse the summer after I was born; by our calendar *waníyetu áŋpawí waŋ t'e,* the year the sun died. So it was clear to us that such a thing as an eclipse was possible. But we were very certain that no *wašíču* could predict such a thing. Or we *were* certain... until the eclipse came on exactly the day he said it would! I remember that eclipse because that was the day when I decided that I had to take my school learning seriously. That day I saw that there was an actual connection between things the teachers said in school and the real world. And by "real world" I mean the real world of earth and sky, not just railroads and cities and things made by the *wašíčus.*

In my classroom at the Allen School I moved on from the stories to talking about the weather and about the plants and about the night sky. In *Lakȟótiyapi,* as you know, these aren't separate things. The constellation *tȟayámni pȟá* is the origin of humanity as well as a group of stars. The big storms of spring and summer are incomprehensible to us without knowing about the *wakíŋyaŋ,* the thunder spirits. What worked so well was showing the children that the things they knew – things their grandparents taught them! – were important enough to discuss in the classroom. And, vice versa, that the classroom was a place where important things could be discussed! We learned that the real world could be discussed in English. We moved back and forth between *Lakȟótiyapi* and English, showing that they didn't have to abandon one world in order to enter the other.

This was a learning experience for me, too. After all my years in school, it turned out there were lots of English words I didn't know. For example, in *Lakȟótiyapi* I could easily tell the difference between the great *pȟeháŋǧila* and the tiny *tȟanáǧila*. I could even distinguish between the *hokȟátȟo* and the very similar-looking *pȟeháŋ ská*. In English, though, they were all just birds to me. I realized that I didn't know one grass from another in English, either. But in *Lakȟótiyapi* every one of us knew dozens of grasses: *hupȟéstola, pȟeží šašá ókhihe tȟaŋkíŋkiŋyaŋ, siphȧwičhakaše, wápaha kamnímnila pheží, pheží wakȟáŋ...* and on and on.

It was just about that time that your friend Mrs. Elaine Eastman came to visit us at the school. She was then the superintendent for all Indian schools in both North and South Dakota. Mrs. Eastman quizzed the students aloud on their English and was amazed at our progress. She said the children in our little school were learning so much faster than any others that she wanted to know the secret of our progress! I kept it a secret, though, because I was pretty sure that she and her superiors in Washington would not be happy if they knew what I was doing. Shortly after that visit I received a formal letter of commendation, citing me as one of the finest teachers in the Lakota schools. I was so proud.

Not for long! Just a few days later I got the results of the new civil service examination for teachers. I had *failed*, along with every Indian teacher in the reservation schools! And then I received another letter from Mrs. Eastman, a letter *firing* me, even though the ink was barely dry on her letter commending me for doing better than all the *wašíču* teachers.

Every Indian teacher in the reservation schools was fired. We were all replaced by *wašíčus* who passed the test, *wašíčus* who had book knowledge but knew nothing of the lives of our students. Speaking honestly, most of them knew nothing even of the *wašíču* world outside of books. The man who replaced me broke his leg by putting it between the spokes of his wagon's wheel. He thought that was a good way to keep it from picking up too much speed driving down a hill!

All these years have passed since then, but I am still hurt about being fired from that job. Part of it is personal. What does it mean to praise my work and then fire me? I knew I was doing a wonderful job teaching, I had the letter from Mrs. Eastman to prove it, but that test made me feel that I wasn't good enough. It made me doubt myself and wonder if my replacement – a man who didn't even know how to drive a wagon without hurting himself – wasn't better than me: he had, after all, passed the test. If he was stupid and still passed, then what was I?

But I also wondered. Did they really *want* us to learn to succeed in their world? If they did, why were they firing people like me? Was it actually possible to remain Lakota in English? My pupils and I worked so hard to express ourselves about the things that mattered, but where were the words? Who would we all become if we gave up our language and stories – these things that made us Lakota – but weren't even allowed employment on our own reservations?

I do not write now to ask you for a job. I gave up teaching when I was let go from the Allen School. Now I am an actor. I dance and attack wagon trains for white audiences at the Miller Brothers 101 Wild West Show. Every day, come show time, I take off my suit and tie and shoes to put on beaded leggings, moccasins, and a feathered warbonnet. It's a show business costume, but at least I am not pretending to be a white man. And I get to sing our songs and do our dances, all of which are illegal back on the reservation! This is the irony of my daily life, playing some version of myself for a crowd of cheering *wašíčus*.

I know you must have thought about these questions, too. That is why I write: to ask about my very survival as a Lakota. How do we go about being Indian in this new world? How do we stand on this earth without surrendering our selves? I would dearly love to hear what you are thinking about all this. Please write me.

Yours truly,
Luther Standing Bear

Johns Island, South Carolina
1916

September 17

At the Avery Normal Institute in Charleston we were taught that every teacher worth her salt keeps a professional journal, so this is mine, the teaching journal of Septima Poinsette. Though I have yet to lay eyes on Promise Land School or even any of my students I will begin writing in it this evening. Today was such an adventure and I fear forgetting the details in the rush of the next few days if I do not commit them to paper immediately.

Promise Land School is right in Charleston County, but it feels like another century or perhaps another continent. The trip here to Johns Island made that very clear. Last week I happened to meet Miss Mamie Garvin, who taught elsewhere on the island a few years ago. She advised that Charlotte and I not make our initial trip by train because all of the luggage we are bringing would necessitate the hire of a wagon from the whistle stop to the ferry and then yet another wagon from the ferry to our lodgings. We need clothes, bedding and school supplies sufficient to last us until Christmas. That is the first time we will be able to return to visit our families. Consequently, we purchased passage from Charleston on a motor launch with a Mr. Leo Ward, and then waited until midafternoon to leave, presumably to accommodate the tides in Bohicket Creek, which he said separates Johns Island from Wadmalaw Island.

We left from Bennet's Wharf on the Ashley River and had a fine time in what Mr. Ward said was Wappoo Creek until the gasoline engine died in the Stono River. I thought that Charlotte would die! I had to keep from laughing as I knew what Mama would think about me spending the entire night in the company of the rough men who were our travel companions. We floated helplessly on the tide until morning when a boatman named Mr. Jerry Blake, sent out by the church elders to look for the missing teachers, finally discovered us. He took Charlotte and I in his little flat-bottomed boat and promised to get word about the engine failure back to Mr. Ward's father, Mr. Scipio Ward, who was the owner of the ferry business. After all our concern about luggage, we had to leave our trunks on the motor launch as they would not fit in Mr. Blake's rowboat! It took many hours of rowing the tidal creeks (poling in the shallower spots.) Fortunately the day was not too warm as we spent much of that time in direct sunlight with only our umbrellas to shade us.

Mr. Blake finally landed us at a sandy spot on Bohicket Creek, opposite Wadmalaw Island, near where we were meant to have arrived. We held our skirts clear of the mud as we climbed out of the bateau and walked though the salt grass to higher and drier ground. It took a moment for our eyes to adjust from the bright sunshine of the marsh to the deep shade cast by the giant live oaks and the Spanish moss hanging from their strangely twisted limbs. Then a new drama ensued. Mrs. Blake rushed up to us and demanded to know what her husband was doing with two young women! It was not easy to convince her that we were the new teachers for Promise Land School. She did not seem much interested in what we had to say, threatening us with bodily harm and calling us names that I will not repeat here. Charlotte missed much of the meanings, since she is unfamiliar with the dialect of these islands, so close to Charleston, yet so different from her upper class home. She could not fail to miss the intent, though, given the ferocity of Mrs. Blake's expression and gesture! I am more familiar with the people's patois, since Mother always sent me to do her shopping from the fishermen and vegetable farmers who bring their goods from the islands to sell in the city. Charlotte's family employs servants to do their marketing so she never had even those short encounters with country folk.

Mrs. Blake finally calmed down when she realized that Charlotte and I were not there to seduce and run off with her husband. She and Mr. Blake then brought us to the home of our hosts, Mr. Myers Bishop and his wife Mrs. Melvina Bishop. Mr. Bishop has his own farm and a little store. Presumably his house is the nicest in the vicinity, but – oh! – Mama would never approve. I must say that Charlotte looked rather chagrined, too, when she saw the peeling paint, the sunlight peeking between the boards and the parsnips in the garden where we city folk would have planted flowers. Also, she and I have to share a bed in the attic. The roof looks tight to me, though, and if our luggage ever arrives, it will be quite suitable.

Because of our misadventure with the boat, we missed the day's church services, so people came calling all through the late afternoon and early evening to meet us, the new teachers. I certainly hope they don't now expect me to remember all their names!

That is enough for today.

September 18

If Charlotte found our lodgings unprepossessing, imagine how she felt when we finally laid eyes on Promise Land School this morning! It is a small, squat log hut, dark with creosote... and redolent with the distinctive, sharp smell of creosote, too. The cabin – for it is no more than that – is divided into two classrooms by a wall down the middle. There are no chalkboards, no books, no supplies of any kind. There are no desks for our pupils, the only seats being rough planks on stumps. There is a cast iron stove in each room for when the temperatures drop, but it appears that *we* shall have to chop wood for it! I have never chopped wood before and I am quite certain that Charlotte has not either. Moreover there is no chinking between the logs that make up the outside wall. Unless we put mud in there, we will have the winter winds right in our classrooms. Did I mention that the windows have no glass? I am sure I don't know where the light will come from once it gets too cold to open the shutters.

In the city of Charleston the county board maintains two classes of schools, one for the white children and one – dramatically inferior – for us. That is why Mama pulled me out of Shaw Memorial High School and paid to send me to Avery Institute. But this Promise Land School is like some third class! I should have known. In town, all the teaching positions in the colored public schools are reserved for white teachers. The simple fact that they allow Charlotte and I to work here should have told me how little regard they have for the country Negroes.

I got right to work mixing up mud to pat between the logs and make the school habitable. When Charlotte saw what I was doing she suddenly developed a case of the vapors and returned to the Bishop's house to recuperate. I hope she gets better in time to help with chopping some wood. In the meantime it is warm enough to open school tomorrow without a fire in the stove.

I spent the afternoon visiting nearby homes. Our teachers at Avery emphasized the importance of cementing good relations with the parents of our pupils and I am determined to begin immediately. I am once again grateful for all the marketing Mama sent me to do out on Henryetta Street. I can understand the people's dialect, and I can make myself understood, too! Father taught me to respect everybody. Mama was well educated as a child and she comes from a seditty family, but Father was born a slave, forced into the Confederate army as a porter, and cannot read or write. He doesn't look down on people who have less than us the way some bourgie Charleston folk do. He always looks for the best in everyone and he would never tolerate my treating these country Negroes the way Mama does.

Still, visiting the parent's homes really made me wonder. Why aren't their houses painted? Why aren't the walls papered? I suppose I shall have to withhold judgment, but I do wonder.

Our luggage finally arrived, just before dinner! We will not, after all be forced to wash our intimate apparel every day. I was quite relieved. So was Charlotte, who was convinced that we should soon see everybody on this island wearing our purloined garments!

September 19, 1916

Today was our first day of school! Charlotte took the first through fourth grades and I took the fifth through seventh. Some of these "seventh" graders look like grown folks to me! In fact, no sooner had the children settled on their benches when one very big boy (with facial hair!) asked me how old I am. When I told him I was eighteen, he stood and left the school without a word. One of the girls said, "He seventeen," and a lot of children laughed. I suppose being taught by someone his own age was a blow to his dignity, but Father always told me that learning is the most important thing one can acquire. And I noticed that some of the bigger girls didn't so much as smile. Could they be my age too?

With neither chalk nor slate I was forced to improvise. Last night I wrote out a reading exercise with a piece of charcoal directly on a wooden board. I shall have to find another approach before too long. I am thinking about dry cleaning bags, but I am quite certain that will have to wait for Christmas. There is no such thing as a dry cleaner out here in the country. Despite all the live oaks and other trees on this island, every bit of planed wood is in use for something and there is not much scrap, so I will have to wash off the board and reuse it. For some reason many of these children could not read the passage I offered them. I gave each of them a chance; no more than a few demonstrated any facility at all. And while there are forty pupils' names on the register I received from the Board, only eighteen actually arrived. I will have to visit more families tomorrow to get the word out that school is in session. Perhaps the Bishops will help me in finding where their homes are. So far as I can tell, there are no street names or house numbers.

One interesting thing that I found today is that all the children have two names. For example, none of them call George Simmons by that name. He is known to one and all as Kofi. Everybody calls Celia Chisolm "Mandy." Thomas Qualls answers to me by that name, but to everybody else as Boney. And he is not a thin boy! Florina and Elvina are twins. I cannot for the life of me find a way to tell them apart. But none of the children call either one of them by those names. Instead, everybody calls both of them Twin! These are just the ones I remember after this one day.

I asked Mrs. Bishop about this when I got back to our lodgings this evening. I thought that maybe these are nicknames, although rather queer ones. She cut a face and said that I should continue to call the children by their "government names." What a curious idea! More tomorrow. For now I have to spend some time wiping down my wooden board and putting a new reading passage on it with charcoal.

September 20, 1916

Today I taught about the rotation of the earth on its axis and its revolution around the sun. Afterward, I had the odd sensation that I was hanging in the air. I was nervous when I started teaching this, because even though I was confident in the lesson plan that I worked so hard on, I could not know what kind of reaction the pupils would have. Now, at the end of the day, I still don't know! The children sat on their benches. They were polite and considerate. They seemed to listen. Some of them even answered questions. But did they learn it? I don't know. And – I must admit, I care – did they find it interesting?

At Avery Normal I saw teachers whose lessons moved fluidly from point to point. I always wondered whether the answers that students give to the teachers' questions are anything more than payments they make for the information that will allow them to pass their examinations. Shouldn't the pupils be asking questions of their own? And why do the teachers always ask questions in a form that is certain to elicit a correct answer?

Given the absence of books, and my uncertainty about the pupils' reading ability, I introduced a unit on poetry by reciting aloud from Edwin Markham's wonderful poem about Lincoln, which was a great favorite of our teachers at Avery:

> When the Norn Mother saw the Whirlwind Hour
> Greatening and darkening as it hurried on,
> She left the Heaven of Heroes and came down
> To make a man to meet the mortal need.

I recited it twice, too, because I knew it was the pupils' first time hearing it and they had no copies of their own to read along with while I declaimed. It was only after my second recitation that I noticed the blank looks on their faces. After lengthy explication by me, and then some prodding, Florina Scott (one of the twins) finally said it was "lonesome," which is – of course – a word in the last line about the death of that president.

16

After school I visited several homes to encourage the parents to send their children to school. The places were far from prosperous, and make the Bishop's house look like a palace by comparison. Moreover, they were cooking without any fresh vegetables at all. What then is the point of growing all this produce if they are not even going to eat it? There is obviously a lot going on here that I do not yet understand.

September 21, 1916

The children call Charlotte "Miss Ivy", but they seem not to be able to pronounce my name. "Miss Poinsette" is beyond them and "Miss Septima" has been abbreviated to "Miss Seppy." I quite like it, but I cannot imagine what Mama would say. I know I should focus my attention on the classroom, but why does nobody on the island use cooking utensils? Even our hostess, Mrs. Bishop, who is well-to-do by comparison with other people, cooks in old tin cans instead of pots.

Our home visits have paid off and we now have 100 children in the school, but that has just created new problems. It is very crowded in the classrooms. And I don't know the students well enough. I am not even certain of some of their names! I don't really feel that I must do some great thing for each one, but I also don't want to harm any of them or hold them back. When I don't know some specific thing about a child it seems easy for them to fade into the crowd, especially when all fifty-five are in the room. I stand in front of the classroom, consumed with the lesson I prepared, and I lose my awareness of the distinct personalities and experiences who sit in front of me. I know that I must do better.

That is why I kept my roll in my hand today. Instead of calling on pupils who volunteered, I asked some of those who never do. The results were quite mixed. I did draw in some new participants, but others wordlessly shook their heads and did not answer. I will continue trying.

The children told me the most astonishing thing today. One of the smaller boys is named Robert Smalls, although his classmates call him Simmy. Robert is extremely quiet and reads very poorly. Gus said he needed to be more like the real Robert Smalls. My face must have betrayed my lack of familiarity with that name, because Gus asked in astonishment whether I had never heard of Congressman Robert Smalls. I confessed that I had not. The children all buzzed about this and Gus told me that Robert Smalls was a colored man from Beaufort

17

who became a captain in the U.S. Navy and then a United States Congressman. One of the twins (I still can't tell them apart) informed me that he had only died the previous year. If this is true, how did I get all the way through Miss Nuckle's School and Avery Academy without learning it? It makes me wonder what else they failed to teach me!

September 22, 1916

It seems that Charlotte and I will not have to be responsible for fuel to keep our classrooms warm after all. Mr. Andell, the school trustee here on the island, paid us a visit this afternoon and said that we should delegate this task to the bigger boys. It is their job to bring in fallen wood and cut it to an appropriate size that will fit in the iron stoves. That is a great relief to me and I imagine it to be a greater relief still to Charlotte who seems lost without her household servants.

I am more frustrated than ever about the apparent lack of learning here on the island. How is it possible that fifty years after emancipation these children and adults are no more literate than their forebears were when they were in bondage? I try to be patient, remembering that my own beloved father does not have his letters, either, but he himself was born into slavery. These are adults who were born after emancipation. Why have they not made it their business to acquire the basics of an education? There are still some truants on my register and I have made little headway in getting them to attend class. Honestly, I have not even made much progress in locating their homes. I went to one house where an elderly man threatened to work roots on me if I persist in trying to get his grandson to attend school instead of going to work. I laughed at his backwardness. As if I should be frightened by some hoodoo mumbo jumbo! But when I returned to the Bishop's house they had already heard about my meeting with this man and they warned me not to antagonize him. These are the most progressive people on this island? To what manner of ignorant place have I been assigned?

I refrained from sharing this story with Charlotte. Who knows how she would react! And we have a mission here. We are teaching in order to bring equality to our people. Even these country folks on Johns Island.

Okmulgee, Oklahoma
1905

When Tustenugge Yarholar returned to his seat in the Mvskoke tribal council's upper house, the House of Kings, Delbert McIntosh was red-faced with anger. Old Tustenugge had implied by his questions – without actually making any formal charges of corruption – that Delbert and his uncle were selling off tribal lands to white people for their private profit. The fact that the allegation was largely true only made Delbert madder. This backward Yarholar from Thlopthlocco Town, of all hick places, didn't know the first thing about leases. Delbert wasn't *selling* thousands of acres; he was simply arranging permits for their use by white cattlemen and cotton planters. So what if he made a few dollars for facilitating those permits? Or, to be honest, a few thousand dollars?

Delbert tried to control his breathing as he looked out the second-story window at the trees next to the Creek Nation's capitol building. He thought he understood what the Apostle felt when he wrote to the Corinthians about "a thorn in his flesh." These backward towns – Thlopthlocco, Talladega, Nuyaka, Eufaula – had been a thorn in the sides of the McIntoshes for a hundred years. They were the hotheads who insisted on starting a war against the white people way back in 1812. Delbert's great-grandpa was the leader of the progressive towns, the ones who allied themselves with the Americans and who fought against the Yarholars and their kin. But when William McIntosh and the progressives beat the Red Sticks at Horseshoe Bend, who took the credit? Andrew Jackson! That was a joke: without the support of Chief McIntosh and his White Sticks, Jackson would have died there in Alabama and never become President. And then, because of these stubborn Yarholars and their endless resistance, President Jackson had kicked the *entire* Muskogee Confederation out of Alabama and Georgia, even the McIntosh family who had helped Jackson win the war!

In 1861, the *wvcenv* turned against one another in their own Civil War. The McIntoshes and other leading Mvskoke families saw it as an opportunity to turn the tables on the U.S. government so they sided with the Confederates. But did these ignorant, low-class Yarholars understand? No. Now they were suddenly loyal to the Americans! Loyal to the same government they fought against in 1812! Loyal to the same government who ran them from their homes in 1832! The Yarholars and their ilk all went to Kansas and organized their own pro-Union militias to fight against the Mvskoke troops. Worse, the Yarholars encouraged the McIntosh family's *estelvste* slaves, and those of the other leading families, to run away and join the Yankee army with them! After the war, the Yarholars and their allies happily agreed to accept these *estelvste* as voting members of the Muskogee Nation.

In the legislative lower house, the House of Warriors, the so-called "traditionals" maintained a strong alliance with the colored delegates. And it gave them a lot more votes since there were so many *estelvste* in the Creek Nation. Today's proposal for the lease of 20,000 grazing acres to Colonel George Miller should have passed the upper house without comment. But instead this Tustenugge Yarholar, this pagan corn farmer who knew nothing of law or business, stood up in the House of Kings to ask a series of questions about the lease. It was galling. Yarholar's own daughter Sunshine had married a Black man, and not even an *estelvste* Muskogee, but a state Negro from Alabama. What was wrong with these people? And what was Delbert going to tell Colonel Miller, who had already given him an advance on his "service fee"?

He was hoping for time to think about this as the House of Kings broke for lunch. But, speak of the devil, when Delbert stepped out of the old sandstone council house and onto Sixth Street, there was Colonel Miller waiting for him with a smile so false and theatrical it seemed masklike.

"Delbert," said the Colonel, taking his elbow as if Delbert were a child who needed help crossing the street, "has our business been resolved satisfactorily?"

Delbert took a moment to respond. Kentuckians. Were they issued the title of "colonel" for leading soldiers in combat? Or was it a designation to let people know you were an asshole? There was nothing to be gained here by telling this man to keep his hands to himself. "I am afraid that there is an unexpected wrinkle."

"Son," chuckled the Colonel. "You wouldn't be trying to renegotiate our deal, would you?"

Son. Delbert had to take another long breath. "Sir, you misunderstand me. If you want me to refund the fee you have paid I will be happy to. I am telling you that there were unanticipated objections raised to the lease." The Colonel had not yet let go of Delbert's elbow. Using his other hand, Delbert now gently extricated himself from the man's grip.

"Don't get your feathers all ruffled, son," said the Colonel with his smile still intact. "They get in the way of good business all the time. Who raised these objections?"

"A delegate from a rural district named Tustenugge Yarholar. He is a member of the Isparhecher caucus and I think he just wanted to score some points with his constituents," answered Delbert.

"Holler what? What is it with these Red devils and their made-up names?" snorted the Colonel happily, as if Delbert would naturally share his contempt for Indians. Then, noticing a reaction cross Delbert's face, he added, "Present company excepted, of course! I always think of you as a white man!"

Delbert decided that this was intended to be a compliment and let it pass.

"Tell me a little bit about this man's family," prompted the Colonel. "You said his name is Yo Ho Ho?"

"Yarholar," corrected Delbert. "He has a married son, Hank, who raises corn, beans and livestock west of here. He has a daughter, Sunshine, who is married to a Negro railroad worker named Ezekiel Payne."

"He has a nigger son-in-law?" sputtered Colonel Miller. His mask of bland amiability had suddenly vanished, replaced by open rage and disgust.

For some reason this question truly offended Delbert coming out of the Colonel's mouth, despite the fact that he had been thinking the exact same thing only five minutes earlier. He breathed deeply and said nothing.

The Colonel must have reminded himself about the importance of his grazing lease because his bland smile returned as quickly as it had departed. "Never mind. Never mind," he said quietly. "Do you think this son Hank would be interested in working for me as a foreman over my hands?" he asked.

Now it was Delbert's turn to smile. This truly was a stroke of genius. A cash income? A position of responsibility outside his father's shadow? Delbert knew Hank Yarholar well. They had been schoolboys together. He was quite certain that this would appeal to Hank and he was quite certain that old Tustenugge would do what he could to look out for anybody who employed Hank, too.

"Oh, yes," he answered the Colonel. "I think he would. And I think that would make all your problems go away. Would you like me to direct you to Hank's place? I will, of course, return your fee since you are expediting this another way."

"Oh, no, son!" said Miller. "I would never renege on a deal. We'll just let you make the arrangements with Hank. You see this through and you will have more than earned that fee."

The two men shook hands on it. The Colonel then turned back to the post outside the council building where he had tied his horse. Delbert walked on to his Aunt Della's for lunch. There was still an hour and a half before the House of Kings reconvened for the afternoon. There would be plenty of time tomorrow to find Hank Yarholar and offer him the ranch job. As Delbert McIntosh walked the streets of Okmulgee, though, one of Colonel Miller's sentences echoed uncomfortably in his head: "I would never renege on a deal."

Linn-San Manuel, Texas
1965

My name is Timotea Hinojosa y Garza. I was born January 26, 1900 right here in San Manuel, Texas. My mother was Dionicia Garza-Singletary. My father was Eusebio Hinojosa-Cantú, a rancher. He was a direct descendant of Juan-José Hinojosa y Ballí, who was granted all the land you see around here, one hundred twenty-five thousand acres, by King Carlos III of Spain in 1769.

I did not cross the river from the other side. Neither did my father and mother, nor my grandparents. We have been on this land since before the American Revolution. We were on this land when George Washington was *don nadie*, a person of no particular significance or value. And yet, here we are today, living on our own land, but treated as if we swam across yesterday.

I put down nothing in these pages that I heard from *fulanita*; everything I write here I have seen with my own eyes, every word spoken I heard with my own ears. That is how you know that all my testimony is true.

I put these words on paper for you, *mis nietos*, my grandchildren, who I love more than anyone I have ever known, even my beloved Narciso, your abuelo, who none of you ever met. I write this also for your friends, the grandchildren of my cousins and neighbors. I do not have much money to give you. I do not have much land. I would gladly give my life for you. These pages then, *are* my life, and these pages I give to you.

Today I see children sit in front of the television as if it were the *retablo* of some new religion where they learn lies about our ancestors and about our adversaries. They watch shows that treat Texas Rangers as if they were an organization of crime fighters instead of a gang of murderers and thieves. They watch shows that treat our own people as buffoons and thieves and sex maniacs. These lies turn my life on its head. I cannot make a television show, so I write this *testimonio*. My life is the life of all the *abuelas*. My life is the story of San Manuel and of the entire Valley.

I begin with my education. I started school when I was four years old. I was too young, but I insisted on going anyway. I followed the other children to the house of the *maestro*, Don Antonio, and listened through the window of his *escuelita* every morning. When he told me to go home until I was old enough, I just ran around the side of the building to where he couldn't see me. I would wait a minute, run back, and listen again. After a few days of that, Don Antonio decided to let me come inside and start my letters and numbers.

23

I loved school from the beginning. Don Antonio used to say that he would teach us until they found a real teacher who knew what he was doing, but I knew that he was the greatest teacher in the world. One of my favorite things was watching him recite poetry. One year he stood in front of the room waving his arms and declaiming Félix Lope de Vega's epic "Jerusalem Conquered." I think some of the older children knew why he was so moved by this poem even if the rest of us didn't. I just remember finding his excitement contagious.

I liked the shorter poems, especially ones by women writers. On Don Antonio's bookshelves I discovered the Mexican poet Sister Juana Inés de la Cruz, who lived shortly after Lope de Vega. I memorized her sonnet *"En perseguirme, Mundo, ¿qué interesas?"* because it was just the way I felt about school and about Don Antonio: "I don't value treasure or riches, so I am always happier to invest in thinking than to think about investing!" I recited that in front of the class and everybody applauded. I felt like a queen that day. I did not yet know that it was the Church itself that took away her books and ordered her not to write. I did not yet know that I was soon to encounter an Inquisition of my own.

Our reading was always from the classics, but our science came directly from the fields and streams around the school. Don Antonio wanted us to watch the birds and learn all their names. Because I had my head buried in books all the time, I only knew the most obvious ones. The biggest bird we saw was the *grulla cenicienta*. I don't know what they are called in English. They still come through every year. They are as tall as a ten-year old child. They have red faces and white cheeks and their wings are six or seven feet across. The littlest birds were the *chupaflores*, which I think the Anglos call hummingbirds. I didn't know most of the birds, but at least I could always tell the difference between a *grulla* and a *chupaflor*!

I had a classmate, though, Doroteo Pérez, who was a wild little boy. His family lived on Rancho Rucio and he was always running through the fields. He knew the names of all the different *chupaflores*. I think he could name a hundred kinds of birds. One year he started catching butterflies and bringing them in and naming them for us. Don Antonio praised Doroteo to the skies for the many birds and insects he could name. I was jealous of all that attention but not enough to get me to take my head out of my books!

We studied the weather, too. Don Antonio's school had a thermometer, a barometer, a wind vane and an anemometer. Every single day we took turns reading all those instruments and describing the sky. We had a brown notebook for recording all our readings. For most of my years in school the job of writing

24

in the weather journal belonged to my friend Marcelina because she had the neatest and clearest handwriting. Up until today I remember the names of all the clouds!

Another important study in Don Antonio's little school was our history. We had no textbooks for that, so we just sat spellbound while Don Antonio explained to us about how Hernán Cortés and his little army of 600 defeated hundreds of thousands of Aztec warriors. He told us how our own great-grandfathers fought the Comanches for our land and how our grandfathers defeated the corrupt Mexican president Antonio López de Santa Anna to win their freedom. He taught us about the Treaty of Guadalupe-Hidalgo that made Texas part of the United States and how some of the Anglos tried to ignore it to steal our land. We also learned about how those same Anglos then tried to break up the United States so that they could buy and sell human beings to work in their cotton fields. We learned the Constitution of the United States and we even had our own practice elections in class. I wanted to run for president myself, but I found out that girls couldn't run. We had to choose between Taft and Bryan. I couldn't figure out how Taft won, because every adult I knew voted for Bryan. That was before the Anglos passed a law that made it illegal for our *papis* to vote. As I write these words it occurs to me that the *gabachos* gave their women the vote right around the same time they took it from us *Tejanos*. That can't have been a coincidence, but I will have to think about it some more.

By now, children, you will be wondering why I am devoting so much attention to all the work we did in Don Antonio's little school. Be assured! It is important to so many of the stories I want to share with you. For now, I will just explain how it prepared me for the next step in my education.

It is not a boast to say that I was the first graduate of that *escuelita* to prepare for high school. Most of the children of ranch hands only attended for a few years, just enough to learn to read and write, add and subtract. Of those who went all the way through, most parents thought the diploma was sufficient achievement, especially for the girls. The sons of wealthier families were sent away: some to Monterrey, a few as far as Michigan. So I do not declare myself the best student ever to come from San Manuel, only the first to graduate from the local school and apply to a Valley high school.

I was thirteen years old when I completed the curriculum for eighth grade. Don Antonio wrote a report of my progress along with a letter of recommendation for me to bring to the new high school in McAllen. It was thirty miles away, a long ride indeed on those roads, but my *abuelo* was so proud of my achievement that he decided that he could bring me every morning in his Model T Ford. He had cousins and friends on the other side in Reynosa and he planned to socialize with them until it was time to bring me home in the afternoon. Shortly after my graduation, I put on my best dress, gathered all my documents, and drove to McAllen with my parents.

I knew something was wrong as soon as we walked into the office of McAllen High School. Everybody there was Anglo and nobody would make eye contact with my father as he stood at the desk for visitors. He spoke anyway, in his courtly manner, saying to the clerical staff, *"Licenciadas, me honran encontrarles. Yo deseo registrar mi hija en esta escuela."*

Somebody shouted rudely, "Speak English!"

He started as if he had been hit. In those days we were still accustomed to Anglos learning our language when they came to our Valley. But he gamely proceeded, "Please, I come to sign my daughter in your school."

This time a *gabacha* stood up from her desk, walked over, and looking my father directly in the eye, said, "No greasers! This school is for white children!"

I was only thirteen years old, from a village, raised to be modest and shy. But I wanted to go to high school and I was not going to let this poorly brought-up and shameless woman deny me. Moreover, all my education to that point had prepared me for a wider world than our little *rancho*, or even the aspiring "metropolis" of McAllen with its 2000 people. So I stepped forward with my official documents and said, "I am a graduate. I would like to show my credentials to your principal."

That *malcriada* didn't like my words or my manner at all. She stood there staring at me. So I waited a minute and repeated, "I am an elementary graduate. I would like to show my credentials to the principal of this school." But I said it much louder this time, as if she had a hearing impairment.

Well, I must have spoken loudly enough to get the attention of the principal himself, because a bald Anglo man in a poorly fitting suit came running from an interior door. He looked us over quickly, glanced at his secretary, and immediately, in good polite Spanish, invited my parents and I back to his office. As we walked past the astonished *gabacha*, I tried to preserve my good manners... in vain: I couldn't restrain a little triumphant smile. Too soon!

Inside his wood-paneled office the rumpled man introduced himself as Mr. Craig. My father repeated his wish to enroll me in the school, and handed Mr.

Craig my papers. Mr. Craig put on a pair of reading glasses and busied himself with examining the record of my work and my recommendation from Don Antonio. He seemed to consider them for a very long time.

Finally he looked up, took off the glasses, and addressed me – in English – saying, "These are excellent reports you have achieved."

"Thank you, sir," I nodded.

"It seems you have undertaken a very serious course of study with Professor Longoria."

I was so proud that I just smiled without saying a word.

"These are all bilingual classes?" asked Mr. Craig.

"Bilingual, sir?" I didn't get his meaning.

"Bilingual, meaning that Professor Longoria taught you in Spanish?" questioned Mr. Craig.

"*I* am bilingual," I said, still confused. Was Spanish more than one language? "Don Antonio made certain that we could all read and write English."

Mr. Craig nodded encouragingly. "But the literature, the mathematics, the science: your teacher taught you all those subjects in Spanish?"

"Of course!" I answered.

"Oh," he said sadly. "I am so sorry. All those years in a bilingual classroom have put you too far behind the youngsters who attend this school. All of our instruction is in English and I am afraid you would find yourself at a profound disadvantage. You really need to attend a bilingual high school."

"A bilingual high school?" I repeated, still puzzled by his use of this word.

But Mr. Craig was still apologizing. "Unfortunately we have no bilingual high school here in Hidalgo County. Or, for that matter, in Starr County, Cameron County or Brooks County. The truth is, most children in our bilingual schools don't continue up to the fifth grade."

It was only later that I discovered that children of Mexican descent were always enrolled in "bilingual" schools in McAllen... even if they spoke English at home. That the whole language question was a trick to keep us out of their schools at every grade level. That I discovered that none of us was allowed to attend any high school.

But at that moment I was just trying to correct this man's misconception about *my* abilities and to get my ambitions back on track. *Mami* and *Papi* were still sitting in the leather-upholstered chairs across from Mr. Craig. They hadn't followed every bit of this, but their stricken looks made clear that they knew something was wrong.

Mr. Craig now returned his attention to my father, saying – in Spanish, "Señor Hinojosa, your daughter is a very impressive student. It would be our privilege to have her attend here. I just feel that it would be so unfair to suddenly force her to study in a language in which she is incompletely prepared. I am only looking out for Timotea when I say that this is not the school for her." And he stood up and extended his hand in a gesture that said that the conversation was over.

My father stood up, too, but he pointedly ignored Mr. Craig's hand. He said, in English, "Mr. Craig, our enemies tell us we are incapable of learning and that they do not want our dirty children near theirs. How are you different than them?" Without waiting for an answer he turned away, took my mother's hand in his and – gesturing at me with the other hand to come along – left that office.

I tried not to look at the nasty secretary on the way out, but I saw that she was now giving me the same little triumphant smile that I had given her on my way in. I turned back and ran in to the principal's office to take my reports and recommendation from his desk. Today, fifty years later, I still have those papers in my bureau. I look at them from time to time. When I take them from the drawer, I hurt just as much now as I did that day long ago. Those papers remind me of what I had hoped to achieve. They remind me of the person I thought I could become.

For many years I carried the shame of that morning. I believed that even I, the best graduate of Don Antonio's little school, was lower than the stupidest pupil of McAllen High School, unprepared even to attend. I believed that, despite the explanations of my parents and grandparents. Even when I saw the trickery they used, even when I saw their lies, it was hard not to feel ashamed of being turned down by their school. The *gabachos* of McAllen were my Inquisition, and they silenced me as the Inquisitors silenced Sor Juana Inés de la Cruz, in my case for being Mexican as well as for being a woman.

In the Texas of today you children are allowed to attend the same schools as the children of the Anglos and you all get to go to high school. And what does that mean? It means that they never give you the books of Sor Juana or Octavio Paz or Miguel Ángel Asturias, not to mention Unamuno or Cervantes. Your teachers never even mention the names of these writers. I doubt that they even know that literature is produced in Spanish. It is the language of this Valley, but they are incapable of speaking it, and they threaten you with a wooden paddle if you do!

They tell you that our ancestors were the villains of the Alamo. They make heroes of murderers and slave traders. They don't teach you any science and math at all because they don't think we are able to do anything but clean their houses, mow their lawns, and sell oranges by the freeway. That is why I write this *testimonio*. That is why every word of this is for you and not for me. I am old now and may not have many more years, but before I go, I want you to know who you are... who *we* are. And I want you to know what they have done to us.

It may be too late for me to become the woman I dreamed of being. But it is not too late for you. Maybe by writing this testimony I can discard the grief and the shame that still envelop me. Maybe by helping you, my grandchildren, become all that you can become, I will be following my destiny at last. That is my hope.

Boley, Oklahoma
1911

"What the hell is a 'shivaree?' demanded Sheriff T.R. Ringo, slamming his newspaper down on the table. The silver star pinned to his leather vest marked him as a lawman. But his permanent scowl - and the enormous Schofield Model 3 revolver on his hip - told everyone, even strangers, that he was also a dangerous man.

"Shivaree?" Mayor T.B. Armstrong repeated, scoffing at the question, then pulled his tan suit jacket back from his prosperous paunch as he put his hands in his pockets. "White man's foolishness," he answered authoritatively.

Ezekiel Payne heard this exchange and smiled to himself. He wondered, not for the first time, how two men, respected by the whole town, could speak with such authority on matters that they clearly knew nothing about?

He was drinking a phosphate at the counter of D.J. Turner's Drugstore at the corner of First and Pecan, and listening in on an impromptu meeting of the town fathers. While Ezekiel sat on a stool up front, the elite of Boley, Oklahoma were gathered around a table at the back of the store, near the large safe that the pharmacist took such pride in. They seemed to meet like this daily. All Ezekiel knew was that every time he came into town for supplies... there they were.

"Shivaree," explained George Perry, editor of the *Boley Progress*, "is a mob that interrupts a couple's wedding night." In a white town, Perry's fair skin and wavy hair would have allowed him to pass. He continued, "Sometimes they just stand outside banging on pots and pans. Sometimes it gets rougher: dragging them outside, dunking them in stock tanks, stripping their clothes."

"Only a white man could think of that," the mayor repeated.

But Sheriff Ringo was, if possible, even angrier than before. He sat up straight and his right hand strayed toward his gun. "I would kill the first son of a bitch that tried that with me," he said, glaring at the men around him, as if any of them had even dreamed of such a thing.

Yes, he would, thought Ezekiel Payne. Sheriff T.R. Ringo would kill a man over much less.

"And that is exactly what happened in Claremore," said their host, pharmacist Turner. Claremore was a good ninety miles away from Boley, clear on the other side of Tulsa, outside the old Creek Indian Nation, which is what all this land, roughly 5000 square miles between the Arkansas and Canadian Rivers, had been before statehood. Claremore was a "sundown town," another reason for nobody in Boley to know what was going on over there. The signs in places like Claremore politely said, "Whites Only Within City Limits After Dark." But the colloquial meaning was clear: "Nigger, don't let the sun go down on your head in this town." Actually, there was a sign with exactly those words only twelve miles east of Boley in the town of Okemah.

D.J. Turner looked more like a banker than a druggist with his dark three-piece suit and gold watch chain. He had his fingers in all sorts of businesses. He also had the only long distance phone in Boley, so he frequently had news from around the state even before the telegraph operator two blocks away at the Ft. Smith and Western railroad depot. He repeated, "That is exactly what happened. A girl from a good family – nice farm, lots of money – married a cowboy, ten years older than her, too. I guess folks in Claremore thought it wasn't the right match. Or maybe some of those men were eyeing this girl and her bank account, too. In either case, they pulled them out of the house and stripped them, stripped them naked. The cowboy, name of Curley McClain, he stabbed one of those men to death." And he nodded at Sheriff Ringo.

"Hm, hm, hm," humphed real estate man T. M. Haynes. He looked at the mayor, then mimicked Armstrong's gesture, pulling back his own suit jacket and putting his hands in his pockets. "That marriage was not destined to be consummated," he said. He chuckled a little. "I think Old Curley McClain must be in a locked car on the Katy Railroad, riding to McAlester Penitentiary as we speak."

Ezekiel, still sipping his phosphate a few feet away, silently disagreed. He had been studying Oklahoma law enforcement since he arrived in the Creek Nation years ago, after mustering out of the U.S. Cavalry. He was pretty certain Curley McClain was already dead. Those local "shivaree-ers" would have lynched the cowboy right there.

"You think wrong," said D. J. Turner. "The white folks in Claremore convened a grand jury – or what they called one – on the spot. And they concluded that no crime had taken place. They said that the dead man fell on his own knife!"

"What the hell?" asked a few of the men.

Was the dead man colored? wondered Ezekiel. But he couldn't be; there were no colored allowed in Claremore. Still, a grand jury declaring that a murder wasn't a crime?

31

It turned out that editor Perry, who had been allowing the pharmacist to tell this story, actually had some more information about this. "The dead man was another cowboy, part-Creek Indian, named Jud Fry. And he wanted to marry that girl, too."

He didn't have to provide any more explanation than this. Everybody knew that the good white folks of Claremore were not going to allow an Indian man to marry a white girl. And if he fought a white man? And he ended up dead? Well, where was the crime?

"Goddamned Indians!" said D. J. Turner. Ezekiel almost answered that, but only almost. Turner's own wife Minnie was *estelvste*, a Black Creek Indian. Her tribal land allotment – and those of her brothers and parents – were the reason why Turner owned so much property around Boley! Where did he get off speaking with contempt about Indians?

But the subject was just too personally painful for Ezekiel, so he stayed quiet. His ex-wife was Creek, *estecate Mvskoke*. She left him – and their child – because he was not. His daughter Nessa – the pole star in his life, his reason for being – was mixed, Native and Black. Who knew what Turner might say to him if he were to call the man out publicly? Who knew how he, Ezekiel, might respond? He had protected Nessa from this conversation her entire life. He was not about to get into it now with some pompous, self-serving loudmouth.

Mayor Armstrong's mind was apparently stuck in a rut today. For the third time he opined, "White folks' business; none of ours."

When the other town fathers nodded and humphed in agreement, Ezekiel Payne took a deep breath. He thought, thought again, then said decisively, "That is where you are wrong."

The men of affairs of the town of Boley all looked across the store at Ezekiel with astonishment, as if a horse had spoken. He was not a member of their social class: not a banker, not a merchant, not an attorney. Certainly he was a thrifty farmer who supplemented his income with railroad work, but he was a single father with no house in town and no wife. Where did he get off disagreeing with them? Where did he get off having an opinion at all?

It was M. J. Jones who finally responded. The young attorney sighed deeply, as if it were one of his adopted children interrupting him. He looked at his

32

colleagues, turned back toward Ezekiel at the counter, paused, then asked haughtily, "Excuse me?"

Ezekiel Payne tended to keep his own counsel. He had spoken little even years before, when he was in the army, among his peers. When he moved to the Creek Nation after his discharge he was an outsider. *Estelvste* who were just as dark as he was called him "state Negro" because he came from the United States. Later he married into a prominent Creek Indian family. He knew that their tribal politics weren't his concern, so he kept his mouth shut there, too.

Boley affairs, though, were as much his concern as anybody's. And these men were dangerously delusional.

"You think we are immune from their lynchings?" he asked. "Sure, Boley is the most prosperous colored town in Oklahoma. But this is still the United States."

Lawyer Jones rolled his eyes and smirked, "What lynchings?"

Ezekiel kept right on in the face of this contemptuous dismissal. "When a grand jury ignores a murder," he explained, "that is a lynching. There is no other word for it. When some Curly McClain continues his life without consequence after taking the life of another man, that is a lynching."

Jones snorted. "Let us accept that flawed premise for the moment," he answered. "Why should we here in Boley care about what a bunch of white folks do way over in Claremore?"

"Way over in Claremore," repeated Ezekiel, shaking his head. "And what did you say when it was Laura Nelson and her son Lawrence, right down there on the North Canadian?"

That comment elicited a kind of gasp, almost as if Ezekiel had punched each man present in his affluent stomach. The incident was still raw in everybody's memory. The Nelsons had lived in Paden, only five miles west, and, being colored people, they often shopped here in Boley. Laura's husband Austin was accused of a theft and the boy was charged with shooting an Okemah deputy during his father's arrest. A crowd of about forty white townspeople broke Laura and Lawrence out of the Okemah jail at gunpoint. They gang-raped Laura and then hanged the two of them from the bridge outside town. To this day an Okemah photographer was selling souvenir postcards of that murder. Ezekiel had seen the postcards, a sight he would never be able to erase from his memory: a crowd of smiling white folks standing over the mother and son's swinging corpses. Ezekiel knew some of those folks, too.

But the Nelsons were not the class of Negroes to be welcome for anything more than occasional shopping in Boley. And so it was no surprise that, after the initial shock of Ezekiel's accusation had worn off, Sheriff Ringo dismissed it. "The Nelsons were worthless, no-account Negros," he sneered, "cattle rustlers and bootleggers. They got no more and no less than they deserved."

The other men only nodded silently, perhaps unprepared to make such a strong, categorical statement, but – on the whole – sadly agreeing with Ringo's judgement.

"That's what they want you to believe, isn't it?" asked Ezekiel. "Was one of you in that house? You know for a fact that Deputy Loney wasn't killed by his own posse? You know how reckless that kind of white folks get when the shooting starts."

Nobody chose to answer this. Why would an upright Negro workingman like Ezekiel Payne defend low-class riffraff like the Nelsons?

It hadn't been the fate of the Nelsons that worried Ezekiel at the time. It was the failure of the authorities in Okemah to even discuss arresting any of the lynchers. The deputy guarding the jail that night claimed they were all strangers to him, which was laughably false. And while the Okfuskee County sheriff made no attempt whatever to apprehend members of the mob that took the Nelsons from his jail, he was highly concerned with an alleged "plot" by local Negroes to "kill all the white people" in retaliation. He and his posse rounded up several hundred over the next few days and held them in a stockade before putting them on a train out of the county. The *Okemah Ledger* said that none of the "better class of Negroes" had been involved, so the townsfolk of Boley had not been personally inconvenienced by the deportation.

At the time, Ezekiel was disquieted by his own passivity. Maybe there *should* have been a plot like the one those guilty white folk imagined. So he confronted the town fathers now. "What about all the other folks they arrested in Okemah afterwards? Were they 'worthless Negroes', too?"

M. J. Jones was clearly offended by the implication that he wasn't a strong race man. "We are doing just fine over here," he said. "And so are *you*! Why don't you just leave the thinking to grown folks?"

This last was intended to be a dig. Ezekiel Payne easily had fifteen years on the young attorney. But it was also obvious to him that he had struck a nerve. "We're doing fine?" he asked. "Okfuskee County passes an ordinance forbidding the conveyance of real estate to colored men, and we're 'doing fine'? We are legally barred from putting our heads down to sleep in Okemah and Henryetta and you say we are 'doing fine'? How long before those people come to take our property? How long before they come to take our lives?"

He had gotten louder than he intended. He could see that Sheriff Ringo wanted to say something, and that was a confrontation from which there might be no turning back. But Mayor Armstrong stood up and turned his back on the conversation, silently declaring it over and preparing to go. D. J. Turner was holding Ringo's gaze with his own and shaking his head as if to say "No." He did not want a shooting affray in his place of business and he knew the sheriff's temper better than most. Ringo turned to follow the mayor. Turner then gave Ezekiel a look that clearly declared him banned from the premises: no more phosphates at the pharmacy. So Ezekiel gathered himself, took a last sip, and headed out to his wagon, which was parked in front on Pecan Street.

He unhitched his horses from the rail and climbed up on the seat for the drive back to his farm on Sandy Creek. As he released the brake, he noticed George Perry standing on the raised wooden sidewalk, studying him. He looked back at Perry. "What?" he asked.

The newspaper editor was quiet a moment longer, and then answered with a question of his own, "Been thinking about this a long time?"

Ezekiel responded with a short, humorless laugh. "You have no idea," he said.

"Stop into my office the next time you're in town," said Editor Perry. "I'd like to share some thoughts with you."

Maybe the town fathers didn't all share a single brain, thought Ezekiel. Maybe there was a way to begin organizing. He wanted to protect Nessa. He wanted to defend the race. That was why he had joined the Army all those years ago to begin with. But for the moment he just nodded and said, "I'd like that, too," and then clucked twice at his horses. The wagon jerked to a start. He made a left on Grant and headed out of town. He couldn't stop thinking about the newspaperman's invitation. Perhaps there was something to be done about their white neighbors and about their growing lawlessness.

35

Camp Walker, Cebu Island, Philippines
1906

When Grant Mims enlisted in the United States Army, Captain Wygant told all the recruits that there were three essential rules to being a soldier: "Obey, obey, and obey." His training sergeant, John Calloway, had publicly agreed with the captain's summary. Later on though, when the white officers were out of earshot, Sgt. Major Calloway confided that there was really only one: "Shit rolls downhill."

That had been seven years ago. Grant was a corporal now and today shit was positively raining on him. Major - no longer Captain - Wygant was bellowing at him, demanding to know what he, Mims, had done to turn Private David Fagen into a turncoat, leading Filipino rebels in combat against the United States. And all Cpl. Grant Mims could think was *Of course.*

Of course it's my fault. Of course I'm to blame for white soldiers treating us like shoeshine boys. Of course I'm to blame for them calling the Filipinos "niggers" and acting like the 24th US Infantry is on the side of the enemy because we're colored. Of course I'm to blame for this vicious war of massacre against civilians who seem to all support the rebels. Of course I'm to blame for the entire boneheaded idea of taking over an immense chain of islands and its seven million people and then treating them like slaves.

Of course. Grant Mims couldn't even blame Calloway for recruiting him anymore. The rain of shit had already flushed the Sergeant Major right out of the Army he was still so proud of.

It felt like a lifetime ago that Sgt. Maj. John Calloway had walked into St. David A.M.E. Zion Church in Sag Harbor on a Sunday morning in 1899, when the flush of victory against Spain still had everybody's imagination on fire. Calloway looked so sharp in his dress blues that he caught the eyes of the young men in the congregation almost as much as the young women. The 24th was temporarily stationed at Camp Wikoff out at Montauk Point, freshly - and triumphantly - returned from service in Cuba. With the regiment's numbers severely depleted, Calloway was looking for patriotic young colored men with a taste for adventure. After worship services, he stood in front of the congregation and shared his heroic tales of the 24th's exploits on San Juan Hill. He told them about suppressing rioting miners in Colorado and Idaho. He told them how he, a colored man, was even being recommended to become an officer. He neglected to tell them about the regiment's duty in the yellow fever camp at Siboney. He neglected to tell them that it was yellow fever and not combat that caused the losses he was trying to make up.

Grant Mims probably would have signed up anyway. What was there for him in Sag Harbor? The East End of Long Island was a place of hard times and scant rewards, especially for a young man of color. If you didn't have land to plant potatoes - and Grant did not - you got a job in the menhaden industry. He had been hauling purse nets on a bunker-seining steamer for a few months. The work was hard and the pay was laughable. It could be worse, too. The fish factories paid even less than the boats and the stench was unbearable. The Army sounded good to Grant. He joined the very next day.

When the regiment boarded the *S.S. City of Para* in San Francisco for the trip across the Pacific, Private Grant Mims was quite certain that they were on their way to liberate the Filipino people from their Spanish overlords. He was equally confident that their service was going to once and for all prove the worth of colored Americans and bring an end to Jim Crow discrimination in the U.S.

So there were some unpleasant surprises when they disembarked in Manila. The first were the greetings they received from the white soldiers they were relieving: "What the fuck are you coons doing here?" was among the less offensive. Grant saw white regulars, privates, address Captain Charles Young of the 10th Cavalry as "nigger" and refuse to salute him, without being chastised in any way by their own officers. He saw the notorious Major General Frederick Funston ride by with a hemp rope hanging from his saddle as if he were a Klansman on his way to a lynching. Truth be told, that is exactly what Funston *was* planning, though of a Filipino rebel. After the twentieth time he heard white soldiers refer to enemy combatants as "niggers" Grant Mims had to ask himself: *What the fuck are we doing here?*

His doubts never interfered with his willingness to carry out orders. When the 24th was sent on a forced march for 900 miles up and down the Cagayan Valley in northern Luzon, Grant dealt with the heat, and the rain and the hunger without complaint. When the regiment fought Pulahan rebels in Tacloban, he wondered why Filipinos would hate the Americans who were freeing them from Spain, but the fighting was hand-to-hand - more accurately knife-to-knife - and there was no time to question them about it. When his brigade was dispatched to Cebu, it was Grant Mims who captured Eugenio Alcachufas, the notorious highland rebel who had killed Lieutenant Alan Walker at Aloguinsan. That's when Major Wygant promoted him to corporal.

None of this stopped his struggling to understand the war. The 24th served for several more months in Tacloban, providing support for the U.S. Marines on Samar. Grant never actually saw those Marines burning the people's farms and houses and churches. He never saw them waterboarding civilians. He never saw them lining up whole families and shooting them. But he heard about it. He heard about General Jacob Smith's orders to kill everybody on the island over ten-years old. He heard that Smith had forbidden the Marines to take prisoners. Older veterans of the 24th whispered that Smith had been in command at Wounded Knee. Grant Mims didn't know what that meant and learned for the first time about the massacre of unarmed Indians in South Dakota. He thought about his Shinnecock cousins in Southampton and it made him shiver. What kind of Army had he joined? But he kept his head down and his mouth shut. So did most of the other soldiers in his regiment.

But not all. Sgt. Major Calloway did his wondering out loud. And in print. Who knew that John Calloway was such an intellectual? He had not been lying that Sunday in Sag Harbor when he said that the War Department was considering making him an officer. Calloway had taken - and passed! with the highest grades! - the Army's exacting examination for Officers' Candidate School. He was one of the founding members of the regiment's Frederick Douglass Book Club. And he wasn't satisfied just to subscribe to race periodicals from back home. He contributed to them, too. Sgt. Calloway's reports from the front were published on the front page of his hometown paper, the *Richmond Planet*.

When copies of the *Planet* with his articles in them arrived in camp, Calloway proudly showed them to Cpl. Mims. He was not shy with his words or his criticism. While they were in Cebu he had written, "The whites have begun to establish their diabolical race hatred in all its home rancor in Manila." And the sergeant major wasn't only referring to the white soldiers' habit of teaching Filipinos to abuse American colored people. Calloway predicted that the status of Filipinos *in their own country* would become comparable to that of colored people in the Southern states. The sergeant wrote that nobody white regarded Filipinos as having any rights at all. Grant Mims looked at the newspaper with both admiration and fear. Did Calloway think he could say all this and still be made an officer?

It really didn't matter what Sgt. Major Calloway thought. Nor did it matter that he had received the highest score in the Army on his officer's candidate exam. It didn't even matter that his long and stellar record of service had brought him the praise of generals. The Army got the last word. The Army always got the last word. John Calloway was not just rejected as a candidate for officer training. They took Calloway's stripes and busted him down to private. Then they kicked him out of the Army he had served for so many years, with a dishonorable discharge, weeks before he could have retired with a pension. They said he was a spy. They said he was corresponding with the enemy. They said that he *was* the enemy. The only thing they didn't do was put him in prison. Corporal Mims thought about all this for a good long time. And he continued keeping his mouth shut.

Calloway was not the only soldier in the regiment who couldn't, though. Private David Fagen, notably, seemed congenitally incapable of silence, under any circumstances. Fagen was a Florida phosphate miner who enlisted in the 24th a year before Grant Mims, when the regiment was in Tampa getting ready to deploy to Cuba. He saw the Army as his chance to get out of standing in the sun all day, chest-deep in dirty water, digging fossil fertilizer out of the ground. Fagen had a joke or a song or a story for every occasion. He was a walking library of mother wit.

Private Fagen even preached Sunday homilies, but they were usually from no Bible that Grant Mims ever read. Fagen preached about the doings of John the Conqueror and the sayings of an African-priest-turned-Seminole-Indian named Uncle Monday. They were a kind of counterpoint to the sermons of the regimental chaplain. Captain George Prioleau was a professor at Wilberforce College and ordained in the African Methodist Episcopal Church. His lessons were always thoughtful and enlightening, an education as well as an inspiration. Fagen's, by contrast, were funny, profane and down to earth. But if you thought David Fagen didn't also know his Scripture you would be mistaken.

One week the chaplain took his text from the Parable of the Talents in the Gospel of Matthew. Captain Prioleau explained to the men that the Master in the story is God and that our talents are gifts from God. If we use God's gifts, said Captain Prioleau, He will reward us, but if we fail to, we will suffer God's punishment. The chaplain urged each soldier in attendance to reflect on what their special gifts were, and how they should best share them. After worship, though, Private Fagen revealed that he had a different interpretation of that text.

"Jesus tells us a story of three servants and how buckra abused every one of them," announced Private Fagen when the service was over. He had an audience of about 15 men, mostly from his own Company I. He walked back and forth in front of them, gesturing with his arms, his voice rising and falling in a preacher's cadences. "Was it enough for buckra that those servants *worked* for him? That they made *money* for him? No, not buckra. He demanded that they *make his money work* for him, too!"

A few of the soldiers rolled their eyes a little at Fagen's imaginative retelling, but most of them chuckled. Fagen was just getting warmed up. He went on, "Now the first servant was an old Uncle Tom. How does the Gospel reveal his character to us? The Gospel says that Tom *doubled the master's money* for him. The Gospel says that Tom gave his master *all the profits* without even keeping a little fee for himself. And, most of all, the Gospel says that master told Tom, 'Well done, good and faithful servant.' You know that good and faithful servant must be an Uncle Tom! And you ask, how did the master reward Tom? Did he let him keep the extra money he made? Did he even give him a percentage? Maybe a tip? You must not know buckra! He told old Uncle Tom to invest *more* money for him and make him even richer!"

There was some grumbling from those soldiers who thought this sounded like blasphemy. Grant Mims's friend, Corporal William Nesbit, was especially irritated. "The word is 'talents,'" he complained. "Where do you get money from that?"

But Fagen wasn't discouraged by this criticism and he went on. "Master did the same with the second servant, took the money he made, gave him nothing but praise, and then put him to work making him even more money."

He paused and looked around. When he saw there were no objections he continued, "But the third servant? He was no Uncle Tom. He knew buckra a long time. He just stuck the master's money in a hole in the ground. That third servant told buckra to his face: 'Master, I know you're a hard man, reaping where you don't sow, harvesting where you don't plant. That's why I *planted* your money and look: here's what grew!' And he gave the money right back to him, the same money that he buried in the ground, the exact same money master gave him, because - as the Bible tells us - money don't grow on trees."

This last comment elicited some laughter. Cpl. Nesbit, though, objected: "Man, that ain't in no Bible."

Fagen remained undeterred. "How do we know that the last servant was telling master the truth? Because buckra says so himself! 'Thou wicked servant!' says he. 'Thou knewest that I reap where I don't sow! Thou shouldest at least have put my money in the bank so I could collect my little bit of interest!'"

Even Nesbit chuckled at this. But Fagen had not finished. "The servants all lose. The servants always lose. If they invest master's money, he puts them to work investing more. If they tell him the truth about himself, he casts them into outer darkness with weeping and gnashing of teeth." Fagen paused, as if he was done with the story. But he had a little more to say.

"What does Jesus tell us is the meaning of this parable?" he asked his listeners. He looked around, waiting for an answer. When none came he concluded, "Jesus says, 'The rich get richer and the poor get skinned.'"

"*What?*" demanded Cpl. Nesbit. "Where does he say this? Jesus never said that. Where in the Bible does it say this?"

Private Fagen looked at Nesbit triumphantly. "'For he that hath, to him shall be given more. And he that hath not, from him shall be taken even that little that he hath!' The Gospel of Matthew, chapter 25, verse 29!" And everybody laughed.

Grant Mims looked it up later. It was pretty close. It was always a mistake to underestimate David Fagen.

The whole regiment resented the injustice that had been done to Sgt. Maj. Calloway when he was busted down to private, and again when he was kicked out of the Army, but it was Private Fagen who couldn't keep his head down or his mouth shut about it. When Major Wygant took the sergeant major's stripes, it was Fagen who insisted on continuing to salute Calloway, even though Calloway was now the same rank as Fagen. Wygant had Cpl. Mims assign Fagen to cleaning the latrines as a punishment, but Fagen just kept on saluting Calloway. Then, the day after Wygant discharged Calloway, just a week short of earning his pension, Fagen shouted Calloway's name in morning muster instead of his own. Grant Mims ordered Fagen to stand at attention there on the parade ground for the rest of the day. Fagen just repeated the stunt the next morning.

And Fagen had more on his mind than Major Wygant or Sgt. Maj. Calloway. They all should have known it. Fagen wasn't the only soldier in the 24th with a Filipino girlfriend. But he was the one who *listened* to his girlfriend - and her parents… and her neighbors… and all the Filipinos he met - so very seriously. He was one of many who already spoke Spanish before they arrived. They had, after all, just served in Cuba and before that on the Mexican border. He was the one, though, who learned Tagalog after just a few weeks in Luzon. He was the one who learned Waray while they were in Tacloban. He was the one who knew more than anybody about why the Filipinos were fighting them instead of welcoming them as liberators. Everybody in the regiment resented the way they were treated by their white countrymen. More than anybody it was Private David Fagen who resented how all Americans - including the regiment - treated the Filipino people they claimed to be freeing.

41

Maybe Fagen was tired of being denied leave to go see his girlfriend. Maybe he was tired of the other punishments, the endless latrine duty, the long days standing at attention on the parade ground. Maybe it was the irony of Chaplain Prioleau preaching about "Do unto others" that Sunday morning. But Grant Mims got his first inkling of just how troubled Fagen was after worship services. Private Fagen was uncharacteristically quiet. Corporal Nesbit looked at him and asked, "What's with you? Nothing smart to say this time?"

Fagen didn't smile. He didn't stand up. He just said, "Jesus said that. He said 'Do unto others as you would have others do unto you.' But that ain't all Jesus said. He also said 'Watch for false prophets. Watch for wolves in sheep's clothing.'"

William Nesbit looked around as if wondering whether Fagen made this up, but the regular Bible readers among the men looked unperturbed by this statement so he stayed quiet. After a quiet minute, Fagen went on. "How do we know which are the false prophets? Jesus says we know the tree by its fruit." And then he stopped speaking again.

"What fruit?" asked Grant Mims now. He was genuinely puzzled.

Private Fagen sighed. "Like the sergeant major. He gave his whole life to this Army. They took his stripes and they took his pension. They almost took his freedom. They say we fight for liberty and justice. Where's Sgt. Calloway's justice? White man says it's a liberty tree, but the fruit? Well, the fruit says something else."

Fagen was warming to his subject and he sat up straight now. "And the 25th. Where's their justice? You all know this just as well as I do." They did. The 25th was another colored infantry regiment like theirs and the story had been everywhere in the newspapers.

"Ofay don't like colored men in Texas, leastways not colored men wearing uniforms and carrying M1903 Springfield rifles," continued Private Fagen. "They say the 25th shot up Brownsville? That's a goddamn lie. Even the white officers said every man and every rifle was in the barracks that night, present and accounted for. But it didn't matter, did it? Army didn't even give them a chance to defend themselves, didn't let those men have a court martial. Teddy Roosevelt gave them dishonorable discharges for not identifying the shooters. Not identifying the shooters? There were no shooters. Unless it was some drunken white cowboys. Kicking soldiers out for nothing? That's the fruit of that tree."

Now he stood, his words rushing out. "You all read the same story as I did in Sgt. Calloway's newspaper, about that man in Georgia, they call him Sam Hose. He went to his boss to get his pay and buckra threw down on him with his gun. Sam Hose killed that devil in self-defense. Two thousand white men came down from Atlanta by train to burn Sam Hose alive. They cut him up. They sold parts of him for souvenirs. And then they went and lied on him, said he raped the man's wife. You all know damn well Sam Hose didn't rape no white lady. He ran away as soon as he killed the husband. He knew what it meant. He knew what they would do to him. And then killing him wasn't enough. They hung two more men for the same crime. Including a preacher. The fruit of that tree is Sam Hose's body. Those other men's bodies are the fruit of that tree."

Not everybody got what David Fagen was saying that day. But Grant Mims did. He was coming to understand all too well what Private Fagen was saying about the Army, what Fagen was saying about all of them. He was coming to understand what Fagen was saying about *him*. He wondered how he would explain himself - how he would *live* with himself - the next time he assigned Private Fagen to empty all the latrines or to stand at attention all day long in the rain and the 90° heat.

He didn't have to. That was the last time any of them ever saw U.S. Army Private David Fagen. The next time they *heard* of him he was *Captain* David Fagen in the Hukbong Pilipinong Mapaghimagsik, the Philippine Revolutionary Army. And so here was Major Henry Wygant, his usually-pasty, fat face inches from Mims, but now beet red; blood vessels ready to explode; spittle dripping from his beard and flying into Grant Mims's eyes. And this ofay motherfucker was demanding to know what he, Grant Mims, had done to make David Fagen switch sides?

Grant Mims was a physically strong man. He could march up and down Luzon, Cebu, and the Visayas with a 70-pound pack, an 8-and-a-half-pound Krag, and forty-rounds of .30-40 ammunition. He was a physically courageous man, too, as he demonstrated in combat against the Pulahanes in Leyte. But he had seen what happened to Sergeant Major Calloway and he was not planning on spending the rest of his life locked up in an Army stockade… or worse. He was not interested in returning to Long Island so he could work in a stinking fish-processing plant. He held his tongue.

Grant Mims never again harbored the slightest doubt that his military service might liberate the people he fought, whether they were Filipinos or Mexicans or American Indians or striking American workers. He never again held out any hope that his military service might improve the lives of other Black Americans. He put in his time and he collected his check. When he could - which was often - he and his friend William Nesbit also collected the checks of their fellow soldiers over games of cards and dice and by betting on the regiment's baseball games and boxing matches. They understood the value of patience and of letting their marks have some wins.

The regiment was ordered to witness the hangings of Privates Edmond du Bose and Lewis Russell who, like David Fagen, joined and fought with the *insurrectos*. Several others were captured and sent to Leavenworth. But the Army never caught up with Captain David Fagen. Sure, the lyncher, General Funston, offered a $1000 reward for Fagen. And sure, a Filipino scout collected by dropping a head off and saying it was Fagen's. But Grant Mims saw that head. So did dozens of other members of the regiment. They had no idea who that scout murdered to get that reward and allow Funston to claim victory. But it was not who Funston said. It was not David Fagen.

Transcript of oral history tape recording with John Howat Walker, April 6

Yes, young lady, I will be happy to answer your questions about Mother Mary Jones. This is a home for retired miners. Every man here remembers Mother Jones.

You say she was a "precursor" for the women's movement? Maybe, maybe not. I just know that she cursed like a sailor. She surprised the hell out of people! Like I said, every man here remembers Mother Jones. Most of them can't speak two sentences without wheezing. That's why they all have oxygen tanks. They were breathing too much coal dust. I can speak for a few minutes still. That's because the coal operators labeled me an agitator and kept my name on a list. I couldn't hardly get a job underground. I spent most of my career preaching for the union. For the United Mine Workers of America. Mary Jones did, too. She was Irish and Catholic by birth, so it didn't strike her as strange to be a woman preaching to men. And threatening them, too. Just like the nuns in the schools she went to.

Yes, I think I do remember that. She did tell me she taught in them schools. Are you telling this story? Or is it me you want to record with that device?

District 12 here was the living beating heart of the union from the very early days when we started it. I was a wee lad back then. I worked in them mines under the flat prairie. I worked in the breakers when my family moved there from Glasgow. I guess I was six. I started underground mining when I was ten-years old. We were trying to organize them Illinois mines. We even got a state arbitrator to say 40¢ a ton was a fair rate of pay for us, but the goddamned operators said *they* couldn't live on it!

That's what I said. 40¢ a ton. That's right. Them operators were always afraid of us being able to feed our children. Like if we aren't starving then maybe they can't afford to do whatever it is the rich do. You think they all entered the poorhouse when we finally won the union? Of course not! Sometimes I think it's about the money for them. But sometimes I think they just enjoy seeing us naked and hungry. Where was I?

That's right. Mary Jones was there, too. That was before she became Mother. She was just a woman who helped us organize our union. Just like Big Mary Septak did for the miners in Pennsylvania. But I'm getting ahead of myself.

Sure, we shut down the mines in central Illinois. The operators refused to abide by the decisions of the same arbitrators they insisted on! They started building fortresses at their train stops. It puzzled us at first. Why build walls to keep us out when we were refusing to go in?

That's right, they had their own train stops. They were shipping the coal by rail. By the carload. Mostly to fire furnaces or to heat people's homes.

No, this wasn't coal for steel making. This was bituminous coal. Yes, this was all underground mining. Some of the mines were 100 feet underground. Some of them a thousand. They didn't start stripping the ground above until later. In them days it was still cheaper for the operators to send us down there to dig and to die. They didn't have the big power shovels yet.

Yes, Mary Jones was there with us. Did I say that already? Them operators were trying to get around the arbitrator's decision. They were bringing in scabs for 25¢ an hour. By train.

What? The scabs? They were colored men from Birmingham, Alabama.

Join the union? No. Those Illinois miners still had too much color prejudice to allow them in. And not just them. Me, too, I'm ashamed to say. That's why we were trying to form a union there. We were trying to protect white man's work. We wanted to get white man's pay.

Sure they were miners. We just couldn't see that at the time. We didn't see that at all. All we saw was their color. All we saw was the operators were bringing them in to take our jobs. Maybe I don't understand this like you young people do today. Maybe it was a different time.

Okay, that's true, too. Maybe the times weren't all that different. I'm sure the colored people already understood it real well back then. I probably still don't understand it the way the colored people do. I'm just trying to tell you the story. That's all.

Of course Mother Jones felt the same way. The whole story of that strike was about how we kept the scabs out. As far as we were concerned it was scabs on the train. It was a crowd of armed St. Louis detectives, too. We shot it out with them. I don't know how many we hit. I do know that train went on to Springfield without anybody getting off. That's how we won the union.

No, them weren't no Sherlock Holmes detectives. They were American detectives, you know? Just gun thugs for the company. Shooters who were paid to kill union men.

Mary Septak? I'll tell you that story. That was in Pennsylvania. Yes, Mother Jones was there, too. I think it was the year before the Illinois strike. It was in the Wyoming Valley.

No, I am not confused. The Wyoming Valley *is* in Pennsylvania.

No. I don't know why. I just know it's up there on the Susquehanna River. They mine anthracite coal there. Well, they did until the river fell right into the mine. Yeah, flooded everything.

Anthracite? It's harder and shinier. You need to force air through the fire. It gives a *lot* more heat, a lot. They used to float it down the river in barges. Then they took it by train to Pittsburgh. Not here. Not Pittsburg, Kansas. Pittsburgh, Pennsylvania. I'm talking about Pennsylvania.

When the mines up there in Pennsylvania first opened, it was Welshmen. The operators brought them from Barry and Cardiff to dig the coal. By the time you're asking about it was mostly Hunkies in there.

What? That's what we used to call them. They were from Poland and Lithuania and Slovakia. At first we didn't know if they were white. They didn't speak English. The operators weren't paying them white men's wages.

I understand what you're saying. I mean the operators were paying them less. By that time... it was around the time of the Bryan-McKinley election. I remember all that silver-gold talk. By that time a lot of them had learned to speak English. We realized they wanted to join the union. So the union sent me and Mary over there. We went to help with organizing. Mary, you know, Mother Jones.

We stayed at Mary Septak's boarding house, the other Mary. It was just a big old frame house, directly across the railroad tracks from the colliery. Mary Septak was strong for the union. She was Polish, but she spoke all them Hunkie languages. She used to give speeches to the miners first in one language and then in another. At least that's what they said she did. It all sounded like Hunkie to me. She was the one who invited us into the district. She heard about Mother Jones. She sent her a letter in care of the union. She asked her to come and help organize her miners.

They called her Big Mary. The bosses and the police were all afraid of her. She would get on a streetcar and give a look at the conductor and he wouldn't ask her for no money. The sheriff was afraid of her, too. But when the two Marys got together? Oh, it was like nothing could stop them. The two of them would get up on a platform, Big Mary in her babushka just towering over our Mother Jones in her glasses and hat. Mother Jones would give a speech. Big Mary Septak would translate it into all them other languages. The miners would just roar. Oh, it was like nothing could stop *them* neither.

They had a meeting up there. In the hills above Hazleton. In Lattimer where Big Mary's boarding house was. Hazleton was a town, but Lattimer wasn't nothing but a coal patch. You had the colliery, you had the company store, and you had the company houses. Big old wood-frame houses, built cheap with lots of small rooms, where the men lived doubled and tripled up. Not much grew up there. The trees were all cut down for lumber for the mine or else they were poisoned by the air. One or the other. Mother Jones said to the men, "You must be the most pathetic things on earth. Are you men at all? Look at the way you let these coal operators abuse you."

You would have thought they would be insulted. Well, you would if you never heard her say these things before. But that's the way she gave a speech. Sure, she ran them down hard. She told them they didn't deserve to be called men. And they loved it. They loved every word. Big Mary translated what she said and they all cheered.

Why, you ask? Because they were *planning* to get up and be men. They were *planning* to demand their rights. They were *planning* to stop the abuse of the Lehigh and Wilkes-Barre Coal Company. They were *planning* to stand up to the Luzerne County sheriff.

That's what the boys loved about her. That's what she called the men: "her boys." That's why she was Mother Jones, because they were her boys. And she would scold them. Like a mother can scold her boys if they aren't acting like men. Or maybe you're right. Maybe she was like a nun. Only a nun for the working class instead of a nun for the church. And just like those big nuns, the mothers, not the sisters. She could scold a boy. She could even hit a boy, if he didn't act like he needed to. Huh. I like that, you know? The union is the church of the working class? I think I might use that.

The meeting in Lattimer. Sure. She told them miners everything. She told them she weren't no humanitarian. She told them she was a *hell raiser*. That's right. I told you she could curse like a sailor. They loved that, too. Because it was hell they were going to have to raise if they were going to beat the coal operators and win a union.

The vote? Hell, no, she didn't talk to the women about the vote. You think Mother Jones needed to vote to raise hell? You think Big Mary needed to vote to raise hell? Them women asking for the vote back then were all married to mine operators. Or to the lawyers and the bookkeepers who served the operators. This weren't about men and women, it was the workers and the bosses. You think the operators let the miners vote? Let me tell you something. Back then the state of Pennsylvania charged the operators 3¢ a day for every Slovak or Italian they had on their payroll. They called it an Alien Tax. The operators had to pay it. Let's say they had 25,000 employees, which is about right. Let's say 20,000 of them were foreign born, which is about right. That's $600 *a day* in taxes. That's what, $200,000 a year, give or take? But those operators weren't cutting into their profits, oh no. They charged the workers themselves 3¢ a day, every day, for the privilege of being exploited in Pennsylvania! That's the kind of insult that those miners had to take. That's why Mother Jones and Big Mary Septak could whip them up by talking them down.

Let me catch my breath. Yes, Big Mary gave her own speeches, too. Honestly, I couldn't tell you. She wasn't speaking English. Mother Jones only told the men what they already knew. It *sounded* different, though, when she scolded them about it. Most of her speech was stories she got right from them. Big Mary had, I don't know, 12, maybe 18 men boarding with her at the Lattimer Mines. We sat at the table with them at dinner. We learned everything about the district right from them. Nowadays people remember the 16-hour days and the 6-day weeks they worked before we got the union. That was all true, and it was bad, real bad. But in Lattimer it wasn't year-round work, you see, it was seasonal. So it was not uncommon for those men to go four months without work! That's four months without any pay at all. Some of them would go elsewhere. Some of them would struggle with odd jobs. Or they would plant vegetables in the hills. And when I say the work is dangerous all you know about is the big cave-ins and explosions. They get the newspapers running to report those because it's an exciting story. The papers don't cover the everyday injuries. They don't cover the everyday deaths. We figured out those Wyoming Valley mines were killing one miner in three hundred *every year!* They were maiming one miner in *one hundred!* Every year! But the operators expected that every day they opened the mines they should have all the men they needed. And they expected to pay them pennies.

Things started to get hot around Labor Day weekend that year. It had only been a national holiday for a few years then. People still celebrated it as Labor Day instead of just barbeque day or end-of-summer day. They didn't like us celebrating May Day because that was all about the Haymarket Massacre so back in '94 President Cleveland proposed a labor holiday the first weekend in September and Congress passed it.

You don't know about the Haymarket?

Okay. I'll stick with Mother Jones. Where was I? Labor Day, 1897. We were sitting at Big Mary Septak's boarding house in Lattimer, Pennsylvania. Big Mary had a long oak table with enough room for all the boarders to eat together. She fed everybody pretty good, too. All Big Mary's food was new to me. That was a special meal that day because of the holiday but it sticks in my mind because of the conversation, planning how to fight the coal operators. She made a soup with sour cucumbers and potato. Then she gave us pickled fish. And I remember cabbage wrapped around a bunch of rice and vegetables and meat, all ground together. When I say these out loud, they sound kind of awful. But, believe me, it was all delicious. And it got all the men feeling optimistic. So Hanusz Tarnowicz, who was there at the table, asks, "Mother, what can we do?"

Mother Jones was waiting for that question. She proposed a peaceful march from Harwood, which was another coal patch, the other side of Hazleton, across Black Creek and up the mountain to the Lattimer Mines. It was the kind of thing she liked, you know? A procession. Now you've got me thinking of her as the nun of the working class. Everything fits: a procession, like the Catholics have for their saints' days. Big Mary was a Catholic, too, and she loved this idea. No picketing. No shouting. Everyone would walk through the district, all peaceable, past all the banks and law offices and the respectable people, petitioning for justice with our bodies.

I don't know who in that house was a spy for the bosses. I know that they always have one. If you're making secret plans for surprise actions the spies are a problem. Same thing if you're just starting out in a district like West Virginia or Colorado where they'll kill you just for talking union. Those places it's like Russia. Everything is a secret. But if you are planning a peaceful public march? In a district where you're already out on strike? It isn't that big of a problem. So I don't know who the spy was, but the bosses already knew about this march before we even discussed it.

No, I don't know. That's just what it felt like.

The operators' guy was the High Sheriff of Luzerne County. He was a gun thug named Martin, I think, James Martin. It was Labor Day weekend. He was off in Atlantic City, staying at the fucking Traymore Hotel. Maybe it's not that big of a deal anymore, but back then it was like the Taj Mahal of Atlantic City.

Atlantic City isn't that big of a deal now? You don't say! Well it was then.

So the general manager of the mines was a guy named Elmer Lawall. He calls Sheriff Martin in a panic. Tells him he has to *leave* Atlantic City right away. Tells him get right back to Luzerne County. I thought it was funny at the time. I should have known right away it was a problem. This guy blames *us* for cutting his vacation short, not his boss at the coal company. No, I mean that. He was his boss. The sheriff might as well be on the payroll of Lehigh and Wilkes-Barre Coal. Yes, there were other anthracite operators in the district, but Lehigh and Wilkes-Barre was the biggest. Their mines were taking two million tons a year out of the ground. That was a quarter of all the anthracite mined in the state. So, yes, Sheriff Martin was like an employee of Elmer Lawall. He had their finances behind him, too. That's how he had one hundred brand-new Winchester rifles in his office waiting for this occasion at $25 a piece! With metal-jacketed rounds! Sheriff Martin was known for dispersing mobs by himself. So you might wonder, why was he equipped for a posse of a hundred? So did we. I don't think he ever had more than four full-time deputies for the whole county. But there he was, arming a hundred local bank clerks and mine superintendents and accountants and lawyers. All to oppose an unarmed procession of miners. The two Marys made it clear. That march was to be peaceful. Nobody was to go armed. They wanted everybody to see the difference between law-abiding, petitioning workers and greedy, recalcitrant bosses.

The march was later in the week. Friday after Labor Day, I think. The miners began in Harwood, about six miles from Lattimer. There were about a hundred of us at the start. The idea was that people would join the procession as we went along. When we crossed Cherry Creek, about a mile and a half into the route, we were met by Sheriff Martin. He had about a hundred of his armed deputies with him. He told us we could not proceed. We said we were simply exercising our rights. He told us we had no permit to march in the streets of Hazleton. So we said we would just go around Hazleton.

Things could have started right there. One of the sheriff's deputies tore a flag off the pole of one of the marching miners. This was an American flag I'm talking about, too, not no Slovak flag. People got pretty angry, but Big Mary said we were there to march to the mine. We weren't there to fight with some pissant deputy. So we all went around Hazleton, across Black Creek and on to Harleigh.

There was a crowd of miners in Hazleton who were planning to join the procession as it went by. They heard what happened so they walked up to Harleigh. They joined the march there instead.

It seemed like the sheriff hadn't got what he wanted, you know? He and his posse jumped on the next streetcars. They hurried up to Lattimer to meet the march again. People on the trolleys said they heard some pretty reckless talk. Them deputies were bragging about what they were going to do. I mean, with all those pretty new Winchesters they were carrying.

Mother Jones wasn't talking, this was the miners' march, not hers.

Yes, the story has a point. Listen, young lady, I didn't go to Chicago to your university and stop *you* from playing cards to tell you this. You came here and asked *me*. I think you young people today should know about this but the capitalist class writes your history books and that's why you don't know anything! I guess you could just write the story of Mother Jones the way you want it to be. I'll go back to my card game.

[There is a click here as the tape is shut off, then another as it starts again.]

Yes, I accept your apology. Yes, I will finish the story.

When the workers reached Lattimer we were about four hundred people in the procession. Sheriff Martin and his posse were blocking the route again. It was just a few hundred yards short of the mine entrance. They were right in front of Big Mary's boarding house. Sheriff Martin stepped out in front of the crowd and ordered them to disperse. Big Mary translated his speech for the miners who didn't speak English, you know, but nobody moved. Everybody just stood there in the road, waiting to see what would happen next. Then, all of a sudden, the deputies started shooting.

Even then none of the marchers ran at first. But when we saw two miners drop – Andrew Jurešek and Mathias Čzaja, yeah, I still remember their names – well, then people realized that those were live rounds we were hearing. They panicked and scattered in every direction. Except for those first two men, every other casualty, killed or wounded, was a bullet in the back. The posse kept shooting and shooting even though the crowd followed the sheriff's orders and dispersed. When all that shooting finally stopped, 19 people were dead on the ground. There were at least another 60 wounded. Nobody really knows. So many people fled up Buck Mountain to get away from the sheriff's posse. Who knows how many left the district? Who knows how many bled to death up there in the woods?

Now do you understand why this story makes me angry? These were unarmed workers, in a peaceful procession and they were gunned down like... I don't know what they were gunned down like, who commits a massacre like that? And why has it been forgotten? No, the story gets worse.

You want to hear about Mother Jones. Yes, Mother Jones spoke some more in the days to come. She demanded justice for the dead. She kept quoting the Bible. "The voice of thy brother's blood crieth unto me from the ground," she said. I think that's what God said to Cain after he killed Abel. I don't really know my Bible. Mary demanded murder indictments. The truth is even those killers knew they did wrong. Yes, they did. Most of them fled that same day, before the grand jury even met. That's right, they all ran to Atlantic City, right back to the Traymore Hotel. The same hotel where Sheriff Martin was before it started. And that was another thing Mother Jones kept talking about in those days after the Lattimer Massacre. She compared the wives and the children of the dead – hungry and grieving, without anyone to care for them ever again, husbands and fathers shot down in the street – with the indicted deputies living it up at the Traymore with hot and cold running sea water. And hot and cold running fresh water. Four faucets in every tub. A fifth faucet for ice water in the sink. Oh, and the next march she organized was all women. Just wives of miners. She was everywhere in those days. They eventually got the union in Lattimer.

Justice for the murderers? No. The trial lasted 27 days. The jury heard testimony from marchers who survived. They heard testimony from the sheriff's deputies. They heard evidence from schoolteachers who saw the entire thing from the door of their schoolhouse. They heard from the coroner how every one of the dead after the first two were shot in the back. No, they weren't convicted. Those murderers were professional people, friends of the coal company. No coal county jury was going to convict accountants and lawyers for killing a bunch of Hunkie miners. Emperor Franz Joséph threatened to sue, because it turned out that all those countries that all those murdered men came from were all Austria. But nothing ever came of that either. All those capitalists, American president or Austrian emperor, they all look out for each other. Mother Jones said that, too.

Now I am tired from all this talking. If you want to hear more you will have to come back another day. If you have the stomach for it.

[Recording ends here.]

53

Cananea, Sonora, Mex.
10 May 1906

Confidential Report from Henry Ossian Flipper
To New Mexico Att'y Gen'l Albert Fall

Dear A.G. Fall,

I regret to inform you that conditions here have deteriorated over the last few weeks. The mine closed Saturday for Cinco de Mayo celebrations. While the Mexican employees were imbibing "High Life" by the keg, outside agitators were stirring them up against the company. I am quite certain I recognized José Quintana. You may remember him from my report on the recent disturbances across the border at Los Cerrillos. We thought we had that situation completely under control. Quintana hadn't even been a member of the New Mexicans' negotiating committee. He singlehandedly brought together the Indians, the Serbs, the Italians, the New Mexicans, the white Americans, and the Bolivians. I still don't know how. Those groups hated each other. Now Quintana is an IWW, traveling from one work site to another, stirring up the ignorant class. He is a fluent speaker of both English and Spanish.

I also saw Abrán Salcido. He is a Mexican national and very well-read for a laborer. He was in the Arizona Territorial Prison at Yuma for leading a strike in Clifton a few years ago. Either they released him or he escaped and came here to start more trouble. He, too, is most probably an IWW and a dangerous enemy. I will secure a copy of his mug shot from the Arizona authorities.

These two, with others whose identities I am attempting to ascertain, were circulating through the beer halls and picnic grounds, making outrageous claims and spreading slanders. They claim that Mexican workers deserve the same pay as Americans. They whine that lift operators don't treat them with respect. (All these borderers think they are grandees at the court of King Alfonso!) They even ask why Mexicans don't receive promotions, as if that weren't evident. Most damning, though, is the fact that the identical trumped-up grievances were heard in every venue. This proves positively that there is a *cabal* organizing to mislead the Mexican employees.

Since Monday when the men returned to work I have seen petitions circulated with the same points mentioned above. They demand equal pay, courteous treatment and promotions. Col. Greene will, of course, reject these demands.

I cannot personally confirm the rumors that some outside power has been arming the IWWs with bolt-action rifles. I have heard rumors that they are drilling in the mountains toward Cuitaca under the command of officers of the Japanese Imperial Navy. None of my informants has actually seen this, but I know for a fact that there are Japanese persons in Hermosillo. I include this as a warning that the IWWs must be considered extremely dangerous and that they may even be in the service of a hostile foreign power, a hostile foreign power which is attempting to stir up the colored races.

Regarding the legal work I am doing for you, the public reason for this confidential mission, I forward under separate cover a translation of the original Huerto de los Brazitos Land Grant, along with a survey map made by me. Note especially that I indicate former river channels. I am quite certain that you and your investors will be able to use this information in the Court of Private Land Claims to prove that your competitors' titles are baseless. If the deeds they purport to own are not forgeries – and I suspect they are – then they refer to now-arid tracts along the *previous course* of the river and are therefore without any value. This survey should cement the validity of your claims.

Please forgive my importunity, but it is now some time since I asked that you investigate the trumped-up charges that led to my court martial and fraudulent discharge from the U.S. Army. How is my case going? I wish for reinstatement, but I would welcome any settlement. There is no question in my mind that those allegations were only made because of my skin color. The other junior officers resented my presence, as they had since the first day I began attending West Point. When our commander's daughter began paying attention to me, they could not bear seeing a white woman speaking to me.

Most of my classmates from the Academy have now attained the rank of Lieutenant Colonel. Even Jim Maney, who is notorious for actually murdering his own superior officer, is still in the Army and a Major. Maney attempted to bully me out into dropping out for all our four years together at West Point. The parallels between my case and Maney's assassination of Captain Edwin Hedberg are galling. Like me, Hedberg was disliked by his fellow officers, in his case for his Swedish accent and for having been an enlisted man before he was commissioned. As with me, they conspired to trump up embezzlement charges and had him drummed out of the Army. Unlike me, Hedberg was reinstated and returned to his rank. The other officers encouraged the enlisted men not to salute him. They themselves disrespected him in every way and at every turn. When Captain Hedberg confronted then-Lieutenant Maney for continually flirting with Hedberg's pretty young wife, Maney drew his pistol and shot Hedberg to death. The court martial ruled this self-defense; how is beyond imagination. And still I remain a civilian, my reputation sullied by a false conviction. I beg your assistance with this matter.

I will write again if circumstances here in Cananea warrant.

Yr obt svt,
Henry Ossian Flipper

Cananea, Sonora, Mex.
27 May 1906
Confidential Report from Henry Ossian Flipper
to N.M. Att'y. Gen'l. Albert Fall
FOR YOUR EYES ONLY

Dear Attorney General Fall:

Thank you for your confidence. As you advised in your letter of 12 May I presented my bonafides to Colonel Greene at his office here in town and discussed innocuous engineering matters. During that meeting he silently passed me a note with an out-of-town location and a time later that day. I went by mule early to survey the area and ensure that it was secure. I watched Colonel Greene arrive by automobile. He was not followed.

It seems that the IWWs, Quintana and Salcido, are working with a local group styling themselves the "Liberal Club of Cananea." This Liberal Club is affiliated with the editors of the subversive journal *Regeneración*, published in St. Louis, Missouri. Those editors, Enrique and Ricardo Flores-Magón, are well-known enemies of public order in Mexico. The Magón brothers are Zapotec Indians, but with their college and law degrees they pass as civilized people, despite their advocacy of anarchism. President Porfirio Díaz put a price on their heads, and that is why they are living in the United States: were they to return here to Mexico, they would be jailed for treason. (It is hard for me to understand why President Roosevelt tolerates their seditious and anti-American literature, or – for that matter – why they want to live in "Yankeeland" if they hate us so much.) The Liberal Club organized the Fifth of May celebration here in Cananea which I referred to in my previous letter of 10 May. I believe the Magón brothers themselves are trying to start a strike here.

Greene is confident that he can convince the workers to drop their ridiculous demands for equal wages, promotions and "respect" since he is very popular with the people here. He is anxious, however, to find a way to squash the

"Liberals" and has the complete cooperation of the local mayor and police. They are all concerned, too, about the possibility of armed IWWs drilling with the Japanese. Greene can enlist the assistance of the Arizona Rangers (who are happy to cross the border), but this requires a *serious misstep* by his adversaries so that President Díaz will understand the arrival of armed North Americans as aid, rather than an invasion. An example of such a misstep would be an open call by the "Liberals" for violence against either the regime or the mine.

Colonel Greene is quite certain that these local "Liberals" are too careful to make an error like this, even though chaos and disorder are their program. This is why he met with me, and this is why it was secret. This is why I headed this letter for your eyes only. Any breach of secrecy on this could have fatal consequences and I humbly implore your cooperation, even with colleagues you trust.

I am now drafting an anonymous handbill in Spanish to be distributed to the Mexican mineworkers. The intent is to mimic, as far as possible, the rhetoric and tone of the "Liberals" and of the paper *Regeneración*, but to abandon their pose of civility. We will, of course, provide our own English translation and give it wide circulation in the territorial press of New Mexico and Arizona. This should assure support for firm measures against the "Liberals" here in Cananea and may even allow the agents of President Díaz to move against the Magón brothers in their sanctuary in Missouri. And, should Colonel Greene's entreaties fail with his employees, the presence here in Sonora of a troop of Arizona Rangers will work wonders in crushing any strike, especially one for which the IWWs are unprepared.

I do not yet have a first draft to share with you. I can say for certain, though, that the handbill will open with a declaration of a strike, which will surprise the workers since they will still be waiting to hear Colonel Greene's response to their "demands." This premature move should help turn them against the "Liberals." I will also include an inflammatory denunciation of the Porfirio Díaz government. This will convince the state authorities of Sonora of the danger the "Liberals" pose and the need to accept help wherever it is offered, i.e. the Arizona Rangers. Finally, I intend to use phrasing that will divide the so-called "colored races" who the Imperial Japanese pretend to support. That should alienate any soldiers of the Negro cavalry sent here to suppress a potential strike! I am working on the details. I will send you a draft as soon as it is completed.

Your obedient servant,
Henry Ossian Flipper

Cananea, Sonora
1906

Like the conversion of San Pablo, the moment of Joey Quintana's calling was so astonishing that its sights and sounds, its textures and scents, remained brightly illuminated in his memory as long as he lived. There was no blinding light from heaven on the Damascus Road, no divine voice. Instead, there was a canvas-covered beer garden in the dusty mining town of Los Cerrillos. There was a cool breeze that had no business inside the moldy tent, and a phantom tap on the shoulder. In the case of San Pablo, his dramatic call led him to spend the rest of his life as an itinerant, preaching the good news of Jesus Christ all over the eastern Mediterranean and founding churches everywhere he went. For Joey Quintana, ever since that afternoon mug of Glorieta beer, he had been preaching the gospel of the international proletariat as an organizer for the Industrial Workers of the World.

When Joey was fourteen he left his home in northern New Mexico with reluctant *bendiciones* from his puzzled parents and a look of silent hurt from his kid sister Piedad. He was searching for a wider world than he could find in the valley of Cañada de los Alamos where he grew up. He was looking for a life beyond planting corn and chiles and raising a few sheep like his father and grandfather and every other man in the village. He tried working on ranches and docks and ships and mines. He traveled to Texas and Montana and California and even China. But after all that, he finally received his vocation only thirty miles from home, working in a copper mine alongside boys with whom he had grown up.

Half the miners in Los Cerrillos were outsiders. The Phelps, Dodge Company recruited them from every place in the world where copper was dug: the Upper Peninsula of Michigan; Cornwall in southwestern England; Bor in eastern Serbia; Sestri Levante near Genoa, Italy; even Kan Hsien on the island of Formosa in China.

The rest of the mine's workers came from the mountain *placitas* of New Mexico. When the U.S. government took away the villagers' timber and grazing lands, all that was left to the people were their irrigated parcels directly adjacent to the seasonal streams. Every year it became harder for a young man to support a family with those little garden-sized farms. Some supplemented their income with cash work for the railroads, cutting fuel and ties in the forests that had once been their own. Some traveled to Colorado to work in the sugar beet fields. Many, though, went underground, digging copper for the wires and coal for the generators of the new electric industry.

These New Mexicans who worked at the Los Cerrillos mine were like a village to themselves. They may have grown up in different places – Anton Chico, San Miguel del Vado, Galisteo – but in the copper camp they were *vecinos*. At home, in their respective *villitas*, all the neighbors came together as one for spring ditch cleaning, without regard for the conflicts that fester in every community. The same here: they were working together to challenge wage cuts from the copper company. All the workers from all the *placitas* of northern New Mexico met together.

The *manitos* selected a committee to represent them in negotiations with the mine superintendent. They expected to be treated honorably, like men. But the superintendent ignored their formal petitions. He told them it was out of his hands. He said decisions about wages were made at company headquarters in New York City. This was a puzzle. How does a man talk to a corporate board? How do you negotiate with its members: people who nobody has ever met, who live in a city two thousand miles away? They really weren't sure what to do next. They needed somebody whose advice they could trust.

That is how Joey found himself one evening after work sitting in Doña Rosa's beer garden with his childhood friend, Bernardo Gallardo, and with Bernardo's buddy, Jesús Vega. Joey was the one who had traveled the world. He was the one with experience working for the big corporations. Maybe, the *manitos* thought, Joey would have some idea how to resist the copper company.

He did.

The instant they asked him, he knew that this was the call he had been awaiting for so many years. This was the work he was meant to do. He smelled the mildew on the canvas and the stale beer on the ground and they suddenly took on a heightened meaning for him, so that these smells would always bring him back to this moment. The hair on his arms stood as if there were a breeze where there was no breeze, as if a spirit was tapping him on the shoulder. It was the feeling of transcendence he had long imagined, but more so, much more so.

Joey said that their first step had to be including all the other miners, of all nationalities, in their discussions. Bernardo and Jesús didn't really like it – who, after all, were these outsiders? – but they did it. The New Mexicans were surprised and happy to discover that the other men wanted to work with them. Even the Serbs and Italians, who had some ongoing murderous feud that nobody else understood, were ready to join together. Joey told the new multinational committee that their next step was to address all the miners at the opening of the morning shift, and to share with them the news of the failed conversations with the superintendent, how he had dismissed their concerns. And they did that, too. In every language.

Things didn't go exactly as planned. Joey certainly never expected that the superintendent and his armed guards would immediately lock them all out of the mine. But it didn't matter, because the miners stuck together and they won back their original wage plus recognition for a committee – of all nationalities – to meet regularly with the superintendent and discuss any new conflicts that might arise.

It wasn't even their victory that gave Joey the most joy. It was the simple fact of all those people joining together to make their voices heard by a distant corporation that valued them no more than the mules that hauled the ore cars. It was the joy of unity over division, of purpose over anonymity, and of resistance over oppression.

Because of that success the Industrial Workers of the World asked Joey to join them as a traveling organizer. That is why he was now in Mexico in a copper camp that dwarfed Los Cerrillos, dwarfed even the great Anaconda camp of Butte, Montana. Colonel William Greene's Cananea mine produced 144 *million* tons of copper a year. There were 11,000 men here.

At first glance, it looked to Joey as though finding unity among the miners would be easier in Cananea than it had been among the many nationalities of Cerrillos. Eight of every ten men here were Mexican. But that was before he realized how many of the men were Yaqui Indians, working here to avoid being sold into slavery on the sugar plantations of Oaxaca by the government in Mexico City. There were conflicts between the landless farmers from Aguascalientes and the cowboys escaping hacienda peonage in Sinaloa. The men from San Luis Potosí were all experienced miners. They were contemptuous of both the farmers and the cowboys because they were novices to underground work. And all of them looked down on the Nahuatl speakers of Nayarit. All these men might be Mexican, but they were apparently as divided as the Italians and Serbs of Los Cerrillos. And this was before even accounting for the Cornishmen, who seemed to hate everybody else, and the Chinese, who everybody else seemed to hate.

Then there was the owner. Despite his unimaginable wealth, the workers admired him as one of their own, a miner who had made it good. It complicated the work of organizing a union. Nobody could tell Joey how William Greene had acquired the title of "Colonel," but that is what everybody fondly called him. He was not an absentee like the Dodges of New York who owned the Cerrillos mine. No, Colonel Green seemed to be around all the time, slapping miners on the back and buying them drinks in the cantinas. The *mineros* all knew that *el coronel* fought off a hostile takeover bid by the Rockefellers even if they didn't exactly know what that meant. They knew he killed a man at the OK Corral in Tombstone, but everyone considered it a badge of honor: they all said that the man was responsible for the drowning death of Colonel Greene's daughter. Nobody had more details, but it didn't matter, that was the story. They knew, too, that the Cananea mines offered the highest pay in Mexico. It was rumored that President Porfirio Díaz himself complained about Greene's generosity to his employees. They said *el señor presidente* was afraid that other Mexicans would want what they got, that it interfered with Díaz's policy of *pan o palo*, bread or beatings. Even when Greene cut the wages of his Mexican workers (but not the Anglos!) he explained that he, too, was facing financial challenges – the Rockefellers, you know? – but they would all endure the hardships together and then soon, very soon, they would all share in his success. And their desire to believe in him prevailed.

Still, there were a few things that rankled, and Joey listened very carefully to the bitter words. Perhaps Colonel Greene himself spoke in good Mexican Spanish, and perhaps he smiled and treated them like friends, but his Anglo clerks and supervisors and support staff did not. The first thing a Mexican miner heard at the start of every shift was a gringo elevator operator shouting: "Squeeze in there you beaner sons of bitches!" If they went to the lumberyard to pick up framing to timber the roof of the cut they were working in, one of the Metcalf brothers who ran the operation was sure to complain: "Don't take so much! This wood is worth more than all you fucking spics put together."

The Metcalfs were also the rental agents for the houses the Colonel rented to his workers. For the Mexican miners, those "houses" were shacks up in the hills, built of nothing but broken-up shipping pallets and scrap wood cast aside by the lumberyard. The Metcalf brothers were completely uncompromising about the high rents they charged and everybody blamed them - not Colonel Greene - for both the rents and the conditions. They were horrible places, especially for children, because the Metcalfs also rented space to brothels and 24-hour gambling dens. Mexicans were forbidden even to enter these segregated establishments, but the Metcalfs put them in the Mexican neighborhoods. The Anglos who frequented them all lived up on the mesa, but their drinking and whoring and gambling was done among the homes and families of the Mexican workers. Every Mexican parent resented their children having to step over the bodies of naked, intoxicated *gabachos* and pools of vomit on their way to school in the morning

Then there was the company's refusal to promote Mexicans. Correct use of a pick and shovel can be picked up by anybody with an able body and reasonable intelligence. But tunneling underground and following a mineral seam safely and economically requires a thoughtful, observant person with long experience and good teachers. It made sense that there were some such men among the Cornish, who claimed to have been mining underground since before the time of Jesus Christ. It made sense that the savviest Cornishmen should be made foremen. But what was true of Cornwall was also true of Mexico. Mexicans had been mining underground for at least a thousand years: before the Spanish conquest, even before the Aztecs. Joey found no shortage of Nahuatl words for every aspect of copper mining, and they were not loanwords from Spanish. And yet there were no Mexican foremen.

Those complaints became the heart of Joey's agitational work: Half of all foremen should be Mexicans. Supervisors should treat workers with courtesy. He added the demand for an eight-hour day and a minimum wage of five pesos a day, which was already the minimum for Anglos. And then he began the slow, patient work of convincing the miners that they could address the company as a group instead of as individuals, that they had things in common, that they were not alone in this new industrial world.

There was a basis for the miners to understand collective action. Back home, in the ranchos and villages the workers came from – as in Joey's home village in New Mexico – everybody knew that together with their neighbors and cousins they were part of something larger than themselves. *Vecinos* all belonged to the same church with its annual saints' days and processions. Some belonged to irrigation cooperatives with seasonal collective work cleaning the ditches. Weddings? Baptisms? Funerals? In times of joy and in times of sorrow, the whole community joined together, bringing food and emotional support. Here in the new town of Cananea, though, capitalism persuaded the members of its transplanted work force that they were solitary and insignificant players in a great battle royal, a war of all against all. It was Joey's job to let each person he met see a new identity of purpose in joining together with one another as industrial workers.

Some of his work took place in the cantinas of Ronquillo, the *barrio* where most of the Mexican miners of Cananea lived. But Joey was not looking to convert every disgruntled miner who had one too many High Lifes. No, he was looking for men who already had the respect of their fellows, for thoughtful men who had begun to develop a working-class consciousness on their own. Vincent St. John, the lead organizer for the IWW, told Joey before sending him here that it was not his place to lead the movement. The job of the organizer was to identify the leaders and to assist them. So most of his work took place in private meetings. Sometimes they met in homes or boarding houses. More often they avoided the eyes of informers and company detectives by meeting in the nearby Elenita Mountains or in the cottonwoods and willows by the banks of a stream called *el Barrilito* just outside of town.

Joey and his potential recruits read and discussed the documents of the movement he represented: "The working class and the employing class have nothing in common. There can be no peace so long as hunger and want are found among millions of working people and the few, who make up the employing class, have all the good things of life." That was the method that Vincent St. John advised. But Joey had his own ideas, too. He insisted that they take time getting to know each other's personal stories. The capitalists might value them only as a pair of arms and strong backs; he wanted them all to value one another as people.

One of the best-read recruits was a miner from Chihuahua named Abrán Salcido. Joey was surprised to discover that Abrán had done most of that reading while he did time in the Arizona Territorial Prison in Yuma. Many of the men in the study group were suspicious of unions. They saw how the predominantly-Anglo Western Federation of Miners excluded them from joining, keeping Mexicans underpaid and keeping the best jobs for themselves. Abrán had seen just that in the copper camp of Clifton-Morenci: when the Anglo union secured an eight-hour day, it actually meant a 20% pay cut for Mexicans and Mexican-Americans! He led a strike – without the help of any union at all – to restore their wages, which was why the copper company had him imprisoned. Instead of opposing unions though, Abrán was now totally convinced of the need for a *new* union… one that included everybody.

Fernando Palomares was a Mayo Indian from Sinaloa. He was completely fluent in Yaqui and had the trust of all the Yaquis in camp. As a boy he had been employed by a utopian commune of North Americans called the Pacific Colony. They taught him about socialism and the class struggle and he never forgot those lessons.

Práxedis Guerrero was the son of a wealthy *hacendado* from Los Altos de Ibarra in Guanajuato, educated in an elite *secundario*, and in a military academy where he became a lieutenant of cavalry. He turned his back on all that. He had worked in copper mines in Arizona and gold mines in Colorado. He had worked as a longshoreman in San Francisco and as a logger in east Texas. Práxedis introduced them to middle-class allies in Cananea, professional and business people who – like him – were affiliated with the Partido Liberal Mexicano led by the Flores-Magón brothers.

The work went well. There was a growing sense that it was *almost* time to select a committee and present demands to the company. And that is why Joey was astonished to get up at dawn one Friday and find that the Mexican miners of Cananea – instead of heading in to work – were all milling around the streets in their Sunday best. There was still a morning chill in the air at this mile-high elevation and the skies were blue. Spirits were high and he heard the word *"huelga"* on every lip. A strike? Who had called it? He asked a passing stranger that question. Instead of answering, the man handed him a leaflet. As Joey read the text, his heart sank. It was both an invitation to the army to crush the workers – *pan o palo*, remember? – and an affront to everything Joey believed about class solidarity. He wouldn't have believed it was possible to be so divisive and so provocative at the same time, but there it was. It said:

> Mexicans!
> What we don't have is a government for us!
> What we don't need is a government of criminal oppressors!
> Throw out all foreigners!
> Curse those who put us on the level of Negros and Chinese!
> Curse the government that favors foreign adventurers over the true owners of this earth!

Who could have written this? Who could have distributed it? If somebody had set out on purpose to split the workers by nationality, they could not have done a better job. But Joey was not about to start arguing with people. If they were striking against the company, he was going to do his best to support it and to help guide it. He was not going to stand on the sidelines quibbling.

The strikers were in a festive mood as they gathered in front of the Ronquillo town offices on Avenida Durango. One after another, men stood up to give flowery speeches about honor, respect, tradition, and patriotism:

"Let us march in the spirit of that golden eagle, the father of our nation, Father Miguel Hidalgo!"

"We must defend the fertile soil of our homeland, watered by our tears and by the blood of the teenaged martyrs who defied the Yankees at Chapultepec!"

"Our silence and passivity now dishonors the heroism and victory of the outnumbered soldiers of Puebla!"

Above all, each speaker prayed devoutly for the assistance of the Virgin of Guadalupe, alluding piously to the mantle of Juan Diego. The crowd cheered enthusiastically for all this old-fashioned oratory. It was everything that Joey feared: looking backward instead of forward, excluding the workers of other nationalities.

As the speeches went on, the temperature soared under the Sonora sun. The high spirits of the crowd, though, did not wilt. Eventually, one of the speakers realized that somewhere in the enormous complex of Cananea there might be workers who were not yet on strike. He urged those assembled to march en masse from shop to shop, calling out those who hadn't heard or who might be afraid. With a roar of assent, most of them began walking east through the dusty streets toward the plaza. They sang – what else? – "*Al grito de Guerra.*" For all that song's martial words, though - about readying the steel and about cannon shaking the earth to its core - everybody still seemed to be in good humor and there were no firearms in evidence.

As they walked up toward Avenida Chihuahua somebody started singing "*La Golondrina*" and the whole crowd picked up the maudlin melody. Joey understood how the wistful lyrics about a storm-tossed bird, far from home, might appeal to homesick people, but he wondered: *Where were the songs of solidarity and struggle? Where were the songs of the proletariat?* These songs were worse than the speeches for reinforcing backward ideas. But there was no time to think about the need for class-conscious songs. They were headed for the lumberyard. They were headed for the Metcalfs.

As the marchers arrived at the complex on 8th Street, the singing died down and the temperature seemed to drop. Standing at the gate, and commanding everybody's attention, was Colonel Greene's foreman, the older Metcalf brother, George. With his foul mouth and his contempt for the people of this country, he had managed to personally affront each man in the crowd at one time or another. Now Gabacho George had devised a new insult. As he stood facing them he was holding a four-inch, high-pressure fire hose. This hose was a necessity to protect tens of thousands of dollars worth of wood here in the arid desert climate, but he was now threatening to use it as a weapon against the workers. The woven linen hose was fully charged, rigid, and dripping with water. Little rivulets turned the dust in the street into worms of mud.

"All you spic sons of bitches can get the fuck out right now!" shouted Metcalf. "Or get wet!" he added.

The crowd hesitated. Ruining one's good suit was not an idle threat to a workingman making three pesos a day. But before anybody could decide what to do, Metcalf unleashed a blast from his hose, knocking the front ranks of the marchers right off their feet and into the dusty gutter. Then, before anybody even had the chance to turn and run, three rifle shots rang out in rapid succession. Two of the marchers were hit by bullets and dropped. George Metcalf had placed snipers atop the stacks of timber.

At once the great, good-humored, and nostalgic crowd of displaced peasants, dressed for a fiesta, vanished. They became instead a murderous and vengeful mob. Metcalf tried to hold them back with his hose, but he couldn't cover all angles at once. They were on him in seconds and he went down under their fists and feet. The miners' matches came out at once, as if Metcalf's use of a firehose against them inspired the idea of a retaliatory conflagration. It seemed only a moment before the entire lumberyard, thousands of board-feet of tinder-dry wood, was ablaze. A few more miners fell from rifle shots, but the gunfire stopped quickly as the snipers fled to escape the deadly inferno.

For a while the strikers watched with a kind of horrified fascination as the flames leaped a hundred feet in the sky. Then they began walking back toward the Cananea plaza, uncertain what their next move should be.

One thing Joey knew from his experience in Los Cerrillos was that the next move would not be theirs to decide. What none of them knew was that Colonel Greene's Anglo clerical-support staff was waiting for them in front of the Hotel Sonora, each carrying a newly-purchased high-powered rifle and hundreds of rounds of ammunition. As the crowd of strikers approached the plaza, they still had no plan. Neither did Colonel Greene's frightened posse, though, and in the absence of any clear leadership, they simply opened fire on the workers, killing a few more miners and scattering the rest in all directions. Across the plaza, ten or fifteen hungover American cowboys, spooked by the fire at the lumberyard, were hiding on the roof of another hotel, the Los Angeles. The sight of fleeing strikers terrified them into unleashing a new barrage of pistol fire. Fortunately they were too intoxicated to hit anybody, but the hail of bullets convinced the workers that Colonel Greene had decided to kill all of them.

Joey's mind raced. Was there some way to salvage this rapidly deteriorating catastrophe? He had not yet run into even one member of the committee with whom he had been working. Their goal was to create the structure of a local organization, but such an organization did not yet exist, much less have the recognition and trust of the mass of workers. He walked toward the mine openings west of town, hoping to meet somebody he knew and with whom he could strategize. Finally, as he got to the Cobre Grande #5 entrance, he found Abrán Salcido. This was a relief. Salcido was easily the most respected and capable leader among the Mexican workers.

They quickly exchanged reports on what each had seen and heard. Abrán had no more idea than Joey how the strike had begun. Nor did he know who could have written the handbill. He disliked it even more than Joey did.

"The Liberals?" asked Joey, referring to the small businessmen and professionals who opposed the Porfirio Díaz government.

"I wondered that, too," answered Abrán. "They have access to a printing press. But they would have included their own demands and they certainly would have insisted on their own leadership. No," he concluded, "it has to have been an agent of Colonel Greene himself."

Joey was skeptical. "Doesn't he have too much to lose? He needs every ounce of copper coming out of the mines just to pay his creditors. How much do you think all that burned lumber was worth?"

Abrán stood up straight with a new thought. "The Rockefellers?" he suggested. "They have everything to gain if he loses control of this business."

Joey smiled sadly. "That could very well be, but if it is, it doesn't help us at all. What difference does it make to the workers which plutocrat runs this town? So, whether it's Greene or whether it's his enemies in Wall Street, we still need to get organized. Unless you have a brilliant tactical idea, I think we have just suffered a big setback. They're going to come down hard on us, and I don't think we have the capacity to resist them yet. Maybe the *federales* are coming to crush the strike. Or maybe the *rurales*. But we know the Díaz regime won't miss an opportunity to make an example of us."

Abrán nodded, then looked up sharply. "You're not leaving us, are you?"

"No," said Joey. "I'll stand with you. But understand: we still need to organize. And it's going to be harder."

It would be years before the workers of Cananea were again in a position to organize a union. And within a month, Greene had been forced to borrow $400,000 from the Rockefellers for operating capital. By the end of the year, they had taken control of his entire business.

When the *rurales* did arrive, they arrested Abrán Salcido, Praxédis Guerrero, the former cavalry officer, and all those middle-class liberals who opposed President Díaz but had nothing to do with the strike. No posse members were charged with any murders. The miners all returned underground to work, but without any more illusions about the company or the people for whom they were working. Joey was called back to the other side of the border. The union leadership wanted him to get a job in the beet fields around Fort Collins, Colorado, to see if there was an opportunity to organize the farm workers there.

Sapulpa, Oklahoma
1905

Hank Yarholar tied off the last strand in this quarter-mile-long roll of barbed wire and returned his fencing pliers to their holster. He took off the thick leather gloves and wiped the back of his neck with his bandana. Then he said, "Break time. That's five miles already." Only a few days had passed since Delbert McIntosh's conversation with Colonel George Miller, but neither Hank nor any of his crew knew anything about that. They only knew this was paid work.

The four men in Hank's work gang said nothing. Zack Berryhill and Island Grayson immediately climbed under the wagon – the only shade for some distance – and went to sleep. Archie Bruner pulled out a pouch of tobacco and rolled two cigarettes. Warrior Bruner filled a couple of tin cups with water from the crew's five-gallon canvas bucket. Warrior handed Archie a drink and Archie gave Warrior a smoke. Then they, too, climbed under the wagon without a word. It was that hot.

Hank Yarholar had a lot of doubts about fencing in all this Muskogee Nation land for a white man. *Wvcenv* had been sneaking into the Nations and stealing native land for decades. With statehood coming, and with the whites controlling the courts, their thefts were accelerating and becoming more brazen. Some were pretending Native ancestry. He had heard even heard of white men marrying *estecate* women and then murdering them for their allotments. So what did this fence mean?

Hank's father, Tustenugge Yarholar, had assured him that no wire fence could ever convey any ownership rights of Mvskoke land. For traditional Creeks, Tustenugge's word was like law. He was a member of the Council of Kings. He commanded a company of Creek Light Horse. And Hank wanted this cash work. He badly wanted the prestige that came from distributing work (and the pay that came with it) to his peers. Still, he could not shake off his discomfort. The premium pay Colonel Miller was giving them for this job only increased that discomfort.

They had just put up a straight line of barbed-wire fence five miles long. When they were done, the enclosed pasture would measure thirty square miles. How many *este mvskokvlke* could all this land support? Why build a fence of barbed wire to keep out other men's cattle and pigs (not to mention wild game)? What was Colonel Miller's intent here? And, really, what had Miller ever been a colonel *of*?

69

What was that saying: Speak of the devil and he will appear?

"Nice work, fellows," said Colonel Miller. "At the rate you're working, we can be done by Saturday."

Hank hadn't seen him ride up, hadn't heard his horse.

Archie and Warrior listened, still silent. Zack's and Island's eyes remained shut. Hank didn't know whether they were feigning sleep or not. "You asked for a good crew who are willing to work," he answered the Colonel.

"I just wasn't certain when I saw that you hired niggers," drawled the Colonel. At that, Island Grayson opened his eyes. Warrior Bruner got out from under the wagon and stood up.

"These men are all Creek Indians," said Hank. "Some of them are my kin."

"I'm from Kentucky," answered the Colonel. "We don't have nigger kin."

The ugly statement sat in the heat like a decomposing carcass.

"Don't you?" challenged Warrior after a moment's silence. Now Archie, Zack and Island got up and joined him next to the wagon. They all looked at the Colonel, awaiting his response.

The Colonel pulled back his coat, displaying the big Navy Colt he wore on his belt. None of the other men were armed, although Hank kept a rifle in the wagon in case they saw wolves. "I'm surprised you Indian boys are even willing to work alongside these niggers," Miller said, apparently addressing himself to Archie and Zack.

"Mister," said Warrior, ignoring the threat of violence in the Colonel's gesture, "maybe you forget we fought a Civil War over this. Or maybe you just forget who won. Maybe you'd rather see some of us working for you for nothing."

The Colonel made no eye contact at all with Warrior Bruner. Instead, looking at Hank, he said, "I took you for a competent foreman who knows how to run a disciplined crew. Was I mistaken? Should I find somebody else to complete this job?"

Hank had been following the exchange between Colonel Miller and Warrior with dismay. He wondered for a moment how his father would handle this, then

70

quickly suppressed the thought. This was his problem. He knew before he took the job that the Colonel was an asshole. He hadn't suspected that he was one of these unreconstructed Confederates. But Miller was a *rich* Confederate asshole, and the money he was paying for this job was a good deal for all of them. There was precious little paid work in the Creek Nation at these rates. Hank had a wife and two boys. The others had children, too. If he could find a way to defuse this little blow-up there might be more jobs for all of them, and more money.

Warrior Bruner, however, wasn't in the mood to defuse anything. "I asked you whether you have Negro kin. You didn't answer me. Maybe you have a little something in *you?*"

Colonel Miller's face reddened and his hand strayed toward his Colt. Hank quickly stepped between the men, his back to the Colonel and said, "Warrior, take your tools and leave; you're off this job. I'll settle up with you later in the week."

Warrior now looked at Hank and said, "Our daddies fought side by side against these assholes. You choose this *wvcenv* over *este?*"

"Take your things and go," said Hank. He was confident that once Warrior calmed down he would realize that Hank had just kept him from being shot.

Warrior shook his head, then took off his battered hat and slapped it against his knee in a gesture of contempt. He headed for his horse, followed – still wordlessly – by Island Grayson. The two men mounted. Warrior looked at Archie Bruner, but Archie looked away. "You, too?" asked Warrior. Then he shook his head, clucked his teeth, and he and Island rode off.

"They certainly showed their true colors," chuckled Colonel Miller, emphasizing the last word.

No, you showed yours, Hank thought. But he said nothing. And, after a moment, he wondered a little about how quickly he had run off his friends. He hoped that they understood.

"Well handled, I think," added the Colonel. "You showed real leadership. Do you think your crew can handle this work for the rest of the day?"

"Of course," answered Hank. He wanted to get Warrior and Island back on the crew by tomorrow. Sending them off was just a show for this *wvcenv*. If Colonel Miller left now, the rest of them could do some more work and he could explain his actions to the others. "Let's get back to it," he told Archie and Zack. We're burning daylight."

"Before you do," interrupted the Colonel, "I would like to discuss another job for you."

Hank was relieved that the discomfort of firing Warrior and losing Island was paying off right away. "Get started with that next roll of barbed wire," he ordered his men. They wrestled it off the wagon and onto the jack they would unreel it from. Hank turned back to the Colonel. "More fencing?" he asked.

"This is a little more delicate," Colonel Miller said. "My lawyer is concerned about the dual governments you have here in the Creek Nation."

Hank felt an ache in his stomach. This was a bad start. Lawyer? Dual governments? He had been feeling so good about being his own man, running his own crew, stepping out from behind his father's oversized shadow. Now, though, he wished his dad, Tustenugge, was with him to hear this and advise him.

The Colonel continued, apparently unaware of Hank's distress. "The Council of Chiefs approved the lease for me to graze cattle here," he went on. "But I hear this is considered Yuchi Town land. So is this the Creek Nation or is it Yuchi Town? Delbert McIntosh tells me they don't even speak Creek in Yuchi Town. Could they say that it wasn't the Nation's land to lease? What if the courts were to decide that only the Yuchi can lease this to me?"

Hank was really sick now. Why the hell was this *wvcenv* lecturing him about his own people? Did he think the Creek Confederation had language requirements? And why was Delbert telling all this to an outsider? The Yarholars had tried very hard to forgive Delbert's family for splitting the Nation in its own Civil War just so they could hold onto their *estelvste* slaves. Were the McIntoshes still colluding with Confederates all these years after the war was over? Hank tried to refocus on the torrent of words pouring out of the Colonel's mouth. They were like molasses: sweet, but opaque. He couldn't understand where Colonel Miller was going with this.

"So I just want somebody to get signatures from the leading men of Yuchi Town acknowledging the lease. My lawyer assures me that it should be a formality since Sam Brown already voted for the lease in the House of Kings and he is king of Yuchi Town."

Sam Brown was *balen gabidan*, as the Yuchi called their *micco*. Hank had gone to school for a short time in Eufaula with Brown's son Sam, Jr. Junior left school after beating up three bigger boys who made fun of him for being Yuchi, but he and Hank always got along okay. The old folks said Junior was now a hand on the ranch of his uncle, Sakasenney. Maybe Hank could speak to Junior about the Colonel's lease.

"I have a document my lawyer drew up, so all they have to do is read and sign. I have sufficient copies for twenty men to return one to me and keep one for themselves." The words were still coming. "I can pay you five dollars per signature."

Five dollars? That was a week's pay. Something had to be very wrong with this for the Colonel to offer so much money. But Tustenugge had voted for this lease. He had assured Hank that it was all aboveboard and legal, that no Creek rights were violated. If Sam Brown voted for it, too, then it should be okay with the Yuchi. And twenty signatures times five dollars? That was a lot of money to turn away from.

"So do you think you can do this? Or should I ask somebody else?"

There it was. Somebody was going to take this job. The Colonel was going to get his Yuchi Town signatures. Why not Hank?

"I'm your man," said Hank. A wave of bile came up from his unsettled stomach and he choked it back down. "I'll get your papers signed."

"Can your men here work without your supervision for a while? I would really like this done now."

Two men on a five-man job? Without a foreman? Wouldn't that seem like Hank wasn't necessary? "Can I get on it tomorrow? That way I can replace my lost men and get my brother to run the work."

But the Colonel just smiled. "I won't take the job from you." Was he a mind reader? "The fence can wait. Send your men home now and I'll pay them for a whole day today. I really want you to get started on those signatures."

Now Hank was nauseous. Colonel Miller's rush to have this done smelled as bad as the high wage he was offering. Should he just forget the whole thing? Should he bring this to Coody Johnson? Coody was clerking for Judge Parker and he knew the law. Hank's father trusted him with all their business in Washington.

73

Then again, he was another *estelvste*. Maybe he would just oppose this because the Colonel was a Confederate, the way Warrior had. The nausea passed. "Thanks," he told Colonel Miller. "I'll get on it immediately."

Hank directed Archie and Zack to load all the tools and materials in the wagon and bring everything back to his place. They shrugged at the changed plan and began re-rolling the barbed wire. Hank turned back to ask the Colonel when he needed the papers finished.

The Colonel had already left. In all that flat prairie, there was no sign of him or where he had gone. Hank looked at Archie and Zack and began, "Did you…" Then he stopped. He mounted his horse, wished the two men *cehekares*, and rode off to the Sakasenney ranch to look for Junior Brown.

Cañada de los Álamos, New Mexico
1913

When, exactly, had this become a village of women, youngsters, and the elderly? Piedad Abeyta stopped near a patch of late-blooming *juve,* arrested in her work by the thought. She was out on the mesa above town when it hit her, gathering *contrayerba, matarique,* and *mastranzo* for her practice. The fiesta of San Lucas was in a few days and that meant harvest season was over. Corn, squash, berries, chiles and apples were all in; the men were all away. Some were cutting lumber for railroad ties, many were mining coal, a few were already tending beets, but not one wife in Cañada de los Álamos had her husband with him.

No, she thought, that wasn't quite true. Seferina Trujillo, Cleotilde Vigil and Choni Maestas all had their husbands with them... just not here. All those women had left the village in order to be with their men. Seferina was with Benigno at the Phelps, Dodge coal mine in Dawson. The others were at the Rockefeller coal mines in Colorado, along with her Epifanio. Oh, and of course there were the *viejos* who no longer worked. They were sitting in the sun together, talking about old times, *resolaniando.* But none of the young men were here. None of the working men were here. None of them would be back before Christmas. When had all this happened? When Piedad was a girl, all the working-age men were here, farming, herding, and weaving. Well, all except her wandering brother José. Now all the village men had become itinerant workers like Joey.

She sat down for a moment to consider the village in the valley from this vantage point. No sooner had she stopped moving than she heard the sound of iron-shod hoofs on the rocky trail below and little Silbestre Jaramillo rode into view on his family's roan mare. This had to be about his mother's cousin, Raquel. It was still early – Piedad hadn't expected her to go into labor before November – but it was Raquel's first baby. Maybe she was just nervous. In any case, Piedad would have to drop what she was doing here and check in on the young mother-to-be. She gathered her things.

Silbestre was not here about a birth, though. "There was a telephone call," he said as soon as he got close enough to speak. That could not be good. The nearest telephone was at the railroad station in La Vega. Calls meant trouble. "They need you in Dawson," added Silbestre. Dawson? Something with Seferina? she wondered. But she put away her anxiety. It would take time to travel. Dawson had to be a hundred miles away and worrying would not make the trip faster. Piedad climbed up behind the twelve-year old and rode down to the village.

The grown-ups in town were no more informative. Old Bonifacio Vigil was sitting out in front of his little *tendejón* with his cronies, Don Apolonio, Don Faustín and Don Porfirio. As soon as Piedad got off Silbestre's *yegua* and thanked him with a small coin, the grocer was up and gesturing toward the north. "Dawson!" he said. "There is trouble in Dawson!"

"What kind of trouble?" asked the *partera*. "A pregnancy?"

"Trouble!" repeated Don Bonifacio. "Elías Martínez said that Gilberto Naranjo got a telephone call!"

This information was all useless. She wanted to know *who called*, not who received the call. She wanted to know who was the patient they were calling about, whether it was a birth or a medical emergency. She really wanted to know why they were calling her so far away, to Dawson. There were plenty of other *parteras* and *curanderas* between here and there. Hadn't Genara Lucero moved to Dawson? "What was the message?" she asked the men.

Don Bonifacio looked at her in disbelief. "Trouble!" he shouted, as if she were hard of hearing. "In Dawson!"

Why had she thought this *resolanero* could answer her questions? There would be more information at the train station. Piedad nodded and thanked Don Bonifacio, then went to her house. She packed both her healing bag and her midwife bag into the valise where she always kept a change of clothes for overnight calls and she folded in an additional change of undergarments. Dawson was far; she might be away an extra day. Then she went next door to tell her mother-in-law that she would be out of town. Doña Luz promised to take care of the children for as long as necessary. In the old days this would have been the responsibility of Pia's *comai*, but in this new world? Choni was up in Colorado with the men. Choni's children were with *her* mother.

Piedad saddled her *golondrino* and tied on her valise. The only child she could find quickly was eight-year-old Anita García, so she hoisted her up in front of the saddle and asked Doña Luz to inform Consolación. Anita's mother would never object to Piedad asking her daughter to bring the horse back home from the train station in La Vega, but she did have to be told and Piedad was running out of time if she wanted to make the 2:30 train.

Finally, sitting on the Denver and Rio Grande narrow-gauge for the two-hour ride to Santa Fe, there was time to think about what she had learned from the telegraph operator: a mine accident in Dawson. They were calling for help from all over, so there was no particular reason to think that her neighbor Benigno Trujillo was hurt. The wait at the station in Santa Fe and the northbound ride on the AT&SF passed without incident. But there were a lot of anxious people waiting for the transfer to the El Paso and Southwestern at the depot in French. The closer she got to Dawson, the more her dread returned.

The town of Dawson, up the canyon from French, was dominated by two huge smokestacks and a towering steel-framed mine entrance, bigger than even the cathedral in Santa Fe. Every man in town was working to excavate the collapsed mine entry. More miners had come from as far as eastern Kansas to help with the rescue efforts. Piedad went to a large tent where an Anglo man in a suit asked, "Are you a miner's wife?"

"Nurse," she answered, knowing that the *gabachos* only understood their own medical credentials.

"Over there," he said, pointing to an area of empty cots. "We are still waiting for the first patients to be brought in."

Waiting. There was nothing to do but wait. Where were the victims?

As the assembled doctors prepared their equipment, Piedad spoke to the other *curanderas* and nurses who had been summoned to deal with this disaster. Over 250 men had descended into the Phelps, Dodge #2 pit the previous morning to dig coal for the big coking ovens. In mid-afternoon, the people of this boomtown heard what sounded like a very loud rifle shot, followed by a deafening roar. Then they saw flames leaping into the sky as high as the surrounding hills. Crews from other shifts and other shafts ran in as far as they could to attempt a rescue, but they were forced to retreat when some of them dropped dead from lack of air. The ventilators would have to be restored before they could return.

So far, only 15 men had made it out. As the day turned into night and the electricians set up emergency lighting Piedad began to wonder if there would be any more. One by one, the crews were bringing out bodies – some charred by flames, some broken by rock fall, some asphyxiated and looking asleep – but there was nobody to care for in this hospital tent. And she was wondering, too, where were the women? There was very little English spoken here for what she had imagined in a corporation town like Dawson, and not much Spanish, either.

She didn't recognize the languages. And the mourners, those crying over the corpses, seemed to be almost all men.

Piedad wasn't sure what time it was when she dropped off to sleep sitting in that makeshift hospital, but as dawn awakened her, surrounded by dozing nurses and doctors, her fear returned: what if there were no living souls to rescue? She went outside to find that the electricians had returned the big fans to service, pulling air through the underground tunnels. The miners, working in oversized relays, had cleared the debris from the mine entry. Rescue crews were reentering the works. She saw men who had worked through the night to reopen the mine collapsed on the ground in exhaustion. So. There was work for her anyway.

Retrieving her healing bag from the hospital tent, Piedad took a bucket of water and a ladle and began walking from one man to the next. Some were fast asleep. She touched their throats for a pulse and their foreheads for a fever and moved on. Some had visible injuries from the haste and darkness in which they had worked. She applied the appropriate balms and dressings of *romerillo del llano* and *añil del muerto*. Some showed symptoms of *susto*: they gazed into a distance that was visible only to them; they sat crying. She gave them water into which she stirred *yerbanis* and *yerbabuena*. All of them would need more treatment later, but this was a beginning and – if she was honest with herself – it felt better to be doing something than nothing.

Like all the others, the sleeping man she approached now was coated in coal dust. His face, his hands, his clothing, and his boots looked like a statue carved from rock, or perhaps a formation from deep under the earth. Nevertheless, she stopped before him and she looked at him, her brow furrowed until something – her staring? – woke him up. His eyes, and his astonishment at seeing her there, confirmed her unconscious intuition: it was Epifanio. It was her husband. It was the father of her children. Why, though, was he here? Wasn't he supposed to be up in Colorado?

Epifanio leaped from the ground and embraced her as if the two of them were alone, as if all the dozens of other people present had vanished from his view. "Oh, how I miss you, *mi amor*!" he said with passion. Three weeks ago when he came home for the fiesta of San Gabriel he hadn't been this affectionate. And that time it had been almost six months since his last visit. She welcomed the tenderness, but questioned it, too. What had he seen underground last night to trigger all this emotion?

He still wasn't letting her go, either. "I miss you so much!" he repeated. He was sobbing now. "Don't leave me, *cariño*! Don't leave me!" Leave him? He was the one who kept running off to find cash work outside the village. She was the one at home taking care of their children and of his parents. What was he talking about?

"All gone!" he was crying now. "They're all gone!"

Piedad was afraid she knew exactly what he meant. Nevertheless, she asked, "Who? Who is all gone?"

"They're all gone!" Epifanio said again. "All those men! Dead! They killed them!"

"Killed?" asked Piedad, pushing him away. "Who? Who killed who?" She thought this was an accident. Why was he talking about killing?

He looked around wildly, as if to see who was listening to them. She looked around, too, although she didn't know why. Nobody was paying any attention to them at all. But now Epifanio began speaking in hushed tones, "The company," he whispered. "They don't care if we live or die. Lose a Greek; replace him with an Italian."

This made no sense to her at all. Greeks? Italians? What was he talking about? Had he lost his mind? And what was he doing here? "*Amor*," she whispered back, trying to calm him, "everything will be okay."

"Okay?" he asked sharply, and drew back from her as if she were a stranger. She might look like one now, too, she thought, covered as she was with the coal dust that he had transferred to her face and clothes during their embrace. But it wasn't her appearance that shocked him. "How is any of *this* okay?" he asked, waving his hand around. His gesture took in the entire horror that surrounded them, the burnt-out mine buildings, the row of corpses, the weeping survivors. He was right. None of this would – or even could – be okay.

"*Amor*," she asked, changing the subject, "how are you here?"

This question calmed him considerably. Good. "We heard about the blast in Colorado," he answered. "We came right away."

This answer raised new questions for Piedad, but their conversation ended right there because a shout went up from the mine entrance. The men she had been tending to earlier now all jumped up, joined by others who had been waiting all around them. People were coming out of the mine. Would she be needed now in the hospital tent?

She would not. There were only more corpses. "George Gelasakis!" shouted a man as he set down a new body in the line of bodies that had started the night before. Hearing that name, several men fell to their knees, crossing themselves and saying something that sounded like, "*Agios athanatos, eleison imas.*"

Then another name: "Umberto Giordani!" More kneeling, more crossing. She heard some say, "*Riposare in pace.*"

"Antonio Bediali!"

"Luigi Marinucci!"

"Duilio Zamboni!"

"Mike Cachulakis!"

And on and on. There were a few Negros. She couldn't say for sure whether the people who ran to those bodies were relatives or friends. There were many New Mexicans, most of whom seemed to have wives and children weeping over their bodies. Jesus Reyes. Patrocinio Chavez. Felipe García. But the vast majority of the names she heard were unfamiliar. And the mourners for those apparently foreign names were overwhelmingly other young men.

"Gus Katis!"

"Giuseppe Nava!"

"Dominic Bruglioni!"

It was as if the roll call would never stop. Each name was accompanied by another broken body. She thought she could not bear anymore. But she had forgotten that there were men from Cañada de los Álamos working here at this mine.

"Benny Trujillo!" Benny Trujillo? Her neighbor Benigno Trujillo? She choked back a scream and stepped up to get a better look, taking Epifanio by the hand. It was true. Benny's mother Teófila sat in the dirt, silent, with her son's head cradled in her lap as if he were her sleeping infant. Her shawl was drawn up over her head and tears streamed down her cheeks. Benny's wife Seferina stood behind Teófila, both arms reaching upward (to God? to Benny's departing spirit?) howling wordlessly in protest against this insult. At Benny's feet stood his friends, Sixto and Amarante. They had recovered his body from the mine. They looked beaten.

Piedad didn't know what to say. She had something in her bag for labor pain and for menstrual cramps. She had something for diarrhea and something for snakebite. She had nothing for this, this… what *was* this? She gave Sixto her water bucket and a rag. He began cleaning the coal and rock dust from his friend's body.

Epifanio whispered hoarsely, "We will make them pay. We will make these *malditos* pay."

There were already at least a hundred men's bodies lined up on the ground now. More were coming out every minute. Smoke still hung in the air. Wasn't this a terrible accident? What *malditos*? Who was going to pay?

Epifanio was now shuddering with grief and rage. Piedad took him in her arms to try to comfort him, but he could not stop shaking. She saw him looking up and down the unimaginably long line of broken men and their mourners. But all that she could see was the small tableau of her neighbors: Teófila holding her dead son Benigno while his wife wailed and his friend Sixto cleaned his body.

Two

Tulsa, Oklahoma
Thursday Afternoon

After walking a few blocks from the Stradford, Special Agent Amos began to find some businesses that – while still prosperous – seemed a little less seditty than those near his hotel. The clientele wasn't as expensively dressed; working people instead of professionals. The storefronts weren't as pretentious. Cafés. A barbeque joint. Boarding houses. Pool halls. And then a barbershop.

Perfect. It was a two-story building with signs in the upstairs windows advertising a chiropractor and an employment office. A red and blue striped pole stood out front and the sign over the door read, "Carter's. Nuff Sed." Walking inside he saw that there were four chairs, all occupied and a crowd of hangers-on sitting on the wall opposite the big mirror. He was certain not all of them were waiting for a cut, and – in any case – he was more interested in picking up some gossip than in getting the shave he was going to ask for. He chose an empty seat, picked up a newspaper, and sat down.

The paper was called the Tulsa *Star*. A banner headline asked, in giant letters, "Why Shouldn't Negroes Arm Themselves?" And below that, in only slightly smaller type, "You Push Us and We Push You!" Apparently Mr. Hoover had sent him to the right city, but this didn't look like any secret conspiracy. Maybe he could just go directly to the publisher of the *Star* and get the intelligence from him.

Once it seemed that nobody was particularly interested in him, Agent Amos began his surreptitious study of the men in the shop: first the customers in the barber chairs, then the men waiting along with him, then the barbers themselves. The mirrors made this easier. He didn't have to turn to look at them and if he didn't spend too long on any one face he wasn't likely to be caught at his assessment.

Amos's attention was drawn very early by a man waiting in the seat nearest the front door. He was a brown-skinned man in his early twenties, and even sitting down it was obvious that he was very tall, with the bulk to match his height. He wore a grocer's apron, which struck Agent Amos as odd: Didn't grocers take off their aprons when they left the store? Did grocers get haircuts during store hours? But then he noticed a .45-caliber Colt semiautomatic pistol at the man's waist, only partially concealed by that apron. And it wasn't really the man's size, or his apron, or even his gun that got Amos looking at him. He was the loudest man in the shop. He had an angry answer for everything. And he would not shut up.

"Mayor Evans ain't the worst white man in Oklahoma," one of the barbers was saying.

"That is a mighty low bar you're setting," objected the big grocer.

"The Klans are against him," argued the barber. "That's why the *Tribune* is running all these crime wave stories, making it look like Evans is in cahoots with cocaine dealers and what-not."

"White man tell you that?" demanded the grocer, angrily. "They get you thinking they're your friend, you'll fall for anything." He was working himself up now, getting to his feet. He was a good six-four.

The barber at the first chair – Carter? – turned right to him and gestured with his straight razor, "Sit down, O.B. I'm not having no mess in my shop."

The big grocer sat back down, but he wasn't done talking. "I don't see a hair of difference between Evans and Tate Brady. Do you?"

"That's true, O.B." said a slender, mustached man with a gold tooth and a long scar down the right side of his face – knife fight? – "Brady may be the Klan in Tulsa. He may be the one took them IWWs from prison during the war and whipped them half to death. But it *was* T. D. Evans and that Arizona YMCA man who jailed them in the first place for not buying war bonds."

There were a few "Mm, hms," and "True, trues." Agent Amos stopped paying attention to the details of the conversation and returned to his assessment of the men in the shop.

He was interrupted this time by the arrival of an older, light-skinned gentleman in a custom-made suit and bespoke shoes. Amos spent enough time with Director Hoover's wardrobe to recognize the quality. And everybody in the shop seemed to know him, too. They sat up a little straighter. The customer in the first chair was just giving the barber his dime and the newcomer headed straight for that chair. "I'm next," objected the grocer loudly.

The light-skinned man didn't even turn to listen. He just sat down in the freshly vacated seat. Now the big grocer was on his feet again. "I said I'm next! Who the fuck you think you are?" And he took a step toward him.

The barber stepped toward the grocer, razor in hand. "You know damned well who he is," he said quietly, half whispering. "Mr. Gurley is my landlord. He owns this building, this whole block, and the next one, too. If he wants his shave now, he gets it now."

"That's how you run your shop?" demanded the grocer, but he didn't take another step toward the barber. Instead he directed his anger toward the customer. "You're my brother," he said, "but you ain't God. And don't think them white folks love you like you love them."

This got the man, Gurley's, attention. He turned in his chair and looked directly at the big grocer, but he still didn't say anything. The grocer looked back at him and spat, "Nothing to say. That's what I thought. Come on, Peg. Let's get out."

He turned to the door and was followed by a one-legged man in an extremely shabby Army coat. This surprised Agent Amos. He had noticed the wooden leg and seen the crutches but he would never have put their owner together with the grocer. The big man carried himself like the proprietor of his own business. Amos had guessed that the cripple was a beggar, in the barbershop to panhandle. His hair didn't look like it had been cut in over a month. Still, the two men left together.

It wasn't until they left that the newcomer, Gurley, spoke. "O.B. came back from that war a little too big for his britches. He thinks he's as good as anybody, doesn't he?" he asked. And everybody in the shop was quick to agree.

Amos said nothing. But he had plenty of thoughts. Uppity vets? Businessmen whose survival depended on going along with the white man? He could have seen this same scene, heard this same conversation, felt this same conflict in any colored barbershop in any city in America. Where had this intelligence about an "African Blood Brotherhood" come from? What made Director Hoover think Tulsa was special?

He waited for a shave because leaving now would make him conspicuous. But he studied the advertisements in the *Star* while he considered his next move.

Boley, Oklahoma
1912

When Ezekiel Payne and his daughter Nessa drove up to his Daddy's house in his two-horse wagon, Abraham Payne was sitting on the front porch, smoking his pipe. Ezekiel said, "Hi, Daddy," but Abraham just nodded. Then he stood and gestured at a single steamship trunk. Abraham Payne was leaving, moving to Africa, and that trunk contained everything of his old life that he deemed valuable enough to keep. Ezekiel hauled it down and hoisted it into the back of his wagon, Abraham Payne climbed up front and sat down next to his only granddaughter.

"Nessa," began her grandpa. "There are some things I have to tell you before I go. I have never told your father these things. I suppose I was trying to protect him, but somebody needs to know."

Ezekiel Payne's Daddy had first moved here before statehood, in 1903, back when this was all still Indian Territory. Abraham Payne was among the very first to purchase a town lot in Boley. The Fort Smith and Western Railroad purchased the land - Abigail Barnett's allotment - from her father Jim with the intention of promoting it as an all-Black town. They held a Juneteenth fair and distributed flyers all over the Black Belt South. They even offered free rail passes to ensure good attendance. The highlight of the entertainment was a traditional ball game between Muskogee and Seminole Indians. Then they held a giant real estate sale with their agents sitting at outdoor tables and "closers" moving in to seal each deal. The salesmen rang a bell every time a purchase was made to enhance the bandwagon effect. Abraham Payne was tired of fighting with the Alabama crackers for the very existence of his store. He bought a home site in Boley that very day and never returned to Eufaula.

By that time Ezekiel had been living in Indian Territory for over ten years and he had already learned that it was not Black Zion. Whites were swarming into the Nations, legally and otherwise. Black Indians looked down on "state Negroes" like him who came from elsewhere. The whites were even aggressively dividing the loyalties of the tribes themselves: so-called "blood" Muskogee were listed on one census, their African-looking kin, so-called "freedmen," were listed on another. Still, Ezekiel knew that the Nations – with all these problems – were a hell of a lot better place for him than Alabama. And he was glad to have his Daddy nearby. The painful estrangement of his wife Sunshine and her "blood" family left his daughter Nessa without any family beyond him. Ezekiel was happy to give Nessa a grandpa.

And Nessa loved her Grandpa. Every day after school she stopped by his house in town before going home to the farm. She would brew him a cup of sassafras tea and tell him what she learned in class and what she did with her friends. He would sit on the porch, smoking his pipe, and listen with intent interest. Ezekiel often thought that nothing he could accomplish in this world would ever be enough for his Daddy. But every little thing Nessa did pleased Abraham Payne. Whenever Ezekiel left the farm for a few days to take cash work on a construction site, Nessa stayed with her Grandpa.

Now, though, Daddy had decided to sell his home and leave Boley. His early purchase worked out well for him financially. The town had grown beyond anybody's most optimistic expectations. There were more than twenty Black towns in Oklahoma and Boley was easily the most prosperous. The oil boom, too, was an unpredictable bonus. So Daddy got four times what he had paid for the property.

Why had he decided to leave? The high-seditty town leaders definitely snubbed him, just as they did Ezekiel. He was never elected to the town council. He wasn't offered a municipal post. They didn't include him in their conversations at D.J. Turner's drugstore. Maybe it was because, for all his business success and political acumen, he didn't have an education like they did. Maybe they snubbed him because his son Ezekiel had been married to a "Native" (their derogation for all Muskogee, both Black and "blood") and had a Native daughter. Maybe Daddy's departure had nothing to do with his exclusion from the Boley elite. Maybe it was just disappointment that this Black Zion had turned out to be a precarious island in a sea of violent white supremacy: lynchings in Okemah and Henryetta, sundown towns established all over the former Creek Nation, Jim Crow laws just like Alabama. Or maybe it was all these things.

In any case, the same precipitous determination that made Daddy come to that Juneteenth fair and invest in a town lot now made him give up his home in favor of Chief Alfred Sam's 30,000 acre Zion in Africa. Daddy sold his Boley town lot and went all in on Chief Sam's plan to help American Negroes return to the mother continent.

Nobody really knew who Chief Sam was. He reminded Ezekiel of a traveling salesman for some "miraculous" drug, drumming up business by presenting a small-time carnival act. Instead of selling "Golden Elixir" for $1, he was selling stock in his "Akim Trading Company" for $25 a share. Included in the share price was a farm in the Gold Coast of West Africa and a berth on a ship to get there.

Chief Sam was a compelling speaker, true, but white folks seemed to do everything in their power to support his view that there was no safe haven here, even in Boley. God knew the crackers in this state provided more than enough evidence to convince Black folk that the "promised land" of Oklahoma was about to devolve into another Alabama. Right after statehood in 1906 the legislature's very first act was to establish Jim Crow racial segregation. They followed that up with a phony literacy qualification for voting… a rule that only applied to Black folks. And the periodic lynchings were a reminder of what would happen to Negroes who forgot their place. When Chief Sam said Oklahoma was no place for us, he was speaking a powerful truth.

The town fathers in Boley (and Rentiesville and Clearview and Redbird and every other Black town in the state) insisted that Chief Sam was a charlatan and a grifter, planning to take the money of the gullible and disappear. So far as Ezekiel could tell nobody had any evidence of this. In fact, sometimes he wondered whether they didn't just recognize a kindred spirit in the African. After all, Chief Sam was a competitor to them, somebody whose business – like theirs – was to convince folks that his venture was a path to safety for you and your children. Every Oklahoma Negro who moved to the Gold Coast was an Oklahoma Negro who was *not* moving to Boley. Every dollar invested in Akim Trading was a dollar *not* deposited in D.J. Turner's bank.

But what he could not understand was why his Daddy was so certain that Chief Sam was on the level. Daddy wasn't satisfied to buy a $25 share in Akim Trading. Oh, no, he wanted to be a real player. He put most of his savings into the enterprise, along with every penny he made selling his Boley town lot and the house he built on it. It was Daddy's money and none of Ezekiel's business, but it seemed less like an investment and more like an awfully risky bet.

Today was the real turning point in that risk. Because today Ezekiel was driving Daddy to the train station to depart for his new life in Africa. Today Daddy was taking the Katy Railroad to Galveston where the first wave of emigrants would climb aboard the S.S. Liberia for the voyage to Accra. Ezekiel and Nessa could write letters to him, but today was likely to be the last time Nessa would see her grandpa in this life.

Earlier that morning when they left their own house on the way to Daddy's, Ezekiel took the reins, clucked his team to a start, and then looked at his daughter. "Baby, how do you feel about saying goodbye to Grandpa?" Ezekiel asked.

Nessa chose not to remind her Daddy that this was perhaps the thirtieth time he had asked this question. "We can always go visit." She smiled.

Ezekiel chuckled. "Sure," he replied. "We can stop by for Sunday dinner after church."

"We still have each other," reminded Nessa.

This really hurt. Nessa had a mother, a grandma and a grandpa, uncles, aunts and cousins, all less than twenty miles away. They had chosen to cut her off when the Dawes Rolls were created. They thought it was more important to ensure that her mother be registered as "Creek by Blood" rather than be left off because she was the wife of a state Negro. Ezekiel was still pained by their rejection of him, he couldn't deny it. But their rejection of Nessa was a wound that would not heal. She was Sunshine's *daughter* for God's sake! Nessa had been the pole star in Ezekiel's life from the day she was born and he still could not imagine how anyone could feel differently about her – anybody who *knew* her, not to mention her own kin! How Sunshine dealt with it, he didn't know.

"What's wrong, Daddy?"

His eyes were filling. "I'm just very sad about saying goodbye to Grandpa," he lied.

"So am I," said Nessa, accepting this, but she looked closely at his face for a few moments more. He drove his team through the dry, wide bed of Sand Creek and said no more until they got to town.

Now Ezekiel tied Daddy's trunk into the wagon bed to keep it from shifting while Daddy climbed up front alongside Nessa. He heard Abraham Payne say, "There are some things I have to tell you before I go. I have never told your father these things. I suppose I was trying to protect him, but somebody needs to know."

What could Daddy possibly be talking about? And if Daddy had protected him, why wasn't he protecting Nessa? Ezekiel was thunderstruck by this pronouncement. Nessa, however, seemed as happy about this as she was about everything to do with her grandpa. She smiled and said, "What, Grandpa?"

Abraham said, "Listen close. You need to know all of this."

While Nessa looked intently at his Daddy, Ezekiel studied them both. He had never before noticed how alike they looked. Nessa was thirteen – still slender, still girlish – with her mother's straight hair and almond-shaped eyes. Daddy was, well, Ezekiel didn't know how old he was. His curly hair was white now. The dark brown of his eyes was fading to gray with age, too. But a steel in both pairs of eyes, a determined set in both jaws, made it clear that these two were kin. Nessa said, "I'll listen. Tell me."

Grandpa nodded seriously and began.

"I was born on the old Mason plantation in Sussex County, Virginia," he said. "My daddy was a carpenter who could make anything from wood: tables and chairs, coffins, dolls, spinning tops, musical instruments. His name was Coffee. He was the one who taught me my alphabet and made sure I knew my sums.

"My mama's African name was Awa, but the white folks always called her Eve. I never found out why. She was a cook in the Masons' house, which meant that she gardened their vegetables and herbs, too. Some nights she worked late and brought leftovers from their table to our cabin, but we usually had our own dinner. She also brought me clothes from the Masons, mostly from their younger son Chambliss who was about my size. I remember her voice and her smell, too. But I also remember she spent much more time with my sisters, Cozy and Emma, than she did with me and my brother Dave. I guess that's natural, but I remember anyway.

"As the oldest boy it was my job to help everybody. I helped my daddy keep his tools sharp with a whetstone and oil. I helped him with his team of mules when he went into the woods to cut lumber. And once I got big enough, say eight years old, I helped him rough out the wood with an axe. I was fixing to learn his trade and I would have, too, if everything hadn't happened like it did.

"I helped my mama, too. I kept the birds out of her gardens and I pulled the weeds out. I picked herbs and I hung them to dry. If she called when I was playing I had to drop whatever I was doing and run to fetch what she wanted, like a strip of streak-o'-lean from the smokehouse to flavor her soup or potatoes from the cellar.

"Certain times of year it was all hands to the tobacco. When they decided it was time to pick, it wasn't like it all had to be done that very second. Each plant had its own right moment and it had to be cut just then to get the best price. Everybody had to help with those leaves, from the littlest chap walking to the oldest grandma: cutting the plants with a knife, laying them on the ground for the right amount of time, and hanging them in the barn to cure. And those are big plants – taller than a man. That was how the Masons made their money and old George used to go into a frenzy every year from the time he decided the leaves were ready until they were sweated and sold and out of his barn."

Nessa had been listening to all this with great interest. Ezekiel, though, wondered why any of this was so important. More, he wondered why it had been such a secret. As if he could read his son's mind, Abraham turned to him with a sour look and said, "Am I boring you, boy?"

Ezekiel bit his tongue to hold back his first response and then said only, "No, sir. Tell Nessa your story."

His Daddy responded to this with a loud, sharp, "Hmm!"

Then he turned back to his granddaughter and said, "That's how I grew up until they murdered my Daddy."

This was new. Abraham gave Ezekiel another hard look and then turned back to Nessa. She was looking at him with her eyes wide. "It was just about time to start cutting tobacco. Late, late summer. I don't know for sure anymore how much of this I understood at the time and what I figured out later; the older folks tried to protect us chaps from a lot. But that year a preacher named Turner in Southampton County had a vision that Jesus put down his yoke and that he, Turner, must take it up and fight Satan. He and his congregation went from plantation to plantation on horseback, killing the white folks."

Nat Turner, realized Ezekiel. He had heard about this, but he never knew his Daddy had any part in the story. He looked at his father, but Abraham was deep into his memory and didn't notice. Nessa was still looking wide-eyed at her grandpa and Ezekiel wondered again why Daddy had taken this moment to share this.

"We only heard about this after the Virginia militia stopped them," continued Abraham Payne. "It all happened about thirty miles away and we didn't have cars back then. Tell the truth, there weren't any trains in that country, either." He paused, looked again at his son and granddaughter, and challenged, "So you want to know what this had to do with my daddy, don't you?"

Ezekiel nodded. He looked at Nessa. She said, "Yes, Grandpa. If you didn't even know about it…" She ran out of words.

Daddy looked at Ezekiel and asked, "What are you teaching this child? Does she know what happens right here in the state of Oklahoma today?"

The truth was that Ezekiel had no idea what Nessa did or did not know about the epidemic of lynchings in the former Creek Nation since statehood. He tried very hard to protect her from all that and he didn't know what she might have heard elsewhere. But he also knew that his Daddy's question was rhetorical and he wasn't planning to piss Abraham off by answering it.

Abraham Payne was already back in the Virginia of his memory anyway. "When the patrollers came around, the Masons didn't do nor say nothing to stop them. They just stayed there inside their big house like they were hiding. Or like they didn't know what was happening right outside their door. I hadn't seen any of these white patrollers before. But they came right up to our cabin with their pine tar torches and they called my daddy out by name. They said, 'Coffee, get your black ass out here before we burn you up in there.' My daddy stepped out the cabin and asked, 'What do you gentlemen want?' But there were no gentlemen there that night, only assassins. They had those old-fashioned one-shot pistols that you loaded with a lead ball. They shot my daddy dead right there in front of my mama and us chaps. And then they rode away."

"Why?" asked Nessa. Ezekiel saw tears in her eyes. There were tears in his, too.

"Why." Abraham repeated her question without inflection. "Because he was the smartest man in the county?" he speculated. "Because he could do things with wood and a knife that nobody else could? Because he could read? Because he was a Negro man and he frightened them by breathing?"

He shook his head. "I don't know why they chose my daddy from the other men on the Mason place. I know that they killed hundreds of us, for months, as far away as the Carolinas. I know the Masons didn't say a word, even though my daddy worked for them. That's what I know. And I know it wasn't but a few months later that one of those same men stole me away to Alabama."

"You were kidnapped?" asked Nessa.

"Oh, they paid money to Chambliss Mason, who called himself my friend," Daddy told her. "Old Man George Mason died so we didn't know what would happen. But those men came again in the night and stole me and my brother Dave from my mama and Cozy and Emma. I never saw not one of them again in this world, though I tried. I tried and tried."

Now the rush of Abraham Payne's words stopped. The only thing Ezekiel could hear was the breathing of his mules, the jingle and rub of their harness, the clip-clop of their iron-shod hoofs on the dirt road. He glanced sideways at his Daddy and saw that his eyes were glistening. Could this story get worse?

It could.

"They shackled Dave and me and chained us together and they marched us to Hick's Ford on the Meherrin River. No, I had never seen or heard of those places before. But I listened closely to the white men who stole us, and to their conversations with the other white men they spoke to. I was careful every day to learn the names of the places we passed through and the rivers we crossed. I knew that if Dave and me were going to find our way home I had to remember the way. Every night I recited the towns and rivers so I wouldn't forget. In Hick's Ford they put us in a cage made of iron in back of the inn where our kidnappers stayed. We were there for four days, and every day they put more boys in that cage. The first few days I couldn't have shit if I wanted to out there in the open for anyone to see. And I was careful to piss out the side as far away as I could. By the time we left that town, though, the whole corner of the cage was a pond of loose shit."

Nessa's eyes were red now and she had begun weeping. Ezekiel no longer had words.

"I think it was living in shit that made Dave sick. He started throwing up the third day we were there. When they chained us all together and put us back on the road I hoped it would help him get better, but he was shitting blood and he died before we got to Rocky Mount. I was carrying him, but they checked on him before we crossed the Roanoke River. They opened his shackles and dumped him in the woods. They dumped him like he was an apple core and not a human boy: my brother. After that I think the only thing that kept me alive was memorizing the towns and the rivers so I could get home to my mama and sisters.

"Every time we got to a town they put us in some kind of jail. I don't remember which were locked barns and which were cages. All I remember was the route. We crossed the Tar and the Neuse and got to Fayetteville on the Cape Fear River. We crossed the Pee Dee River at Pee Dee Town. The Black, the Catawba and then the Congaree at Columbia."

He recited all these names from memory as if they were the words to an old hymn, sung many times. "The Edisto and then the Savannah to Augusta. The Ogeechee, the Oconee and the Ocmulgee at Macon."

Nessa had stopped weeping and frowned curiously at her grandpa at those last three rivers. "Okmulgee?" she asked. "Like here?"

Okmulgee was a town about forty miles away. Before statehood it had been the capital of the Muskogee Nation and the site of their council house. Finding names from back home had puzzled Ezekiel when he first got to Indian Territory. His brother-in-law, Nessa's Uncle Hank, had finally explained to him how the entire Nation had been dispossessed of their old homes in Georgia and Alabama, how every place in what was now Oklahoma had really been *new* Weleetka, *new* Okfuskee, *new* Nuyaka… But the Muskogee never used the word "new" because these town names referred not to places, but to the communities of people who lived there.

Abraham Payne allowed his first hint of impatience with his granddaughter. "Honey, you let me tell my story. I'm getting to it."

Nessa didn't seem disturbed with this. In her eyes her grandpa could never err.

"After Macon we went to Columbus and crossed the Chattahoochee River. From there, the road followed the bank of the river two-and-a-half days until we got to Eufaula." He stopped speaking and looked, first at Nessa and then at Ezekiel, to be sure there would be no new interruption for this town name, which was also the name of a town here in Oklahoma. Neither said anything, so he went on.

"They locked us up in a jail in Eufaula. Dave wasn't the only boy who died on that long walk and there were only ten of us left. All of us looked pretty bad, but now they allowed us to bathe and gave us haircuts. They started to give us food, too: fried eggs with streak-o'-lean, grits with fatback and beans. At the time I didn't know why, but I was about to find out."

Ezekiel knew. He had never heard this from his Daddy before, but he had heard it from other people of Abraham's generation. Maybe Nessa knew more about this part than either man suspected, because she was welling with tears again.

"The day they auctioned us, like livestock, my kidnappers got themselves all dressed up. They looked so happy that day, so business-like and prosperous. Us, though, they stripped naked. Then they rubbed our bodies down with grease. There was a good crowd of farmers there that day. I watched them closely, because I knew I was going to end up with one of them, but most weren't bidding. It seemed like most of them were just there to watch, like we were the best show in Barbour County. And it wasn't just white folks, either. Some of them were Muskogee Indians, too." He looked at his son with a smirk. "That's right, son, Graysons and McIntoshes, and even some Yarholars in their turbans."

Ezekiel's eyes widened. His former in-laws – Nessa's mother and grandparents and uncles – were Yarholars. Could they have…?

"Boy, I told you that you would always be a nigger to these people," Daddy said.

Ezekiel looked at Abraham Payne angrily, cutting his eyes toward Nessa as a warning. His Daddy knew full well how he had tried to shield the girl from the fact of her abandonment by her mother and her mother's family. But apparently Abraham intended this piece of horror for his son only and did not make the connection more explicit. For now.

"I was bought that day by Mr. Jack Knowland. He bought boys named Tyler and Sam, too. By the very next morning, he had us in his cotton fields. The first day they called themselves teaching us. The next day the whippings started. They whipped us for missing weeds with the hoe. They whipped us for breaking the stems with the hoe. They whipped us for not making as much progress as the person in the next row, even if that person was a grown man. Hell, they would whip a grown man for not doing more today than he did yesterday. That was just their way in that country. Those white folks acted like the whip was a part of the day that could not be left out. You might as well say they worshipped the Devil instead of God and that those whippings were their evening prayer to him.

"I remember when the white folks kicked the Muskogee Indians out of that country. It wasn't much past the time I got there. Every one of them had to leave, and those Graysons and McIntoshes took their Black folks with them. That's right. Lost their land, but kept their Black folks. Brought them right here."

Ezekiel was thinking about these revelations. No wonder Daddy was so skeptical of his Yarholar in-laws. And no wonder he was such a hard man. Why hadn't he told Ezekiel any of this before? But then he looked at Nessa and thought about all he withheld from her, how badly he wanted to protect her from ugly truths.

94

Nessa, meanwhile, looked like she was now ready to say her piece. But Abraham said, "Let me finish, girl. Soon I'll be on that train and on my way to Africa. Maybe I can find my folks there, maybe not. I don't even know how much time I have left on this earth, but I cannot leave you here without leaving you what I know. When old George Mason stood indoors and let those men kill my daddy, when young Chambliss Mason took money from the men who stole me, I learned that there is not one white man you can trust. Not one. I don't know whether they honor their words to one another. Maybe. Maybe not. But I do know that none has ever kept his word to me, nor to any other Negro I ever met. All they want to do is steal from us: steal our land, steal our crops, steal our bodies. They act like they're better, but they know they're not. That's why they fear us so much. They know they're demons and they fear God's judgment."

He intoned these words as though he had been thinking about them for a long time. "I want to tell you about Indians, too. The white man has killed them and robbed them. But everything I've seen – back in Alabama and here in Oklahoma – tells me that the minute that white man points them at us, gives them a sign that he'll let them join in robbing us, those Indians jump right in. Your mama's folks aren't as bad as some. But there's a reason they don't call you kin. You need to know that."

And just like that, Abraham Payne had crossed the one firm boundary that Ezekiel had enforced since the day the Yarholars cut off Nessa, their own blood, in order to make certain that her mother was listed as "Indian" on the white man's list. He had done everything in a father's power to keep this rejection, this ultimate horror from destroying his precious daughter's spirit and wellbeing and grace. Now the day went silent and cloudy. All Ezekiel could hear was the pounding of his own blood in his ears... no squeaking of wagon wheels, no jingle of harness, no clip-clop of hoofbeats. He could still see, but the sky and the earth were blurred from the tears in his eyes. Would that sky open in a pillar of flame? Would that earth open and swallow them?

This was just the way it had been that day at Ezekiel's father-in-law's house: vision clouded, sound muffled. Nessa was about six, playing outside with her cousins. Old Tustenugge Yarholar thanking him for being a good father and a hard worker. His brother-in-law Hank remembering a ride Ezekiel gave them once to the train station. His wife, Sunshine, explaining that according to the government, being married to him determined her status, made her no longer an Indian. Ezekiel, mystified by all of this, then slowly realizing what they were saying to him. That his marriage was now over. That the life he thought he was building with Sunshine could be disposed of in a few thank-yous: thank-yous for things he had done for the Yarholars as a matter of course. That precious Nessa – their own blood – was no longer family.

But there was no fire in the sky, no hole in the earth. Ezekiel turned back to his only family and found the two of them still sitting with him in the wagon, his beloved Nessa looking expectantly at his stubborn daddy, apparently waiting for the answer to a question that he, Ezekiel, had missed while thinking that the world would now end. Abraham said, "That's right. When Senator Dawes came around to make a census of the Creek Indian Nation, they made *two* lists, not one. One list was for Creek by Blood and the other for what they called Creek Freedmen."

Nessa nodded. She knew this already. Ezekiel was still reeling at the fact that Abraham had revealed his most closely guarded secret… apparently without it destroying her.

"Your friends Roxana, Clarissa and Abby and their families were all listed as Freedmen. Mostly everybody who looked African was listed as freed, regardless of whether their ancestors had been slaves of Creek families or whether they were always free members of the tribe. There are exceptions, too. Legus Perryman is *estelvste*, all you have to do is look at him and you can see that. But him and all his kin around Tulsa got on the "by blood" list because he was elected chief. Those McIntoshes and Poseys may have called him nigger when they were inside their houses, but in council, he was their chief."

Nessa was nodding seriously, as if nothing had happened, as if the earth had not broken in two. Ezekiel, though, was still stunned into silence. Abraham went on, "Creek who didn't look African, or who nobody *said* was Negro, were all listed as Creek by Blood, even if they looked white. They introduced fractions, though, like half-Creek or quarter-Creek. And it had to be Creek: if one parent was Creek and the other was Cherokee, that made them half-Creek."

Ezekiel's tears were gone now and he could hear clearly. Daddy was talking general history now, not tearing scabs off unhealed wounds. But he still scanned the sky for a tornado; he still listened for early warnings of an Oklahoma earthquake. He feared Abraham Payne was not done. "Your mama was married to a State Negro," Daddy continued, "not a Creek Freedman. *You* were a State Negro. The Yarholars were afraid that would make your mama a State Negro. Old Tustenugge is a proud man, proud to be a full-blood Creek. He needed his daughter to be a full-blood, too."

It was all Ezekiel could do now not to toss his Daddy from the wagon and horsewhip him. How dare the old man destroy his granddaughter like this?

But it was not only his Daddy who would surprise Ezekiel today. Nessa, having listened to all this without comment, now said, "The Walkers told me that Daddy and Mommy weren't getting along. They said that *I* chose to be with Daddy."

Ezekiel felt the ground shudder underneath the wagon, so he quickly reined his team to a stop. Both Daddy and Nessa turned immediately to him –Nessa worried, Daddy irritated – and Nessa asked, "What's wrong, Daddy?"

Ezekiel waited for the aftershock. Nothing came. But the world now looked red and Ezekiel realized that the earthquake had not been in the ground; it had been *inside* him. He realized that he was seeing through tears of blood. "How dare those people discuss our family business with you? When did this happen?"

"Oh, Daddy, I've known about Mommy and her family since before we moved to Boley. I wasn't an infant. And Grandpa Tustenugge's name is always in the newspaper, too. I just thought you didn't want to talk about it because it hurt your feelings."

This last revelation was… well it was like both a hurricane *and* an earthquake. *She* had been protecting *him*? And a Biblical flood, too, because now Ezekiel was weeping uncontrollably. Nessa embraced him. Even stubborn, aloof Abraham Payne remained silent instead of making a disparaging remark. The horses waited patiently.

After what seemed a very long time, Ezekiel's tremors stopped. He regained his breath. His eyes cleared. He said, "Nessa, I love you more than anybody on this earth. Thank you for caring for me." She kissed his cheek without a word.

Ezekiel turned to Abraham Payne and went on, "Daddy, I love you, too. I understand why you are going to Africa, but please know that I will miss you very much."

Abraham Payne said nothing. It was familiar and painful. Ezekiel had been straining against Daddy's silences for years. They made him feel like he had been weighed and found wanting. But today Daddy had revealed his own pain: the death of his father, his helplessness to save his brother, his failure to return to his mother and his sisters. Today Daddy made Ezekiel face his worst fear and Ezekiel learned that it would not kill him. For the first time in his life, Ezekiel felt the possibility that his Daddy's silence could be a sign of something other than judgement. He clucked his horses back into motion and continued to the train station.

Johns Island South Carolina
1916

November 27

So much of note has happened since yesterday that I *must* confide it all to the pages of this teaching journal before the intensity of the memories fades! I want to be able to refer later to these notes. I also hope that by putting them in writing I can clarify my thinking on these events.

For the last two months (has it really been such a short time?) I have been busy taking in new sights and sounds; I have done precious little reflection. When I re-read my first impressions now they seem all wrong: it is as if I was seeing everything through the lens of Mother's prejudices about two-for-five folk instead of looking at the living people who were in front of my eyes.

I have been utterly preoccupied with what Promise Land School does not have! We do not have a chalkboard or chalk. We have no books of any kind. The school lacks even stout walls to keep out the cold winds of autumn! The privy smells. The well is suspect. Miss Ivy and I must chop wood for the stove every morning. We are cast out on this island and – in my worst moments – I despair that nobody remembers our presence here.

But yesterday I remembered our blessings. In the morning, before worship, Mr. Flood Wilson came up to me and asked, "Miss Seppy, would you be willing to teach reading to some of the men after their working hours?" How quick I had been to dismiss them all as without ambition! They work so hard in all weathers and yet they are prepared to make time for elementary education! I am ashamed of myself for seeing them in such a bad light.

During worship I prayed that Jesus would help me to discern the blessings in our challenges here. It came to me as a revelation: if the school board never visits, then we are free to teach the children what we want. If they do not provide us with books, then we are free to use whatever we can. And if they value the children so little as not to know even how many they are, then we are free to value each one as if he or she were our own. I felt unchained by these epiphanies, as if a great weight has been lifted from me.

This morning even splitting and stacking fuel for the school stove felt like light work. I nailed a large paper bag to the front wall of my classroom, and once the children were seated and I had called the roll I asked, "Who will tell me a story?"

My request met with silence. This was not what I was supposed to do. I was *supposed* to say things to them and then make them parrot my words. I was *supposed* to write things down and make them read those things back. I was not *supposed* to ask them to say anything to me other than what I had already said to them. And so they sat mute. I was quite certain they had heard me, so, instead of repeating my request I waited in silence.

After an uncomfortably long time, perhaps a full minute, Junie Harris asked, with a laugh, "You want to hear a story, Miss Seppy?"

My heart sank. I dreaded what I would hear now. He is the rudest and crudest of boys. But I had opened this door so now I had to give him a chance. "Yes, Junie. Please tell us your story."

With a smirk, Junie began. I copy this now directly from the paper bag, where I wrote as he spoke: in his words, as he told it. "Once there been a Ibo man what been a great fiddler. He know better than all them people what for do with a fiddle. When he lean back and draw he bow, nobody can keep from shuffle he foot. One day he going for play at a party. He have he fiddle in a bag. Bruh Bear and Bruh Tiger take he track and run him through a swamp. The man was scared, but he wouldn't drop he fiddle. He climb a tree and fix himself in a branch. Bruh Tiger begin for crawl up the tree for catch him. The man holler and try for scare the beast, but he wasn't scared. He keep on the climb up.

"Then the man draw he fiddle and he bow and begin for play with all he strength. Bruh Tiger obliged for stop for listen to him and the tune sweeten Bruh Tiger. He turn around and come down the tree. Him and Bruh Bear grab hands and set in for dance. The faster the fiddler play, the faster them dance. Them gone round and round till them dead tired. At length them drop for ground for catch them wind. The fiddler slip down the tree and leave. Bruh Tiger and Bruh Bear ain't have strength for follow him and so he music save him."

I wrote this on the paper bag as he spoke. I wrote it just as he spoke it. I wrote "he" for "his," "ain't" for "didn't," and "Bruh" for "Brother." Several times I asked him to wait to let me catch up. He looked suspicious... or maybe just puzzled. The other children laughed again and again. They laughed at Junie's story and – I think – at the fact that I allowed him to tell it without interruption or reprimand.

When he was done the class was silent again. I called on Mazalea Gaddis, my best reader: "Mazalea, will you come forward and read Junie's story?" And, to the awed wonderment of the class, she did just that, from my penciled notes on the paper bag, exactly as he had told it!

I asked, "Who else will come forward and read Junie's story?" This time it was me who was dumb with awestruck wonder, because who should raise his hand but Hamilton Brown, who the boys call Bubba! I had seen no indication before today that Hamilton knew so much as his alphabet. Each time I called on him he silently shook his head no. But here he was, confidently walking forward.

I was right. He could not read the words written on the paper bag. But he stood facing his classmates and repeated what Junie said (and what Mazalea read) almost word for word! Bubba was a prodigy. His memory was astounding.

Two more children read Junie's story aloud to the class, haltingly and with a few errors. Throughout, Junie sat with a smile of great satisfaction and pride. As I write these words I remember our readings in Pestalozzi back at Avery Institute. He said it may be *smart* to pay attention to some children more than others, but it's not *right*. Pestalozzi said I owe it to the child to give him more than what is necessary for what I imagine will be his station in life. But this goes way beyond recognizing Junie and his gifts. Because *giving* the children what is necessary (or more) implies that *I* am the one who holds everything of value. Have I truly been seeing *any* of the children of Promise Land School? Or have I only seen what I think they lack? Have I seen any of the adults of Johns Island? Or have I only seen the turnips they plant in their yards where I would put roses?

There was one more revelation, too. After school I planned a home visit to Sibbie Rivers to discuss her academic progress with her mother. This time I checked with the Allens before embarrassing myself calling the mother by the child's surname. Sibbie's mother is Mrs. Eva Singleton. I ate dinner at the Allens before going. I do not like to impose on people for food when they seem to have so little themselves.

Mrs. Singleton was just serving a crab stew to her four daughters when I arrived. And who should be sitting at the table with them? Sibbie's classmate, Blue Gamble! I have not written much in these pages about Blue. He is mostly silent in class and likes to sit hunched down on his bench as if to reduce his chances of being seen by me. Seeing him at Sibbie's house made me wonder why he wasn't eating in his own home.

And then I remembered: Blue may speak infrequently, but every time he does, it is about food. In early September I gave the children a spelling test. I called out the word "fish." Blue immediately yelled, "Porgies be def!" Once during recess Exodus Jefferson told the boys about tripping on a tree root on his way to school. Blue asked, "Did you drop your lunch?" I wondered, have I ever seen Blue carrying or eating lunch?

Mrs. Singleton generously ladled out a second helping of stew. Boys and their appetites! How many other mothers are feeding Blue Gamble?

I am ashamed of the judgments I was so quick to make on my first days on this island. The people along Bohicket Creek make so much of so little. They are generous with me and I have responded to their open hands with mean-spirited condescension. I pledge myself to do better.

Trinidad, Colorado
1916

Army travel had one very strict rule: Hurry up and wait. For two years, Private First Class Osceola McKaine and the 24th Infantry had been on garrison duty in the Philippines, which mostly consisted of cheering for their baseball team against the teams from white regiments. Suddenly– suddenly! – they absolutely had to leave. Immediately! The soldiers hurried 400 miles by train from Tacloban to Manila and then… nothing. They sat and played cards and speculated about their destination for over a week while they waited for a ship. Pfc. McKaine used the time to read *Conquest: The Story of a Negro Homesteader* by Oscar Micheaux.

When they finally boarded a troopship, their transport back across the Pacific took another two weeks. More cards. More speculation. While his bunkmates threw up over the rail, McKaine reread *The Histories* by Herodotus. He was characteristically excited by the story of King Croesus and the Delphic Oracle and spoke to anybody who would listen about the parallels with their position as Negro soldiers, proving their worth by serving a country that rejected them. By the time they landed in California, there was not a man in the regiment who hadn't been told – twice! – about enigmatic prophesies, ambiguity, and multiple interpretations.

Arriving in San Francisco they received orders to establish the Presidio as their new home: posting regimental signs, hanging flags, marking the homes of their white officers, laying out a baseball field for their team. That lasted a month. Just as they began to settle into a routine, they were ordered to pack up again, and they hurried across the Sierras and the Rockies to Fort Russell. No, not San Francisco, but Cheyenne, Wyoming would be their permanent base.

That lasted six days.

Now this train. The card playing began anew, along with the speculation about their ultimate destination.

"Don't be sore losers!" Sergeant Grant Mims laughed at two more defeated opponents as he gathered up the well-worn deck. He wore his customary predatory smile that rarely reached his eyes. It was hard to tell sometimes whether being a soldier wasn't a part-time job he did when he wasn't too busy playing cards.

"How sore could they be?" asked his partner, veteran First Sergeant William Nesbit. "They haven't been in those seats an hour. These two didn't take a trick we didn't give them." With his wavy hair and narrow features, he could have been mistaken by a stranger for a white man. Pfc. McKaine sometimes wondered whether that wasn't the quality their white officers looked for when choosing which enlisted men to promote to sergeant. Nobody made that mistake about Sgt. Mims, but he, too, was fair-skinned. Nesbit had enlisted around the same time as Mims, right after the Cuban war. They quickly became inseparable, especially in games that blurred skill and chance.

Their opponents stood up from the table. Private Luther Rucker, a tall, dark-skinned Georgian with a baby face, stretched and complained, "There's such a thing as too much talk."

"Too much talk," repeated Sgt. Nesbit. "When you two actually win a game – hell, when you win a hand – we'll see what your opinion is on too much talk. Rise and fly! Who's next?"

Sgt. Mims finished gathering the cards and began shuffling. He looked up and down the train car, then summoned Pfc. McKaine. "College Boy! Let's see if you and your friend Baltimore can give us a little more competition than Rucker and Bivens."

The train clattered and shook as "College Boy" McKaine and Private Charles Baltimore carefully moved down the aisle, holding the seats for balance, and sat down at the table. Pfc. McKaine had been awarded that nickname in part because he went to Boston College for a year, but mostly because he read so much. Now he looked out the window as the train rattled through a truly spectacular gorge and wondered briefly why he was playing whist instead of enjoying the scenery. This game had been going on almost without stop for weeks now: from Leyte to Luzon, across the Pacific, over the Sierras and through the Great Basin, now south through the heart of the Rockies.

"Where are they sending us this time?" wondered Sgt. Nesbit.

Mims stopped dealing and gave his partner an impatient look. "Nesbit, I have the same answer to that as the last thousand times you asked: 'When has the Army ever told us anything?'" He set down the last four cards in the center of the table.

Each man picked up his cards and began considering them. Osceola's partner, Charles Baltimore, was actually from Pennsylvania, not Maryland. Unlike many of the other men in the regiment, most of whom had been denied much formal education in the Jim Crow schools, Baltimore was a high school graduate. Now he ostentatiously rearranged his cards – by suit, low to high – to signal his partner. But McKaine seemed to ignore him, apparently preoccupied with his own cards. "I know exactly where we're going," he said in his confident baritone, in the loud voice he used when he wanted everybody to hear.

Mims looked up. "You been chatting with the general again, Mac?" he chuckled.

"Oh, I have an even better source of intelligence," McKaine said airily. Baltimore pounded urgently on the table, still focused on the cards. "Two, hearts, uptown," added Mac, who was, after all, paying attention to his partner's signals.

"You reading dispatches?" asked Nesbit. "Three no."

That bid got Baltimore's attention. He looked again at his cards, looked Mac in the eye, and said, "Four. Down."

This struck Mims as very funny. He looked again at his cards. "Really?" he asked. "Pass! You boys make it…" he hesitated. "A dollar on that?"

Baltimore's eyes went wide. "That's a day's pay!" he objected.

"Are we playing cards here or just socializing?" asked Nesbit. "Why bid if you're afraid to back it up?"

"Five dollars," said Baltimore calmly. "Oh, and hearts."

Sgt. Mim's eyes flashed angrily. He was supposed to be hustling these youngbloods, not the other way around. Osceola McKaine made no effort to contain his smile at the trap his friend had set for Mims and Nesbit.

But Mims was still curious about the College Boy's inside information. "Where *are* we going?" he asked.

"Columbus, New Mexico," answered McKaine, "and then down into Old Mexico after Pancho Villa."

"How could you possibly know that?" asked Baltimore of his partner. He studied the kitty, then pulled two cards to replace two from his hand.

105

Mac pulled out a copy of the *Denver Post*. "Because I got off the train to take a walk when we stopped in Denver."

The other three put down their cards and looked at the headline: "Wilson Orders US Invasion." They were quiet for a moment. Then Mims smiled and asked, "You sure about this, College Boy? Doesn't that leave room for…" he paused for comic timing… "ambiguity?"

They all laughed at that, even the College Boy himself.

Baltimore started flushing hearts. Mims and Nesbit watched closely for errors. But Mims had something else on his mind, too. "I don't know how I feel about invading Mexico," he said, breathing audibly as he gave up his four. "Mexico is a sanctuary for the colored man."

This exasperated Osceola McKaine. "What?" he asked sharply. He dropped the two and took the book.

Charles Baltimore now played the five of spades. "Come on, Mac, Mims is right. They not only protected Jack Johnson from lynching, they treat him regular. That's more than you can say for this Army."

"Johnson is the heavyweight boxing champion of the world," objected William Nesbit, sighing heavily as he dropped the king. "'Course the Mexicans take good care of him. How do you think they treat you, Negro?"

"Sorry, partner," objected Mims, "but I think that kind of talk is real ignorant. Lots of colored folks have moved to Mexico. Isn't that true, Mac?" For once he deferred to young Pfc. McKaine. Sometimes there were perks to being known as the intellectual of the regiment.

McKaine nodded and played his jack. "It is, but I wouldn't fall in love with Mexicans. Let me remind you that most of the so-called white folks in Brownsville, Texas are Mexicans."

Brownsville was a sore subject for the older noncoms and Osceola McKaine knew it. Sims and Nesbit had both been in the service when Teddy Roosevelt summarily discharged 167 soldiers from their sister regiment, the 25th. Every colored person in America knew that the men of the 25th had been framed. They were accused of an off-base shooting on a night when even the white officers knew – and swore! to an official inquiry! – that every single soldier was in the barracks and accounted for. When nobody would rat anybody else out (because

106

nobody had done anything) President Roosevelt kicked *all of them* out of the Army without even the pretense of a trial. The townspeople of Brownsville simply didn't want armed, uniformed Black men anywhere around them. That was the beginning and end of the case.

"I don't know if that's true," said Grant Mims, "and I don't know how you would know, either, since you've never been there. Not to mention the fact that you were still in short pants when it happened. I do know that Brownsville is in Texas and we're talking about Mexico." The play had come to him. He dropped his three of spades, but only after a long hesitation, and with obvious reluctance.

"I'll tell you what I know," said William Nesbit, who was still less interested in defending Mexico than his partner seemed to be. "These Mexicans all act real friendly when there's no white men around, you know? *Gabacho* this, gringo that? But the minute ofay comes back it's all 'Nigger, nigger, nigger.'"

They were approaching the crucial books, so Baltimore caught Mac's eye for a second before dropping his solitary spade, the ten. Then he said, "I've seen that. I have. I've also seen some colored soldiers who love serving in New Mexico and Arizona because they get to treat Mexicans exactly the way ofay treats us. You feel me?" And he pounded the table.

Mac nodded. When he took the book with his three it was clear that he understood both his partner's observation about Black men who wanted to play the Imperial American when they were on the border, and his communication about which cards remained in his hand.

Sgt. Mims dropped the five. One more chance.

And then there was no more chance. William Nesbit took the last books, but McKaine and Baltimore had made their bid. Osceola gathered the cards and began shuffling.

His partner was smiling broadly now. "I think I will put off taking your five dollars," announced Private Charles Baltimore loudly, and he gestured with his hand as if he was urging Mims to put his wallet away. Sgt. Grant Mims had not made any move for his money. He may have been hoping Baltimore had forgotten the bet. He may have been thinking of not paying. But Baltimore continued, a little louder, "I think when we get to Columbus you can treat the entire 'B' Company to a beer at La Esmeralda!"

"B" Company cheered. Everybody else laughed. Mims groaned.

Osceola McKaine was still thinking about their upcoming deployment to Mexico. "This is our opportunity," he said, and not to the men at the card table, but to everybody in the train car. "A popular war? All the newspapers there to tell our story? This is how we will prove ourselves to America. This is how we advance the colored race."

Sergeant Mims shook his head. Was this youngblood really so naïve? His mind recoiled from the carefully-buried memory of his own aspirations when he first deployed to the Philippines, just seventeen years before. He preferred to think of himself as realistic, not disillusioned. If he could make just three more years he could retire with a pension. That would be achievement enough.

But "College Boy" McKaine was still rousing the troops. "Pancho Villa, alive or dead!" he shouted. "Let freedom ring!"

"B" Company was still cheering. For racial equality? For a beer in New Mexico? Time would tell.

Inceville, California
1913

Dear Chief Alchesay,

My name is Luther Standing Bear, an Oglala Sioux from South Dakota. We met eight years ago when Chief Geronimo appeared at the Miller Brothers 101 Wild West Show in the Indian Territory and you came up from Arizona Territory to visit him. Please permit me this correspondence with you. Please share your thinking about some issues that have been troubling me.

I am so sorry I did not take the opportunity to speak with you when you were there in Oklahoma. Like everybody, I was interested to see Chief Geronimo and so I lost track of things that are usually important to me, both my manners and my curiosity. You will remember that the white people's newspapers were filled with stories of Geronimo riding in President Roosevelt's inauguration parade that March, with wild language about how even a glance from this elderly man would be enough to kill his enemies. When he arrived to appear in the Wild West show with us, all the white people were trembling with excitement and fear.

I remember seeing something similar many years ago in Philadelphia when our Sioux holy man, Sitting Bull, appeared on stage. Sitting Bull spoke in our Lakota language about his desire to meet President Cleveland and to have his children educated in white peoples' schools. The host then "translated." According to him, Sitting Bull talked about how he killed Custer, and how he wanted to do the same to all the white people in the audience, too! They cheered wildly for this lie, and for the strange thrill of being threatened by Chief Sitting Bull. I still don't really understand it. My brother Henry used to perform in the Wild West shows in Coney Island. He tells me that the white people in New York pay good money to go on rides that hurl them around a track and shake them and drop them from a height. They all scream in terror, and then they pay to do it again. I think seeing Chief Geronimo was like one of these "rollercoaster" rides for them.

Even the Indian employees at the ranch were interested in Geronimo, and not just the performers in the Wild West show, like me. A lot of the Creeks and Cherokees who manage the Miller Brothers' cattle operations stopped work to meet the train when the old man arrived. My Creek friend Hank Yarholar made fun of the others for it, but when Geronimo's train came to the station, so did Hank! So, let me apologize for not realizing who you were and for not speaking to you then when I had the opportunity.

109

Geronimo was traveling with a translator named Jasper Kanseah. I knew Jasper when he was a young student at Carlisle Indian School and I was a graduating senior. During his visit to the ranch, Jasper and I took some time to catch up about people we both knew, teachers and students. But then he told me about you and about the other Apaches. His stories so captured my imagination that they stayed with me up to this day. I now feel the need to write you and share some of my own.

I never knew that Jasper actually fought alongside Geronimo. I didn't know that they surrendered together. I had no idea that he was held in prison in Florida and Alabama before he came to school with us in Pennsylvania. Thirty years ago I was there at the Custer fight when the soldiers fell into our camp at Little Big Horn, but I wasn't old enough to carry a gun. When I started at Carlisle School it felt like a great act of bravery to walk into the white man's school. Listening to Jasper's stories really made me think about how little we learned from one another while we were at that white mans' school and how much we still need to listen to each other's stories.

That was not the end of Jasper's surprises. "We finally surrendered to the soldiers because two of my cousins who were scouts for the Army said we could go back to the reservation in Arizona. But the soldiers put us on a train to Florida instead. They arrested my cousins, too."

"Wait, they arrested their own scouts?" I asked. I have had a lot of experience with white people's dishonesty but I had to make him repeat this.

"Not just those two," he said. "They arrested *all* their scouts. They arrested every Chiricahua, even those who had stayed behind when we left the reservation. We all went to prison together." He told me that they were all still prisoners, twenty years later.

I asked him how the families were able to live together in prison for years after being on opposite sides. Jasper laughed and told me that you, too, had been in the Army. He told me that you were a head scout, and that you tracked Geronimo for the soldiers and met with him and encouraged him to surrender. You can imagine my astonishment. I saw you two embrace one another as brothers. I do not understand your language, but I could see the smiles on your faces as you spoke. How is it possible that you could have served Geronimo's captors and yet remained friends?

Please understand that I do not take his side against you, or yours against him. I understand how difficult and complicated our decisions become when we are trying to serve our people in the face of an adversary with endless wealth and numbers. I will share this story of my own. About fifteen years ago my people heard stories about the Prophet Dance. Maybe you heard about it, maybe not. They say it was all over Indian country. It was a simple round dance and it came from the vision of a Paiute man from Nevada. The Prophet Dancers hoped that their prayers would bring back the buffalo herds and let us live the way we had before the whites came with their railroads. I didn't believe it, but many people on our reservations in the Dakotas did. I suppose dancing was better than waiting to freeze and starve while the agents stole our food! That winter the dancing went on for days.

The whites say that we are a superstitious people. They mock our beliefs. But what about them? The Indian agents were absolutely terrified of that Prophet Dance. They treated it as a physical threat, as if we could actually make them vanish with our prayers! How else can I explain their reaction?

The government sent soldiers, first by the hundreds, then by the thousands, just to stop the dancing. They encircled the Prophet Dance camp. After they took away everybody's weapons they opened fire on the dancers and their families with rifles and machine guns. They murdered hundreds of my relations that day. My brother Ellis saw this, because he was there, serving alongside the soldiers as a Sioux policeman. He could do nothing to stop the massacre. Instead, he ran away, because he was afraid they would kill him, too, even though he was in their uniform.

As soon as I heard about the killing, I rode out to the dancers' camp to see. It was winter time. There was snow on the ground. I found the bodies of my cousins still frozen and twisted on the ground with the pitiful few clothes they had been wearing. There were hundreds of them, spread over miles where they had tried to escape the soldiers. I cannot remember all of them: it is beyond me now. But I remember Rattling Wind Woman. She was the daughter of Red Head, the Keeper of the original Pipe gifted us by White Buffalo Calf Woman a thousand years ago. She was a beautiful woman, married to Chief Black Shield. The soldiers had stripped her of her blanket and who knows what else when they killed her. She lay naked in the drifting snow, holding her infant daughter, also dead. I have to stop writing you as I recall this. It was a day that shook my heart.

When our people heard what had happened, many, many Sioux fled from their homes and into the Badlands. Who knew whether the soldiers were done killing? Maybe they planned to get rid of all of us! Lots of people thought it would be better to die fighting than just to be gunned down in the snow with empty hands like our relatives. And the soldiers really were planning to go out and fight them. There could have been a lot more deaths.

My father, Chief George Standing Bear, thought he could calm people on both sides. He wanted to prevent any more killing. He rode into the Badlands stronghold to talk, holding our sacred pipe as a token of peace, but the people in the camp were frightened and angry. They were in no mood to see that pipe. One man actually shot at my father while he held the pipe! My father succeeded in bringing our people back to the reservation, but the bitterness of that day still divides us after all these years. Even now there are those who hold grudges against our family because my father chose to talk about peace after the Army massacred our relations; those hoping to avenge the sacrilege of a rifle shot at my father while he was holding the pipe of peace. I long ago gave up asking who was right and who was wrong. Now I only want to know: How do we get back to being a single people? How do we face the new challenges of today while remaining Sioux?

My father told me long ago that if we do not restore the sacred hoop, the circle of our nation, then our future is doubtful. Seeing you with Geronimo told me that you understand something that we still do not. It looks to me like you two understand the need to reconcile the divisions of the past in order to work together for the future. If you and Geronimo can embrace as brothers, it makes me optimistic for the Apache people. I only hope that we Sioux can learn from you.

But that is not all. Kanseah told me that you are working to create your own school at Fort Apache, one that you will control, and where you will have your own teachers. I was a member of the very first class at Carlisle Indian School. I went there without even knowing it was a school, just to show that I was a courageous enough boy to ride into the home of the white man. After I had been there a year my father came to visit and he told me that he wanted me to learn everything I could about the language and ways of our enemies. He said we could no longer survive as a people without understanding them. I took his words to heart, but it was hard. When the white priests threatened us with their Hell, it seemed to me that we were already living in it.

Alvan Kills Horse was a cousin from my band. He was twelve years old when he died at Carlisle. He arrived the year after I did and began coughing after only a few weeks. By November he couldn't get up from bed. The consumption took him right after Christmas. They told me to write a letter home to my father, saying that Alvan was now in a "better place." And I did, I wrote that letter. I was fifteen, far from home, and dependent on the teachers for my wellbeing, but I am still ashamed of that letter.

Alvan was not the only friend to die there at Carlisle. There were so many. Lelu Little Chief got diarrhea as soon as we started eating school food. He never got better and he was dead three months later. Fannie Charging Shield got pneumonia that fall. She lived only four months. Sam Flying Horse, too. Then there was James Cornman. He didn't get sick at all. He insisted on speaking Lakota in the classroom, which was against all their rules. The teachers beat him every time they heard him, then they chained him up in a third-floor closet. When they found him dead in that closet, they said he had a brain hemorrhage. But they didn't say why.

In the summers at Carlisle, nobody went home. We were all sent out for work experiences, mostly with local farmers who fed us as little as possible and worked us around the clock. Our second summer, Herbert Littlehawk went to work at a Bucks County dairy. Herbert never returned. We never found out what happened to him. We could only guess.

I worked hard to be a good boy at that school. I wanted the approval of my teachers. I wanted my father to be proud. But so many of us died, of strange food and strange illnesses. They tried to take away our names, our speech and even our way of being in the world. Some say they succeeded.

I still think my father was right about learning to speak and to read and write in English. But I am certain there must be a way to do this without destroying our bodies and souls. That is why I am so interested in learning about your work to open your own school. Have you had any success? What kind of subjects do you want them to teach? Will the curriculum include Apache traditions and customs? Or will you leave that to the parents and just teach the white subjects in the school? And how are you managing to convince the agents of the Bureau to allow all this? It seems they no longer want to kill us, but they certainly don't want us to be Sioux, either. And I don't think that being Sioux is something *I* can do, by myself. I think it is something that *we* have to do, within the circle of our relations.

Here is what I remember: When my father sent me away to school, I was still a boy. I only got to go on one buffalo hunt in my life, when I was eight years old. What I remember most about it was that it was something *we all did together*. People did not go after buffalo with a friend, like they did for deer and elk; the entire camp prepared for this hunt together. Even a successful hunt by just two or three men could leave the people hungry if it meant that because of their chase the herds went elsewhere. The night before the buffalo hunt, the whole camp was silent, even our horses. The dogs didn't bark. The babies didn't cry. There was no shouting from tent to tent. That is how important it was that nothing happen that could spook the buffalo herd.

On the morning of the hunt we gathered our horses, still in silence. Nobody was allowed to ride out without the say-so of the leaders. When we got near the buffalo, we had to wait quietly until everybody was in place. I remember hearing the words, "Let's go!" And then – for many minutes – I heard nothing but the hoofbeats of hundreds of one-ton animals running over the ground. I couldn't see far, either, over the dust they raised, but I could smell the horses and the buffalo and the trampled grass.

We all rode as fast as we could after the running buffalo and I was now also truly on my own. Each of us did our own part in the midst of that large hunt. Each of us measured our own success by what we could bring back. I was proud to kill a buffalo calf that day. I was not proud that it took me five arrows to bring it down. But I was most proud to be riding with the men and to be doing something that made us Sioux.

Jasper told me that you, too, believe that to be Apache is to do important work together. He said you won't lease tribal timber and grazing lands to outsiders, even when they offer good money to the tribe, because you believe that running cattle and cutting timber are occasions for cooperation. He told me that you see lumberjacking and cowboying as dangerous jobs, done in the company of men, benefiting the whole people: jobs in which young men can test themselves and in which they can prove themselves.

I know that you are a busy man. I know that leading your people demands all of your time. But I would really appreciate your thoughts on these questions, along with anything else you can share with me about our path in this new century.

Yours truly,
Luther Standing Bear

Pawnee, Oklahoma
1913

Hank Yarholar was leading this little posse, but he was happy to let the white cowboy Curley McLain ride out front, even if Curley had no idea where they were going and no particular skill at tracking the men they were following. Really, there was no way that Hank was going to let Curley's horse behind him; he didn't trust Curley enough to turn his back on him. Curley had murdered a Creek man named Jud Fry and he made no secret of that fact. There was never a trial either: the other *wvcenv* cowboys convened a "grand jury," decided that Jud had accidentally fallen on Curley's knife, and that was that. Hank was not interested in becoming the victim of another "accident" so he avoided Curley when he could and kept him in sight at all other times. He felt the reassuring weight of the short-barreled Wells Fargo Schofield revolver in his jacket pocket, looked again at his bolt-action Spanish Mauser in its scabbard, and spurred his horse.

Hank wished Zack Miller would let him pick his own crew. Zack's daddy, the Colonel, always had, but the Colonel was dead now, and Zack – who had inherited all the Colonel's bad temper and none of his shrewdness – was in charge of the Miller Brothers' cattle operations. The Colonel had known all his riders by name, but Zack only knew them by the numbered brass badges he gave them all. "Number 23, I want you to take a crew out and bring back those cattle and the thieves. Cattle alive, of course." Zack had laughed at his own little joke.

Along with Curley (Miller Ranch number 78), Zack had sent Hank out on this mission with Will, Tom and Archie: numbers 157, 201 and 25. Will and Tom were virtually useless for this kind of work. Will Rogers was Cherokee, a good rider and an excellent roper, but he was from a well-off family and – as far as Hank could tell – he didn't need to work at all. In fact, he worked rather sparingly. He was not really someone you could count on in a tight spot. But he was good company, always ready with a joke or a story.

Tom Mix was a ladies' man from Pennsylvania. He was married, to his second or third wife if the rumors were accurate, but nobody left him alone with their own wives, sisters or even mothers. Tom rode well, exceptionally well, but Hank suspected that he, like Will, would be useless in an actual emergency… unless, of course, he could blind his opponents with his dazzling smile. He bragged of having been in Cuba with President Roosevelt but – again – the gossip was that his Army unit never left New Jersey. Hank was certain that Tom really wanted to work for the Miller Brother Ranch's show, the 101 Wild West. There were a lot more ladies watching that work than this.

The only man in this posse who Hank would have chosen to ride with him was Archie Bruner. Archie was *ennake*, some kind of cousin or other. Hank had never quite figured out the relationship, but they had grown up together. He suspected that Archie liked riding with the other men even less than he did. Archie had been silent for a few hours, but now he spoke up. "How many head are we supposed to be following? This track don't look like more than one or two. Is it worth it?"

Before Hank could answer, Curley McLain turned around his little sorrel mare and asked, grumpily, "Difference does it make, 'skin? Outlaws is outlaws."

'Skin? Wow. Straight, no chaser. Hank slowed his breathing and refrained from reaching for his revolver. Archie, though, replied immediately. "Outlaws is outlaws?" He spat. "Maybe that's something you know about. Like when you robbed Stribling's cattle? Or when you killed Montgomery for Colonel Miller? Or maybe like the Colonel himself robbed *our* land and paid us to fence it for him." Hank had worried all day about having to fight whoever stole the cattle they were trailing. Now it looked as though the possemen were going to kill each other first.

"You got a lotta sand for a red man," said Curley. "Don't he?" he asked Tom, the only other white man in the group. Tom looked away. Hank suspected that Tom Mix was more comfortable shooting airborne bottles than he was mixing it up with armed men. But it didn't matter. Curley McLain was a killer.

Now Will spoke up. "We red men all have a lot of sand," he said. "The white man took all the actual soil. Sand is the only thing left."

Curley looked at Will quizzically for a second, then smiled as he got the joke. Will continued, "They told us the land was ours as long as grass grows and water flows. But now that they discovered oil underneath, those treaties no longer apply. I guess it's because 'crude' doesn't rhyme with 'grow' and 'flow.'" Curley laughed out loud now. So did Tom and Archie. This was Will Rogers's great gift. He could always get people laughing and he could defuse a tense situation with his humor.

Curley turned and rode on, followed by Tom and Archie. Hank caught Will's eye and said quietly, "Thanks. That was diplomatic."

Will grinned a little and said, "Diplomatic? Diplomacy is the art of saying 'Good boy!' to a mad dog…" he paused a beat before delivering the punchline,

116

"until you can find a rock to bash his brains in." Then he rode after the others. Hank shook his head, chuckled and followed. He wondered how soon he would need a rock for Curley McLain.

A few more hours passed in silence before Hank raised a hand to signal the other riders to stop. Curley was still riding point, but he, too, stopped when he didn't hear the footsteps of the other horses behind him. They were approaching a line of willows, meaning a creek, but what got Hank's attention was a faint whiff of wood smoke... and the still fainter odor of something else: roasting meat. He gestured Tom and Curley to the left. He gestured Will and Archie to the right. He himself rode straight ahead to where he thought the fire was.

As he got closer Hank saw a half-butchered steer with the 101 brand still visible. No doubt, it was from the Miller Brothers Ranch. He also noticed two horses tied to trees: a roan and a pinto. Why did that pinto look so familiar? While he puzzled that out he drew his Mauser from its scabbard and quietly dismounted. He walked carefully toward the creek until he found the fire and the people near it. Boys. Only boys. No more than fifteen or sixteen years old. Maybe *mvskoke estelvste*, maybe not. Either way they were Negro.

"Don't move," he said. "Put your hands up."

"Don't shoot," said the older boy. He put his hands over his head, but he stood up.

"He said 'don't move,' nigger." This was Curley McLain. He was still on his sorrel mare, riding straight down the middle of the creek from Hank's left with his double-action Colt in his hand. "Tell us where you stashed the other cattle so we can kill you and leave."

"That's not much incentive for truth telling," said Will Rogers, walking in from the other direction. The two boys by the fire were swiveling their heads from side to side now, eyes wide.

Will's comment seemed to have gone over Curley's head. He stopped his mare and pulled back the hammer on his Colt. But now Archie arrived next to Will. Unlike Will, who was not displaying any weapon, Archie was holding his lever-action carbine. He wasn't pointing it at the boys, though. He was aiming directly at Curley McLain. "These are the Samson boys. They're kin to Warrior Bruner and Warrior's kin to me. Nobody's killing them."

Hank thought he had a pretty good imagination and he had been in his share of desperate situations, but this was deteriorating beyond his worst nightmares. Nobody's killing *them*? Hank was starting to think that nobody was going to *survive* this. He thought quickly, but came up with nothing. Maybe Will Rogers had another joke?

Curley McLain still had his gun on the standing boy. "I've got six shots, 'skin," he announced. "I can get four of them off before you get your second round in the chamber."

That was bullshit, but it was irrelevant. Once Curley and Archie shot each other, anything could happen. He didn't even know whether these Samson boys were armed. And he didn't want to have to shoot Curley himself, but Archie was his kin. "That's my cousin you're threatening," he said, but he didn't take his Mauser off the boy by the fire.

"What about you, Tom? Are you a white man?" asked Curley.

"Last I looked," answered Tom. "But I'm not fixing to die over another man's cow." Nevertheless, Hank noticed that Tom Mix's right hand had strayed to the Smith and Wesson revolver at his hip.

Will tried again: "Careful, fellas. We're in Oklahoma. One stray pistol shot and we could set off a gusher bigger than the Nellie Johnstone. Our families will be rich, but we'll all drown in oil." This time, though, his witticism got no reaction at all.

Hank thought the situation couldn't possibly get any worse. But then another voice spoke up, a familiar voice, though one he had not heard in a long time, a voice that explained why he recognized that pinto he had seen tied to the tree. Hank's heart sank. This was worse. Nobody knew where the man was hiding – behind a tree? *in* a tree? – but everybody was afraid to take their eyes off each other and look. "How about I decide who dies today?" asked the authoritative voice of Hank's former brother-in-law, Ezekiel Payne.

"Is that you Ezekiel?" asked Archie.

"It is," answered the man Hank had last seen the day his sister, his parents, and he kicked him out of the Yarholar family. In his mind's eye he saw the look of utter betrayal on Ezekiel Payne's face that day.

"You still carry that big Henry?" asked Archie, smiling.

"I do," answered the man Hank had exiled from his life.

Hank saw Curly McLain's eyes go wide at the mention of the .44 caliber lever-action repeater. But he was no more relieved himself. He had rejected Hank's daughter Nessa as if she were not his own blood. What must this man think of him?

"Everybody listen carefully and do as I say," said Ezekiel. "Boys, ride out south. You know where to go. Kitt, take my horse. Hap, you ride yours." The boys were both gone in an instant.

"Now," said Ezekiel, "you, white man with the nasty mouth. You're the one that killed Jud Fry, aren't you?"

"That 'skin killed himself!" objected Curley.

There was a very loud report and a bullet took off Curley's hat. "Holster your piece, shut up and dismount," said Ezekiel.

Curley followed the instructions without providing any more commentary. "Now you two start walking back to New Ponca. Take your horse, Big Hat," he said to Tom. "Leave the sorrel."

"You're a horse thief!" objected Curley.

"Oh, you'll get your horse back," answered Ezekiel. "Just not right now. Go!"

"Good one, Ezekiel!" laughed Archie Bruner, lowering his carbine as the two white men left. "Am I glad to see you!"

But Ezekiel wasn't having it. "Hank," he ordered, "drop your rifle." Hank did so without delay.

"What's wrong, Ezekiel?" asked Archie. "We're all friends here."

"Oh, we're friends now?" Ezekiel emerged from his cover, a thicket right near the creek. "Because friends abandon each other when its inconvenient, like you did when Hank fired Island and your cousin Warrior to please Colonel Miller?"

Oh, God, thought Hank despairingly. He didn't know how Ezekiel even heard about that. Island and Warrior hadn't returned to work, true, but they never complained to him about it, either. What did Ezekiel have in mind for him now?

"Take your funny Cherokee friend and head back to Claremore," Ezekiel told Archie. "Or wherever you think you'll be safe from Curley McLain. That man is a rabid dog."

Archie looked unhappy with this turn of events, but he shrugged and turned to leave. Before he took a step, though, he turned back to Ezekiel. "Wait, what about Hank? I can't leave without Hank."

To his credit, Ezekiel did not gesture with the big gun. He did not mention Nessa. He did not mention Hank's sister, Sunshine, Ezekiel's ex-wife. He just said, "Hank and I have some things to talk about."

Archie looked briefly at Hank, then back at Ezekiel, then at Will Rogers. Will said nothing. Finally, Archie and Will left.

Hank and Ezekiel stood silent by the fire until it was clear that they were alone. All Hank noticed was the smell of the cooking meat... and the big gun in Ezekiel's hands.

Finally Hank asked, "How is Nessa?"

He was sorry he had asked the question the moment the words passed his lips. He looked away. If there was one thing that could turn Ezekiel Payne murderous it had always been protecting his daughter Nessa. But no rifle shot came, nor even a harsh word. Instead, Hank heard a sob. He looked up and saw that Ezekiel Payne was weeping.

"I don't know, brother," said Ezekiel. "I don't know how she is. I don't know what it means that she never asks about her mother or about her grandparents or about you. Is she silent because she's trying to take care of *me*? I just don't know."

"But how are *you*, brother?" Ezekiel went on. "How are you on her birthday? How are you at Christmas?"

Now Hank forgot the big Henry rifle, forgot his fear. He teared up, too. "I am so sorry," he said.

"Save your tears. Save your apologies, too. You chose sides."

Hank looked at him curiously. *Sides*?

Ezekiel composed himself. His tears were gone. "You chose sides when you went to work for that Confederate colonel. You chose sides when you fired Island and Warrior because of their color."

Hank didn't remember it happening that way at all. He remembered Warrior implying that Colonel Miller was, himself, part Negro. He remembered the Colonel's anger and his big Navy Colt. He remembered saving Warrior's life. But he said nothing.

"You chose sides when you helped that colonel steal the Yuchi Town land. You chose sides when you helped him fence it in."

Hank had been regretting those things since the day he did them. But Ezekiel Payne wasn't even *Mvskoke*. He was a state Negro and he had no standing to make these criticisms.

"You all chose sides when you decided that we colored men didn't need a vote in Oklahoma as long as *you* got one. You chose sides when you decided that we colored men couldn't ride in a first-class train car so long as *you* could."

Hank was uncertain about all this. Hadn't there always been friendship between Thlopthlocco Town and the *estelvste*? When *had* he stopped being friends with Island Grayson? When had he stopped visiting with Warrior Bruner?

Ezekiel wasn't done. "You chose sides when you decided that Nessa couldn't be your kin. And I mean *you* chose sides. You chose sides when you chose a white man's definition of Muskogee over your own blood."

This was too much. Hank was tired of being lectured by this man who couldn't even speak the *Mvskoke* language properly. "What are you going to do about it?" he asked angrily.

"Do about it?" repeated Ezekiel Payne. "I'm not going to *do* a God-damned thing. I *have* my daughter. I know who I am and I know who she is. I'm not trying to please a white man or to let him decide who I am.

"I just saved your life, and Archie Bruner's life and probably his Cherokee friend's life, too," continued Ezekiel. "I know I saved the Samson boys, because

121

no matter what *your* intentions were, that murderer Curly McLain was going to kill them just because he could. I think you know it, too.

"So take your horse," said Ezekiel. "Take Curly McLain's horse, too. And take your gun. Go back to Thlopthlocco Town, or wherever. You need to live with yourself."

"You gave your pinto to the boy," objected Hank. "How will you get back to…" His words ran out. He realized guiltily that he didn't even know where Ezekiel lived, where his own niece Nessa lived.

Ezekiel gave him a harsh smile. "Don't worry about me. I'll be fine. You need to watch your back for Curly McLain. You need to look out for yourself. You don't know who you are and you don't know where you're going." And with that he left, Henry rifle in hand, disappearing up the creek, around the bend, into the trees.

Hank picked up his Mauser and walked back to his horse. It took him only a minute to replace his guilt with more anger at the man who made him feel it. *Fuck Ezekiel Payne*, he thought. *Fuck that estelvste.*

Linn-San Manuel, Texas
1965

When I sat down a few weeks ago to begin composing this testimony for you, my grandchildren, I was thinking only about our losses. I was thinking about all of you growing up in what is now no better than a *colonía*, surrounded by the children of landless *mojados* from deep inside Tamaulipas and from Zacatecas. And then I remembered this Psalm of David: *Aunque acampen ejércitos contra mí, no temblará mi corazón. Aunque me embistan en batalla, entonces mantendré firme mi esperanza.* "Though armies camp against me, my heart will not fear. Though I am attacked in battle, I will firmly maintain my faith." God has given me many blessings, and the most important of them are you, *mis nietos*. How then shall I forget the blessing he gave me in the form of your grandfather, without whom I should never have had your mother or any of you?

There was a time before I was a widow. So please, allow me to tell the story of your *abuelo* out of order. Let me skip ahead to this moment of joy, before I return to narrating my horrors.

I actually met your grandfather before he went to fight in the Great War, the day of my cousin Encarnación's wedding. He was flirting with all the girls while we were setting out the food. I don't think I would have noticed Narciso Garza at all among that crowd of jokesters, but he was wearing the uniform of an officer in the United States Army. I thought I would ask him why, but he seemed so full of himself that I didn't want him to think I found him interesting.

The next time I saw Narciso was after the War, at the Vela family's *capilla*, the Church of the Holy Family, over in Laguna Seca. The orange blossoms were blooming in Doña Carlota's groves and their smell was strong: so fresh, so sweet. Today the county is filled with groves, and every time I smell the blossoms it reminds me of my first real conversation with the love of my life.

That night all the prominent families of the county were there and we were trying to decide what to do about the upcoming primary election. Boss John Closner expected our votes again, as always, but some people were tired of his stealing and thought we might be better off with an honest sheriff like Judge Edwards. There was also a contested primary for governor that year. Pa Ferguson was running for re-election, but he, too, was embarrassed by all kinds of financial scandals and William Hobby was running against him, promising a clean up.

Most of the speeches that evening were not at all about what they pretended to be. Anastasio Villareal, for example, supported Sheriff Closner. He reminded everybody how the sheriff protected Mexicans during the *rinchada*, the terror I will describe to you in another chapter. But that was not the real reason that Don Anastasio sided with Closner and everybody present at the meeting knew it. When the St. Louis, Brownsville and Mexico Railroad laid its tracks across the county, Closner gave the Villareal family the mule-team contract to freight construction supplies. We all saw the new house Don Antastasio built with the money he got from the sheriff's cronies at the railroad. We all saw his wife's new clothes when she came back from shopping in New Orleans.

Domingo Fonseca, on the other hand, supported Judge Edwards, and he was eloquent in his denunciations of Closner's corruption. But he, like Don Anastasio, was only concerned with justice insofar as it affected him personally. Everybody in that room knew about the trips he took across the border with Judge Edwards to find legal documents that would allow Edwards's gang to secure old land grants at pennies on the dollar.

When the conversation turned to votes for women, I felt it was time for me to stop listening. I had to speak up. Don Nicolás Zamora was chairing the meeting that evening. When I raised my hand he looked as though he was going to choke. The prospect of a woman actually addressing his meeting embarrassed him so badly that he immediately looked away and called on Marcelino Ballí. I, however, was not raised by my parents to be ignored. I stood right up and started to speak before Marcelino could even open his mouth.

"*Mis vecinos*," I began. "Is it not strange that we discuss a woman's right to vote and yet do not hear the voices of the women in this room?" The few other women present – and some of the men – chuckled at this. Don Nicolás frowned but said nothing.

I did not want to antagonize or divide those present by accusing anybody of favoring this candidate or that for reasons of personal gain. I only wanted to discuss the way this election would affect all of us, the families who had been in the Valley the longest. "This year we hear many flowery words about the right of women to vote. I myself am a great advocate for women's rights: to own property, to serve on juries, and to make contracts, too. But I ask that we pay close attention to the language that has been used in this campaign. The supporters of William Hobby speak about 'decent' women and how these 'decent' women will prevent corruption in government. Is there any person here who doubts that by 'decent' they mean 'Anglo'? These same people demand an end to the sale of liquor and beer and they say that it is the curse of foreigners

124

and indecent people. Is there any person here who doubts that by 'foreign' and 'indecent' they mean us? How many counties in Texas have instituted a white primary to ensure that no Negro can vote? Is there any person here who doubts that what the 'reformers' mean by 'cleaning up politics' is to deny us the vote as well?"

The ladies and gentlemen in the room had been listening intently and with interest until I compared us to Negroes. Several men began shouting angrily and Don Nicolás took advantage of the commotion to silence me completely. "Thank you, Señorita Hinojosa, for your interesting observations. Don Marcelino?" And just like that the conversation returned to its previous direction. It didn't matter anyway. Governor Ferguson lost his primary by the most lopsided margin in history and Judge Edwards took over Hidalgo County. The white ladies won their right to vote and every one of us *Tejanos* lost ours. It is only now, almost fifty years later, that I begin to think we might get it back.

But that is not the story I set out to tell. When the meeting broke up, the other women my age who were present gathered around and complimented me profusely on my courage and clarity in saying what needed to be said. I suspect that some of them actually meant it. But standing nearby was a tall, slender man in a suit of the latest style. Ermenegilda Ballí took my hand and said, "Timotea, permit me to introduce you to my cousin, *Licenciado* Narciso Garza." And then turning to him, "Narciso, this audacious woman is my friend, Timotea Hinojosa y Garza."

I gave him the withering and disinterested look I had learned to share with all the self-important young men who presumed to ask for my time in those days. He was not discouraged. "Garza?" he said, and smiled. "Perhaps we, too, are cousins."

This flimsy attempt to manufacture a connection between us completely exasperated me. "In this Valley we are all cousins," I said quietly. Then, quite against my own conscious intention I added, "My mother is Dionicia Garza-Singletary." I was immediately sorry I had given him a reason to continue the conversation.

But Narciso did not follow up the genealogy. Instead, and to my pleasant surprise, he said, "I thank you for your comments and I am sorry they cut you off. It's too bad that pride forbids these people from understanding the evidence of their own eyes and ears. The Anglos of this Valley lynched more of our people in the last few years than the Anglos of the entire state lynched Negroes since the end of the Civil War. You are certainly right that they mean to take our vote."

"Lynch." It was a word they used when a mob took an accused person from jail and killed them without a trial. I had never thought before to use that word for the murder of my father, a murder I will narrate to you shortly. But this Narciso made a good point. And it meant that he was not just complimenting me in the way of young men, but that he had actually listened and agreed with me.

"*Licenciado*?" I asked.

Now he smiled like any other young man trying to impress a girl. "University of Michigan Law School." And it worked. I *was* impressed.

"Are you visiting here in the Valley?" That was all wrong. I had not intended to express any interest in seeing him again. I had actually meant to establish that he was just an outsider, passing through. Something about him was making me continue this unwanted flirtation.

But my confusion seemed to elude Licenciado Garza. "No, I am back from the War in France and I plan to establish a law practice here in the Valley... perhaps in Hidalgo County. That is why I attended the meeting here and that is why I remained silent."

It was the mention of France that jarred my memory. "Have we met before?"

Narciso had smiled before, but this seemed to please him immoderately. "Yes, we have!" he said. "We were introduced at the wedding of my friend Anselmo to your cousin Encarnación. I was beginning to fear I made no impression on you at all. While I thought of you every day I served in the Army!"

That was too much for me. Of all the nerve, to feed me an obvious piece of flattery as if I were some silly young thing! I did not bother to hide my frown and said nothing in return.

Narciso realized his error as soon as the words escaped his mouth. The funny thing is that later, after our own wedding, he repeated this claim and insisted on its truth. I accepted the story from him then. Today, so many years later, I don't know what to believe. Perhaps it was the truth. In either case, in the time we had together we loved each other very much.

126

That evening, though, he quickly changed the subject back to the serious content of our meeting. "You didn't get the opportunity to finish your address to the meeting tonight. Do you see a path forward for us?"

I swallowed my irritation because I really did want somebody to hear my thinking on this. "The *gabachos* have us fighting with them in defense of our land, but that fight also keeps us divided. There is always some cousin somewhere who can establish a hereditary claim to a ranch that an Anglo wants… a cousin who is willing to sell for a few dollars. Then the family splits: Tía Fulanita supports the sale because the money goes to her favorite nephew and Don Fulano opposes it because he grazes his cattle on that land. It all turns into a big mess. I think we should be paying more attention to elections. We are still the majority here, and we still have the vote. Did you see us tonight, arguing between Closner and Edwards? Why aren't we electing our own people instead of choosing which *gabacho* isn't as bad as the others? Is José Canales the only person our community can find to represent us?"

Narciso was nodding seriously as I spoke but there was the hint of a smile at the corners of his eyes. "Am I amusing you?" I asked, a little angrily.

"Not at all!" he protested. "I am smiling because what you are saying is exactly what I have been thinking. I don't just want to open a law office… not to help Don Fulano sue Tía Fulanita, anyway!" He laughed. Now I was smiling, too. "I want to choose a place where I can use my law degree to represent *all* our people. And that means just what you said: running for office. I have all the respect in the world for José Canales, but he is falling into the trap you described at the meeting. He supports prohibition of alcohol. He supports women's suffrage. He behaves as if he can convince these 'reform' *gabachos* that he is one of them."

"I did not speak out against women's right to vote!" I interjected sharply. "Only against these white women who think they should have it instead of us!"

It was at that precise moment that Ermenegilda Ballí cleared her throat, reminding both of us that she was still standing there. I had quite forgotten and it was apparent that Narciso had as well. "Chicho," she asked him, laughing lightly, "is this really what you want to discuss with my friend Timotea?"

"Well…" he stammered, "yes, it is. But I would also like to ask whether I can call on you sometime."

My courtly manners returned. "If you were to come visiting at the home of my *abuelo*, Don Carlos, and if he were to invite you in to speak to him in his *salón*, perhaps I would join the two of you in conversation."

And with that I found my cousin Ramón with whom I had gone to the meeting. He was speaking rather deferentially to old Don Nicolás, apologizing – I suppose – for my scandalous insistence on expressing a point of view in public. Don Nicolás had a contract with the county for maintaining the roads and Ramón was hoping to hire himself and his mule team to do some grading. This was, of course, before any of those roads had been paved. In any case Ramón was clearly working very hard at erasing the bad impression I had made. We made the rounds to say good night to everybody who was still there and then drove back to San Manuel.

Narciso and I married six months later, at La Capilla de la Lomita. It was the beginning of a wonderful marriage to a man who I loved and who respected me. He had a good law practice. He was decent and hard working. I am not ashamed to reveal that my pulse raced when he came home to me each afternoon at the end of his working day. Intimate lives are just that, but let me say that ours was full and exciting and very satisfying. I was always one to chuckle at the girls who were so interested in boys. I had not known that such feelings existed.

A year later your mother was born and I named her Dolores, and not only for all the losses I have already described. I thank God for bringing me Narciso, for giving me my daughter, and especially for blessing me with all of you. But I must return now to my testimony and to the time before the terror. The Anglos of McAllen tried to get me to give up on my schooling, but I was not so easily dissuaded.

Transcript of oral history tape recording of John Howat Walker, April 10

So you came back did you? I thought you were tired of me. I didn't think you wanted to hear about the war that capital waged on labor in those days. I thought you had your own idea of who Mary Harris Jones was. I thought you wanted me to shut up.

Yes, I am glad to see you. I'm tired of hearing these donkeys tell the same jokes over and over again. You come around with your machine and ask me these questions about Mother Jones, and – for a minute, at least – it's like she's not dead and forgotten. It's like her life might mean something, and my life, too. So, yeah, even when I argue with you I am really happy for this chance to tell our story.

Oh, no. That was far from the only time we were there when the capitalists turned the guns of their hirelings on the workers. Have you not heard of Ludlow? Yes, I was there. So was Mother Jones. She was everywhere that children were hungry. Everywhere men were standing for their rights. Always in the field. Our national president tried to get her to stay and work in his office. Or at least he did until Mother Jones told the miners not to give him a $10,000 house. Sure, she said if his family needed a fancy house he should get a job where he could afford it. Why should coal miners, who couldn't clothe their own children, support him like some plutocrat? Why should a miner's wife, living in a drafty coal-patch shack, sacrifice to buy a nice place for him? Oh, he hated when she said that. He held it against her for the rest of his life. He did. I think he and the other union officers *wanted* her trapped in the national office. Instead of out in the field, you know, so they could control her. But she lost her husband and all her children years before. She really didn't care much about the paycheck. She only cared about the working class.

Me? Oh, that was another story. No, they didn't offer me those kind of leadership jobs. In fact, when the miners elected me president of District 14 the national office barred me from the position. That's right, some coal operators accused me of taking bribes from them. You know, to soil my reputation with the members? But the national office pretended to believe it. Mary stood up to them about that, defended me, you know. That's another thing they held against her. But nobody could tell stories like that about Mary. The members always supported their Mother Jones. That crowd at the national office could never do anything against her.

What did I do? Oh, what did I do when they took my job with the union away? Why I went back to work in the mines! The day a union man is too good to work, the day he's afraid to toil side by side with his members, well, that's the day they should turn him out of office. You know, John Mitchell and I started in the same mine as children. But when the miners told him he couldn't take a check from the bosses as well as from the workers? That's when he quit the union.

Mother Jones? No, she never quit.

Oh. Money. No, she never took a dime nor a meal nor a night's stay from the bosses. When she could get it she took an organizer's pay from the union. When she couldn't, she depended on the hospitality of the miners' families. Sometimes she had to work in the mills, too, or, anywhere a working-class woman could get a job.

What? That's right, I was going to tell you about Ludlow. This happened years after the story I told you about when you were here last Friday. Let me think, it was 1913, maybe 1914. It was just before the war broke out in Europe. Those Colorado coal camps were hell. The Rockefellers ran them like the tsars ran Russia. And dangerous? I told you how deadly the Pennsylvania mines were. Colorado was twice as bad. So we were slow and patient about organizing there. A union man going into those camps openly would never be seen or heard from again. Nobody would ever find their graves, neither. We did the work in secret until we knew we had enough people.

No, Mother Jones wasn't there until later, when the strike was on. Let me get to that part of the story. You can't understand why they put her in jail, just for entering the state of Colorado, if you don't know there was a strike on, can you?

It took us a long time before we were ready to present our demands to Rockefeller. All those years we had organizers quiet-like in the Colorado mines, and you want to know something? Most of what we were asking for was already the law in the state of Colorado! It was Colorado law that miners had a right to elect a check-weighman to make sure they were paid for what they actually mined. It was Colorado law that the company had to pay the workers in money.

In money, you know, U.S. dollars.

No, they weren't paying them in money. They were paying them in *company* money. Scrip, they call it. It could only be spent in company stores and company boarding houses. Company gin mills, too, because that was before Colorado went dry.

And it was the law that workers had to be paid for dead work, too.

Dead work. Dead work is the work to maintain the mine.

Right. Because the company only paid us by the ton of coal. We still had to put up timbers to shore up the ceiling. We still had to blast and dig to get from one part of the coal seam to another. We still had to dig rock so the tunnel would be big enough for us to fit in. No, they only wanted to pay us for tons of coal. Oh, and that, too. The coal companies decided that coal tons were 2,200 pounds. I don't know where they got that from. They were cheating the men on weight anyway. They built in another 10% cheat with that extra two hundred pounds to make a ton.

So we presented our demands to the operators. They rejected them all, so the men went out on strike. The companies immediately evicted them and their families from their company houses but we were ready for that. That's right, that was another reason it took us so long to get organized there in Colorado. We rented land. We built tent platforms. We bought tents. We put iron stoves in every tent so that the strikers could have a safe place to live.

I'm getting to her. She'll be back in the story soon.

So we made these tent cities where the miners and their families could be away from the Baldwin-Felts. Baldwin-Felts was one of them detective agencies.

No, I told you, not Sherlock Holmes detectives. They weren't solving mysteries. They were perpetrating crimes on the working class.

What do I mean? Shooting at the strikers. Shooting at their families. Beating people up. Murdering them when they could get them alone. They built an armored car with a machine gun mounted on it. They drove around the camps shooting in all directions. They burned down the tents and platforms in the Forbes camp while everybody was at a funeral. In Ludlow the families had to move to holes in the ground under the tent platforms. Them Baldwin-Felts snipers were in the hills taking potshots right through the canvas walls of the tents. The governor decided to protect the law by bringing in the National Guard, but it weren't no National Guard he brought in. It was Baldwin-Felts in Colorado National Guard uniforms.

Yes, here's where Mother Jones arrived. Now, understand, I wasn't there for all of this, you know, they locked her up by herself, but she told me the whole story later. You'll get it when I tell you the story. So the governor announces that Mother Jones was banned from the Colorado coalfields. She wasn't even in Colorado at the time, she was in West Virginia. This news made the papers everywhere, though. You know Mary, she couldn't let that stand at all. She was on the next thing smoking to Denver.

Yes, the exact same day. She got a room in a hotel and bought a train ticket to Trinidad down there in the coalfields. But there were detectives watching her room at the hotel. And there were detectives at the train station. So she left her luggage at the hotel. She went to the rail yards, *before* her train pulled into the station. She told a section hand and he told a porter and they had her into her sleeper and fast asleep in her berth before the train went into the Denver station for boarding!

Of course, they knew Mother Jones. What workingman didn't in those days? Her reputation was everywhere men were fighting for their rights. In the morning the conductor stopped the train before Trinidad to let her off. She walked into town and saw an entire company of Colorado National Guard watching the station for her. But they didn't see no Mother Jones get off that train. She was already at the restaurant having her breakfast! Soon enough, the Guard found out she was in town.

I told you, there were always informants. The capitalists pay and somebody is weak. Secrets are hard to keep. So right away they arrested her. They locked her up in the Catholic hospital, Mt. St. Rafael. The nuns fed her, but there were ten armed guards just for her. Two at the door of her room. Two more down the hall. Two at the elevator door on her floor. Two at the elevator door downstairs. Two marching up and down outside the hospital. She was locked up there for two months and not allowed a letter or a newspaper or an attorney. She was locked up like the Count of Monte Cristo. The nuns saw her, and the guards saw her, but that was all.

Finally, we got a writ of habeas corpus. But she didn't know we did that, because they were keeping her incommunicado, you know? All Mary knew was that after being held in solitary all that time, one night, in the middle of the night, a colonel of the Colorado National Guard came for her. And when he took her out, suddenly none of her guards was anywhere to be seen. She thought it was all over. She thought they were spiriting her away to murder her. But instead they took her by train back to Denver and straight into the governor's office.

He had instructions for her. Orders, really, as if she was the servant of the bosses like he was. Like he could tell her what to do. He said sure, she was free to go, but not back to the coalfields. What do you think she said? She told him what she thought of his instructions. She got right back on a train for Trinidad!

Yes, isn't this what I have been telling you? She cared nothing for herself. Mother Jones did what she thought was needed for the entire working class. She knew what it meant to disobey his orders. The detectives followed her onto the train. Forty miles before Trinidad, at Walsenburg, the National Guard got onto the train and arrested her. This time there was no hospital, either. They put her in a rat hole under the Huerfano County Courthouse. They kept her there in the dark and cold for a month and they fed her bread and coffee. They were hoping she would die there. It took a month for us to find out where she was being held. And then to get another writ of habeas corpus to get her released.

I told you before. She usually made her speeches by saying back to the people exactly the words that the people told her. The women of the southern Colorado camps told her the most awful stories. Those stories were her speeches. It was all, "Oh, Mother did you hear?" and "Mother, listen!" and "Mother, it's an outrage!" and each was some horror she had heard. Machine guns firing into the tents. A girl assaulted by soldiers. A man captured and made to dig his own grave. What did she add? Mother Jones added the class-conscious summation to all these outrages. She would say, "It's an outrage that Rockefeller should own the coal that God put into the earth for all of us. It's an outrage that soldiers protect the mines against workers who ask to be paid more than just a crust of bread." She said, "It's an ocean of outrage." That was the gift of Mother Mary Jones, to tell the workers what they *already knew*, but to let them see it in a new way. And since you asked me whether she was the Mother Superior of the working class, I remembered another thing she used to say. She told them, "Fight like Hell until you get to Heaven!" That doesn't sound like any nun I ever heard about.

So that went on from New Year's until Easter. The Greeks and the Hunkies in the Ludlow camp, and there were a lot of them, were celebrating Easter the week after everybody else. I don't know why. I think the Greeks and Hunkies have a different Easter. Anyway, the Baldwin-Felts came to camp early the next morning. They demanded that two of the miners surrender to them. They had no arrest warrant. They just insisted, so the miners said no. That was the signal for the gun thugs surrounding the camp to open fire. Some of the women and children immediately fled into the hills. Others hid in the pits under the tent platforms. The men who were armed tried to return fire. By late afternoon they were all out of water and ammunition. All they could do was try to cover their own retreat into the hills.

Dozens of strikers and family members were killed by machine gun fire. Then, before the sun set, the Baldwin-Felts came into the camp. They set fire to all the tents and all the platforms and all of the miners' possessions that they didn't steal. But that weren't all. Four women and eleven children were hiding in a cellar the men dug under one of the tent platforms. It was meant to be a shelter from the bullets. When them Baldwin-Felts assassins set fire to the tent, it just sucked all the air out. Every single one of them in that pit suffocated to death. Four young mothers. Eleven innocent children. It was an ocean of outrage. I need to stop talking now. I can't remember that day and just talk as if, as if... I just need a minute.

What did we do then? Why we armed every man we could in the whole strike district! You're damned right, we did. The Rockefellers were trying to kill us; we weren't going down without a fight. We sent a committee of wives to see President Wilson. We held a mass meeting in Denver. Not just of workers, but of everybody who cared about human life and the rule of law and who opposed John D. Rockefeller and his gunmen who spit on American freedom in the name of profit.

What? Private life? I don't understand what you're asking me. You want to know what? Wait, are you asking whether I was *fucking* Mother Jones? She was forty years older than me for Christ's sake! She was like my grandmother! Why do you think we called her "Mother"? Where do you get this shit?

No, I will not apologize for my fucking language, are you kidding me? Look, young lady, if I misunderstood your question, I'm sorry for that, but I have no idea what you're getting at here. First you ask me about her private life and when I say I don't understand you say you want to know about her intimate life and our relationship and I don't know what else you could be asking me except were we fucking.

Have you been listening to anything I have said here? We were engaged in a class war for half a century. No, that is not a figure of speech. It was a war, a shooting war. Those Baldwin-Felts in Ludlow were wearing the uniform of the state of Colorado. After those ladies went to see President Wilson he sent the U.S. Army against us. That happened again and again. The U.S. Army broke the Pullman strike in '94. They broke the strikes in the Idaho mines in '92 and '99. Arrested everybody with no regard to a crime or a charge and held them without hearings or anything. But whether it was Pinkertons or National Guard or the

U.S. Army it was the armed agents of the capitalist class and they came against us every time we organized. It was a war, do you see? They were waging war on us long before we even realized it. Mother Jones was a leader because she could show the working people how the capitalists were waging war. Not just profiteering on our sweat and blood. Not just starving our children. Making war. And that is who Mother Jones was, the mother of the working class. Why are you asking me questions about intimate life? I think you're looking for something that wasn't there because you don't want to look at what was.

Look at the Cabin Creek war. Oh, you don't know about that either? Why aren't I surprised anymore? This was in West Virginia, two years before the story I'm telling you about in Colorado, but it was the same story: another blood-sucking coal company, another captive governor sucking off the operators' titty, more Baldwin-Felts and more machine guns.

What? You must never have had any children yet. Is there a polite way to describe that? The Baldwin-Felts were evicting miners from their homes. They were beating union members. They were machine-gunning people's homes. Mother Jones organized a march to the state capitol. She invited the governor to come speak to her on the steps. He didn't come, of course. Like the rest of them, he was afraid of her. Afraid of an eighty-year old woman. She scared all of them. But she spoke to him anyway, in front of everybody, just like he was there. She spoke to him for an hour. She told him that if he wouldn't protect the rights of West Virginia miners they would have to do it themselves. There was a thousand miners there that day to hear her. She told him that the union movement was a command from God Almighty. She said if he didn't believe her he should look for a star in the east, because it was there for anyone to see, just like when Jesus was born. She told him that Jesus had organized a union of enslaved Israelites and that God was going to break the people's chains again.

What did they do? Why they locked her up, of course, that's what they did. That time they kept her hidden for three months until she could smuggle out a note and let the world know where she was.

Yes, I was there. Yes, I remember. I must have been forty. That is exactly the point I have been trying to make to you. It was a war, there were lots of battles, the enemy kept using the same tactics because that's what they knew how to do, to starve us or to shoot us.

Now I *really* don't understand your question. She was Mother Jones. It wasn't a role she was playing, she wasn't an actress. Why can't you hear the things I'm telling you instead of asking about things that don't matter?

You know, I'm about the age now that she was then. I'm sitting here in this rest home playing cards with the boys at the same age that she was still out raising hell and risking death and arrest. But today we have a third of wageworkers in this country union members! Back then it was maybe one in twenty at most. We coal miners built the entire CIO. Us. It was we who built the steel union. We built the auto union and the rubber union, too. We have three-quarters of a million miners in the UMW today. We negotiate with the operators and we work under contract. The work is still dangerous, sure, but today a union miner can make a living. He can feed his family and live in his own home. So maybe I can rest instead of getting shot at like she did at my age. Or maybe I am just not the man she was. Or woman. I don't know.

Yes, you got me upset. Maybe I don't know what it is you want to hear about. It feels like you just don't like the truth, but that's what I'm telling you.

No, I won't calm down. We'll see about another day. If you come back we'll see whether I'm ready to talk to you then. [Recording ends here.]

Walsenburg, Colorado
1914

The preachers of the gospel of the international proletariat could be as sectarian as those of any other religion. Most of Joey Quintana's fellow IWW organizers were strict in their condemnation of all competing churches. They gave speeches ridiculing the Christian faith. They sang satires of hymns, turning the "Sweet By-and-By" into "you will eat by and by," and mocking "Christian soldiers" who would "slay their Christian neighbors." But Joey never did. He believed in an inclusive revolution, with room for all faiths. The hours immediately after his conversion in Doña Rosa's cantina had been spent convincing Serbs, Chinese, Chippewas, Bolivians and his fellow New Mexicans that they had a common goal in winning recognition and a living wage from the Phelps, Dodge copper company. He had never forgotten the need to accept people's differences.

Way back in the days of the Bible, Paul the Apostle argued with the evangelists of his time over the same thing. He said that the good news of Jesus was for everybody. When Joey was a child in Cañada de los Álamos the *hermanos* taught him San Pablo's words: *"Ya no hay distinción de judío ni griego, porque todos vosotros sois una cosa en Jesucristo."* Paul didn't demand that converts to Christianity be circumcised or that they follow the laws of the Old Testament. And Joey Quintana didn't ask the workers he recruited to give up their beliefs or their customs. Far from it. Instead he asked them to join one another's celebrations!

In the most magic moment of his life miners of every nationality walked off the job together and ate rice and beans and peppers while they danced to the ballad of Juan Cortina. And it was not just food and music that Joey wanted to share. Mother Jones warned the coal bosses that if they hanged her, she would stand before the Almighty and tell him to damn the exploiters of the working class. Why would he call this superstition? Bishop Spalding preached that socialism was the Kingdom of God; Joey shouted, "Amen." Collective joy in sharing and resistance *was* Joey's proletarian gospel. He had been carrying it for eight years now, from mine to mine, from farm to mill, all over the Southwest, northern Mexico, and beyond.

Now he was sitting in the Denver office of the United Mine Workers with District Leader John Lawson. He had come to volunteer his help with the big coal strike in southern Colorado. Lawson studied Joey with a frown, not bothering to hide his suspicion. "Ain't you an IWW?" he asked. Yes, even within the union movement there were sectarian conflicts.

"I am," answered Joey candidly. "But it looks to me like you could use a man who speaks Spanish. Especially somebody who knows *la gente*. I heard half those strikers are locals."

Lawson nodded. It was only seventy years since all those mountains were still part of Mexico, so "local" meant Mexican. Joey knew that Lawson really wanted to know whether Joey was here to steal his members, but he was clearly having trouble getting to that question. "Why are you here?" Lawson asked instead.

Joey took a deep breath. "They say you have a Croatian organizer down there. They say the strike leader is Greek. That's great. But neither of them speaks Spanish. Honestly, I just want to help."

Lawson looked at his fellow district officers. He looked back at Joey. Finally he said, "Things have gotten worse than you know down there. That organizer? Mike Livoda? The sheriff beat him almost to death. Mother Jones went to help and now she's disappeared off the face of the earth. We don't know if she's alive or dead. And those aren't National Guardsmen down there either, they're out-of-state gunmen in Colorado uniforms. Are you willing to walk into that?" he asked. And, his real question, "Are you willing to shut up about the One Big Union?"

Joey nodded seriously. "I understand," he said. "And I understand your conditions."

Lawson took a deep breath, frowned again, and said, "Welcome aboard. You have any problem with religion?"

The question came as a surprise. "I do not. Why do you ask?"

Lawson ignored the obvious answer, the well-known and aggressive anti-clericalism of the IWWs. "This weekend is Orthodox Easter," he said. "'Pascha,' they call it. Last week it was Easter for the Mexicans and Italians and the Welshmen, the Catholics and the Protestants. This weekend they'll celebrate again, with their Greek and Slavic brothers and sisters."

Joey couldn't have been happier. Nothing pleased him like people sharing each other's rituals in working-class unity. But all he said was, "What do you want me to do?"

To walk alone into danger. The officers of the United Mine Workers wanted Joey to go to the strikers' camp in Ludlow. They wanted him to hand-carry messages from the District 15 office and from the national office in Indianapolis because telegrams could be intercepted or forged. They wanted him to seek information about Mother Jones, who they hoped was still alive. She had not been charged in any court. They presumed she was being held incommunicado somewhere in southern Colorado. She had to be ninety and – tough as she was – if she was locked in some wet basement, then her health was at risk. They were asking a great deal, but in this country the life of a union man was always at risk *y prefiere morir de pie que vivir de rodillas.*

So a few hours after Joey's interview in Denver, and thanks to a sympathetic brakeman, he was jumping off a southbound C&S freight, just south of downtown Walsenburg. There was a chance that Mother Jones was being held here. Leaving the tracks behind him, Joey found a group of children playing ball on West Fifth in a neighborhood that he thought was predominantly *Hispano*.

"Do you kids know where a fellow can get some lunch?" he asked.

They conferred. "You got any money, mister?" questioned one.

"Sure," he answered. "Do I look like I'm begging?"

They briefly looked him over. Fresh haircut and shave, clean suit and coat. They laughed. "Doña Lola serves meals at her hotel on South Main," said one little boy. Joey noticed that he wore a skullcap and had fringes hanging from beneath his shirt. Maybe these kids weren't all *Hispano*.

For some reason the boy's recommendation caused a flurry of recrimination among the gang. After a minute of intense argument, another boy, who looked like the twin of the one with the fringes, said, "Dave shouldn't have told you that!"

"Shut up, Amir!" shouted the boy with the fringes.

"Why not?" asked Joey.

They all looked at him in silence for a minute. "Tell him, Chuy," said Amir, turning to the first child, the one who asked him if he had money, and who Joey was now starting to think was the only *Hispano* in the crowd.

Chuy looked up the street, then down, as if to see if there were any informants nearby, then said, quietly, "That's where all the soldiers eat. That's General Chase's headquarters. You want to stay away from them."

Joey knew the general's reputation very well. John Chase had been abusing the workers of Colorado for a decade now, in the hard-metal mining districts around Cripple Creek and down here in the coal-mining region. He was best known for holding prisoners locked up indefinitely, without any criminal charges or legal justification at all. He had also pioneered the practice of deporting union men from the state of Colorado by dumping them out of rail cars in neighboring states, in the middle of nowhere. "General" John Chase wasn't just a tool of the bosses; he was a vicious and deranged gangster whose attacks on union workers made even his corporate masters uncomfortable.

"Why is that?" asked Joey nevertheless, curious about what the children would tell him.

The boys now lost their inhibitions and began shouting their answers at once:

"He rode a lady down on his horse!"

"He beat a man unconscious with his pistol!"

"He made a boy dig his own grave!"

"He put an old lady in the basement *under* the jail!"

The *old lady* got Joey's attention, but he didn't want to betray any special interest in her. That might make them clam up. He said, "Sounds like those soldiers are in charge here. Don't you have any local cops?"

Now they all turned and stared silently at Chuy, the *Hispano* boy. "Chuy's dad is the town marshal," said the boy named Dave.

"What do you know about it?" demanded Chuy. "If he goes against the general, the soldiers could kill him, too."

They all looked away and nodded their agreement with this. Then he added, defensively, "Anyway it's my dad who is sneaking her food. He brought Doctor Beshoar in so she wouldn't die when she got sick. He's the one who is keeping them from killing Mother Jones."

That was all the information he needed. Joey promised the boys that he would be sure to avoid any soldiers and thanked them for the tip about Doña Lola's. He crossed the irrigation channel then turned up Fourth Street, crossing Main and not stopping even when he reached the red brick train depot. There were Colorado National Guard watching the station; they might ask questions if he purchased a ticket. They certainly wouldn't let him send a telegram about Mother Jones. Ludlow was still 25 miles away, almost to Trinidad. Joey scouted out a quiet spot near the tracks where he would be out of the sight of the coal operators' armed thugs. He sat down to wait for the next southbound freight. But he had a bad feeling.

Ludlow, Colorado
1914

In many ways this tent city was now the most dangerous place on earth… dangerous to the body, dangerous to the soul. Perhaps that is why Piedad Abeyta needed to be here.

For months the Colorado National Guard, dug in on the high ground outside the camp, had made a habit of firing random bursts with their machine guns at irregular intervals. One child had been murdered. Everybody now had basements under their tent platforms to shelter from the bullets. Under Piedad's tent the strikers dug a deeper cellar so that she could attend to lying-in mothers without fear of the uniformed assassins. The young shopkeepers and junior attorneys who usually made up the Guard had actually all gone back to their homes in Denver and Fort Collins and Boulder. Their replacements were gunmen and cutthroats from other states, men utterly without remorse or shame, hired by the Baldwin-Felts Detective Agency and sworn in by the governor of Colorado. Six months earlier they were all employed by the coal companies of West Virginia, murdering striking miners and their families in the Cabin Creek and Paint Creek districts. Now they were here in Ludlow to do the same.

When they weren't shooting at the women of the tent city they were soliciting sex from them. Piedad had prepared teas of *yerba mosquera* and *mastranzo* for more than one young woman who made the mistake of thinking that some uniformed gangster was wooing her, only to find herself stripped, raped, and abandoned in the dark. They returned to camp, bleeding and humiliated, where Piedad treated them until their monthlies returned. Nor were mature women exempt. Even mothers with children in tow were subjected to the most vulgar and outrageous verbal assaults as soon as they left the compound for any reason. One of the Welsh wives, Mrs. Thomas, was knocked on the head with a rifle butt and then brought in to jail by no fewer than fifty of these *sinvergüenzas*!

The men weren't immune from attack, either. One father who went to Trinidad to shop for his family was captured by the so-called Guardsmen and forced at rifle-point to dig his own grave. The assassins laughed uproariously at his terror and then allowed him to return to the camp: stripped of his groceries, stripped of his clothes, stripped even of his belief that he was a human being. Piedad could no longer count the number of men she had treated for beatings they received outside the camp. If they weren't beaten, they were robbed, apparently just for the fun of it, because – from what she could see – the gunmen had no shortage of food.

With the promise of spring in the air, it was no surprise that so many of the New Mexicans, both single men and families, were leaving. The farms of their mountain villages were calling. Here in Colorado the beet fields would soon need workers. Why stay in this hellhole, striking against Rockefeller and his coal mines, when you could find other work? Even some of the Italians and Slavs were moving on now that winter was over.

And yet. And yet. Something more than $5 a week in strike benefits was keeping Pia and her husband Epifanio here in the camp of the mineworkers' union. Her work as a *partera*, of course, was a piece of it. Two of the young wives were due around *Semana Santa* and they had asked her to deliver their babies. That would definitely keep her past Easter. But that was not really the whole story either.

Her husband Fani had seen it from the moment the strike began and all these people with no common language moved into the camp together under the guns of the *gabacho* soldiers. In the snow and in the wind, even before the tents arrived by train, the miners found a way to communicate and to share: *frijoles* and *chiles*, hardships and joys, festivals and funerals. This was why he asked her to join him on this desolate plain. She met and cared for the wives and children of coal miners from places she had barely heard of. There were families from Italy and families from Wales. There were families from Zacatecas. Then there were the people called "Slavs" and who knew where they were from? Montenegro? Serbia? Bulgaria? Everywhere there were Greeks, although for all she could see, Greeks were a nation of men. There was not a Greek woman in camp and the men lived together in groups of five or six. Some cooked for themselves and others paid to eat with families from other nations.

All the men in this camp were armed (or they all had been until the Guardsmen seized many of their weapons) but the Greeks were mostly ex-soldiers. Piedad never quite got the story of their war, but apparently they had been on the same side as all these Slavs, thank God. In any case, they were extremely well-organized in defense of the camp. The leader of the Greeks was a man called Louis Tikas and he was really the leader of all the nationalities. You could pick him out at a distance by his smile and his red bandana. Everybody loved him. He never ate until he knew everybody was fed. He never slept until he was certain that everybody in camp was okay.

It was that spirit, embodied in Louis Tikas, that kept Piedad and her husband Epifanio here in this camp, that kept them on strike, that kept them in the union. It was as if all these strangers from all these places were more than kin. It was a collective magic that kept them all warm and dry through the harsh Colorado winter. It was like the Kingdom of God on earth.

And here suddenly was Louis Tikas, with his Croatian buddy, Mike Livoda, asking Piedad's assistance with their religion, a religion she did not understand at all. The Greeks and the Slavs hadn't celebrated Christmas until *Día de Reyes*, and apparently their Easter was a week after everyone else's, too, even the Welshmen. She did know that they each had churches of their own – one for the Greeks, one for the Slavs – in Pueblo, an hour away by train, but people were afraid to leave camp now and they wanted to celebrate here. What in the world, though, did that have to do with her?

"We really could use your help with an *epitaphios*," said Tikas. Was she supposed to know what that was?

"*Sí, señoras*, we need a *plashchanitsa* for our observances," agreed Livoda enthusiastically, as if translating the Greek into his language (and throwing in his little two words of Spanish) would help her to understand. They both obviously knew what they were talking about, though neither seemed to have a word for it in either English or Spanish.

"*¿Qué dicen ellos?*" demanded her friend Choni, with whom she had been sharing the task of hanging laundry.

"*No sé, todavía,*" Piedad responded. Her head was beginning to spin again. How many languages was she expected to master?

"It's a cloth," explained Louis Tikas. "We use it for Friday and Saturday of Holy Week. It has a picture of our Lord lying dead, with his mother and Mary the Magdalene mourning him, and with John and with Joseph of Arimathea. We will carry it through the camp at the head of our procession."

Asención was demanding her attention again. "*Ellos necesitan una bandera,*" translated Piedad, "*como llevan los Penitentes en sus procesiones... Con las imágenes del santo entierro y María y Magdalena y José de Arimatea.*" But she hadn't yet figured out what this had to do with her.

"*¡En el viernes santo la hermandad también lleva el santo entierro!*" said Choni excitedly.

That was true, thought Pia. She had been to Choni's church at Santa Cruz de la Cañada for a wedding and seen the man-sized carving of an entombed Jesus in its niche in the wall. She had heard that the brothers carried it in their Good Friday procession. Maybe this religion of the Greeks and the Slavs wasn't as different as she thought.

And with that insight came an epiphany. She realized in a momentary blast of clarity what Louis and Mike were asking of her. They had seen the little drawings she made for the children in the camp. Who hadn't? Sometimes it seemed that every one of the two hundred or so tents had one of her pictures in it. They wanted her, Piedad Abeyta, to *create* this banner of Christ being entombed! Was this a job for a woman? At home, a husband and wife were given the task every year of caring for the church. The wife would repair or remake the clothing for the *bultos*, the carved images of saints. And, of course, the wife would clean the altar cloths. But to make this sacred image from scratch?

She wondered. And then, suddenly, as if one monumental revelation in a day was insufficient, the idea for the banner appeared complete in Piedad's mind, fully-formed, and requiring her only to make a physical copy! There, in the center, she saw Benigno Trujillo, dragged from the collapsed Stag Canyon #2 shaft in Dawson. There, on the side, knelt his mother Teófila clutching Benny's broken and lifeless body. There was Benny's wife Seferina, standing over him, shrieking, both arms lifted to Heaven. And there behind him were his friends, Sixto and Amarante, who had pulled him out, mute and defeated. That moment had been identical in appearance to the removal of the Lord from the Cross. She had been there. "Yes," said Pia to the men. "Yes, I will be honored to help you with your banner."

"Thank you," said Louis Tikas. "You'll see. This will mean so much to the people. Please let us know what you need and we will get it for you: cloth, needles, thread, colors. It will be beautiful."

"It will," assured Piedad.

After explaining what she had agreed to, after finishing with the laundry, Pia sat down with paper and pencil to outline the picture she had seen in her mind. All she had to do was close her eyes and there it was, waiting to be made.

Pia began working the following day. One of the Slavic women gave her two yards of blue silk that she had been saving to make a gown. Using her pencil sketch, Piedad cut out patches from old clothes in the shapes of the faces, of the garments, and even of halos for the figures in her... she tried to remember the Greek name... *epitaphios*. Paints allowed her to add features and expressions, but a lot of the emotion in the scene was evoked by the body postures, and they were just as she remembered them. When she was busy with other work, such as visiting the sick and injured, or calling on the pregnant women in the camp, her neighbors stepped up by tying strands of yarn to the edges of the banner to create a fringe. Asención was especially active in this task, but Cedi Costa and some of the other Italian women helped, too. The banner for the Greeks and Slavs was like everything else in the camp, a labor of love for everybody.

Piedad discovered that there were words that belonged on this banner, just like the banners of the confraternities back home. This is how she discovered that the Greeks and the Slavs didn't just have their own languages… they had their own alphabets! So she carefully copied what the men gave her onto the cloth in pencil. Then she embroidered the symbols in gold thread. On the top was:

Племенити Џозеф, узимајући доле Тхи највише чисту тело од дрвета, нисам умотајте у чисту постељину са слатким зачинима, а он је положио у нови гроб.

On the bottom was:

Ιωσήφ, λαμβάνοντας κάτω σου πιο καθαρό σώματος από το Δέντρο, το έκανε τυλίξτε το σε καθαρά σεντόνια με γλυκά μπαχαρικά, και αυτός που σε ένα νέο τάφο.

She had no idea what any of this meant, of course. All she could say about it was that she hoped she had copied all the letters correctly!

Pia had not yet finished the banner when *Domingo de Ramos* arrived for the Catholics in camp. Father Hugh came from the Church of the Holy Trinity in Trinidad to offer mass to the Mexicans, the New Mexicans, and the Italians. The Welshmen, Greeks, and Slavs did not take communion with them, but everybody who wanted them received palms.

As Holy Week went on, though, Piedad grew sadder and sadder. By Good Friday she was disconsolate. Part of this was certainly the observances. Father Hugh was in camp again, leading them through the Stations of the Cross and this was anything but a happy time, thinking about the Passion and the way Jesus was tortured. But she also missed her children, her parents, her aunts, her uncles, her cousins. She missed her neighbors. Everybody would be back in the village now. All the mountain trees would be in bloom: the red flowers of *acezintle*, the yellow of the *robles*, the furry little cat's tails of the *sauces* near the creek. She remembered the excited voices working together to clear the *acequías* so that they could begin irrigating the fields and she remembered the smell of the earth as they opened the gates and let the water in. She could taste the *chiles* and she

146

could smell the tortillas roasting. Why, oh, why were they in this place by the tracks, surrounded by killers? That afternoon, just before the procession for the Stations, she ran into Lieutenant Karl Linderfelt, one of the worst of these assassins. And what did he say to her? "Don't worry about the cross, bitch! I'm your Jesus Christ. I'll show you real soon."

She could not get these disgusting words out of her ears. They affected her all through the observance, through the night and into the next day. She kept hearing his insinuating tone, too. She wanted to go home.

Easter Sunday in the camp reminded her of why they were here. She didn't know where people found the ingredients for the food they prepared. It was as if their faith had produced a magical banquet from the cans that the union delivered. Mrs. Thomas made sausages and bread coated with melted cheese. Piedad had never tasted cheese like this before and the combination, simple as it sounded, was like a religious experience itself. Cedi Costa baked cookies and candies from ground almonds and sugar that drove the children wild. Pia's friend Choni made enough *tamales* with lamb and *nopales* and her secret seasoning for every person in the camp. It was a day of joy, as Easter should be. They all celebrated together and it helped Pia realize, once again, that this was a family of a kind that she had never experienced before. When Monday morning came she rededicated herself to finishing the banner and to making it as beautiful as she could.

And then they got to do it all again for Greek Easter! On Friday afternoon the entire camp gathered as the Greeks and the Slavs processed from the big communal tent, up and down the "streets" and back. At the head of the whole procession was the banner that Piedad had created with so much work, and so much devotion, and so much love. It was carried by Mike Livoda and by Louis Tikas. She guessed that the chants were in Greek and in Slavic. She understood nothing but she could see who was taking turns singing. Choni stood with her, holding her hand, and Fani smiled at her proudly. The banner was perfect.

That night there was another procession. The men chanted, "*Agios athanatos, eleison imas.*" Where had she heard those words before? Once again, Mike Livoda and Louis Tikas carried her banner, and after walking around the entire camp they held the banner shoulder-high at the entrance to the big tent, so that everyone entering had to bow underneath the image of the two Marys, the Beloved Disciple, and San José de Arimatea preparing Jesus for the tomb. And even though Piedad had made this *epitaphios* with her own hands, from start to finish; even though she had cut the cloth, and applied the paint, and sewn the stitches; even though she had been hearing the story it depicted her whole life...

still she wept as if she was seeing it for the first time. She wept for the broken coal miner Benny Trujillo and she wept for the broken Son of God. She wept for the families and friends in Dawson and she wept for all humanity. She realized with a start that what she had created was not a banner at all, but a shroud: a shroud for the burial of God himself.

Sunday was – again – a day of feasting. The Greek men had acquired a sheep from a *rancho* up in the canyons. They began roasting it after their midnight service was over and by noon the smell alone was making everybody happy. Before that was even ready they served a soup made of *casquería,* eggs, and lemons. She would never have thought of lemons in a soup, and it was like a new idea of what food could be. The Slavs made rice with onions, carrots, spinach, tomatoes and parsley. Some of the women made shiny, round, braided breads with a hard-boiled egg dyed red and baked right into it!

That afternoon there were baseball games and dyed eggs called *pisanica* for the children. And there was singing. Oh, was there singing! Elías Baca played his guitar and sang a brand-new *corrido* about Rockefeller and the Colorado National Guard and about all of them together in this camp. There were mandolin players and violinists of every nationality. Every time somebody would start a song, in whatever language, the players who knew the song would join in immediately. But after a verse or so, the others would pick it up, too! And the people? If the song was in their language, they sang right along. And if it wasn't? Maybe they didn't understand the words, but they could sing along anyway, couldn't they? And that is what they did. They all sang together long after the sun went down.

Piedad knew now that these people could *never* be defeated. Maybe they spoke different languages. Maybe they worshipped differently. But if they could all sing together in one voice, then no coal company and no hired killers could ever beat them. And there was no place else that she would rather be than here with her husband Fani and his union brothers.

Boley, Oklahoma
1914

"Daddy, I am a grown woman! You cannot hold me prisoner in this house forever!"

He caught himself before responding to all the hyperbole in Nessa's complaint. Grown woman? Prisoner? Forever? She was seventeen years old and she left the house every single day. In fact she hadn't missed school for any reason in over three years. Ezekiel Payne knew, though, that anything he said to her right now was just going to make her madder. So he kept his silence and waited for Nessa to explain herself beyond, "I'm going out tomorrow night." That was the pronouncement with which she opened this one-sided argument.

"Daddy, why won't you let me go out?" He hadn't said no to her. All he had asked was, "With who?" But contradicting her would only fuel this display of outrage. So he waited some more.

"When I was little you let me go everywhere. I used to bring water to the railroad workers all by myself. Now you watch every move I make." This was all true. Had he been delirious to allow her around those men? No, it was the territory that changed, not him. All those track workers either knew him personally or by reputation. He trusted them around Nessa and trusted them to watch out for her around strangers. Well, being honest, what he actually trusted was that they knew him well enough to fear what he would do to them if they let anything happen to Nessa.

But now? Strange, wild white boys were everywhere and he no longer went anywhere unarmed. After the big Ida Glenn gusher south of Tulsa, the Creek Nation had been overrun with roughnecks and roustabouts that nobody knew. As far as Ezekiel could see they were young men with neither kin nor conscience. Everywhere the oil derricks went they were followed closely by bootleggers, brothels, and betting houses. In Boley proper the sheriff and his constables kept all that nastiness out of town and kept order among the folks that passed through. Anywhere else? Even in the towns that had their own police he didn't trust them to look out for a pretty, young Negro woman.

"Daddy, are you even listening to me?" demanded Nessa.

"Yes, I am, honey. Please tell me who you are going with and where you want to go."

149

It was as if he had not just asked the exact same question, only moments ago. Nessa immediately stopped pouting and put on a great big smile, as if she had already won the argument. And, in truth, that smile melted Ezekiel, like it always did. But he still wanted an answer. So he looked at her and waited.

"There is a dance at Weleetka Colored School. I want to go with my friends."

Weleetka meant riding through Okemah, a sundown town, and that was risky. But Ezekiel knew that the real reason Weleetka put a lump in his throat had nothing to do with the hazards of travel for a colored girl. No, the real reason was that Nessa's mom and her whole family lived near there, out on Alabama Creek. Ezekiel felt a weight on his chest just thinking about those people.

His feelings – though not their origin – must have shown on his face because Nessa got argumentative again. "Daddy, Weleetka is only five stops away on the train. And you know Principal Gladney at the school."

Yes, he did. And he had decided long ago that his problem with the Yarholar family should never become Nessa's. So he smiled and said, "I know, baby. Which friends?"

Once again, Nessa's pout vanished and her eyes lit up. "Roxana Barnett, Clarissa Johnson and Abby Walker." Why had he even asked? This was Nessa's tight little circle from the age of ten when they first moved to Boley. They were all *estelvste* girls, African Creeks. Even though Ezekiel, like most of the men in Boley, was a "state Negro," Nessa's mom, Sunshine Yarholar was *estecate*. Like her friends, Nessa was fluent in Mvskoke as well as English, and grew up eating *safke* and *sakkonepke* stew. From their first day at the Boley school, Nessa and her circle banded together to defend themselves from the queen bees of the leading Boley families with their condescending attitude toward "natives."

"Boys?" asked Ezekiel.

"Daddy, we can travel to Weleetka by ourselves," insisted Nessa.

"No," said Ezekiel sadly, "you cannot." After a second he added, smiling, "And I don't think you're planning to, either."

Now Nessa looked up at the ceiling. He had her. She hesitated a moment, then said, "You know some of the boys." Ezekiel was afraid that the key word here was "boys." How could he trust these trifling little boys with the man's work of protecting his Nessa from the lunacy out there? She wasn't finished speaking, though. "I want to introduce you to somebody new," she added. "His name is Rector Beauchamp and he is studying to be a teacher at Seminole-Creek College."

"Who are his people?" asked Ezekiel.

This question was everything to Ezekiel but its significance escaped Nessa completely. "I never know what you mean by that," she said. "It sounds like something the seditty people would ask," she added, turning up her lip in contempt.

Too true, thought Ezekiel. The Kings and the Lees and the Partridges and the other first families of Boley undoubtedly asked that same question about him. And, given their thinking about "natives," they clearly thought their sons were too good for his Nessa, never mind she was the prettiest and smartest girl in town, at least in his opinion. "Fair enough," he admitted. "Where is he from?"

"Rector grew up in Haven," Nessa said.

Ezekiel had never been to Haven. It was a colored town, like Boley, but something stuck in his mind about it. He couldn't remember whether it was a good something or a bad something. "I will have to meet this boy," Ezekiel said.

At that Nessa's smile spread all the way across her face. "Yes, you will!" she answered.

"What?" asked Ezekiel suspiciously.

Nessa laughed. "Yes, you will have to meet him, because he will be knocking on the door in…" she looked at her grandpa's mahogany clock on the mantle, "… less than five minutes!"

Now Ezekiel started laughing, too. This girl really did have him figured out.

"But," she added with a little frown, "you can't do that thing you do to scare every boy I introduce to you!"

"What thing?" asked Ezekiel with feigned innocence. "If these boys are scared, maybe they're feeling guilty about something."

The knock on the door came right then. Ezekiel answered it to find a tall, sturdy-looking, dark-skinned boy, wearing a brown wool suit, white shirt, and a black

151

tie. The only trace of vanity he could see was a crisp, new, wide-brimmed stockman's hat, probably a J.B. Stetson from the look of it. That hat came right off as soon as he saw Ezekiel. The boy held his hat in his left hand, looked Ezekiel directly in the eye, extended his right, and said, "Mr. Payne? How do you do? My name is Rector Beauchamp, and I am a friend of your daughter, Nessa."

Ezekiel took the boy's hand in his, noting that it was not as soft as those of these town boys in Boley. Maybe he was acquainted with honest work. He said, "I am pleased to make your acquaintance. Why don't you come in and visit with us."

The boy held his grip for a moment, then said, "Thank you," and stepped up and through the door. He had an inch or two on Ezekiel and maybe twenty pounds. Ezekiel found this reassuring, but withheld his judgment.

"Please sit down in the parlor. Nessa, bring your guest a glass of water and a slice of pie."

"Sir, I don't need to eat," said the boy.

"What you need and what we offer are two separate things," smiled Ezekiel. "Have a seat."

While Nessa went to the kitchen to get refreshments, Ezekiel studied the boy from his boots to his haircut and back. The boy only smiled at this scrutiny. "Son, why are you here?" Ezekiel demanded.

"Sir, I came to ask your permission to accompany your daughter to a social at Weleetka Colored School. We will be traveling as a group, but I would be escorting Nessa."

"Are you her beau?" demanded Ezekiel.

For the first time since he arrived the boy looked uncomfortable. "Why n-no, sir, I mean, begging your pardon, it's not that I'm not interested, but…"

Ezekiel remained silent while the boy struggled for the right words.

"Sir," he finally got out, "I am hoping for the opportunity to better make your daughter's acquaintance."

"And Nessa's acquaintance requires a dangerous railroad trip?"

The boy seemed utterly at a loss to understand this simple question. "Dangerous railroad trip?" he repeated.

Ezekiel didn't think this was going well. "Son, Okemah is a sundown town. Castle is full of oil roughnecks. I do not expose my child to those dangers lightly."

Now the boy nodded seriously, understanding. "Sir, I make that trip often to go to Clearview. I do understand the dangers and I think I understand your fears although I am not a father. When I say that I wish to *escort* Nessa, I know the meaning of that word." And here he patted his right hand to his hip, where a revolver would have hung had this not been a social call.

Ezekiel wasn't certain if he was reassured by this gesture. But the boy wasn't finished speaking.

"I know that I am new to you. But I swear that I do not take the responsibility of accompanying your daughter lightly. I swear that she will be safe with me."

Ezekiel thought about this for a minute. Then he asked, "Boy, are you one of these Negroes that think Indian girls are fast?"

The boy frowned, "*Estecatet omis. Semvnolet omis.*" So he was native himself. And then, as if the more he thought about Ezekiel's question the more he disliked it, he added, "*Vpohkvci eyaceko vne.*"

This time Ezekiel nodded seriously. "Then you will understand why I asked you. In this town I deal with prejudice against my daughter all the time."

The boy was not assuaged by this explanation. "Sir, I understand that you don't like people making certain assumptions about Nessa. I am concerned about the assumptions you are making about me."

And with that, Ezekiel relaxed; he liked this boy. Nessa walked back in then with two plates of pie and saw the angry look on the boy's face and her father's smile. "Daddy," she asked, "what are you doing to Rector?"

"Getting to know him," answered Ezekiel. "You have my permission to travel to a social with him."

She lit up. "Oh, Daddy, thank you. I knew you would like Rector."

He just cleared his throat. The boy looked puzzled for a moment, but when Nessa sat down next to him and gave him a plate of pie he relented. And when he tasted the filling, a mix of *kvco* and *svtv semvnole*, he exclaimed, "This pie is delicious! I have never had one as good!"

Nessa beamed.

Namiquipa, Chihuahua
1916

85°, but really it could have been worse. When the regiment was in Leyte your sweat never evaporated. The men would strip, wring out their uniforms, and put them back on, still wet. Here, in the desert in Chihuahua, at least they stayed dry. The sun was a killer, though, and Corporal Osceola McKaine had instructed his squad to hang tarps and to stay under them when possible. They brought pines down from the mountains and created pitched canvas roofs ten feet off the ground, which was a distinct improvement over the constant exposure to the beating sun. Lieutenant Herman seemed uncomfortable with the reduced visibility this afforded, but he was more uncomfortable without shade so he allowed it. Soon, every platoon in the regiment was doing the same.

Yes, they were vulnerable here. They were sitting in an exposed plain, just east of the Río Santa María. The officers referred to the position as a "fenced stockade," but the "fence" was really just a pile of brush ringing the camp. The hills were miles away, but it felt to all the soldiers like an enemy could just sit up there and study them. That's why the 24th maintained their own watchers: half-squads rotating on lookout five miles away to the northeast, northwest, southeast and southwest. Each of those elevated positions had spotters with binoculars and signalmen with heliographs. That way there were no telephone lines that could be cut or that could reveal their position to the Villistas.

It was hard to stay alert in their little stockade near the village of Namiquipa. During the first month of this "punitive expedition," especially while the 24th was walking south from the New Mexico border, they had endured intermittent attacks by Pancho Villa's irregulars... no, the accepted word was "bandits." It was important to the officers that the enlisted men always called their adversaries "bandits." The combat phase was over for Company B. Their "stockade" was now a glorified fuel depot. Every day motor trucks arrived to deliver gasoline. All day long other trucks arrived to refuel as they carried food (and more fuel!) to more stockades at more depots farther south. And of course trucks arrived carrying food for him and his men. It was Cpl. Osceola McKaine's job to ensure that they all maintained a high level of military alertness while acting as pump jockeys and warehousemen.

That is why he closed his eyes and sighed before shuffling the cards one more time and dealing. His partner was, as usual, Pfc. Charles Baltimore. Privates Luther Rucker and Gabriel Joyner were back at the table with them after two days exile at Cerro Pelón for poor play. In their case it had been a renege by Joyner. The rule at this table was rise and fly. Weak players weren't just kicked out from under the tarp; they were kicked out of town. Privates Reuben Bolden and Jesse Sullivan had once been judged by the senior noncoms to have played so badly that they were not sent any food at their lookout post for two days!

"Mind if I sit in?" Osceola McKaine opened his eyes to see a rather portly colored civilian with gold-framed glasses and a neatly trimmed goatee, maybe fifty, maybe sixty years old.

"And you are?" asked McKaine.

"H.O. Flipper," the man said.

Flipper. McKaine knew there was a reason he should recognize that name. He saw it in the stranger's eyes, too. The man expected to be recognized. But the corporal just said, "It's a pleasure to make your acquaintance, Mr. Flipper. What brings you here to Namiquipa?"

Before the stranger could answer there was the distinctive roar of a Jeffery Quad and soon a whole train of the four-wheel drive motor trucks pulled into the yard. Drivers and guards all wanted fresh drinking water and McKaine's crew took care of them and fueled their vehicles while he and the convoy's sergeant exchanged paperwork and mild insults. It took about forty-five minutes before the trucks left, the noise died down, and the road dust began to settle.

Throughout the fueling operation the strange civilian watched with keen interest as the troopers of the 24th Infantry cranked the gasoline pumps, poured water into the trucks' radiators, and topped up the air pressure in the truck tires with hand pumps. The first words from Flipper's mouth when the truck train left were, "Wouldn't it be easier for you if you suspended those gasoline tanks and let gravity do the work for you?"

That set McKaine back a second. It would, indeed. Why had nobody else thought of that? But he wasn't about to be distracted from identifying this man. "Mr. Flipper, I asked you what brings you here."

"I'm an engineer," the visitor said. "I work for the Sierra Mining Company. We're looking at a property on the hill above El Terrero."

This wasn't a huge surprise. There were American mining concerns all over northern Mexico. The US Army might be barred from the railroads, but the employees and products of the mines seemed to be riding freely back and forth between the border and the capital city.

"Copper?" asked McKaine.

"Oh, no," answered Mr. Flipper. "The big copper deposits are in Sonora, west of here. In Chihuahua we look for silver."

Until that last word was uttered this conversation had been exclusively between Mr. Flipper and Cpl. McKaine. Now, eyes opened wide all around the card table.

"Silver?" repeated Pvt. Joyner. "We could find silver on that hill?" He had just spent two days at the lookout on that very site. He was obviously regretting the time spent checking the horizon instead of the ground.

"No," answered Mr. Flipper. "Any silver would require milling and potassium cyanide processing to extract it from the rock. Silver prices rose from 50¢ to $1 an ounce over the last five months, so all that would be worth it to a company like Sierra Mining."

If the word "silver" awakened the soldiers, then the mention of "potassium cyanide" put them back to sleep. But for Cpl. Osceola McKaine it somehow triggered the memory he had been seeking. "Henry Ossian Flipper," he said, then he laughed. He leaped to attention and – to the bewilderment of the troopers – snapped off a parade-ground salute. "Lieutenant Flipper!" he said.

"I'm a civilian," protested Flipper mildly.

McKaine turned to the other soldiers and dramatically announced, "You are in the presence of a living legend. Henry Ossian Flipper is the first colored graduate of West Point. He was an officer with the Tenth when Major Young was still wearing short pants. Now the newspapers claim that he is the brains behind Pancho Villa, or maybe that he is Pancho Villa himself!" And he laughed again.

The other infantrymen seemed puzzled by this news. Were they supposed to be impressed by this civilian?

"Are we supposed to arrest him?" asked Luther Rucker.

"I have been asking that for six years now," said Flipper angrily. "I have been in El Paso the entire time. The press had every opportunity to interview me, or at least to notice that I wasn't riding up and down Mexico at the head of an army, yet they could not stop repeating this monstrous libel!"

His fury surprised everybody. Pvt. Rucker just commented, "Who ever knows why buckra say what buckra say?"

This observation seemed to agitate Flipper even more, but before he could reply another group of vehicles roared in, this time from the south. They were Dodge touring cars with the tops down, three of them. Out jumped ten white soldiers wearing the insignia of the 6th Cavalry, one civilian, and one young white officer wearing the gold bar of a second lieutenant. Instead of a holstered Colt M1911 semiautomatic pistol he wore – on each hip! – a big .45 caliber revolver with ivory grips. Despite the fact that he had been riding in a car and not on a horse he had a saber hanging from his utility belt and hand-worked silver spurs with immense star rowels on his knee-high boots. But as astonishing as the young lieutenant's costume was, it was not what silenced the men in the depot, nor was it what they were staring at. In fact they didn't notice any of it until later.

For as the cars pulled into the depot there was only one thing any of the men could see. For the rest of their lives, try as they might, none of them would ever be able to stop seeing it. Tied to the front right fender of each of the three automobiles was a dead human being.

Osceola McKaine had seen the dead. He had even seen other soldiers looting the dead, stealing little mementos and souvenirs. He found it repellent, but he had seen it. But a corpse as a trophy? Covered in dust stirred up by driving on a dirt road? As the hot engines ticked and steam rose from the radiators the flies began to discover the dead men strapped to the cars' hoods.

McKaine realized suddenly that somebody was speaking – shouting, actually. He looked toward the voice and saw, for the first time, the twin revolvers, the saber, the spurs, the arrogant young white face.

"Fuel my vehicles, boys!" yelled the costumed lieutenant happily.

Cpl. McKaine stepped forward with his clipboard and saluted. "Sir, we will be happy to. I will just need your name and unit to authorize the transfer of supplies."

"I," said the man, "am Lt. George S. Patton, Jr." He said this as if the name was supposed to mean something. "I am personal aide de camp to Brigadier General John Pershing. I am currently attached to the Sixth Cavalry, pursuing General Julio Cárdenas. Successfully, as you can see!" he added, smiling broadly and gesturing grandly at the dusty corpse tied to the front of his car.

Cpl. McKaine saluted, then turned to his men saying, quietly, "Fuel them up, fellows." He started preparing his paperwork. But this Lt. Patton wasn't finished: "Look at these!" he pointed to the cartoonish silver spurs. "I don't think *he'll* be needing them anymore!" And he gestured again at the dead man on his car. Apparently he had robbed the dead man, too, after killing him.

The infantrymen fueled the cars and refilled the white cavalrymen's water jugs. McKaine noticed that his guest, the former Lt. Flipper, was nowhere in sight. Patton's civilian scout wondered loudly to nobody in particular where the whores were. Patton was still demanding their attention for his trophy... in particular, to a bloody wound on his head. "That's where Emil finished him off," he said, apparently referring to the scout. "I knocked him down with my Peacemaker, but Emil delivered the *coup de grace.*"

It must have been the young lieutenant's first time in action. McKaine simply stopped listening and finished his business. Finally the cavalrymen got back into their automobiles and drove away.

The dust of the speeding vehicles hung in the air for a long time. The men did not return to their card game while its sour taste remained on their tongues. Cpl. McKaine picked up the cards, repacked them in their box and sat in silence. After a few minutes, Pvt. Gabriel Joyner said, "When I was a boy, back home in Oklahoma, they hung a mother and son from a highway bridge outside of town. Wouldn't let us take the bodies down, either. They sold picture postcards of them for souvenirs."

Another soldier, Elisha Underwood, who had been watching silently until now, nodded. "When my Daddy was a boy the Jefferson County sheriff arrested him for vagrancy on his way to the store to buy groceries for my grandma. They put him to work in the mines for the Pratt Coal Company for six months. The guards thought Daddy's friend George had a big mouth, cause he kept saying Daddy hadn't done anything wrong. They hanged George from a tree. Sold photographs of that, too."

The men were wordless, eyes unfocused, each looking into some private memory. Then McKaine's partner, Pfc. Charles Baltimore, added a story. "I saw a picture in the paper of a colored man they burned alive in Waco, Texas. Hung his body downtown. It looked to be thousands of white folks in that picture, cheering like it was a show."

Pvt. Rucker shook his head and asked, "Whoever knows why buckra do what buckra do?"

Silence returned. They did not see Lt. Flipper again. They wondered a little about what had made him leave.

It was a good long time before they went back to their cards.

Namiquipa, Chihuahua
1916

La traición aplace, mas no el que la hace, thought Pedro Rascón y Tena.

Pues, it had to be worth something, or why do it? Sure, Pedro could have gone to the Yankee lieutenant with other names, but there was no profit in most of them. Candelario Cervantes, for example, really was a general in Pancho Villa's army, but he didn't own anything Pedro wanted. Cervantes was a sharecropper on the gringo newspaperman Hearst's ranch. Maybe he was worth a lot to the gringos, but what was he worth to Pedro? Why bother exposing somebody with no land? Pedro couldn't take anything from him: nothing of value to confiscate, nothing of value to gain. The same could be said of a dozen other members of the Army of the North, most of whom were right here in town, right now, guns hidden somewhere. The only pay-off for those denunciations would be the lasting enmity of their children. Why bother?

Tomás Camarena, however, was a different story. Camarena owned a little ranch outside town, down the Río Santa María in Cruces. Camarena had the ear of the Carrancista governor, Francisco Treviño. Most importantly, Camarena had done exactly this to Pedro himself when the Orozquista troops were occupying the town. Honestly, the only downside of denouncing Camarena as a hidden Villista to the gringos was that it was a complete lie. But Pedro was quite certain that these North Americans would never figure that out. Just as they would never figure out that Pedro himself had been a member of Pancho Villa's army. Frankly, he couldn't see how the United States could be such a rich country. These *norteamericanos* couldn't figure out anything. Most of their officers didn't even have a few words of Spanish!

That's why Pedro was filled with confidence as he strode toward the fueling depot that the gringos built on the edge of Namiquipa to serve their new road. There were no truck trains at the moment, but – as usual – a group of *moreno* soldiers sat in the shade of a tarp playing cards. They really did love their cards, he thought.

As he entered the compound one of the soldiers, a white man with fair hair and sergeant's stripes on his sleeve, threw down the seven of *bastos* and said something to the others with an unpleasant laugh. His partner smirked at the unhappy faces of their opponents, then looked at Pedro. "*¿Qué quieres, Pedro?*" he demanded in a surly tone.

How did this Yankee soldier know his name? But Pedro was not to be deflected from his purpose. He doffed his hat and bowed elegantly; maybe these gringos understood good manners even if they didn't practice them. "*Me llamo señor Pedro Rascón y Tena. Yo estoy encantado encontrarles. Yo quiero denunciar un bandido.*" He put special emphasis on this last word. He was pretty certain it was one that they all knew.

The soldiers at the card table all looked to one of their companions who had been lounging in a chair nearby: the only one of them who spoke Spanish? The sheer amount of back-and-forth told Pedro that there was more to it than just translating his words. Just what, however, he could not say.

The nasty sergeant who had played the winning card was speaking loudest and longest. He must be the senior non-commissioned officer here. And, Pedro now realized, since only their officers were white, these *yanquis* must consider him to be a Negro, regardless of the fact that he looked like a *güero*. The only words Pedro could make out were "Pancho Villa" and "*pistola.*" He worried a little. Perhaps this wasn't going the way he imagined, but there was no sense backing out now. He was in it already and as his Papa always said, *el que no chilla no mama.*

"How do we know it's not you who is the bandit?" asked the Spanish-speaking Yankee now.

Pedro could not have looked more outraged by this accusation if it had been false. Until just a few weeks earlier he had been a corporal in Pancho Villa's Army of the North, what the gringos insisted on calling "bandits". He had thought that word himself just a moment ago, but it felt different when these Yankees said it. Still, what he said was, "I am prepared to show you exactly where his weapons are hidden."

The light-skinned sergeant was looking at Pedro searchingly as he said this. Could he have been mistaken? Did all these Black soldiers speak Spanish? But they turned to the man who had been questioning him now for another translation.

There was another long exchange among the soldiers. Finally, the light-skinned sergeant began shouting orders. Immediately the soldier who had been speaking to him in Spanish stood up, along with a tall, dark-skinned man who had been sitting next to him. Pedro noticed the stripes on his arm and thought he looked very young to already be a sergeant. The soldiers at the table had already lost interest. The light-skinned sergeant was smiling unpleasantly and shuffling the cards. As he began dealing, Pedro wondered again briefly what game it was that they were playing. But he turned his attention to the soldiers who were now walking toward him.

The soldiers had still not given their names. Did all these gringos really have such bad manners? Perhaps he could shame them into polite human interaction. "My name is Pedro Rascón y Tena," he tried again.

"*Encantado*," answered the Spanish-speaking soldier. "I am Corporal Charles Baltimore. And this," he pointed to his friend, "is Sergeant Osceola McKaine. United States 24th Infantry."

The man called "McKaine" didn't even glance at him. He looked around the enclosure, then spoke in a strong baritone. Pedro concluded that he was calling names because four more soldiers quickly joined them. But the arrival of the last man made the hair on the back of his neck stand up. His uniform looked like the others, but his features…

Now Pedro truly was insulted… and a little frightened. Was this man an Apache? He turned to the soldier named Baltimore and made his formal objection: "I am a gentleman and a man of reason. Do you now expect me to be accompanied by a barbarous savage? My father and his fathers before him carved this oasis out of the desert by fighting these murderous cutthroats!"

The tall sergeant now stared directly at Pedro and raised his voice, "This is Sergeant Luke Riley, United States Army, do you have a problem with that?" Pedro understood none of this, because it was in English, but the wide eyes and the angry tone were unmistakable. This "Sergeant McKaine" was shouting, but – even more rudely – he was standing too close and looking directly into Pedro's eyes. Did the man understand Spanish? Had he understood Pedro's objection? Or was he just responding to Pedro's tone with his own?

The Apache advanced with a big grin. He wore a red bandana instead of a necktie but was otherwise in the same uniform as the *moreno* soldiers. Pedro had difficulty swallowing as he noticed the enormous .45-caliber semiautomatic pistol this *bárbaro* wore on his belt and the happy gleam in his eye. Switching his lever-action carbine to his left hand, the Indian extended his right hand to Pedro, while saying something in English. Did these *morenos* actually expect him to shake hands with *gente sin razón*?

Yes, they did. His translator, Cpl. Baltimore, now completed the Indian's introduction. "He says that he is happy to make your acquaintance."

Pedro hesitated, then took the Apache's hand for a bare moment. He wished he were carrying his weapon now instead of leading them to where he had buried it, pretending it belonged to Tomás Camarena. Meanwhile, the Indian said something to the tall sergeant, "McKaine," at the same time gesturing toward his pistol, which sent them both into a fit of chuckling. Pedro looked to Baltimore for an explanation, but the soldier merely shrugged. *"Está bien,"* he said. Pedro was quite certain that all was not well, but now he really had no choice other than to continue with his plan.

When Villa's men returned to town from the north, with the gringos in pursuit, Pedro had cached his 1895-model Mauser and eighty rounds of ammunition near an arroyo about three kilometers south of town, halfway to El Molino. In preparation for denouncing Tomás as a "bandit" though, he moved the rifle – keeping the ammunition for himself – to a bend in the Río Santa Maria near Armera, four kilometers on the other side of town. He wanted the location to point toward Tomás, not him. When they got there, he pointed to the *álamo* tree under which he buried it. *"Allá está,"* he said. *"Allá está la escopeta del bandido Camarena."*

"And just how did you come by this information?" questioned Cpl. Baltimore.

Pedro had, of course, anticipated this exact line of inquiry. "He beats his wife. He beats her like an old mule. She is my wife's cousin through her maternal grandmother's family and they have always been close. His wife told my wife. My wife told me." Keep a lie close to the truth. The relationships were real. So was Camarena's violent streak. Everybody knew these things. If the *gabacho* soldiers checked his story, people would corroborate it.

Two of the soldiers who had not been introduced, both privates, began digging while the others watched for an ambush. They didn't dig long before finding Pedro's rifle, carefully wrapped in oilcloth; Pedro hadn't bothered to bury it very deep. "Just as I said," he told Cpl. Baltimore.

Now the loud sergeant, McKaine, began giving orders. The Apache and one of the *morenos* roughly grabbed Pedro by the arms while a third lashed his wrists together tightly with a piece of sisal twine. "What is the meaning of this outrageous behavior?" Pedro bellowed. This was definitely not going the way he imagined.

There was another exchange of words between McKaine and his translator, then Baltimore said, *"Lo siento, amigo,* but your story is just too convenient. You may think we're idiots, but we're not. That is your gun and it's you who is the bandit."

And with those words, the full, unfeigned outrage of Pedro Rascón y Tena rose to the surface. "¿*Cómo atreven Uds?*" he demanded. "How dare you?"

The loud sergeant smirked and the Apache chuckled, but Pedro hadn't even begun to say what he wanted. "How dare you come to my country and intervene in a revolution you don't even understand? How dare you pretend to represent law and order when you are fighting for the mine companies and ranchers and bankers who have been stealing our land and our minerals and our labor for years? You're not even pirates yourselves, you're just armed killers working for the newspaperman Hearst and for Senator Fall and for all of the real bandits."

Pedro wasn't sure what had come over him. The gringo soldiers were looking at him curiously. He knew this tirade wasn't likely to keep him alive over the next few moments. It definitely was not going to help him get Tomás arrested or help him get Tomás's land. But he couldn't stop himself. "How dare you call us murderers when your Texas Rangers murder thousands of our people on your side of the border for no reason at all? How dare you call us bandits when you loot our petroleum to fuel your cars? How dare you call us barbarous when you bring barbarians here to massacre us?" He gestured with his head toward the Apache.

He wasn't done. "You call us uncivilized, but you murder us and then strap us to the fenders of your cars like trophies. I saw this with my own eyes and you cannot deny the truth of my words. You call us uncultured, but you come here, to our country, without a word of our language. Who are the uncultured ones? You call us lazy, but we are the ones who make you rich, digging silver and gold from the mountains for you, and tending your herds of cattle. Who are the lazy ones?" Pedro paused for a moment here and noticed, for the first time, that Cpl. Baltimore had been doing his best to keep up a running translation for the others.

"There is one thing that I truly cannot understand," Pedro continued. "Why do you, Black soldiers, cooperate in all of this? They will not let you become officers in their army, not even in the separate regiments where the whites keep you away from other soldiers. Why do you fight for them? Seventy years ago they stole half our country because we would not let them enslave your grandfathers on Mexican land. Why do you make common cause with them? They murder you, too. They make public festivals of murdering you. Why do you forgive them?"

165

Now Pedro *was* finished, and he waited for Cpl. Baltimore to finish explaining to the others what he had said. To his surprise, the loud soldier, McKaine, did not look ashamed as Baltimore reached the end. Instead, he seemed to get angrier, if that was even possible. He began yelling at his fellow soldiers. Pedro couldn't even imagine what he could be saying. How could this man possibly defend what anybody with sense must know to be indefensible? McKaine pointed at him as he shouted. But Pedro also noticed that the other soldiers seemed unimpressed with what McKaine was saying to them.

Now Cpl. Baltimore turned back to Pedro. "I'm not even going to translate all that," he began. "My friend truly believes that we can prove ourselves to the white man by serving in his army. He truly believes that the white man will have to treat us equally when he sees that we *are* equal. My friend reads a lot. Sometimes he believes what he sees in books more than what he sees in front of his face."

For a long moment all Pedro heard was the soft growl of a leopard frog and the quiet rustling of the bright blue *damiselas* fluttering over the stream. Then, Baltimore gave a few peremptory commands. The soldiers cut the rough cord that bound his hands. McKaine looked even more unhappy than before, if that was possible. "Leave the gun." Baltimore told Pedro. "Take off."

Pedro walked quickly down the river, careful not to run, but wanting to put as many trees as possible between himself and the soldiers. He couldn't wait for these *yanquis* to go back to their *pinche* country. The sooner the better.

Namiquipa, Chihuahua, Mex.
22 March 1916
Confidential Report from Henry Ossian Flipper
To US Senator Albert Fall

Dear Sen. Fall,

The presence of thousands of US troops in the Punitive Expedition has allowed me to travel freely south of the border to investigate conditions there. Our copper mines were operating well and you should expect to see several very profitable quarters so long as prices hold. With the war in Europe I see no reason for worry there. Recent increases in silver prices, along with the successful adoption of potassium cyanide extraction encouraged me to survey several former mine sites. I suggest we purchase the mineral rights and bring them back on line. As you know, our competitors don't have the maps showing them where mining took place in former times. My decades of surveying here mean that we do. I think we should act while we still have that advantage.

The war against General Villa is proceeding much as the newspapers report. After initial setbacks, General Pershing was able to establish an efficient system of motor truck supply trains, with fuel depots at regular intervals, all guarded and manned by Regular Army infantrymen. The entire call-up of National Guardsmen seems to be in reserve on the American side of the border, which I think wise given both the rigors and temptations on the Mexican side and the complete lack of discipline of these weekend soldiers.

There has been little contact between the bandits and our troops. Villa gave his men a few months vacation at home, meaning there are no bandit concentrations for our soldiers to attack. I do not know what they are reporting in Washington, but everything I see here tells me that this Punitive Expedition is, and will be, a failure. The troops here will no more capture or kill Pancho Villa than they will the man in the moon. He will return to the field as soon as the American public gets tired of this game and forgets why we followed him into Mexico in the first place.

I visited Namiquipa in order to look at the condition of an old shaft called La Venturosa in the hills above a village called El Terrero. I will not give too many details here, but the andesite extrusion looks promising. Namiquipa is considered by Pershing's staff to be the most revolutionary town in Mexico. There are over two thousand American troops occupying the area right now and they have searched high and low for revolutionaries, with very limited success. I am not at all certain that any of the ten or so "Villistas" they arrested actually

167

were followers of Villa at all. The Army has no real sources of information and the locals view American soldiers as "innocents abroad." They use our presence and our naïveté as an opportunity to settle personal scores. Each time a Mexican steps forward with "intelligence" about a "bandit" you can bet the accused has something the accuser wants.

Still, so many of Villa's bandits came from this area – I would guess a hundred of the five hundred or so who attacked Columbus – that the odds are good that *all* of the people here supported the invasion of New Mexico. Now we are arming some of them as a sort of "civilian home guard." Who knows what side they are actually on.

I was interested to note the presence of mercenaries with our troops. Emil Holmdahl was acting as a guide to a motorized team of cavalry scouts searching for General Villa's second in command, Julio Cárdenas, whom they found and killed. It is hardly a surprise that Holmdahl knew where to look, since only four months ago he was Villa's personal machine gunner. This is the same Emil Holmdahl who worked as a mercenary for Lee Christmas in countless banana wars. I do not know exactly when Holmdahl switched sides, nor how much Pershing is paying him. I only know that a man who turned on one employer so quickly can do the same with the next employer. I took care that he not be able to identify me. Given the preoccupation of the penny press with my supposed work for Villa (some even claiming that I *am* Villa) I thought it discreet not to allow Holmdahl to sell my scalp as he obviously did that of Cárdenas.

Yet another mercenary who has switched sides is the Jew, Dreben. As of two years ago Dreben was in the employ of Kaiser Wilhelm's secret service, smuggling arms into Mexico for the Villistas. He was working for a German spy named Felix Sommerfeld, another Jew, who was simultaneously running the Mexican secret service. I first met this Sommerfeld when he was posing as a mining engineer in Chihuahua. I saw through his pose immediately; he knew nothing of mines or engineering. I believe Sommerfeld is now in New York City, working secretly for the German Naval Attache. Dreben, though, is Brigadier General Pershing's chief scout. Where his actual loyalty lies is anybody's guess. He is a Jew.

You asked that I identify promising young officers. General Pershing has on his staff a Lieutenant George S. Patton. You may recognize him from the sporting news because he represented the United States in the last Olympic Games before the European War. I looked up his results for your information. He placed seventh overall in swimming, fourth in fencing, sixth in equestrian and third in athletics. His advocates say his shooting score was perfect, which would have

168

given him the gold medal but the judges disagreed, saying one shot completely missed the target. Even so, he ranked sixth overall after five Swedes.

Patton has a positive ambition for combat. He managed to get himself reassigned from the 5th Cavalry to General Pershing's staff by appealing directly to Pershing. He then maneuvered an attachment to the 13th Cavalry to be part of the hunt for Villa. When I saw him he had been given a scouting party of troopers from the 6th Cavalry to capture Villa's immediate subordinate. This Patton is filled with loud bravado but I foresee a bright career for him, especially if – as I fear – Wilson decides to enter into the European War. Take note of him.

You have advised me also to always be on the lookout for investment opportunities. General Pershing uses trains of motor trucks to supply his troops, over 600 trucks in Mexico alone. That is more than ten times the number of motor trucks that the entire US Army owned just one year ago. Members of his staff all travel in automobiles. The Signal Corps scout the ground from airplanes and send messages by motorcycle. His engineers have built or upgraded over 400 miles of roads for motor truck service. All these vehicles require fueling depots everywhere and they lead me to think about petroleum. The big booms of ten years ago do not begin to address the potential this material has. If coal mines were the fuel for the industrialization of the last century, if copper mines have been the *sine qua non* of our nation's electrification, then petroleum will be the money maker as America motorizes. It is not just the lubricant of the automobile, it is its fuel as well. The War Department may join the Navy Department as the chief consumers of petroleum fuels. That will be a tremendous opportunity for a smart investor. It will be still more so if the warring powers in Europe are making the same switch to mechanized transport.

On a more personal note. During my travels I ran into Major Charles Young who is now an officer with the Tenth Cavalry, my old outfit. Young graduated from West Point twelve years after I did and is now the highest-ranking Negro officer in the US Army. I could not help but look at him and wonder where I would be now if I had not been the subject of false charges and a rigged court martial. I ask again if you can use your influence with the War Department to have me reinstated. It would mean so much to me.

Your obedient servant,

Henry Ossian Flipper

Three

After striking out at Carter's barbershop, Bureau of Investigations Special Agent James Amos wasted a few hours surveilling Tulsa's underworld. His first impression of Greenwood, the Black Wall Street, had been of a booming legitimate business community: hotels, restaurants, banks, real estate offices and lawyer after lawyer after lawyer. A closer look revealed a thriving shadow economy, too. He sat in cafés and hotel lobbies, drinking coffee and checking his pocket watch as if he were expecting to meet somebody. He witnessed fast-talking men negotiating oil leases and seeking loans to finance cotton planting. He overheard conversations about rentals for businesses, new and old. There were country people everywhere, in from the hinterlands to shop or to see a physician. But he also soon figured out where to get corn whiskey and beer in this allegedly dry state. He saw which hotel bellboys had a side business in cocaine and morphine and which were bringing women up to the guests' rooms.

This information was all useless, of course. He wasn't a prohibition agent. Maybe the local Ku Klux Klan was agitated about "cocaine fiends" and "sex maniacs" but he had been sent here by John Hoover to find radicals. So far they seemed to be in short supply. Agent Amos's last assignment was New York City. If he wanted to find a radical in Harlem, all he had to do was step out on the corner of 135th Street and Lenox Avenue. If the weather was decent, there would be Hubert Harrison, standing on a ladder, and explaining anything from Darwin's theory of evolution to Einstein's theory of relativity, with stops on the way for the Great Pyramid of Giza, the Empire of Songhai, and the skin color of the historical Jesus. If Harrison wasn't there, Asa Randolph was. And you could walk up to 144th Street and down to 115th and find more speakers, many in colorful costumes, and most of them far less informative than Randolph or Harrison. The uptown streets were like a free university.

By contrast, Black Tulsa seemed to be all business. Walking up and down Greenwood Avenue, Special Agent Amos found not one street speaker. The closest he came to Harlem-style politics was the office of the Tulsa *Star*, at the corner of Greenwood and Brady. When he saw the sign for the paper, Amos remembered the copy he saw in the barbershop and the fleeting thought that maybe all the radicals were on their editorial staff. But all that he found there were two men reading the next day's edition pasted to the wall and arguing about the headline story. Apparently a streetcar conductor shot a colored bandit to death during an attempted stick-up the week before, but now there were questions about the story and the conductor was being held for a murder trial. The men were arguing about whether an Oklahoma jury would find a white man guilty of killing a Black man. Amos wondered what kind of place Oklahoma was if even trolleymen went about armed.

He did find one piece of intelligence, a handbill glued to the wall near the posted newspaper. It was an advertisement for a meeting addressed to "New Negroes" and demanding, in giant boldface letters, a "DRIVE FOR JUSTICE." It was signed by a list of local professionals, all identified by their occupation. Most of them were attorneys, along with a few physicians and two journalists. Amos was quite certain that none of them were in the "African Blood Brotherhood" he had been dispatched to find. But if he knew his radicals, there was no way that they would miss an opportunity like this meeting to broadcast their beliefs. The meeting was called for 7 pm at Myer's Hall, which turned out to be only a block away on Archer Street. Special Agent Amos decided to take a break from intelligence gathering and have an early dinner.

He walked away from the main Greenwood business district, in the hope of relaxing a little and was charmed to find "Real Mexican Chilli" advertised at Perkins Café. He sat alone at a booth and chatted a little with the waitress who turned out to be Mrs. Perkins. The "real Mexican" seemed to be Mr. Perkins, a loud man, but a terrific cook. The "chilli" was perfect: savory, balanced spices and better than anything he expected here in the Wild West. And they recommended a boarding house at Archer and Detroit. If Agent Amos stayed in Tulsa he was going to have to get out of the hotel where so many eyes could see his comings and goings. A rooming house with a nice Christian lady was a much better idea.

Although he had now been working for hours, Amos felt restored by his time with the Perkinses as he walked back down Greenwood Avenue toward the meeting. He arrived in front of Myer's Hall just a few minutes before the start time. A crowd of men in suits and Stetsons was milling around in front, not quite ready to go in and sit down. Agent Amos walked through the scrum as if he were not planning to join them, carefully taking in the faces without ever making direct eye contact with anybody. He crossed the street to the Bell and Little Café and sat at the counter where he could watch the group through the big front window without them seeing him. He ordered a cup of coffee and a slice of pecan pie, which he picked at desultorily in order to give him time to study the "new Negroes." No Garveyite leafleters. No Socialist newspaper salesmen. No sign of an "African Blood Brotherhood."

171

Eventually the sidewalk in front cleared and even the stragglers filed in to the hall. Amos gave them another twenty minutes before paying for his pie and coffee and crossing the street. He didn't want to attract any attention when he slipped in and sat down in the back of the room.

He found the seat he was looking for on the left aisle, third to last row: no overhead light, one step from the exit. The speaker up front was going on about some local political situation and the names he referred to meant nothing to Special Agent Amos. Much of his talk was about abstruse oil leasing statutes, too, although he seemed most exercised about unequal law enforcement in the surrounding counties of the former Creek and Cherokee Nations. Amos did a head count. There were forty-seven men in the room, which he thought was a lot for a small city that seemed so apolitical. If there were an "African Blood Brotherhood" here, one of them was bound to be in this crowd. And he was bound to speak up. Things would clarify themselves once the speech was over and the inevitable questions came from the floor.

Special Agent Amos stopped listening and began studying the people present. He didn't think he could tell anything about them, especially from behind, but he wanted to remember each of them in case some became persons of interest later in the evening. He had committed some detail or other about every man in the room to memory when the speaker finished whatever he was saying and the crowd applauded politely.

A dark-skinned man in a seersucker suit, probably in his thirties, spoke from the floor, "So why should we wait for these Harlem Negroes to start a colored stock market?" the man was asking. "We have more capital than they and more venture opportunities than they..." Amos stopped listening again. This was radical politics in Tulsa? It sounded like a sales pitch to him and Director Hoover was not interested in prosecuting colored Ponzis. It did confirm his feeling from earlier today that Tulsa Negroes were all about business, legal or otherwise. He scanned the crowd to see who was responding to this.

The next speaker was a familiar face. It was the barber's landlord who he had seen earlier in the day, Gurley. There was no mistaking him, his bespoke suit, or his superior tone. "Some of you don't know how good we have it in Tulsa." There was a loud guffaw at this, but Amos couldn't identify the heckler.

Gurley continued, "We have our own police here in Greenwood." They did? That was unusual. "And we have a good relationship with Chief Gustafson. I hear you talking about problems with the law in Okmulgee County and Rogers

172

County and Creek County. Don't you think we should try to keep this good thing going here in Tulsa?"

Now the heckler stood up and turned around. Another familiar face: it was the grocer they called O.B. He really did have a problem with Gurley. "White police walked right into my store and rousted my customers. Stole from me, too, and smiled about it. You tell me there's something good about that," he said angrily.

Gurley shook his head. "You know damn well we got that police fired. I went straight to Chief Gustafson as soon as I heard about it. He's not a police anymore. Why do you want to stir these folks up about something we already took care of?"

Amos lost interest in what was clearly a personal conflict between the two men. Maybe he would find this "Brotherhood" out on the sidewalk after the formal program. His attention was recaptured by the unmistakable sound of a Jamaican accent. A tall dark-skinned man in tweed was talking about Mother Africa. But he wasn't advocating armed self-defense. He was flogging shares in the Black Star steamship line. Amos had investigated Garvey in New York. He was convinced that this was just another Ponzi scheme.

Tulsa. It really did seem that this city was all about the money. If there were, in fact, any armed subversives in town, they were definitely not at this meeting. Special Agent Amos quietly slipped out of the auditorium and headed for his hotel. Maybe he would have better luck tomorrow.

Inceville, California
December 14, 1915

Misúŋka Henry,

Greetings younger brother! It's me, your big brother, Luther Standing Bear!

Thank you for your letter and your good wishes. I miss all of you so much. Being so far away, I really appreciate hearing any news at all from home. I feel a little better knowing how everybody is doing. I am always proud to read about your work with the Society of American Indians and to know that you are among the leaders of our people. It is good to see that you are still so close with Chauncey Yellow Robe after all these years. I admit that I have mixed feelings about his job as disciplinarian in the *wašíčus'* school in Rapid City: proud he is there to look after our children, hurt that they took my classroom away from me, and wondering why they still insist on taking our children from their homes and parents. I hear Chauncey sends his own daughters to the Rapid City public schools with the *wašíču* children. I am curious why the girls don't attend the Indian school where their father works and where they could be in classes with their Lakota cousins. How he raises his daughters is not my business, though. I am very glad to hear that your own children are all doing well.

I won't write too much about my work here in show business. I know how much you and all the SAI folks disapprove of it. There is something new every day, though, and I sure do meet some interesting people. Last week we were shooting a movie called "The Wolf Woman" near Venice Beach. It will be one of these stories about a beautiful seductress who ruins every man she meets. The star is Louise Glaum who often plays these "vamp" roles. During a lunch break some of the other men and I noticed a stranger following her. He was a sharp-dressed white man – three-piece suit; wide, pink tie with matching pink hatband and spats; pointy, two-tone shoes – and he was talking steadily while trying to put his hands all over her. Miss Glaum walked him right over to us and said, "Boys, will you please rid me of this thing? It's been following me for ten minutes." I don't have to tell you that he took one look at us and ran right off. He was not happy to discover that her friends were a band of "warlike Sioux." I'm just joking. And she is a very nice lady. I suppose she only wants to be the "vampire" when the cameras are running!

People always ask me about William S. Hart. Is he such a "straight shooter" off the screen as he seems to be in his movies? Is he really such a great rider, or is that a film trick? I can tell you that he is as much a friend as a *wašíču* can ever be, which is not much. We do look out for each other on and off the set, but he

174

has that white man's attitude toward "injuns" (as he calls us) and toward Mexicans and colored, too. He *is* a good rider, though, and his pinto, Fritz, is the best stunt horse I have seen. He rides Fritz over logs, through tunnels, and off cliffs. Those tricks are as real as can be.

In defense of my work in the show business, I will just say that it gives us the opportunity to sing, to drum, to dance, to wear our traditional clothes and to speak our own language. All that has to be worth something. I have a nice house, overlooking the Pacific Ocean, about twenty miles west of Los Angeles. Most of the Oglala who are here working for Mr. Ince live in a camp up the hill from my place. As you may know from your work with Major Brennan, there are about forty families here from Pine Ridge under contract to make movies. Besides acting in his moving pictures, part of my responsibility to Mr. Ince is to care for all our people, keep them safe and healthy, and make sure the children are in school.

I also have a little business of my own. I run an archery amusement five miles down the coast at the Santa Monica Pier. It's good fun, provides employment for some of our people and gives me an outside income, too. We had some Japanese tourists in there recently who challenged me to a shooting contest. I suppose they thought that no "red man" could compete with a samurai. I publicized it in the papers, drew a big crowd, and charged admission to watch. Then I put every arrow in the bull's-eye. None of them could match that.

The big news this week was the party we had for my birthday. You must remember Richard Davis Thunderbird from Carlisle. He was one of the *Šahíyela* boys we met during our first year at school. He lives here in California and works in moving pictures, just like me. He organized the party for me, and invited Indians from every film production company around. And when I say "big news," I mean that literally. We made the front page of the *Los Angeles Times*. They called the party a "pow-wow" and said that we scared the neighbors. I hope that's not true. I invited all of them over so they wouldn't feel left out, but none of them came. We made a lot of noise, and the party went on all through the night. You know how that goes!!

We had food, drumming and dancing from most of the different tribes who were there. I can't even count all of them. I know that the Iroquois at the party had never seen the *Omaha Wačhípi* before, not to mention danced it, but before the night was over Jesse Cornplanter was putting some of the Oglala men to shame. And then he taught us something called "false face", which I guess from the name is a masked dance. I did it, too! I learned an Apache *bigotali* and I don't remember what else. The most surprising thing was when a Paiute man from

Oregon tried to teach us *Tuŋwéya Wačhípi*! As if we didn't already know it! Then Thunderbird told us that according to their tradition the *Šahíyela* taught us Lakota how to perform the *Wiwáŋyaŋg Wačhípi*! I listened to his claim without arguing, even though father taught us that we received this gift long ago directly from *Pté Ská Wiŋ*. It was a night for fun, not contradicting each other, and I guess it is possible that even in the buffalo-hunting days we may have learned songs and dances from one another. After all, we acknowledge where we got *Omaha Wačhípi* right in the name.

I was especially interested in a dance we learned from the Winnebago guests that they called the Drum Dance. They were certain that we Lakota would already know it because their grandparents all taught them the same story, that the dance was gifted to them by a Sisseton Dakota Woman named *Wíyaka Siŋté Wiŋ*. They thought we would all have learned it from her, too. Apparently she was given the dance in a vision while she hid from soldiers, probably during the Civil War. It requires a big drum and it is meant to bring together all the tribes. This fit in with my idea that we should be building unity among ourselves by sharing who we are instead of by pretending to be somebody else, especially when that somebody will never accept us anyway.

At the height of the party Thunderbird gave a speech in my honor. He told all the guests how long he and I have known each other, since we were young boys in the first class at Carlisle. How we both left our families to study in Pennsylvania, how we traveled with the big Wild West shows, how we each taught school on our reservations and how we met again in California working in the moving picture industry… we truly have been in and out of each other's lives for over thirty-five years. It is a very long time and I am proud to have him as a friend.

One joke he made has been on my mind and on my heart for the last few days. He referred to the party as "intertribal" and I – like everybody else – thought he meant that the guests were Lakota, *Šahíyela*, Winnebago, Apache, Papago, Mohawk, Ute, and whoever else all these people are. He got a big laugh when he listed the tribes: Ince, Republic, Paramount, DeMille, Universal… the moving picture companies that we work for. But it's true. We all live near the studios where we work and we socialize daily with the other Indians at our studio. The only reason most of my friends here are Lakota is because Mr. Ince asked me to recruit what he called "a whole tribe" from Pine Ridge. Among ourselves we call the Ince Indians a *"thióšpaye,"* as if we were all blood relations. Even the *wašíču* actors, who don't speak Lakota, use this word!

This idea of new "tribes" is reminding me a lot of our school days. When we were boys and new at Carlisle I stuck very close to you and the other Lakota boys, not least because when the teachers weren't around to slap us for speaking our language we could understand each other. I knew Thunderbird was *Šahíyela*, and an ally, but I couldn't speak *Tséhesenéstsestotse* so I left him with the other Cheyenne. It was only after we each learned English that we were able to become friends. It amazed me how much the Cheyenne boys had in common with us, despite our different languages. The white people had a totally different understanding of how this world came to be, but those guys knew all about White Buffalo Woman, the Great Race and the center of the earth. I became a Christian, just like Colonel Pratt wanted, but I often wonder whether we Indians are now the only Christians left in this country. The Whites certainly never treat us in a very Christian manner. Why would we want to become like them in any way?

I saw a poem by Zitkala Sa in your magazine that I think touches on this. She wrote:

> I've lost my long hair, my eagle plumes, too.
> The will-o-the-wisp learning, it brought me rue.

This is exactly why I am searching for something new. Maybe *ptéhčaka* is gone forever and we can never live again by hunting the great herds that used to darken the grasslands. Maybe boys can no longer make their names and young men cannot impress their in-laws by raiding our enemies for *súŋkawakháŋ* and then gifting them to people who would otherwise have to walk. But there must be some way for us to remain Indians.

So this has me thinking again about what it may mean to be Lakota in this 20th century. You remember that when we got to Carlisle they put us in the tin shop, which is easily the most useless skill I have ever learned in my whole life. At least Thunderbird was put in the print shop. I am quite sure there will never be a time when there is no demand for skilled printers! This was all a part of Captain Pratt's plan to "Kill the Indian; Save the Man." (On a side note I have been remembering the first few times I heard him say this. I was so frightened by those words that I shivered.) We were all supposed to drop everything Indian about us: clothes, hair, language, beliefs. Now I hear that Carlisle is actually teaching "Indian" crafts to the students. Is this just another way to profit off our children's labor by selling something that has become very popular in *wašíču* markets? Or is the new school administration actually acknowledging the value of something we invented?

In either case, it seems strange that our old teachers are now touting our traditional crafts as our contribution to American culture instead of condemning them as evidence of our barbarism. I can tell you, though, that here in the show business we are working to bring those crafts to a high standard. Each of us is responsible for our own regalia. Richard is in great demand as an actor in no small part because he and his wife make such high quality costumes for him to wear. Their beadwork and quillwork are extraordinary. And he never repeats himself; he makes a new outfit for each new moving picture!

Do I seem in this letter to be especially touchy about being in the moving picture industry? It is because I read your magazine from cover to cover every time it comes out. I saw what your friend Chauncey wrote about show business: "demoralizing, degrading, degenerating." But I can't believe he said that the government encourages it, because you know as well as I how hard it is to get permits to go wild westing or to work in moving pictures. The only thing the government "encourages" is our getting in debt to the stores and banks so that we are always a year behind, working this year to pay for last year. Oh, and working for free to build fences around ourselves! I took it personally when Chauncey wrote that we are out here getting drunk. When I was with Buffalo Bill's Wild West I had the job of keeping our people sober, and I took it very seriously... so seriously that a lot of the men complained about me. I do the same thing here at Inceville. It is my job and my calling, too. And when Chauncey wrote those words about "performing the naked war dance" I really had to wonder: What is he so ashamed of?

It is not as though I have no idea what all of you are complaining about. Way back in the days when I was a boy, working for the summer at Wanamaker's department store in Philadelphia, I went to see Sitting Bull, *Tȟatȟáŋka Íyotake*, in the Buffalo Bill Wild West. The master of ceremonies introduced him as the man who killed Custer at Little Big Horn Creek. I knew that was a lie: I was there at *Pȟežísla Wakpá* when the soldiers fell into our camp and I know that it was the younger men who killed Custer. After the introduction, Sitting Bull gave a short speech saying he was on his way to Washington, DC to meet with the president. But did the interpreter translate Sitting Bull's words? No. He made up some nonsense about Sitting Bull threatening the lives of the audience, which seemed to make them strangely happy. So, yes, I know what it means for us to be turned into show savages for the amusement of a white audience.

I read what Chauncey wrote about the motion picture they made at Wounded Knee. It was twenty-five years ago this month that the *wašíču* soldiers massacred our people there. You were still at school so I don't know what you heard about it in Pennsylvania, but I was back from Carlisle and living at *Sičháŋǧu*. Our brother Ellis was right there at Wounded Knee when it happened.

Some of our *Mnikȟówožu* relations had traveled down from *Čhaŋphá Wakpála* two weeks earlier. They were starving and freezing because the agent up there at Cheyenne River was stealing all their supplies, then selling them and putting the money in his own pocket. They were frightened, too. When the police murdered *Tȟatȟáŋka Íyotake* at Standing Rock, all of us wondered who they were planning to kill next. The army, though, acted as though the flight of the *Mnikȟówožu* to Pine Ridge was an act of war! Tens of thousands of soldiers suddenly arrived by train, coming from a thousand miles in every direction.

What unsettled me even more than the army was the press, the newspaper reporters and photographers. There were hundreds of them! Do you remember the Harry Thaw case in New York City? The Trial of the Century? He was a millionaire who murdered a playboy architect, Stanford White, because White raped Thaw's wife years before, when she was fourteen. I remember how the courtroom was filled with reporters, each one hunting for some new salacious detail to feed the public's appetite for scandal. Well, if you can believe it, Wounded Knee was even worse than that. Every newspaper and magazine in the country sent reporters out to Pine Ridge. There were whole camps of them, just waiting for some act of violence to write about. They acted as if we were a spectacle, but they were hoping for a war. And the photographers? They wanted some violence, some bloody spectacle, even more than the print reporters. Then, when the Army massacred our people, they all got what they had been praying for. At least, that's the way they covered it.

I rode out to *Čhaŋkpé Ópi Wakpála* the next day. I have never forgotten what I saw on that field. I have never forgotten the bodies of our disarmed cousins – men, women, and children – piled up in the snow where they were murdered by the *wašíčus* and their guns. I have never forgotten seeing the body of our great mediator *Uŋpȟáŋ Gleška* twisted and frozen on the ground. How could I forget, even if I wanted to? Those photographers turned the scene into picture postcards! They insisted on selling souvenir photographs of the dead for months afterward! I believe every one of the *wašíču* soldiers bought those postcards, showing them standing with smirks on their faces and guns in their hands over the corpses of our Lakota people piled into a mass grave. That picture sold so well, made so much money for the photographer. It must have made the *wašíčus* feel so powerful. I cannot think of it without getting sick.

Chauncey calls the Wounded Knee film – which the producers said is a "re-creation" of the last "battle" of the Sioux – a disgrace and a misrepresentation and an injustice. He's right. I agree. I have been begging Mr. Ince to allow us to write a film, to let us decide how best to represent ourselves. He says he agrees with me, but we never quite get around to making that movie. Instead, every day, we make something else that is silly and wrong. So I do get your point.

But I don't understand why we have to allow the *wašíčus* to define us in other ways, either. They like to talk about the bad "traditionals" who still live in tipis and speak our parents' tongue and follow the pipe. They act as if giving gifts is some kind of sin. (And I guess it is if you worship money instead of Jesus Christ.) Then they like to talk about "progressives" who speak English and have paying jobs and go to church. Father was a "progressive" when he sent us to school in Pennsylvania. You and Chauncey and everybody in the Society for American Indians are "progressives."

I was a "progressive" when I taught school at *Wagmíza Wakpála* and lived in a frame house. But when I went wild westing with Buffalo Bill I turned into a backward Indian again. This is how the *wašíčus* divide us! For how many years were we supposed to be ashamed that Father rode into the stronghold after the massacre and convinced the people to surrender to the soldiers? To this day? Ellis was a policeman; for how many years is that supposed to make me an enemy to the traditional party?

Why did the *wašíčus* outlaw our sacred Sun Dance? How does it hurt them unless they truly believe that it renews the power we receive from White Buffalo Calf Woman? I have heard that in the woods on *Pȟežúta Ȟáka* Creek near Kyle the so-called "traditionals" still dance *Wiwáŋyaŋg Wačhípi* every July in secret. That doesn't hurt me. How does it hurt you? If they plant wheat or herd cattle or even work for wages during the other fifty weeks a year, why does this dance make them enemies to any other Lakota? And the thing the agents hate the most, the giveaway: Why is generosity such a sin?

When you were working for the Sears and Roebuck Company in Chicago, as you used to, how did that hurt the dancers? How does your running the Pine Ridge YMCA hurt them now? I can see how Chauncey Yellow Robe might be hurting them, by taking their children to the boarding school at Rapid City and cutting their hair and stealing their language, but that is his choice.

I was a progressive at Carlisle, but I did not come home so progressive that I could not speak our parents' language. I taught school at Rosebud and Pine Ridge, but I never taught the children that they were worthless. I kept a store at father's place in Pine Ridge, but I never tried to cheat our people. I never progressed that far.

I do not mean these reflections as criticisms. I do not see you as an adversary. Neither of us have progressed that far. You are my brother and I love you. I just feel that until we heal the wounds that divide our people we risk losing who we are as Lakota while not being allowed to be *wašiču*. That is why I was so happy to read in your letter that you are working with the old chiefs to get back our sacred Black Hills. For years the educated young men like you and I have left that to the traditionals, acting as if it was only a dream of the past. Maybe in taking this case to court with them you can restore us as a people.

Please give my love to everybody, especially Nettie. If you visit Ellis, tell Paul and Susie that I miss them. I miss you all.

Love,
Your Brother
Luther Standing Bear

Des Moines, Iowa
1917

To: Maj. Nicholas Biddle
Military Intelligence Branch
From: Confidential Agent Maj. Walter Loving

This Wednesday through Saturday past I visited the Colored Officers Candidate School at Camp Des Moines in Iowa. This is a two-hundred acre complex in the flat prairie south of the city. It was until recently the home of the cavalry and the accommodations are more than adequate. There are in attendance 1000 highly-educated college graduates and 250 enlisted men from the four colored regiments in the Regular Army. They have been enthusiastically received by the residents of Des Moines, both white and colored, as evidenced by the parade the people of the city gave them. There is also a souvenir book for sale about them, including photos of all the training companies and biographies of every man at the school.

The overall mood at the camp is very positive and pro-Army. Candidates are so enthusiastic that there is little discussion of either the segregated nature of the facility or the small number of candidates when compared with the huge number of volunteers. Rather, the colored men in Des Moines are personally buoyed, both by the fact that they were the ones selected and by the large number of highly-educated, "talented-tenth" Negroes present. They have been visited by Dean Kelly Miller of Howard University, Dean William Pickens of Morgan College, and President Robert Moton of Tuskegee Institute. All of those educators spoke to the whole camp about the importance of what the men are doing for America and for the colored race.

The one negative note in camp is the prevailing belief that Lt. Col. Charles Young should be in command of this facility. He is the highest-ranking Negro in the U.S. Army and was recently in command of cavalry in the Mexican expedition. I repeatedly heard a rumor that Lt. Col. Young's health problems were fabricated by the Department of War in order to avoid promoting him. Nevertheless, Lt. Col. Young, too, visited Camp Des Moines and rallied the troops around the importance of their contribution to our war effort.

You asked in your letter of 16th last how the candidates are responding to the mutiny by some members of the 24th Infantry in Houston. A few dozen members of the class here are detached from the 24th for this training and everybody else relies heavily on them for both facts and opinion.

The most important source of both appears to be a young Regular Army sergeant named Osceola McKaine. He corresponds both with members of his own battalion, who remained in Columbus, New Mexico throughout, and with some in the Third Battalion, including Corporal Charles Baltimore of I Company, the Military Policeman whose beating and arrest by Houston police precipitated the affair. Sgt. McKaine's version is that Cpl. Baltimore's arrest was an example of race prejudice by local law enforcement, but that marching into town to free him was both a gross dereliction of duty and bad for the Negro race. He has urged all his questioners to demonstrate their loyalty to the United States by excelling as officers and thereby to make a case for just treatment. According to his white trainers he has been an exemplary candidate and they are recommending him for commission as a First Lieutenant.

Regarding "secret" organizations among the candidates: I found no evidence of subversive or antiwar groups such as the IWW or Socialist Party. There is no "chapter" of the N.A.A.C.P. here, although most candidates read its journal *The Crisis*, which has taken an active interest in their success and is a strong supporter of this war. Indeed, as we discussed when I was last in Washington, its editor, Dr. W.E.B. DuBois campaigned for a position in Military Intelligence Division as a captain. And, of course, Major Joel Spingarn of M.I.D. is the former chairman of the N.A.A.C.P. Consequently, I could not consider it a dangerous organization even if it were present.

The "secret" organizations you are hearing about in the camp are the "Greek letter" groups: college fraternities. The ones here in Omaha are Alpha Phi Alpha, Kappa Alpha Psi, and Omega Psi Phi. A very large proportion of the men here pledged these fraternities when they were students; so many that all three have established so-called "war chapters" here at the camp. They have each recruited a few new members. Some are graduates of colleges where these fraternities had not yet arrived. A very few (Sgt. McKaine is one) are non-commissioned officers from the Regular Army. I attended a meeting of each. None of them are doing anything to undermine the good order and discipline of the camp. Rather they seem to provide mutual support for their members amid the rigors of training. Their openness to my visits seemed evidence to me of the lack of secrecy.

As per your instructions I am departing in the morning for New Mexico to look into allegations of unrest among the 24th Infantry. I will report from there.

Houston, Texas
1 September 1917
Confidential Report from H.O. Flipper
Senator Albert Fall
For Your Eyes Only

I have completed my tour of Chihuahua and Sonora to investigate the state of the mining industry and the war. I am sorry to report that the optimism I expressed in my last report no longer applies. The prospects for *any* investment - new or old have changed drastically and for the worse. The latest issue of *Mining Journal* estimates that 85% of the works in Chihuahua are now idle as a result of the new government and consequent uncertainty about the owners' titles to their property. Even their ability to ship ore that has already been mined is in doubt. From my observation that estimate may in fact be overly rosy. I think the true number of shuttered works is now closer to *100%*. In traveling the state since my last report I found *no* mines still operational. Leonard Worcester remains imprisoned by the authorities for selling ore from the Granby mine. Moreover, Villa (wherever he is) is still threatening to confiscate mines that are not up-to-date on their taxes (to him!), even though the operators no longer have any revenue from mining to pay those taxes. I am quite certain you are informed about this because all the big players, from Rio Tinto to American Smelting to Empire Zinc, are there with you in Washington, DC, lobbying the U.S. government to overturn the Mexican government's new mining law.

I suggest an alternate strategy. These abandoned mines are only "distressed" in the sense that they have been closed. I did not find excessive amounts of water in them, nor have the works been vandalized. If you were prepared to "play ball" with the current government in Chihuahua, you could easily take over the properties of all your competitors, just for the price of the present year's taxes. Let the other companies cry foul. The U.S. Department of State will not be determining the ownership of those mines. It will be the State of Chihuahua. I located some very interesting properties in the vicinity of Namiquipa that could be had for no more than a "consulting fee" to members of the local communal authority.

In my last report I mentioned the enormous opportunities that seemed to be opening in petroleum. Therefore, I returned to Texas via the state of Tamaulipas. It was a reminder to me that the oil fields of Tampico are only 300 miles south of Brownsville. Mexican petroleum production *doubled* after the beginning of this war in Europe, but conditions in the area have since deteriorated dramatically. Nothing can be done without a bribe to one or more low-level officials. Payroll robberies have become routine, and many of the bandits seem to be Carrancista soldiers. All the Americans there think that getting rid of Carranza will solve these problems. The biggest proponents of this view are William F. Buckley and your good friend Harry Sinclair. I do not agree. At this point anti-American sentiment crosses all Mexican party lines. Buckley has been loudly denouncing the mental competence of Mexicans in general, and he does it in front of all audiences, which will not help him secure the cooperation of whoever finally emerges on top after this civil war. Throughout Tampico, Mexicans of every social class and political party remain angry about President Wilson's armed occupation of Veracruz two years ago. No alternative to Carranza exists who will be a friend to the Americans in the oil fields.

There may be one immediate bright side to this. Edward Doheny, the Los Angeles oilman, is so angry with Woodrow Wilson that I think you could lure him over to the Republican Party despite Doheny's lifelong allegiance to the Democrats. And Doheny is (or was), by far, the biggest oil operator in all of Mexico. But that is the only good news. Don't expect any new change of government in Mexico City to stabilize conditions in the oil fields. No party is going to reduce taxes on oil. It is the sole significant source of income in the entire country. It is likely to remain so for the foreseeable future

You asked me to look at our troop dispositions, but as you will have read in the newspapers, events have overtaken my reports. I wrote you that I visited the 24th Infantry (colored.) I found them ill-disciplined and preoccupied with card games. Since then, we have witnessed the mutiny of a large portion of the 3rd Battalion here in Houston. I must attribute this catastrophe to two causes.

First, is the abusive behavior toward them of white Houston, and especially the Houston Police Deparment. *In my presence* a white police officer bragged that in Texas the fine for killing a vulture is $25 but killing a n----- only costs $5. The mutiny itself began when two white police officers pistol-whipped and shot a colored military policeman for asking where they were holding a soldier they had arrested. That military policeman was forced to patrol *unarmed.* The commissioned officers of the 24th were afraid to issue sidearms to their own men for fear of antagonizing the white police!

Second, is the poor leadership shown by the white officers of the 24th. Both Captain Shekerjian and Major Snow have offered their lack of control of the men as a *defense* for what ultimately occurred. When the shooting began, Major Snow actually fled, thinking that he was the target. I feel confident that the men of the 24th could be turned into a superior military unit if led by officers who understand them. The War Department always interprets this to mean white Southerners with experience running Negro work gangs. I suggest Negro

185

officers instead. Colonel Charles Young had notable success with the Tenth Cavalry. I humbly suggest myself for the Twenty-Fourth. Please consider proposing this to Major General Scott. He was a year ahead of me at West Point and may remember me.

I will be returning soon to El Paso. You may contact me there with any further assignments.

Yr obt svt,
Henry O Flipper

Linn-San Manuel, Texas
1965

My beloved grandchildren, I can tell you that although those bigots barred me from McAllen High School they were not yet able to derail my education. Mr. Craig and his *gabachos* kept me out of their school, but they did not take away my intellect and they did not take away my pride. Perhaps my teacher, Don Antonio, could not create an entire high school just for me in San Manuel, but he could provide me with the books I needed to teach myself and he could make time to tutor me in the subjects that required explanation. And that is what he did.

In mathematics we worked with Torroja Caballe's *Lecciones de Geometría Descriptiva*. My geography text was Miguel Schulz's *Compendio de Cosmografía y Geografía Física y Política*. For science I had *An Introduction to the Study of Chemistry* by Ira Remsen. That chemistry book and *American Literature* by Albert Smyth were the only textbooks I had in English. How do I remember these titles and authors so well a half-century later? Because these books remain on my shelf to this day, a reminder of who I was meant to be! You can see them in my house if you look.

Every day I devoted the hours after our morning meal and before the afternoon siesta to my academic work: reading my books, writing my lessons, doing my problem sets. In the late afternoon I visited Don Antonio at the *escuelita*. He checked my work and my understanding and assigned me more for the next day. I was still horribly disappointed by my exclusion from McAllen High School, but I felt that I was making every effort to keep up and I was secretly dreaming of attending a university.

My private ambitions and misfortunes loomed large to me, but I was not so self-absorbed as to be blind to larger calamities in the Valley. They were about to become mine as well. I have mentioned our struggles to retain the family estate in the face of constant legal maneuvers by the Anglos who wanted to steal our land. By this time all of the landowning Mexican families had become well practiced in U.S. law. We had to be! How else were we to keep from becoming landless beggars in our own homes? We might have lost the tremendous grants of our ancestors, but we could still count on working and keeping our ranches.

What we failed to see was that the new arrivals – the Anglos who came to the Valley around the turn of the twentieth century – also had new tactics. The Kings and the Kenedys and those like them who moved to our country in the 1850's and '60's had learned our language and even married into our families.

These new *gabachos* had no intention of doing either… or even of abiding by their own laws. The Lanes, the Cleggs, and the Doughertys were all cattlemen at first. They became lawmen – of a sort – in order to acquire the land they wanted, as I will explain to you.

My teacher, Don Antonio Longoria, was the husband of Antonia, daughter of Don Jesús Bazán. Don Jesús's ranch, Santa Guadalupe, was a portion of the old San Ramón Grant. Somehow, using the name of one of my father's Cantú cousins as a "partner," a *gabacho* named Sam Lane had gained title to an adjacent pasture, which he named "Sam Lane Ranch." He immediately offered Don Jesús $100 for his property. That was less than a penny an acre. Don Jesús was always a gentleman, so he simply rejected this offer politely. He had no intention of giving up his ranch anyway and he chose to ignore the insult.

When Don Jesús wouldn't sell to him, Sam Lane brought suit in Hidalgo County Court, claiming that the Bazán ranch belonged to Lane's "partner", Martín, through his descent from Leocadio Treviño. Judge William Dougherty – one of Sam Lane's friends and another of these newcomer *sinvergüenzas* – found in favor of Lane, but Don Jesús, expecting that outcome, had already prepared an appeal. The Superior Court judge overturned the ruling on the grounds that "Judge" Dougherty had failed to cite any evidence or any law in his decision. I would be surprised if Dougherty owned a law book at all… or, indeed, if he could have read one if it accidentally found its way into his hands! The higher court also castigated Dougherty for even hearing the case, given that he had all sorts of financial arrangements with Sam Lane. Look the case up. If the records still exist and haven't been mysteriously lost, they will show that Judge Dougherty was using his position to steal the ranch for himself.

So you see that there was bad blood between Don Jesús and his Anglo neighbors and that it wasn't personal. It was about real estate. If only we knew then what we eventually learned we would have prepared differently. And let me tell you: this was only what was happening right in my neighborhood. There were stories just like this up and down the entire Valley.

Meanwhile, there were troubles on the other side, too. The people of Mexico had finally tired of the corrupt regime of President Porfirio Díaz. They overthrew his government, hoping for freedom and prosperity. But the opposition splintered - so many generals, all looking to be the next Díaz - and instead of a peaceful Mexican republic they had years of civil war. Soldiers, detectives and police devoted all their attention to their political opponents, meaning *no* attention to actual law enforcement. This affected us on the U.S. side, too. One day, while I was riding with my father, a gang of horse thieves from across the river rode up and surrounded us. These bandits were not even capable of roping the horses they wanted to steal. Our horses were too fast and too independent, they never could have caught them, so they made my *papi* do the roping. I watched with shame and horror while they forced him, at gunpoint, to rob his own best horses for them! In those days, the authorities on the other side were so preoccupied with politics that all these thieves had to do to evade justice was make it back across the river.

If they had only stolen from us *Tejanos* perhaps the law on our side would have looked the other way, but the Anglo ranchers were also getting raided. Governor "Pa" Ferguson assigned a company of Texas Rangers to Hidalgo County to stop them. But do you suppose these Rangers worked to stop the robberies? Pa Ferguson named Sam Lane as one of those Rangers – yes! the very same Sam Lane who was trying to steal the ranch of Don Jesús! – and Lane's ranch was their headquarters, for which he was paid handsomely. During the time of which I am writing you never saw Sam Lane without also seeing Ranger Captain Henry Lee Ransom right next to him. Old Mr. Sam would drive his open-top Ford Model T up and down the roads while Captain Ransom rode shotgun – literally! a sawed-off double-barreled 12-gauge across his lap! – in the passenger seat, and three more armed Rangers in the back.

Captain Henry Lee Ransom has been dead now for over forty years, but I still have to cross myself and ask for the Holy Mother's protection when I think of his name. *Ruega por nosotros, ahora y en la hora de nuestra muerte.* He loved to tell stories about his days in the Philippines. When he knew that we children were nearby he would describe, with great gusto, how he murdered Filipino babies, telling the other Rangers, "Nits make lice!" while looking directly at us and laughing as if he had invented this unspeakable joke himself. The younger children did not know what he meant when he said this, so I pretended that I didn't understand either in order to avoid being forced to explain his abominable threat.

Ranger Captain Ransom had been a prison guard at one time, too, supervising the convicts building the Texas State Railroad. His prison anecdotes always ended with the sentence, "Nobody will ever find *his* body." I wondered how many unmarked graves this monster had dug until I realized that he made the inmates do the shovel work themselves before killing them. And all this horror had only been preparation for his promotion to Chief of the Houston Police Department. In that position he didn't even bother to dispose of the corpses. He just shot people down in public, day or night, and left their bodies lying in the streets. It wasn't until he casually assassinated a prominent attorney in front of dozens of witnesses that he was indicted for any of these murders. When the governor sent him to us, as the head of a company of Texas Rangers, Captain Ransom was out on bail and awaiting trial for that killing in Houston.

None of this was in my mind that Friday afternoon in September. I was sitting in the shade by the *escuelita* waiting to speak to Don Antonio. The academic year hadn't started back in for the children yet; it was still farming season. But now that I was a private student and not bound to the school calendar I didn't take any time off from my studies. I was hoping to discuss some math problems. Don Antonio was very busy helping his father-in-law with the ranch, but he still found time to meet with me one or two days a week. *La Señora* Antonia was in the house stewing an old rooster with *chiltepines* and *hierba dulce*. I was helping her daughter, Ernestina, pat tortillas and we had chosen the coolest spot near the house to work. There was a little late afternoon breeze and we could smell Doña Antonia's cooking all the way over where we were. I can smell it even today in my memory.

My mind was on the exciting prospect of starting a new year of science – physics instead of chemistry – but Ernestina wanted to talk about the *baile* that was coming the following week. The families down the road in Faysville celebrated the feast day of Santa Teresa with a big outdoor dance. There would be a band, plenty of food, and – if previous years were any guide – everybody between Matamoros and Rio Grande City would be there. But Ernestina wasn't interested in everybody. She was interested in a boy named Eligio de la Garza.

"Timotea," she asked, "do you think Eloy likes me?"

Are we twelve? I wanted to respond. But she was twelve, so I just said, "I think Eligio likes all the girls, but I think he likes himself best."

"Now you're just being envious, Tea," said Ernestina, and she made a face.

I said nothing about that. Envious? Envious of a farm boy? Envious of Ernestina? But I felt badly for belittling her, so I asked, "What will you be wearing to the dance?"

The sour expression disappeared as quickly as it had arrived. "I sewed a dress myself, from a pattern in *Delineator* magazine! It's a gold satin with a high waist, a boned bodice and a pleated skirt, longer in the back than the front!" she told me excitedly. "Do you want to see it?"

I did not. "Yes!" I said with a smile, though. "Let's just finish these tortillas first."

190

I remember a cloud crossing the sun, darkening the sky, at just that moment. I can't say if that is truly what happened or if it is a trick of my memory, anticipating what was about to occur. What I know for certain is that, just then, Ernestina's *papi* and *abuelo,* Don Antonio and Don Jesús, came over the rise to the east. My teacher was wearing his range clothes and riding his sorrel mare, Rosinante. His father-in-law was on his prize gray stallion, Tigre. Obviously the horse thieves who robbed my father had not yet been to their ranch! I heard the low rumble of an automobile coming up the road from the west and in a second we could see Jim Lane's Ford with the Rangers aboard. They got up to the gate of Rancho Santa Guadalupe just as Don Jesús and Don Antonio were reaching the same spot, but inside the barbed-wire fence.

I saw Don Jesús turn and lift his hand in greeting. I saw Captain Ransom raise his shotgun. I gasped for breath.

One instant Don Jesús was sitting in his saddle, silhouetted against the sky. The next instant his body was lying still on the dusty ground. Less than a second later, Don Antonio's head flew apart in a cloud of blood, brains and skull fragments. His torso, too, fell from his horse, but more slowly, as if through water. The sound reached me after the sight. I heard two loud blasts. The Ford didn't slow down or speed up. It just continued down the road toward the east until I could no longer see it.

Ernestina threw her tortillas into the dirt and ran down the lane, weeping, "*¡Papi! ¡Abuelo!*" A moment later her mother, Doña Antonia followed her, shrieking, "*¡Mi amor! ¿Qué te han hecho?*" My legs seemed not to be working, though. I tried to stand, but instead, I fell into the dirt. Somewhere nearby I heard somebody screaming uncontrollably. Everything around me was oddly unfocused and my face seemed to be soaking wet. It was a while before I realized that the person screaming was me. Tears blurred my vision. Mucus dripped from my nose. I struggled to breathe.

After some interminable time I finally stood and walked down to the gate to comfort the wife and daughter of my teacher. I could not look at his torn and shredded remains. And who would comfort me?

Do you see now how my story is the story of all our people? I lost my teacher that day. The assassins gunned him down without provocation or pretext. And my loss, the loss of my mentor, was also the loss of all the children in the school, was also the loss of the Santa Guadalupe ranch, was also the loss of law in our Valley. The assassins were wearing badges and they never even faced a grand jury inquest. Outside of our few homes, it was as if the murder never happened.

Ernestina and her mother remained in that house, but it was a house without men. They are there to this day, *mis nietos queridos*, everybody knows Doña Antonia. The rest of that land became the property of the murdering thief, Sam Lane. The school building is still standing, so well was it constructed, but no child's voice recited an ABC inside the classroom ever again. There was no teacher. And so years went by without any education for the children of San Manuel. Even when the Anglos passed a law requiring all children to go to school, they didn't mean our children. They didn't apply that law to us and they didn't fund schools for our children for many years. They passed child labor laws, too, but they were very specific: they didn't include farm labor; they didn't include us.

My education stopped that very day. I have read other books, but I never learned any physics. My mathematics stopped at geometry. I will tell you what I *have* learned, though. I learned that Satan is a *gabacho*. I learned that – here in Texas – *he* is the law. And I learned that, however much God may love us, Satan hates us even more.

Ranger Captain Ransom was shot to death a few years later. Satan? He is still here.

Littleton, Alabama
1911

The steel car accelerated down the track into the darkness. Down, down, and still down, with the only light flickering from the carbide headlamps some of the other convicts had lit on their canvas caps. Nobody spoke; at least nobody that Jimmy Fike could hear over the clack of the wheels on the rails, the banging of the car on its axles, the rattle of the shackles on their ankles, the clatter of the chains connecting the men's shackles one to another. Jimmy struggled to maintain his poise but finally, overcome with a horrified awe as they descended still deeper into the earth, he said, to nobody in particular, "Where the hell are they sending us?"

"You got that exactly right," said a voice inches from his ear. It was the man the others called Pap. Jimmy hadn't realized anybody could hear him, but they were piled into this coal car like fish in a can and the chains didn't leave much space between them, either. "Ofay saving money," Pap continued. "He sending you directly to hell without the cost nor the bother of a hanging."

Jimmy did not answer and he refrained from the shiver he felt: both at the cool damp of the underground air as the coal car slowed to a stop, and at the other man's macabre words. In his nineteen years on earth he had never given much thought to what an ant colony looked like from the inside. Now, as he looked around the little shafts and tunnels and rooms leading away from the end of the track, he thought maybe he knew. He said nothing to Pap, though. Who knew what kind of man he was and what he would make of a show of weakness from Jimmy. Somebody pulled the pin on the u-bolt holding the car door shut and the prisoners spilled out on the wet, rocky floor.

"You're with me, fish," said Pap. Jimmy was reluctant, but he had little choice about it. The men were, after all, chained together. Pap began crawling through an entry that seemed too small for a possum and Jimmy followed.

"They keep us chained down here, too?" he asked. "Where they afraid we'll run to?"

"Even chained there's runaways down here," answered Pap, wriggling through the tiny space. "Disappear down an unused shaft and nobody ever finds them."

This was hard to credit as anything but a ghost story to scare the new convicts, so Jimmy didn't respond at all. He shivered a little, though, at the thought of emaciated ghosts haunting the mine.

"You don't believe me," said Pap, reading Jimmy's mind. "Boy, you will not live to see the light of a day other than Sunday. Men die from falling rock or they die from choke damp. They die from shackle poison or they die from consumption. But they all die."

Jimmy knew what consumption was and he could easily imagine being crushed here by falling rock. But choke damp? Shackle poison? He was not going to let this Pap see him frightened or ignorant. He was not going to ask for an explanation.

"Right here," said Pap. Right here? They had emerged from the tiny tunnel and were now lying side-by-side in a space just about long enough and wide enough for them but not even as tall as the pick handles were long. *What* was "right here"? Pap continued, "That there is the coal," and he gestured with his pick. "We start breaking it off like this," and, incredibly, he began chopping at the rock with the pick, swinging in a short horizontal motion while lying on his side.

Jimmy Fike could plow a field behind a team of bad-tempered mules. He could chop cotton with a hoe, or a tree with an axe. He could dig a ditch with a shovel, swing a hammer or a pick. He had learned all those skills from his daddy and he had worked from the time he could walk. But he had never imagined using a pick in an underground room so small that he couldn't stand. Forget stand: he couldn't even sit up in this room. Had the prison guards partnered him with an insane man? Pap just warned, "You better get swinging that pick, boy. You don't want to find out what they have for you if you don't make your weight." So he did.

It was only a few weeks since Jimmy left his home in Oakmulgee. There was nothing there for him. When Jimmy was a little boy his daddy owned his own place. They had a few hogs; planted corn and greens and beans; and hunted the woods for deer. They even put in a few acres of cotton every year that they could sell for cash to spend in the store. But before Jimmy's thirteenth birthday a white man named Cosby stole his daddy's land. Jimmy didn't really know how, but he had heard his parents talking about a bank loan, a corrupt judge, and court costs. They hadn't been thrown out of their house, though. Daddy just had to pay rent now, on his own farm, to the thief that took it. And Cosby made them plant every square inch in cotton, *his* cotton, cotton that hungry children couldn't eat and that Daddy couldn't sell because the cotton factors and gin operators were all Cosby's friends. It wasn't a life that Jimmy wanted to follow his daddy into. Maybe it was Jimmy getting bigger, but it looked like his daddy was getting smaller year by year after he lost his farm.

And that wasn't the only thing that made Oakmulgee seem hollow. Up to the age of twelve, Jimmy went to school every day at Mt. Olive Church. At least he went every day that Daddy didn't need his help in the field. But then there was no more school, and not just because Jimmy had gotten too old. No, Perry County stopped giving money to the school and without that there was no money for a teacher. All the young chaps stopped going, too. No learning their figures so they could argue with the white men, said Pastor Mosely. No learning to read the word of God. But after lots of talk, nobody had an answer to the problem and the school remained shut.

Then even the Oakmulgee Post Office closed. Daddy said the white men in Montgomery didn't want a colored postmaster. It was a responsible federal job and it paid well and there were no white folks in Oakmulgee to take it. Hell, there wasn't but one white for every four colored in the whole Perry County. But that didn't mean the whites were going to let a Black man have a decent job. After that P.O. closed, though, Jimmy noticed families start to leave. Most said they were going to Birmingham, but a few talked about Chicago. A colored man could make a living there, they said. And Jimmy started to think about how he could get there himself.

His daddy didn't want to hear anything about it. Daddy had empty dreams about buying his farm back. How? They were getting deeper into debt to Cosby with every cheating settlement for every harvest. When Jimmy pressed him for details, Daddy just shouted at him: about Jimmy's responsibilities to the family, about Jimmy's obligations to him. "What do I owe you, old man?" he asked angrily one day, shortly after he turned nineteen.

Daddy stood up with an ash-wood plow tongue in his hand and asked, "Boy, you think you're man enough that I won't whoop you? If you do, then get out of my house."

And that is exactly what Jimmy Fike did. As he walked to the county seat in Marion he calmed down, but did not change his mind. It felt like leaving was exactly what he needed to do. Daddy's harsh words had just made it easier. Once he was settled and had his own place outside Perry County he could send for Daddy and them. The thought satisfied him.

Jimmy had been to Marion before, but they had always traveled by wagon. The walk was longer than he thought, so he slept in Cleveland Mills on the way, in the woods near the church. By the time he arrived in the county seat it was late the next morning and he was hungry, so he went to visit the home of a girl he knew there, Janie Williams.

She answered the door with a smile, but didn't move to let him in, asking instead, "Jimmy Fike, why you look like you slept in them clothes?"

"Well, good day to you, too, gal!" he answered, hoping to shame her into a more hospitable reception.

It worked. "Come on in, Jimmy," she said, stepping aside. "Let me get you some bacon and biscuits and you can clean yourself up."

Over lunch they caught up on mutual acquaintances: who was doing what, who was doing who, and – most interesting to Jimmy – who had left Perry County. "How are you going to get a train ticket?" asked Janie.

"I just know I'll figure something out," he said. "I think I'll go over to the depot this afternoon, keep my eyes open, and work out a plan. Thank you *so* much for this meal. It means *everything*. I don't want to impose too much but do you think I could stay here with you tonight? Maybe a few nights?"

Janie put an angry look of mock exasperation on her face. "Why, Jimmy Fike, do you take me for a woman of low repute?"

He started to fumble for an apology before realizing that she was joking. "Thank you, Janie. Thank you for being a friend. Don't think I'll forget you when I'm settled in the city and start making a way for myself in the world."

"I'ma hold you to that," she said, and then shared another dimpled smile.

He helped her clean up the kitchen before leaving for the Gulf, Mobile and Northern depot on Washington Street, promising first to be back in time for dinner. There was no sign of any train, neither arriving nor departing, but as Jimmy studied the schedule posted over the door he noticed a little knot of men a short way up the tracks near a red brick tool shed. He didn't recognize any of the faces, but he walked over to introduce himself and find out what he could about getting a train out.

As he got closer Jimmy noticed that the men were mostly young, not far from his own age. They eyed him suspiciously. He didn't want to come across too country, so he refrained from waving and saying his name. He just nodded a hello as if he knew them. A tall, sharp-dressed man stared rudely, then, without removing his cigarette from the corner of his mouth, spat, "Who is *this* country-ass Negro?"

Jimmy Fike was no stranger to bullies, nor to folks who thought living in town – even a small, backward town like Marion – made them superior to the farmers out in the county. He knew how to deal with them, too. He put a smile on his face and continued walking until he was close to his questioner, uncomfortably close. He held his eye contact until the stranger took the cigarette from his mouth and exhaled… turning away from Jimmy's gaze to do it. Then, having made his point, Jimmy answered, as if the man's question had not contained an insult.

"I'm Jimmy Fike. I'm looking for a train out."

"So are we," answered the man, in a milder tone. "I'm Jesse Suther, but they call me Benny. This here's Willie and Burke." He gestured to the other two young men and each nodded in turn. "No trains today. We're just enjoying a game of chance." He opened his left hand to display a pair of dice. "Would you care to join us?"

No, Jimmy would not care to join them. He didn't know them, didn't want to show them the pittance of cash he was carrying, didn't want to risk losing it to them: chance, cheating, or strong-arm didn't matter. He was no rube. He just said, "I'll watch for a while," which carried the possibility that he might join later.

Jesse shrugged, took a long draw on his cigarette, and then switched the dice to his right hand. He rolled, got ready to shoot, and then froze. As did they all. Because behind them they heard a voice telling them all to do just that. And appearing from both directions in which they looked to run came armed white men, pistols drawn. Looking behind them, to the source of the order, they saw a third white man: husky, mustached, mid-forties, in a nicely-tailored, blue three-piece suit and a big, black J.B. Stetson beaver fedora. His silver Smith and Wesson .44 was still in its holster on his hip. Jimmy Fike knew him by face, but the Stetson and the .44 caliber revolver would have been enough to identify Perry County Sheriff C.W. Cox.

The man called Burke tried to run around the side of the tool shed they were caught up against, but one of the deputies clubbed him to the ground with his pistol. None of the others moved. Jimmy just hoped he could survive the next five minutes alive. After that… well, he was committing no crime by visiting a friend in town. He hadn't boarded a train. He hadn't gambled. This might turn out okay. He said nothing, though. Any explanation he offered was just going to be treated as backtalk.

Sheriff Cox had nothing to say to them after his initial instruction to freeze. He did, however, have more to say to his deputies. "Chain these cigarette dudes and lock them up. We'll let Judge Prestridge sort them out in the morning." And once he saw that his deputies had secured the four men, he walked away without another word.

Cigarette dudes? wondered Jimmy Fike, but he said nothing. He badly wanted to ask one of the deputies if there was a way he could let Janie Williams know that he would not make it to dinner, but he knew better than to say anything about that, either. He was shackled to one end of the chain holding them all together, so when one of the deputies kicked him in the ass and said, "Move, nigger!" he understood that to mean lead the coffle back up Washington Street to the red brick county courthouse. Slaves built it for the white men before the Civil War, Jimmy knew. His kin. On the way they passed plenty of local Black folk, all of whom looked away. No way to get a message to Janie, but maybe one of them would recognize him and let her know. They passed by the Military Institute and Judson College, two more places that thought the Civil War had never been fought, or – perhaps – that Alabama had actually won.

But they didn't stop at the courthouse. They kept walking. A block past they made a right on Green and then a left on Pickens. There was another brick building, one that Jimmy hadn't seen before. It was the county jail. Their shackles and chains were not removed. Nobody took their names or their photos or their fingerprints. They were simply brought to a cell where they were locked in together. The young man named Burke yelled for food for about an hour, but they were not fed. They did not even see a deputy again that day.

It was late the following morning when they were led, still in chains, back to the courthouse. The only defendants in the room were Jimmy, "Benny", Willie, and Burke. There were no spectators. Sheriff Cox quickly dismissed the two deputies who brought them over. In a few minutes, with no ceremony, no "All rise", they were joined by an old, bald-headed white man in a black robe. "Howdy, Judge," said Sheriff Cox. Judge Prestridge, then. Jimmie felt that soon he would have the opportunity to clarify everything and get himself free.

The conversation, however, did not turn to criminal charges. Instead, Sheriff Cox said, "I got a telephone call from T.C.I., yesterday. The miners' union caught them by surprise and they're short of hands. Said they'll pay $20 each."

Judge Prestridge seemed to be especially interested in that number. "$20?" he asked.

"$20," repeated the sheriff.

"How much do these boys have in their pockets?" asked the judge.

The sheriff shrugged and shook his head. "We didn't bother to search them."

"Okay, you," the judge said, pointing to Jesse Suther and looking for the first time at the four young men in chains. "What's your name, boy?"

"Abraham Washington," said Suther.

Jimmy Fike quickly brought his double take under control. If either of the white men noticed, though, they showed no sign. Instead, Judge Prestridge banged his gavel and said, "Abraham Washington, I find you guilty of vagrancy. Can you pay a $5 fine?"

Suther smirked a little and took off his shoe. Out dropped a gold Indian head $10 piece. He shuffled as far as his chain would allow and placed it on the rail in front of the judge's podium. The judge nodded and pointed to the sheriff who reached into his pocket and took out five silver dollars as change. The judge then added, "Court costs, $10. Jail room and board, $2. Deputy costs, $5. Have you another $12?"

Jesse Suther lost his smile. Sheriff Cox pocketed the gold and silver coins. The judge banged his gavel again and said, "Court costs, five months. Jail room and board, two months. Deputy costs, five months. I hereby sentence you to one year of hard labor to be served at a venue of the sheriff's choosing. Next case!"

Jimmy Fike had attended elementary school for parts of eight years and he knew that what he had just witnessed was not a trial. Where was the evidence? Where was the testimony? Where was the deliberation? Where, for God's sake, were the attorneys? But the judge was pointing to him now and it was time to speak up. "Your honor," he said, "I am Jimmy Fike. My daddy is Henry Fike from Oakmulgee and we work for Mr. John Cosby."

The judge stopped his gavel, which had been on its way down again. He turned to Sheriff Cox. "Is that old J.P. Cosby, who has the place on Dutch Creek?"

The sheriff shrugged again. "I can find out."

"Do that," said the judge. "We both have to be re-elected. Can't do that if we're stealing folks's niggers." Then he turned back to Jimmy Fike, banged his gavel and said, "Case postponed until such time as we can figure out if anybody gives a shit about you."

Jimmy Fike's shackles were separated from the chain and he was returned to his cell at the jail. He never saw Jesse Suther or the others again.

Over the next few days he saw more young Black men come and go from the jail. "Young men" was an exaggeration really; most of them were no more than school age. Nobody was ever fed. He didn't know what that meant for them, but the bacon and biscuits from Janie Williams's griddle grew more and more delicious in his memory. He wondered if that would be his last meal on earth.

One day he was finally chained together with a group of five men who had been brought in the previous night and marched over to the courthouse. When the judge walked in, Sheriff Cox pointed to Jimmy and said, "This here is the nigger who says he belongs to J.P."

Judge Prestridge snorted. "I finally caught him on the telephone yesterday," he said. "Cosby said Jimmy Fike walked out on his daddy, talking about taking a train to Birmingham." He laughed again and turned to Jimmy, "Boy, this must be your lucky day. I find you guilty of gambling, disorderly conduct and resisting arrest. I hereby sentence you to 18 months hard labor. I also sentence you to six months for making us hold you so many days and for the cost of that telephone call. Twenty-four months to be served in the mines of the Tennessee Coal and Iron Company, so you will be going to Birmingham after all. We'll throw in the train ride for free." And down came the gavel.

Jimmy never exactly saw Birmingham. He was transported in an iron cage with the other five men who had been with him that morning at the Marion County Courthouse. And here he was, still chained, scratching with an iron pickaxe at a twenty-four inch coalface in a three-foot-high chamber with a man called Pap who seemed to take pleasure in forecasting Jimmy's death.

Later that day he found out what Pap meant when he warned about not "making weight." They loaded all the coal they dug into a steel car like the one they rode down in. At the end of their shift, hours after Jimmy had concluded that another minute of work would kill him, they pushed their car to a place where other miners' had their own cars. They hitched them together and rode them back up to the mine entrance. There, another convict pushed each car onto a scale and called out a number to the watching guards. "Four tons!" "Four-and-a-half tons!" "Five tons!"

But when a slight, sickly-looking convict got a weight of three tons, two guards stretched him over his car. A third guard pulled down a three-foot-long strip of leather, wide as a razor strop, and tied to what looked like a shovel handle. Then he set about whipping the man. He whipped him as if he were trying to separate one part of his body from the other. He whipped him as if his place in heaven was dependent on putting somebody else in hell. The echoes of the prisoner's shrieks reverberated from distant reaches of the mine shaft. And the guard didn't stop. Nine. Ten. The flesh under the surface was a different color than the skin, much lighter. At first the blood seeped out, but then it began to flow in earnest. Sixteen. Seventeen. The guard, apparently too tired to continue the beating himself, now passed the strap to another. Twenty. Twenty-one. The slight prisoner had stopped shrieking and lost consciousness. Twenty-four. Twenty-five. The two men holding the unconscious convict dropped him right where he was. He was not the only man whipped, either. Of the thirty-or-so miners at that weigh station, eight were flogged into bloody insensibility. Jimmy only escaped because it was his first day.

He learned over the next few days that the beatings were intended to increase tonnage. He learned that you couldn't get to a weight and be satisfied. Once the guards knew you could make that weight, they expected more. And then more. The quality of the seam you were digging didn't matter, either. The steel mills of Birmingham needed coal.

Jimmy learned what choke damp was one day when four men never returned from a chamber on his level. When he was sent in to pull their bodies out, he found them looking as peaceful as if they had simply gone to sleep. There had apparently been no warning because he guessed if there had been, they would have left immediately. He once experienced the rotten-egg smell of poisonous stink damp, too, and he did not stay to experiment.

He learned about shackle poison directly. The shackles made sores on his ankles. Those sores never healed and the swelling seemed to spread up his leg and down to his feet. In the bunkhouse he saw prisoners with more advanced sores. They seemed constantly to be either burning with fever or shivering with cold. Several died, and Jimmy had no idea whether they were returned to their families or whether there was a cemetery there at the mine.

He learned about rock falls early. The ceilings collapsed somewhere at least once a week. If the bosses thought there was still more good coal in the direction of a fall, they sent you in to clear the rock and the bodies. If they thought the seam was played out, though, that was where the men remained, buried deep under the surface. No prayer. No final words. Pap had not been trying to scare him with ghost stories. This truly was hell.

Jimmy even learned what Sheriff Cox and Judge Prestridge had been talking about when they discussed a mine "union." The revelation began one morning, as the convicts were being marched from their quarters to the shaft entrance before dawn. Jimmy saw a crowd of men, both Black and white, standing on the other side of the fence shouting. It was hard to hear what exactly they were saying, but they were really angry and he made out that they were calling him and the other convicts "scabs."

He turned to Pap and started to ask for an explanation, but Pap only signaled him to be silent. He had a rule about not speaking in places where the guards could hear. It was only later, when they were a quarter-mile underground and squatting in a five-foot-high chamber with two others, that Pap began to answer his unspoken question.

"That's the union."

The word triggered something in Jimmy's memory, but he didn't place it immediately.

Pap went on. "The miners got together to get a higher pay. The company wouldn't give it to them so they walked out."

Jimmy couldn't have been any more astonished if Pap had told him that all the white folks had magically turned into dry leaves and floated away on a breeze. There were miners who were paid for this work? There were miners who could walk off when they wanted? There were people who went underground by choice? There were – and this he struggled to formulate even as a thought – white men working alongside Black men in these mines? He was struck mute by these revelations.

But if Jimmy was too awestruck to comment, Riley and Thane were not. They were the other two men working the coalface with Jimmy and Pap. They were both from some place called Letohatchie in Lowndes County. Jimmy had never worked out if they were brothers or not. Like him they weren't yet out of their teens. Like him they had been sent up here without trials, for the crime of not having a white man to speak for them. And it was this that set Riley off about Pap's terse explanation of what they had all seen aboveground.

"What kind of fool Negro trust an ofay to have his back?"

"My question!" agreed Thane.

"I can't speak on that," chuckled Pap. "Maybe one of you men of the world has experience working freely alongside white men?"

Pap's gallows humor must have escaped them, because it drew no reply. But there was more puzzling them about what they had seen and heard than just Black and white working together. "Why they yelling 'scab' at us?" asked Thane.

Pap had an answer for this, too. "Walking off a job only hurt the boss if everybody go. If you don't stand up with your brothers, you're a scab."

This revelation shocked Jimmy back into the ability to speak. "They think we *choose* to be here?" he blurted.

The thought was so ridiculous it got the other three men over their anger and incredulity. They all began laughing. If anybody could figure a way to walk off this job, everybody would have done it on his first day. There was not much use in thinking about the meaning of this union. Still, Jimmy kept trying to remember what he had heard about it. *What was it the sheriff had said to Judge Prestridge?*

The shackle poison on Jimmy's ankles got worse. He could see streaks spreading up his legs toward his crotch, and they were tender and painful to touch. He was often weak and there were days that he could not make weight, so that meant whippings. It seemed like he couldn't heal from those whippings, either. Sometimes he shivered with cold and sometimes he thought he was burning up. The scariest thing, though, was that no matter how much water he drank he seemed to have lost the ability to piss. Was Pap right? Was shackle poison going to get him before he finished his prison sentence?

No, it would not. Nor would choke damp, nor stink damp, nor rock falls, nor tuberculosis. It was fire damp, methane. One second all the prisoners were working. The next second a spark somewhere – miner's lamp? steel wheel on steel track? shovel against rock? – set off an explosion of the methane gas that develops in pockets around a coal seam. The fireball spread through every corner of the mine. Some prisoners were blown apart by the shock wave. Others were incinerated by the flames. Some were just asphyxiated when the fire robbed every nook and cranny of its oxygen. And then there were those who were killed in the minutes after the fire by afterdamp, carbon monoxide poisoning.

Which took Jimmy Fike? Was his body blown to atoms by the explosion itself? Was he vaporized in the intense heat of the fire? Perhaps he simply fell peacefully asleep where he was working, as the fire elsewhere in the mine invisibly took his breath away. Maybe he choked, violently gasping for air. Who knows? His body was never recovered. His "grave" is the chamber where he and Pap were working that day, in a section of the mine the Tennessee Coal and Iron Company decided was insufficiently productive to bring back into use. One hundred twenty-eight prisoners died in the fire: boys as young as thirteen, men as old as twenty-eight. There were no marked graves for those who were removed. Their bodies were tossed into the mine waste.

Over the years Janie Williams tried to forget about Jimmy Fike, but she could never get over her suspicion of men. She saw how they could eat a big breakfast, promise to return, and then forget all about you. Jimmy's daddy never forgave his son for abandoning him, either, although he held out hope until his dying day that Jimmy would return home so that he could have the satisfaction of cursing him and refusing to accept him back. Sheriff Cox was able to use the supplementary income he earned by selling young men to the steel company to send his own sons to Princeton University. One became a US Senator, the other a partner in an Atlanta law firm. And Judge Prestridge? He gained such a reputation for fairness and for knowledge of the law that he was appointed to the United States Fifth Circuit Court of Appeals in New Orleans. There is an endowed chair in legal ethics named after him at the University of Alabama School of Law in Tuscaloosa.

Transcript of oral history tape recording of John Howat Walker, April 12

It's good to see you again. No, I am okay. Yes, I am enjoying telling you these stories. It does. It makes me feel like I matter again, like time hasn't passed me by. Listen, is there any chance we can get out of here today? I'm tired of looking at these same four walls every day. Sure, of course I can walk, but we could take a cab, too, right? I don't know, over where you're staying? I bet you're over on Broadway, at the Stilwell. That place used to be a big deal around here. Teddy Roosevelt spoke from that balcony. So did Eugene Debs. Clarence Darrow, too!

Susan B. Anthony? I don't remember. I guess if you say so. You're the historian, right?

To eat? I would love to go to Jim's. You haven't been yet? It's close, about ten blocks up from the Stilwell. It opened before the second war. Maybe 12 years?

No, not like the Stillwell. But it's good. You go there for the steaks and the onion rings. I haven't been there since I moved into this old folks' home. I would really like it. Okay, after we talk.

District 20? I will try to tell that story. I didn't get down there to Birmingham that much. Not even when I was working mostly for the international. I went to Alabama back in… it must have been '08, because T.C.I. had already been taken over by J.P. Morgan and Judge Gary.

I know you want to hear about Mother Jones. I don't know no other way to tell this. You're not going to understand what I say unless you hear the story. I will explain what's T.C.I. and what it has to do with the panic of '07. Please just give me a chance to tell it my way. I think you'll understand and you'll still have time to find out what an onion ring is. You'll see.

Mother Jones was a lady. She was known for her straight talk, but she didn't talk as harsh as I do. I'm going to start with the panic. '07 wasn't anywhere near as bad as the big depression of the '30's. It didn't last as long. It didn't change the country as much. But it was bad in its time. I think people forgot how much things did change because of that panic. It started in the Wall Street banks. They were playing games in the stock market. Now, I couldn't explain exactly *how* it began. I wasn't paying close attention to what those plutes were doing with the money they stole from us workers.

Tell the truth, I didn't quite understand it. It was something to do with copper. Them metal miners were in a different union than us. WFM. The banks that backed the copper jobbers failed. That started a run on all them New York banks. They couldn't come up with the cash to give every depositor who wanted their money. Like that movie with Jimmy Stewart. Except these were the evil Lionel Barrymore kind of bankers.

You don't know what I'm talking about? It was just a few years ago, not before your time. It was called, um, "It's a Wonderful Life," that's what it was called.

Well, of course you didn't see it. Nobody in your social class did.

What do I mean? The professors and lawyers and town merchants, like you. That movie lost a ton of money. The FBI didn't want anybody to see it. It showed how bankers like Lionel Barrymore are all thieves. They said it was Red propaganda.

No, I am not making this up. Nobody will ever see that movie now.

What was I talking about? Right, the Panic of '07. J.P. Morgan stopped that bank run. But he made the other bankers agree to a deal with him first. Before he used his money to help them. Turned out it wasn't just a couple of banks speculating in copper mines. It was *all* the banks. They were speculating in all kind of stocks. One of them held lots of T.C.I. stock. T.C.I. That was the Tennessee Coal and Iron Company. They owned most of the steel mills in Alabama. They owned the mines, too. Owned the iron and coal mines in Alabama and Tennessee. The mines that fed the mills. So this bank was borrowing from other banks. Their only collateral was all this T.C.I. stock, get it? Morgan and his friends Frick and Gary already owned U.S. Steel. They had more than half the steel production in America. They took T.C.I. stock for the money to save that bank. So after the Panic, they owned T.C.I., too. Instead of District 20 going up against the Birmingham, Alabama bosses, they were going up against J.P. Morgan. Miners used to call the Birmingham operators the "big mules." But J.P. Morgan? Well, he was as big a mule as you could find.

That's what I mean. When I got to Birmingham in '08 the UMW found itself up against a new enemy. T.C.I. was never a friend to the miners. At least T.C.I. had a union contract, though. After 1907, U.S. Steel took over. Then T.C.I. said they would not make contracts with any union. Hell, after '07 T.C.I. said they would not allow any man who was a member of a union to even work in any of their mines. No, nor their mills, neither. They called that an American Plan. We call it a yellow-dog contract.

Why? Well, because you would have to be a yellow dog to agree to it. But I'm getting ahead of myself, aren't I?

Organizing was always harder in District 20 because you had to have two local unions. Two sets of officers. Two unions for every workplace instead of one. Sure, the white men couldn't be in the same local with the colored. Even if they were working in the same pit.

No, that was their custom down there. Anyway it was against the law for them to meet together.

What's that? Well, yeah, a lot of things we did were against the bosses' laws. But you know this wasn't the same. Well, it just wasn't. And, I'll tell you another thing, they had prison crews in all them mines and they were *all* colored and none of them prisoners were in the union. How is a man supposed to get his rights when he's competing with prisoners?

Oh, yeah, the other colored? They *all* joined the union. Yes, they were as strong union men as anybody. Stronger, really.

I do, I get what you're saying. I guess it's not the way I thought about it then. Like I said before, I think that color prejudice rubbed off on me, too.

Mother Jones? No, she wasn't immune from that either. I remember her imitating the way they talk. I also remember her telling how the prison system was corrupt in West Virginia, because they would lock a white boy in the same cell with Negroes. I remember her telling about the shame of the metal miners in the Rockies where the U.S. Army sent Negro soldiers to break their strike and lock them up. I'm thinking about this now and seeing that color prejudice was a poison that infected our union. No, I didn't see that then, not at all. Neither did Mother Jones. At least not that I can remember.

I'll tell the story anyway. And, no, I don't mind the interruptions so much. They help me understand better. Even if I was there and you weren't. Okay, T.C.I. said they wouldn't negotiate with the union. So everybody walked out. No, the miners, not the prisoners. They had shackles on their legs. And on their necks. They couldn't go anywhere. Of course, no sooner do they go out on strike than the operators start bringing in more prisoners to replace them. They just sent out word to every county in the state of Alabama. They said they needed hands.

Before you could turn around the bosses brought in train-carloads of colored prisoners to Birmingham.

Crime wave? I don't get your question. They were just sending more prisoners to scab on the union. Why would I know what they were locked up for?

The newspapers down there were full of how we were preaching social equality. Because Black and white were striking together. I ask you, how are you supposed to get a contract if you don't work together? That's why we have Italians and Hunkies in the union. That's why we print our newspaper in Italian and Hunkie and English, too. If we don't stand together we'll never get a contract. But that doesn't mean we're for equality.

What's wrong with equality, you ask? I guess it just seemed like that's what they were accusing us of.

You're right. This story is hard to tell without seeing how many ways I fell for that color prejudice. And I guess I still do.

And that reminds me. You keep asking about women's rights. Mother Jones always said that what matters is *workers'* rights. They had a newspaper writer down there. Her name was Dolly Dalrymple. She was for the ladies' right to vote. She kept saying that she was ashamed to see Black miners calling white miners "brother." In the union this was always what we called our fellow workers. She said it made her ashamed. She said it was a scandal that the miners' union ladies auxiliary let colored women participate. So what do you say about that? She's the kind of union-busting plute that supported ladies voting back then.

And I guess you heard of Booker T. Washington. He was the biggest colored man in the United States back in those days. He was like the Jackie Robinson of his time.

Why are you laughing? I'm a baseball fan, sure. I follow the Pittsburg Browns. I used to be able to go to JayCee Park to watch their games, too. Now it's a little too tiring for me to sit in the stands for nine innings. We almost made the championship last year. I was there three years ago, the day they lost game four to the Independence, Missouri Yankees. I was tired afterwards. I felt bad that we lost. But it was good to be at the park, so I remember that as a good day. You know Don Gutteridge is from here?

208

Of course you don't. He only went to the World Series with the big club, the St. Louis Browns.

You don't follow baseball? Your loss. How did I get onto baseball anyway?

Booker T. Washington? He didn't play baseball, leastways not that I remember. I think you lost me.

Oh. He hated the unions. Booker T. Washington always said that the colored man should be friends with the operators. He certainly was, himself. I don't know that the everyday colored man got the same opportunities that he did.

My point? I don't remember. Wait, I think it was… oh yeah, the white bankers and white newspaper editorial writers were always telling us white men that we had no business being in unions. Just like that, the big Negroes told the colored people the same thing.

You don't see the difference? I give up. Why do I feel so tired today? What was I talking about?

Right, District 20.

The truth is that most members in District 20 were colored. Are you happy now? But so were all those scab convicts, so think about what that means before you start throwing this in my face. No, the district president and International Rep were never colored, they were always white. The *vice* president was always colored.

Why? Well, isn't it obvious? If we just had an election like everywhere else every district officer would have been colored because they were most of the members. You still don't see? If the officers were all colored then no white man would join. They would have said it was a colored union!

Sorry, but that's what they would have said, you see? The colored understood that, that's why they always elected a white president for the district, but they always got a colored vice president. It was like a gentleman's agreement. Otherwise they couldn't have had a union at all. Otherwise the steel companies would have won by dividing everybody!

Anyway, there's more to the District 20 story than just the whites and the colored. They had all kinds of special tricks down there. They liked to pretend every miner was an independent businessman instead of a company employee. That way there was no call to agree on a wage, only on a tonnage rate.

You're right, they had that tonnage rate trick everywhere else in coal country, too. But in Alabama the miners were allowed to hire their own helpers for a lower rate. Hell, they were encouraged to do it. That way a miner and his own buddy could fight each other instead of fighting the operators. The operators were laughing all the way to the bank about it. Like everywhere the operators didn't pay for dead work, like timbering. They only paid for tons of coal. But there in Alabama they said you were operating your own business. So it was up to you what kind of safety precautions you chose to take or not! And that weren't all. You had to *bribe* the foreman for a good coalface to work at. You didn't pay him, you'd find yourself lying on your side trying to swing a pick in a 30-inch seam. You had to bribe the foreman to get a coal car sent to where you were. You didn't, you'd find yourself wasting time waiting instead of loading coal.

Oh, they had all kind of tricks with that contracting system. But it didn't take much to see that you weren't nothing but an employee. Try to take a day off to be with your family like any other businessman. They'd remind you real quick that they were the bosses. You better be there six days a week or lose that job! Try to find a better price on your tools. Try to buy somewhere else instead of paying their prices at their store. You'd find out that the market applied to them and not you! Hell, try to find a better price on groceries! Or a better place to live than their company shacks! If West Virginia was Russia, then I don't know what Alabama was. That's why you found miners escaping to West Virginia from the Birmingham district like they found freedom.

But none of that was the worst. The worst was the convicts. See a convict would undercut a free man's wage every time! Choice? Just look at the facts. The operators could drive the convicts hard enough to dig and load coal for 80¢ a ton. No free man could compete with that. Just the threat of it was enough to hold free men's wages down. And whipping? They whipped the convicts every single day if they didn't make their target. Whether it was five tons a day or four tons a day or whatever their target was. They whipped them with a razor strop on the end of a rope! They whipped them if they didn't "Yes, sir" and "No, sir" quick enough to please them. No free man would allow a foreman to whip him for nothing. The convicts did! Old Man DeBardeleben, he was one of the big mules down there. He had his own coal company. He said they wanted to keep the miners competing with convicts to keep costs down. He said it right in the newspaper for anyone to see.

Of course we thought it was the convicts' fault. Who else's fault was it? They were the ones making it hard to earn a living wage. They were the ones making it hard to organize the union.

No, I do understand what you're saying. It just wasn't the way we thought about it then.

Then the operators decided they wouldn't allow a union at all. That's when the men organized and walked out. That was July, 1908, after U.S. Steel took over the Tennessee Coal and Iron Company. The men struck all the mines down there, not just T.C.I. All the operators had got together and decided to break the union. Those operators were surprised, too. Even though they got every county sheriff to send them more convicts they couldn't replace the striking miners. And they couldn't break the unity of the strike. They tried to starve us, too. Old Man Louis Pizitz, he was the only businessman who would even sell to us. He helped the strikers stay together because he was still doing business with us after the strike started. That's right. He owned a big dry goods store on Second Avenue. He kept sending the miners food when everybody else cut them off. That's why Sheriff Higdon said a Jew is a nigger turned inside out.

I know you don't like that word. I didn't say it, he did!

Well, maybe it will help you understand the kind of thinking we were dealing with down there.

The companies did what they always did to break the strike. They brought in gun thugs from out of state. They paid the newspapers to write editorials attacking us. They threatened to call up the Alabama National Guard. That was the same kind of thing we had to face everywhere in coal country. But this was Alabama, so the operators had their own special Alabama ways of breaking that strike, too. The newspapers went crazy when they saw colored men embracing white men in front of women and children. Oh, God, they didn't like that. No. They kept reporting about colored and white marching together in parades and picket lines. The mine guards lynched Bill Miller. He was a local president in the district. And Jake Burrows, who was another union leader. That's right. They arrested them on some phony-baloney dynamite charges. Then they pulled them out of jail and hung them from trees. The governor accused the union of standing for social equality, which in Alabama in those days was a real serious accusation. Come to think of it, that's a serious accusation in Alabama today, too, isn't it? But let me tell you the story.

The coal operators sent a delegation of Birmingham business leaders. You know, store owners and bankers and all them. They met with the District 20 strike committee in August. The big mules were getting scared. They never thought the miners would stick together that long. They thought they would be able to break the strike with their convicts. And it wasn't working, because the union was holding strong. But they didn't offer a negotiation, no. They just came with a threat. Those businessmen told us that if the strike didn't end, they would make Springfield, Illinois look like six cents.

Now that doesn't mean anything to you anymore today. Back then we knew exactly what it meant. Springfield was a coal town. The headquarters for District 12. That same week there was a race riot in Springfield. The mob broke into a pawn shop. They stole guns and ammunition. They burned down a restaurant. They burned down the restaurant owner's car. They went and they burned down the whole colored neighborhood of Springfield. When the firemen came, they cut their hoses so they couldn't put the fire out. They shot a bunch of them Negroes dead, too. So when our union officers heard them mention Springfield they knew exactly what those respectable people were threatening them with. They were threatening them with shootings, beatings and burnings. All those respectable business and professional people were threatening union coal miners with mass murder. But the coal miners didn't give in. They stood up anyway.

Finally the governor called up the Alabama National Guard. Now they were jailing the strikers by the dozens instead of a few at a time. They were burning down our tents. That's what it took for them to break our strike. It was ten long years before we were able to start organizing in that district again. So J.P. Morgan and Judge Gary got what they wanted, which was no union at all in Alabama.

No, I told you, Mother Jones didn't spend much time down there.

No, I don't think she used that word you don't like. She did call them darkies, though, and she did accents and everything, you know, like "I done talked to the Lawd" and all that. And she didn't like Chinamen, neither, didn't want them in the country. But she was never down on the colored. She said they knew the value of freedom because their daddies had to run from the bloodhounds. But now that I'm thinking about it, when she was getting old and couldn't travel no more, she asked that when she died she be buried in the Union Miners Cemetery in Mt. Olive, Illinois. And she was 100-years old when she died and that's where they buried her, in District 12. And that is a white district in the union right up to this day. And the coal miners who died in that strike you made me stop talking about the first day you were here, the Virden strike? Those miners who died when they were shooting at the colored coming from Alabama to Illinois? That's who she's buried next to, so go figure.

You know what? Can we go to Jim's Steak House another day? Thursday is meatloaf day here. Our cook makes a really good meatloaf. It's my favorite meal of the week.

No, why would I be tired? I just really like the meatloaf. We can go another day. I don't want to disappoint you. I know you were looking forward to going out. I know you wanted to try them onion rings. Let's do it another day. But come back, you know?

Yes, I enjoy telling you these stories. And I like thinking about Mother Jones again. It's been a long time.

[Recording ends here.]

Ludlow, Colorado
1914

After gathering his intelligence about Mother Jones in Walsenburg, Joey Quintana waited by the train tracks for a long time. By the time he actually hopped an empty freight car going south it was the next morning. He was disappointed to miss the excitement of Orthodox Easter and thought he would be arriving in the strikers' camp on an especially sleepy Monday morning. When the train slowed for the switches at Delagua Canyon, Joey jumped clear and dropped to the ground amid the clacking of the steel wheels on the tracks, the banging of the cars on their axles and the roar of the steam locomotive. That's why it wasn't until the train was completely away that he began to hear the rattle of machine-gun fire and the steady reports of dozens of rifles. This was not the random sniper fire he had been hearing about. This was a full-scale battle.

Joey pressed himself flat against the dry, scabby ground, then looked to see where the shooting was coming from. In the foothills to the west, on the roads leading up to the mines, he saw several machine gun emplacements. To their north and south, uniformed Guardsmen were shooting at anything they could imagine as a target in the tent city the union had built for the strikers, even shooting at the tents themselves. Closer to Joey's position, armed strikers were returning fire, but there were very few guns and they were either very low on ammunition or extremely disciplined, maybe both. Only when a Guardsman actually stood up in his position did you hear a shot from the workers' side.

Joey also began to discern the sounds of weeping. He noticed one group trapped behind a stone wall. It looked like a few families: a crowd of children of various ages, several women, a couple of men. None of them had guns. The children seemed petrified until one boy suddenly jumped up and ran from the shelter of the wall. He looked to be eleven or twelve years old. He got five steps before his head exploded in a cloud of blood, brains and skull. The other children just cried harder.

The shooting continued for another half hour: steadily from the Guardsmen, less and less frequently from the strikers. Guardsmen were beginning to tentatively move closer to the camp, still keeping low, still seeking cover, but they were drawing less fire. The miners were definitely low on ammunition. Just as it began to look as though the positions of the strikers and their families would soon be overrun, another freight train came through. Using the momentary cover it provided, dozens of men, women and children immediately ran east into the shelter of some low nearby hills. Now it looked as though only a few armed union men were holding their positions in or near the camp, apparently to allow the others to escape.

That was when Joey saw one of the strikers, a Greek with a red bandana around his neck, waving an undershirt as a white flag. The Guardsmen held fire and the miner walked toward them, unarmed. He had both hands in the air, the white undershirt in his left. As the man reached the soldiers, an officer clubbed him to the ground with his rifle butt. Then Joey saw the other soldiers point their rifles and fire. When the smoke cleared, they took turns kicking his lifeless body.

Meanwhile, other Guardsmen were running into the now-unprotected camp. Joey could hear their whoops as they began looting and torching the tents. He saw two soldiers fighting over a bicycle. He saw others stuffing jewelry into their shirts. He saw religious icons and Bibles tossed into a bonfire. Treasured family photographs, children's toys, clothing... all were incinerated. Some kind of cloth banner was dipped into the inferno, then held aloft to the amusement of the arsonists. Soldiers all around the camp pointed and laughed as it burned. They smashed tea sets. They opened and emptied cans of food with their bayonets and ground the contents into the dirt with their boots.

When sunset finally came the plains grew darker, but the scene was still illuminated by burning tent platforms and smaller fires that were fed by what had been – just a few hours before – the possessions of striking coalminers and their families. Even after Joey was finally able to look away from the flames, he still could not shut his ears to the shouting and revelry of the National Guard, demons drunk on their great victory. All through that cold night Joey sat by himself, shivering and hungry, waiting for morning.

Perhaps it was another sunny day elsewhere. There, by the railroad tracks, though, smoke and ash hung over the cinders of the strikers' tent city. The Guardsmen had withdrawn to who knows where. Slowly union families reemerged from their hiding places in the hills to pick over the wreckage for anything that might be left of their little possessions... of their previous lives. Joey went to see if there was any way that he could help.

Twenty or thirty people were frantically pulling away burnt timbers from one particular tent platform, so he went to join in that work. A "hospital cellar" they explained to him. This tent had been given a deep basement so that the midwife could assist mothers in childbirth even when the troopers were taking random potshots at the camp, which had apparently been their entertainment before this last wholesale assault. The people were anxious to save the midwife and some expectant women from this cave. Joey was not optimistic that they would even be able to identify the charred bodies he expected to find.

But Joey was wrong. One by one, weeping rescue workers passed up bodies that showed no sign of burns or even smoke. If anything, they looked as if they were asleep. There had been no fire in that deep pit. No, the fire had raged *above* the basement, sucking out every molecule of oxygen. The people underneath had been protected from flame, heat and smoke. They had simply dropped in their places, asphyxiated. First to be handed up were the children. So many children.

"Frankie!" shouted a man at the sight of one infant.

"Elvira!" screamed a woman as she cradled another in her arms.

They began laying them out in a long, neat row, each one still and perfect as if they were napping. Eventually the men in the basement began the more difficult work of carefully recovering the bodies of grown ups.

"Cedi! My friend! I will never forget you!" By her clothing and hair, the dead woman appeared to Joey to be a southern European, maybe Italian. The woman rushing to her had a strong Welsh accent. A man tried to restrain her from embracing the corpse, but the Welshwoman pushed him roughly aside, then lay in the dirt, her arms wrapped around the body of her departed friend, wailing, her tears wetting her face and that of the dead woman.

"Here is the midwife!" called a voice from below. Joey went with two others and got a grip under the woman's arms. He gently hoisted her up from the pit and carefully set her on the ground.

It was only then that he looked at the woman's face and recognized his sister Piedad. All the blood left his head. He felt a sudden freeze and he began shivering uncontrollably. He pitched face forward into the dirt. How was she here instead of Cañada de los Álamos? Where was Epifanio? How did he not know that she was in a strike camp? How did he not know? How did he not know?

No, this could not be. Of course not. Pia was home in Cañada. Pia *was* home, the definition of home. He looked again at the woman's face to confirm his certainty that this was another stranger, a stranger like Frankie and Cedi and Elvira and the others that he had just laid out on the ground. Why couldn't he see this woman's face? He tried and tried, but he was blinded by an ocean of tears. People nearby were touching him. They were talking to him. What were they saying? Why couldn't he hear them over the roar of horror and grief that deafened him?

For years his faith – his hope for a better world, his proletarian internationalism, his joy in the struggle – carried Joey Quintana through jailings and beatings and hunger. He saw Arizona Rangers massacre two dozen copper miners at Cananea in Mexico, but he carried on because *sin lucha, no hay progreso.* He was in McKees Rocks in Pennsylvania when mounted state troopers rode down a crowd of desperate factory workers, beating twenty-six of them to death with their long wooden clubs, but he knew it was an act of desperation by the bosses, and, indeed, the workers won a wage increase only days later. He understood the evictions and the shootings that the bosses ordered to be the death throes of an evil capitalist system and so he bore them with grace.

But Piedad? Piedad, the healer, the giver of life? Piedad, who had helped so many mothers bring their children into this world? Piedad, his beautiful baby sister? There could be no meaning to this. There could be no appropriate revenge. Killing Rockefeller, who ordered her murder? Not enough. Killing every capitalist? Not enough. Even the birth of a workers' republic would not bring back his sister. Joey shook with sobs and screamed without words. When they saw that he was unresponsive to their words, unaware of their embraces, the others left him – wracked with convulsive grief – on the muddy, bloody ground.

Cañada de los Álamos, New Mexico
1914

Joey Quintana remembered nothing of the trip back to Cañada de los Álamos. Piedad's husband, Epifanio, was near Trinidad attending a union meeting when he got word of Pia's murder. He returned to camp immediately to bring his wife's body home. Epifanio must have brought his temporarily paralyzed brother-in-law, too. Joey barely remembered the wake: the *dolientes* – little girls when he was growing up, now women with husbands and children – counting their rosaries and reciting *"Dios te salve, Maria;"* the brothers of the confraternity keening the drawn-out notes of their chants, *"Salgan, salgan, ánimas de pena"* and *"Considera con desvelo"*; the people coming and going all through the night. He didn't even remember the walk to the *capilla* for the funeral. The rushing noise in his ears would not stop. His vision remained blurred.

The *viejitos* began singing *Adiós, acompañamiento.* "Good-bye, parents. Good-bye, children. Good-by, family. Good-bye, friends. I'm leaving for my true home."

Joey hated this song now just as he had when he was a boy: *Who were these mourners to pretend to say good-bye to themselves? Who were they to pretend they had an idea what their imaginary next life would be?*

When the brotherhood came to the verse about "This world is a delusion" Joey positively bristled. He looked up and saw the *reredos* behind the altar with its carved wooden *bulto* of Christ crucified, and its loving paintings of the Virgin of Guadalupe, the Lady of Sorrows, San José with the Christ child, and some other saints whose identities he couldn't recall. *They were the delusion*, he thought. *This life on earth, with all its suffering and exploitation, is the only life we have. The monopoly capitalists delude us about their thieving system and they delude us about our rewards in the "sweet bye-and-bye."* He wanted to scream at these old men for mocking his sister's senseless death with their superstitions. But he stayed quiet, as he always had during their services.

Bonifacio Vigil stood to deliver a eulogy. In Joey's memory Don Bonifacio had always been old: directing spring ditch work as *mayordomo* of the *acequía*, organizing the butchers for the winter *matanza*, leading the brothers in their processions. Now he just sat around in the sun in front of his little store with his *resolanero* buddies, talking about how much better everything used to be and about how little respect today's youth had for tradition. *Please.* Joey prayed that he wouldn't deliver another of the stupid flowery orations he had sat through so many times as a boy.

But Don Bonifacio was a believer in the traditions. "Gratitude," he began, "the most noble and sublime sentiment that God granted to the human heart and which is its most beautiful adornment, has been the fountain of human society: ancient and modern, they have all drunk the inspirations of public recognition."

Was this baboso kidding? Joey couldn't listen. The roaring in his ears got louder, drowning out the *anciano's* driveling nonsense. Occasional phrases got through his blocked hearing: "the last of the misfortunes and the first of the glories," "much-needed example to disabuse us of human misery." Joey was starting to shake now, not with grief, but with anger. He didn't know how he was going to keep himself from physically assaulting the old man.

"Christ dies every day," Don Bonifacio was saying.

What? Every day? What was this crazy viejito talking about now? The candles on the altar flickered and smoked as if a breeze had somehow entered the windowless chapel. Joey looked at the villagers around him, but nobody seemed to have noticed.

"He asks us to do his work. He asks us to see him in one another. He says, 'I was hungry and you gave me food, I was thirsty and you gave me drink, I was a stranger and you sheltered me, naked and you covered me, sick and you visited me, imprisoned and you came to see me.'"

This was all familiar stuff; Joey had heard it all before. *What did that have to do with Jesus dying?*

"The people asked him, 'Lord, when did we do these things? This feeding and sheltering and clothing, when did we do this for you?' And the Lord told them, 'When you did this for the least of my brothers, you did this for me.'" Here, Don Bonifacio paused and look around before continuing with a series of questions. "Why did He say this? Why did He tell them they did all this for him? Did He say this because He wanted them to see Him in the hungry, in the thirsty, in the stranger, in those with no clothes, those who are sick, in the prisoner?"

This seemed to Joey to be the plain meaning of the story. He thought now, for the first time, that the Brotherhood wasn't just about the secret prayers in their *morada* or about the Holy Week processions. They had always quietly provided for people in the village who had little, whether it was meat from their own herds or corn from their own plots. They were always sharing firewood. Joey's parents had always done this, too, insisting that he help them by working for the neighbors. He remembered being sent to clean Doña Inocencia's ditch on hot days when he wanted to go swimming.

Don Bonifacio was still speaking although his voice sounded altered, as if it belonged to somebody else. "That is the truth, but it is not the whole truth. We always hear people call good deeds 'God's work.' If you care for the sick they say you're doing God's work. And that is true, that is literally true. It's God's work. It is *God's job*! That's why the Proverb says 'What you give to the poor is a loan to God.' You took care of His business! He'll pay you back! It's God's job to feed us! The Psalm says, 'The eyes of all wait on You; You give us food in Your time.' It is God's job to feed us, so when we feed the hungry we are doing it for Him!" The old man was getting more and more excited with his idea. The candles on the altar continued to flicker. Joey wondered what had happened to the formal language of the eulogy. He wondered, too, what any of this had to do with Piedad's death.

Don Bonifacio answered as if he could read Joey's mind: "Who did more for God's children than our sister here?" he asked and pointed to the open casket. In response, the people began wailing.

"Nobody! Nobody!" shouted the *viejo*. "Did she visit the sick?" he asked. "With the aid of God, she *healed* the sick! Did she feed the hungry? Every day. Did she cover the naked? Always. And that is not all. She attended the births of all you young people here who were born after she came of age. She birthed babies up and down this valley and across the mountains, too. I cannot count the number of children she brought into this world. I cannot count the number of mothers she cared for. And what did she ask in return?"

Every living person in northern New Mexico knew the answer to that last question. *Muy poco*. Mind you, Piedad always took a little something. She didn't want to make poor people feel like charity cases. But it was always a token: some chiles, some fresh eggs, a bag of beans. She traveled up and down the mountains caring for the sick and assisting with childbirths and she received just enough to keep on doing it.

"That is God's work," Don Bonifacio said. "That is God's job. Piedad did it for Him. And that is why I say that when these *alimales* – these beasts disguised as men – murdered our Piedad, they murdered God, too. Just like the Roman soldiers who came for Jesus Christ, the Colorado National Guard came for Piedad."

220

Joey's eyes were clear now, perhaps as clear as they had been since that long-ago day in Cantina Rosa. His ears were unstopped; instead of the roaring sound of his own blood, Don Bonifacio's words rang like alarm bells. The flames on the candles had grown tall, reaching toward the ceiling. On the *reredos* behind the altar, blood ran uncontrollably from the wounds of *Cristo crucificado*. San José shook with tears as he held the child.

"It is not just Piedad, though," said the old man. "They murdered God when they murdered the babies. They murdered God when they murdered the Greek who spoke for the miners."

Joey was riveted. *Had the Brothers spoken like this before? Had he simply failed to pay attention?*

"Their guns murder our God," continued Don Bonifacio. "But so do their mines and so do their laws. They assassinate our Lord Jesus Christ when they starve the children with the miserly wages they pay their fathers. And they assassinate Jesus, too, when they steal those pennies back with their cheating company stores and their overpriced company houses. They murder Him with their so-called 'accidents' in the mine shafts and on the factory floors. He dies again and He dies yet again."

The old man was starting to sound like Mother Jones herself, thought Joey. *Any minute now he would start mocking the mourners for failing to fight the bosses.*

But that was not where the old man was going with this thought. "Our sister's name is Piedad. Piedad can mean mercy. It can mean piety. It is also the name we give to the image of Mary, mother of Christ, holding her son's broken body in her arms. They tell me that the day before she was murdered, Piedad gave the Greeks a banner of *la Piedad*, of Mary with her son, for their Easter worship."

Joey was starting to lose the thread of Don Bonifacio's eulogy. The old man, though, was warming himself up again: "Holy Friday is always followed by Easter Sunday. The Crucifixion is always followed by the Resurrection. Christ dies, Christ rises."

What? wondered Joey. *Were they expecting Piedad to climb out of her coffin?*

"Our sister Piedad died fighting the *principados y potesdades*, the principalities and the powers." Now Don Bonifacio looked directly at Joey. "You may think they are flesh and blood, these Rockefellers, these Dodges, these Baldwins and

221

Felts. But tell me: What happens when one of these flesh and blood men dies? Tell me what happens even if one of them changes his heart! Are they not immediately replaced by another? The profits they worship, the punishment for those who work, the rewards for those who don't… all these continue regardless of the names of the men who serve them and those spirits – of greed and of exploitation – they are not flesh and they are not blood."

They're not "spirits" at all, thought Joey. *This is monopoly capitalism, not Satan. And where is Piedad's resurrection?*

Don Bonifacio was still apparently listening to Joey's thoughts, for he went on, speaking to everybody, but looking right into Joey's eyes: "Every person here can be Piedad's resurrection, if you will only take up her work, take up God's work. For one person here that will be her work as a healer. For another it will be her work as a midwife. For a third it will be caring for her orphaned children. But she was not murdered for that work. Satan did not kill her for being a mother, or for being a *curandera*, or for being a *partera*. No, our sister Piedad was murdered for her work struggling against the principalities and the powers, against the governors of darkness on this earth. They killed our sister – the best of us – for standing with the weak against the strong. If you will take up *that* work, then Piedad will remain with us. That is the truth of the Resurrection."

"Amen," responded the congregation, crossing themselves.

The procession to the *camposanto* began immediately. They walked down the rocky, open path from the chapel toward the shade of the *mimbres* and *encinos* in the village. Periodically they would stop for a hymn and to place stones at the *descansos* on the route. Joey, though, was lost in thought. He had never heard the crucifixion and resurrection explained in quite this way before. He wondered, in fact, whether he had actually heard it now. Nothing in his previous experience with Bonifacio Vigil or any of the other men in the Brotherhood suggested that they understood the Gospels in this way. And how did any of that square with Don Bonifacio's wordy and ridiculous introduction, with all of its "visible precepts" and "pitiful exceptions"? Had he, Joey, simply imagined this eulogy, one that recalled him to the awakening he received all those years ago in Los Cerrillos?

But there was a problem with that theory, too. Joey had been perfectly happy with the gospel of One Big Union. He had never given much thought to how it might fit with the gospel of the Church. He had never heard a priest say any of the things that Don Bonifacio said, either. Or what he thought Don Bonifacio said, anyway. How could Joey have made this up? Out of what?

And then he had a darker thought. *If the Crucifixion happened once, then the Resurrection was forever: one Holy Friday, an eternal Easter Sunday. But Don Bonifacio said* (at least the Don Bonifacio who Joey heard said) *that Jesus is murdered every day. That means that we are called to pick up his work – to be his Resurrection – every day! No happy ending. No eternal triumph. No proletarian republic. Just the endless work of struggle against the tirelessly dark powers of this earth. And that vision was profoundly different than a new society, than the abolition of the wage system.*

Don Bonifacio's eulogy was inconsistent with anything he had ever heard from the Brotherhood or from any Catholic priest. But it was also inconsistent with what he had heard from any IWW or from any socialist. So where could these ideas have come from? The road was climbing back up toward the mesa now. The head of the procession was arriving at the *camposanto*. Joey looked back and could not see its end. So many people had come to mourn Piedad that they were still emerging from the trees around the village.

They sang another hymn, *"Tened piedad, Dios mío,"* then they took Piedad's body from the cart. The Brothers had already dug a new grave near those of the Quintana *bisabuelos*. Just before they closed the casket, Joey caught a final glimpse of his sister's face and he realized who had preached that eulogy to him. *Piedad. It was Piedad, herself.*

They were Piedad's ideas. They were Piedad's words. She had gone to join Epifanio in Ludlow. She had stayed to fight the coal operators. She was caring for the mothers and children of the striking miners. She was the one who took these gospels so seriously. She was the one who saw the face of Jesus in the striking miners. She was the one who had died for them.

Now he, Joey Quintana, would have to carry on her work. It was much like the work he had been doing since that day in Rosa's Beer Garden in Los Cerrillos. But he now knew that this work would never be finished.

He helped shovel the earth over his sister's body, no longer the home of her fighting soul. With each shovelful he pledged himself to carry on, not just *his* work, but that of Piedad as well.

Linn-San Manuel, Texas
1965

Do you think that the assassination of my beloved teacher, Don Antonio, by Ranger Henry Ransom, may his name forever be cursed by God, ended our nightmare? Please, grandchildren, pay attention to my testimony, so that this story may not be forgotten. Please do not let this horror be for nothing.

Over the next day or so, as word of the murders spread through Hidalgo County, family and neighbors came to pay their respects. There was a lot of talk at the *velorio*. People debated what to do about the killers.

We still did not understand that there would be no redress, no justice. We still thought there was law in the Valley. We didn't know that well-respected men of the community could be shot dead with impunity, as if they were rattlesnakes or coyotes or rabid dogs. So a cousin of Don Jesús, Heraclio Pizaña, went to the sheriff, demanding that Ranger Captain Ransom be arrested and tried. What happened? I hear you ask. Children, think! What do you think happened? Another Ranger, one of Ransom's men, shot Don Heraclio dead – on the spot – right in front of his brother Aniceto's eyes.

How did the Rangers cover up these murders? The *gabacho* newspaper, the *McAllen Monitor*, wrote that five Texas Rangers were ambushed by fifty to a hundred "bandits" and that they killed three of them in a "furious gunfight" before the others ran off! Don Antonio, Don Jesús, and Señor Pizaña – men of reason, pillars of society – were thus magically transformed into dozens of armed criminals! And the ambush? Was it when Don Jesús raised his empty hand in greeting? Was it when Don Antonio's mouth opened in astonishment at the depraved execution of his father-in-law? Or was it when Sr. Pizaña petitioned the sheriff for justice? These cowards, who shoot unarmed men without provocation, tried to make themselves into courageous heroes!

They scared the Anglos with those stories, too, as if *we* were the murderers and *they* were the victims. Captain Ransom told the *Monitor* reporter that we Valley Mexicans planned to kill "all the White people." He said "hundreds of weapons" had been shipped to us by Pancho Villa. The last words in that article were a vile threat against us from Ransom: "A bad disease calls for a bitter medicine. There is only one solution for this, and that is why Governor Ferguson sent me here." Yes, he called my teacher and his father-in-law and Don Heraclio and *all of us* a "disease." And he made clear his intent to murder every one of us.

The day that article came out Don Aniceto Pizaña stood up in our little church in San Manuel. Only gentlemen of substance were in the pews: ranchers like Don Aniceto and my father, attorneys, physicians, merchants. I was outside, listening at the window with a large crowd of *vaqueros*, clerks, and other young men. Don Aniceto described the assassinations of my teacher and his father-in-law. He related the murder of his own brother Heraclio in front of his eyes. He reminded the men of the *gabachos'* fake lawsuits and their endless malicious insults. Then he asked: "How can we remain indifferent and quiet in the face of these abuses? How can we permit such offenses against our *raza*? Have we lost our humanity and our patriotism? No! They may be sleeping, but they are easily awakened!"

And then the men in the church rose to their feet and applauded. Don Aniceto raised his hand and said, "I pledge, by my brother's blood: enough patience, enough suffering. We are men. We desire freedom and we will be free!" And with that, the young men outside joined the applause of those in the church and shouted their approval. It was clear to me that they intended to pursue justice by their own hands. And I agreed, God forgive me. Not knowing what was to come, I agreed.

Don Aniceto led a raid on the King Ranch the next week, at Las Norias, thirty miles away from San Manuel as the crow flies. The men expected to find Rangers there; the *rinches* always acted as if they were a personal security force for the King Family and their million-acre ranch. Norias was a private train station, just for the Kings and their businesses, on the Gulf Coast Lines. Our men shot it out with a few soldiers of the US Army who had been sent there. When Don Aniceto realized there were no *rinches* present, our men left. They had nothing against the soldiers and no interest in fighting them. Later two companies of Rangers arrived, led by the *bruto* Henry Ransom and his assassin friend, Monroe Fox. But did all those Rangers set out on the trail of our men? Of course not, they were too cowardly.

Yes, those *matones* wanted revenge for the attack on the train station. But they weren't willing to pursue an armed man like Don Aniceto who could shoot back at them. Captain Ransom said over and over – and I heard this with my own ears – he would kill all the "bandits" or anyone who *looked like them!* Think about that. It's not hard to figure out what he meant.

And that is exactly what he did that day, when the actual raiders of Norias got away with no *rinches* in pursuit. No, instead of following Don Aniceto, the Rangers murdered four *kineños* that day: regular, workaday employees of the King ranch! Ransom was afraid to ride after the raiders, but his Rangers pulled

Abraham Salinas and Juan Tobar out of the bunkhouse and shot them dead. When Eusebio Hernández and Doroteo Pérez rode back to the station from working on the fence, the Rangers shot them dead, too. How do I know who was murdered? Because those *asesinos cobardes*, those cowardly assassins, *posed for pictures with the dead!* Couldn't I recognize the face of Doroteo Pérez, my classmate from Don Antonio's *escuelita*? Didn't I know the boy who could tell us the names of all the birds and all the butterflies? They sold that photograph up and down the Valley, with *el gordo*, Captain Fox, and his hired killers sitting in their saddles and their ropes around the dead men in the dust. That postcard of Doroteo, murdered and dragged in the dirt, was a souvenir for the assassins and for all the *gabachos* who wanted to see every one of us murdered. I cannot forget it.

Captain Ransom said the Rangers captured and killed Don Aniceto himself that day. If it weren't for the memory of the men the Rangers did kill, I would laugh. Don Aniceto was never captured. He led many more raids. I attended his funeral just a few years ago, with hundreds of *viejos* who remembered him as our leader. They couldn't capture our brave warriors, so they killed the men they *could* capture. And that meant more families who were ready to fight the Rangers.

Our next big raid was on the Gulf Coast Lines railroad itself. The men loosened the track and tied a wire to the rail. As the locomotive approached, they pulled it free, derailing the entire train! Naturally the *rinches* couldn't find the men who had done this. So, again, they arrested whoever was nearby. Four men who had the misfortune to live nearby were taken from their homes. Captain Ransom had his Rangers hang these innocent prisoners from trees and then riddle their bodies with bullets. The Rangers threatened the families that if they buried the murdered men – their husbands and sons and fathers – they, too, would be killed! The bodies remained in the trees for weeks. The smell was notorious. Finally, the families begged an Anglo undertaker from Brownsville to take the bodies down, thinking that if a *gabacho* removed the dead, perhaps the *rinches* might not kill them.

Right around this time, the town marshal in Elsa arrested Rodolfo Muñoz – who we all knew as nothing more than a thief – for attempting to rob the local bank. Rodolfo Muñoz was not one of us: not a friend of my father's, not one of Don Aniceto's men, not a respectable member of our society. All that he had in common with us was that he was Mexican, but that is all that mattered to the Texas Rangers.

The town marshal was holding Muñoz for trial in the Elsa lock-up. One night, after midnight, two Rangers came and took Muñoz from his cell. They said that they were bringing him to the county seat for arraignment. In the middle of the night? Why not do this at noon? Why not do this in the morning? Why wait until after midnight? I was in the car with my *abuelo* the next day when we found the body of Rodolfo Muñoz hanging from a tree by the side of the road.

The Rangers claimed that they were stopped by "masked gunmen" who took Muñoz from them and hanged him. These brave *rinches* who each claimed to be able to fight fifty men. Everybody knew this was a lie. There were no "masked gunmen." There were no "persons unknown." They killed Rodolfo Muñoz themselves. They killed Rodolfo Muñoz because they could. They killed Rodolfo Muñoz because he was a Mexican. We asked the marshal to arrest the *rinches* for murdering his prisoner. The Rangers told the marshal that if he tried, they would kill him too. He believed them.

By the time six months had passed, half of the men who attended the meeting at our church in San Manuel were dead... murdered by Texas Rangers. And it was not just the men who promised to fight who were targeted by the *rinches*. Men who knew nothing of this conflict were murdered as "bandits", too. So were men who swore to steer clear of the controversy. My cousin Josefina begged her father to leave his ranch and seek shelter in Brownsville while the Rangers were on the trail, on their campaign of assassinations. Oh, but Don Aurelio was a stubborn man. *"El que no la debe, no la teme,"* said he. I have done nothing wrong; why should I be afraid? When the Rangers came to his home, Don Aurelio went out on the porch to welcome them, as a friend. Captain Ransom shot him dead. His men shot Josefina's brothers, too. Then they stole the boots off Don Aurelio's feet. They stole his boots.

My father did not go so quietly. After the Norias raid he moved us temporarily to stay with our Cantú cousins in Reynosa, across the river from McAllen. But he would not abandon his friend Don Aniceto. As soon as we were safe he returned to Texas. It was just at the time that Luis de la Rosa and some of his men derailed another train a few miles north of Brownsville. Again Captain Ransom sent his Rangers to murder some innocent men, track workers on the St. Louis, Brownsville and Mexico. De La Rosa, of course, was already safely back in Matamoros, but some *vendido* told the *rinches* that my father had returned to our home in San Manuel. So even though my father had been across the river at the time of the derailment – a fact that could have been testified to by hundreds of men – Ranger Ransom decided that my father must die.

It took fifty Rangers to kill my father. They surrounded the house, firing many hundreds of rounds through the windows and walls. I know this to be true because our neighbors saw it and told me. Some were even courageous enough to testify under oath to what they saw, although they knew the Rangers might kill them for speaking. My father held out for hours, but in the end, they rolled a blazing wagonload of hay up to the side of the house. My beloved father, heir to the twelve leagues of La Fería, was burned alive by these *demonios*. I had lost my teacher and now I lost my father, too. I was like Jeremiah in Babylon, truly an orphan, and my mother a widow.

My father and Don Aniceto had made a promise to seek justice for my teacher, Don Antonio, and for Don Jesús and for Aniceto's brother Heraclio. In the end, they failed. But Captain Ransom made his own promise: kill the "bandits" or anybody who looked like them.

Before that year was out the Rangers had murdered so many of our men that I could not even guess at the number. It must have been thousands. Some were neighbors, people we had known all of our lives. Some were refugees from the other side, people fleeing the violence of the civil war in Mexico, people who thought there would be safety in Texas. Only God knows who all those people were. It is beyond me to remember even all the victims who I knew personally. There were so many.

And that is why I return to the memory of Doroteo Pérez. When we were children, I begrudged him the praise of our teacher, Don Antonio. I loved our school and I loved our teacher and I wanted to be the apple of his eye. Doroteo could not read like I could and he was not as quick as I in mathematics. But, oh, did he know the names of every creature of the field! And, oh, how I resented hearing how wonderful was this knowledge, knowledge that could only be acquired by wandering the *resacas* and *lagunas* of our Valley, knowledge that could never be earned by a bookworm like me.

Doroteo teased me for my reading. He even teased me for being the pet of our teacher, which frustrated me so much when all I could hear was Don Antonio lauding Doroteo – barefoot Doroteo! – as some kind of a scientific genius. This was a boy who I looked down on for his ragged clothing. This was a boy with whom I competed for our teacher's regard. This was a boy whose father worked for my father.

So I don't need a number for the murdered. Five hundred? Five thousand? They murdered my teacher, Don Antonio. They murdered his father-in-law, Don Jesús. They murdered my *tío*, Don Aurelio. They murdered my own father, Don

228

Eusebio Hinojosa-Cantú, *que descanse en paz*. They murdered so many more. Some will say that it was only an evil few, that not all *gabachos* are demons. But I saw the postcard of Doroteo! I saw it for sale in the shops! I saw the grinning gringos buy their souvenir photos of him lying on the ground like some pile of rags, or perhaps a piece of firewood, with their ropes around his broken body! Tell me that they didn't all kill Doroteo and I will concede your point. But do not tell me that his death did not make them all feel like better people. Do not tell me that they didn't all enjoy looking at his corpse in the dirt while their *rinches* smirked above him on horseback. Don't try to tell me those things, because I know better. I saw with my own eyes. I know that the only thing that makes them feel human is to see us stripped of our lives.

Charleston, South Carolina
1917

July 16

What a surprise each new day is! Who knew this morning when I left Mother's house that tonight I would be writing in this, my teacher's journal, as if it were a schoolgirl's diary? But let me begin at the beginning!

I left work at the laundry early this evening to attend a lecture at Emanuel A.M.E. Church. Just because school is out for the summer doesn't mean I am no longer a teacher. It is my professional obligation to keep my mind active and Charleston offers rather more than Johns Island in that regard. The speaker this evening was the editor of the magazine, *The Crisis*, Professor W.E.B. Dubois. Dr. DuBois turns out to be a very light, short, slender, bald man. For all the thunder in his written words he is rather soft-spoken in person. I was so glad I arrived early and got a seat on the main floor near the front! His accent was new to me. I suppose this is the way Massachusetts patricians speak, which is, after all, what he is.

Glancing over this physical description I fear I am doing him an injustice. I make him sound unprepossessing and Dr. DuBois is anything but. Something in his eyes maybe. Or perhaps it was what he had to say, because I am certain that after hearing him speak I will never see the world in quite the same way again.

Since April all the talk in town has been about the European War and of the part our race shall play in that war. Some are for, some against. Before I left John's Island for summer break Mr. Flood Wilson told me, "Miss Seppy, no German never done nothing to me. And if he did, I forgive him!" That probably sums up the views of most island folk. The Charleston County draft board seems intent on filling its quota of young men for the army with their less-valued colored tenants, the same people they have been in the habit of arresting for nothing and putting on the county's road crew. Once in the army, these young men are issued shovels instead of rifles and assigned every menial task. So, for country people, this war looks like nothing more than another chain gang.

But Dr. DuBois inspired me with his vision: he discerns an opportunity for us to *seize* our citizenship! He said, and I wrote this in my notes as he spoke to ensure that I would not forget a word, "That which the German power represents today spells death to the aspirations of Negroes and all darker races for equality, freedom and democracy. Let us not hesitate. Let us, while this war lasts, forget our special grievances and close our ranks shoulder to shoulder with our own white fellow citizens and the allied nations that are fighting for democracy. We make no ordinary sacrifice, but we make it gladly and willingly with our eyes lifted to the hills."

Those poetic words, these *Biblical* words, rang something deep inside me like a bell. I don't think I will ever forget them. And the church rang with applause, too, long after he finished speaking.

Then, from a few rows behind me, a voice called out, "Will Professor DuBois take a question from the audience?"

"Why Mr. Owen," responded Dr. DuBois, "what a pleasant surprise to see you here in Charleston." Returning his attention to the audience he introduced his challenger, "Please welcome Mr. Chandler Owen of New York City."

Mr. Owen looked to be about thirty, and he was quite the dandy with his tan suit and his wavy brown hair. He strode to the front of the room, and then, turning his back on Dr. DuBois – a little rudely, I thought – in order to face all of us, said, "I have these questions for you, Dr. DuBois: How are we to trust a President who brought the abhorrent Jim Crow laws of the old Confederate states into our national capital as Mr. Woodrow Wilson did? How are we to trust a President who screened the libelous moving picture "Birth of a Nation" in the White House and advised every American to see it as Mr. Woodrow Wilson did? How are we to trust a War Department that wouldn't allow Colonel Charles Young, our only serving colored graduate of West Point, to lead the segregated officer training school in Iowa? How are we to trust a War Department that – even as we meet here tonight – is preparing to hang 64 colored soldiers for defending their rights as men against brutal, bigoted policemen in Houston, Texas?"

In just those few words this Mr. Owen had tapped into all the fears of the educated Negroes in the hall... *my* fears, if I am candid. I looked to Professor DuBois for a reassuring answer, but – before he could respond – we all heard a baritone voice from the rear of the auditorium say, "I would like to address those questions!"

I turned, along with every other member of the audience, to see who spoke. I saw a line of men in uniform standing in the back, behind the last row of pews. The speaker was one of them: a tall, dark-skinned man, maybe a few years older than I, with the most arresting eyes I have ever seen. He wore an olive drab jacket with silver bars on each collar and strips of cloth wrapped tightly around his trousers from his knees to his polished boots. He walked quickly to the front of the room without awaiting permission.

Standing to the side, facing both the dais and the audience, the handsome soldier spoke in a strong voice: "I am First Lieutenant Osceola McKaine of Sumter. I am a veteran of the Philippines and of the recent campaign in Mexico. I have already fought for my country in two theaters of war and I am on my way to a third. I am prepared to earn our freedom by any means necessary."

That last phrase took my breath. But there was more. "I attended that segregated officer training camp in Iowa along with a thousand professional men, the best of our race, and two hundred fifty of the finest colored soldiers in the US Army. We met daily, during every free minute, to plan for our success. This World War represents the largest assembly of the American people in history. Before it is over, I believe there will be more Americans under arms than in both armies combined during the Civil War. We will not convince President Wilson, or anyone else, of our manhood by standing aside and watching. We will – we must! – win over our white brethren by standing beside them and by shedding our blood with them."

He looked directly at Mr. Owen then, and said, "You speak so confidently about an execution that has not yet been decided and you use the lives of men you don't even know to make an argument against Dr. DuBois. But the soldiers of the 24th Regiment in Houston are not an abstraction to me. I cannot see those men as a debater's point. That was my unit. I served alongside those men. Corporal Charles Baltimore is my friend. Sergeant William Nesbit trained me. If, God forbid, any of them *were* to be executed, then I would mourn them *personally* and by name."

He turned back to the audience and said, "We are Americans.We fight against the corrupt monarchies of the Old World. We fight against the race prejudice and brutality of the New." His volume had increased imperceptibly, and now he almost shouted, "For the arms of the wicked shall be broken, but the Lord upholdeth the righteous!"

The crowd leaped to its feet with thunderous applause. I, too, was standing and clapping. Mr. Owen of New York City looked as though he was about to respond, mouth open and all, but he glanced around the cheering audience - apparently thinking better of it - and remained silent. He looked at Dr. DuBois, but the professor politely avoided looking at him, only smiling a little while standing and applauding the soldier.

232

The program was clearly over. I saw Pastor A.E. Peets of Emanuel Church, along with several of my teachers from Avery, walk up and surround Professor DuBois. Principal Cox took DuBois's arm as if asserting the primacy of their friendship. Reverend J.J. Starks and some others who I knew to be Benedict College alumni were speaking quietly with Mr. Owen. The circle of people around Lieutenant McKaine, though, was easily the largest. The other uniformed soldiers stood near him in silence, as if on guard. I recognized Mr. G.W. German, the president of the dockworkers' union, pumping McKaine's hand and pounding him on the back. I supposed many of the others in that crowd were also longshoremen and members of his union. G.W. seemed ready to enlist in the army right then and there! I also saw several young ladies of my acquaintance standing nearby as if hoping to be noticed. I will not list their names.

I wondered what the parents of these belles of colored Charleston society would think of their daughters conducting themselves like this. And then my face got very warm, because I realized I was doing the same thing! I, too, was standing and hoping Lieutenant McKaine would see me. I hurriedly grabbed my bag and left.

It was still early evening and I had planned to have a little fun. Morris Street Baptist Church was sponsoring a lemonade social. I had no personal chaperone, but since the deacons of the church were sponsoring, Mother had approved my going.

The music was very lively. I conversed happily with Hazel who is home for the summer from Fisk. I say "happily" since so many of my Avery classmates seem to have adopted their seditty parents' prejudices about my family and barely acknowledge me with a greeting. Hazel, though, remains a true friend. I was catching her up on stories about my year on John's Island when up walked two soldiers who had apparently been invited to the social.

"Miss Singletary," said the taller one to Hazel, "what a very great pleasure to encounter you here. Please allow me to introduce my comrade, Second Lieutenant Vernon Daly of Cornell University."

I smiled a little. Wasn't it just like these bourgie types to add their college to their name as if it were some title of nobility?

Lt. Daly – or was it Cornell? – smiled nicely and took Hazel's gloved hand for a moment. Then Hazel turned to me and said, "Septima, this is Montgomery Jason from Spartanburg. Mr. Jason, Lieutenant Daly, this is my classmate and friend, Miss Septima Poinsette."

Both men briefly took my hand. I did not care for Mr. Jason's smile. It lasted a little too long. Mother always says: "Men are here to ask; women to refuse. If you accept their favors, they will mark you." That saying came straight to my mind with Mr. Jason's smile so I did not return it.

Without a moment's hesitation he turned back to Hazel and asked, "Miss Singletary, would you care to dance with me?" And off they spun.

Lt. Daly looked a little surprised, but he bowed slightly and asked, "Miss Poinsette, would you do me the honor of joining me on the floor?" Well, how could I say no to that? I curtsied and took the hand he offered and was pleased to discover that he was a graceful dancer indeed.

When the band played the final notes of "Hesitation," Lt. Daly bowed again, deeply this time, and thanked me. I was thinking how much fun this was and curtsied back when who should walk up but the handsome, passionate soldier from Professor DuBois's lecture. "Vernon," he said to my partner, "please do me the great favor of introducing me to your lovely dancing companion."

Vernon Daly smiled and nodded. "Lieutenant McKaine, this is Miss Septima Poinsette. Miss Poinsette, allow me to introduce you to First Lieutenant Osceola McKaine of the US 367th Infantry, my friend and now my superior officer."

I felt my face get warm again, but I remained outwardly composed and merely said, "I am charmed, Lt. McKaine."

McKaine showed me a long, beautiful smile. Why didn't this bother me as Hazel's friend Mr. Jason's had? Lt. McKaine said, "Miss Poinsette, may I bring you a glass of lemonade?"

I thought, *If you accept their favors they will mark you*. But what I said was, "Yes, thank you." And, after thanking Lt. Daly, off we went to the refreshments table.

Two hours later I realized the time. What hadn't we discussed? I told him about John's Island. He told me about Pancho Villa. I told him about Avery Institute. He told me about Boston University. I told him about Charleston. He told me about Sumter. The party was still in full swing because that brilliant young company does not – by and large – have to get up early. I, however, am due to work at the laundry at 7 am! So I asked Lieutenant McKaine to be excused. And he accompanied me home!

And here I sit, writing. The clock at the Citadel is just now striking 2 o'clock, but I am too excited to go to sleep. Oh, how I hope to see Lt. Osceola McKaine again before he leaves for war!

Spartanburg, South Carolina
1917

To: Maj. Nicholas Biddle
Military Intelligence Branch
From: Confidential Agent Maj. Walter Loving

As per your instructions of the 11th I visited the training camp of the 93rd Infantry Division in Spartanburg, South Carolina. The situation is far from what was described to you by Senator Tillman. The colored trainees are highly motivated and conduct themselves professionally on the parade ground, on the rifle range and on maneuvers. They are as good as any novices I have encountered, and you know that I have drilled soldiers for almost 25 years.

They have, however, encountered problems with merchants in town when they are granted liberty. They have been barred from business establishments, spat on and cursed. I not only witnessed this; I experienced it myself. I was also ordered off the sidewalk. I was not in uniform, of course, but *they were*. The sight of soldiers in the U.S. Army being disrespected in this fashion *during wartime* was extremely disturbing to me.

Thus far the only incident I uncovered of soldiers physically resisting this treatment occurred the day I arrived, and the resistance came from white soldiers, not from the 93rd. I did not witness it myself. I was informed that two privates of the 369th Regiment walked into a pharmacy and ordered Coca-Cola with ice cream. According to my informants the proprietor said to them: "I don't serve [here he used a disrespectful term for colored men.]" He told them to get out of his place of business, using an interjection which cannot be included here. Several white enlisted men from the 105th Field Artillery, who are also training at Camp Wadsworth, were at the counter while this exchange transpired. One of these men told the proprietor, "Those are American soldiers. You can't treat them like that." The proprietor ordered these white soldiers out, too, using the same vulgar epithet, so they damaged some of his store fixtures. My informants in this case were the two colored infantrymen, but their story was corroborated by multiple white artillerymen when I located them. None of the white soldiers admitted to having torn up the store themselves, of course, insisting that the damage had been done by "friends."

Regarding these incidents I think it might be wise to continue training the 92nd Infantry division in a more salutary climate, i.e., one where merchants do not insist on treating uniformed colored soldiers as criminals. Camp Upton, in New York comes to mind. I would also be remiss in not reminding you that the hair-raising stories you forwarded to me come from Senator Benjamin Tillman. He is on record as saying that if the Negro cannot be subordinated he would favor lynching every one of us. He calls us an ignorant and debauched race and compares us to baboons. He has a long and well-known history of libel and violence – including incidents right on the Senate floor – and that does not tend to support his credibility.

While in South Carolina I attended a public meeting in support of the war effort at a large colored church in Charleston. The speaker was Professor W.E.B. DuBois, editor of *The Crisis*. Dr. DuBois spoke stirringly to a large audience, calling for colored Americans to stand shoulder to shoulder with our white brethren in this war. He was challenged strongly by Mr. Chandler Owen, the New York socialist who – along with Mr. A.P. Randolph – publishes a seditious antiwar magazine called *The Messenger* in New York City. We have both these men under surveillance and monitor all their mail. I was curious to see how Dr. DuBois would answer Mr. Owen's questions, but the gauntlet was picked up by a colored officer of the 367th Regiment instead.

In my report from Camp Des Moines I mentioned a candidate officer named Osceola McKaine. He is now a First Lieutenant. This same Lt. McKaine was the man who stood up and demolished the arguments raised by the socialist, Mr. Owen. He received great applause from the audience. The Charleston longshoremen are all union members and therefore inclined to Mr. Owen's opinions, but they were especially roused by Lt. McKaine. As I wrote in that report, Lt. McKaine was previously a sergeant in the regular army with experience in the Philippines and Mexico. He is a real leader. I recommend he be considered for a captaincy.

I now depart by evening train for Washington, DC. I may arrive in your office before this report.

Four

Special Agent James Amos left his rooming house the next morning to find an altogether different feeling in the streets of Greenwood. He didn't know what had changed, but he understood immediately that something was wrong. Instead of the polite greetings and business-like atmosphere he saw the previous day, people were stopping one another for intense-looking conversations. Their eyes were haunted.

A man could always use a shave, so he decided to try his luck with another barbershop, this one with a sign on its big glass window saying "C.L. Netherland" in gold leaf. Unlike Carter's, this shop had no second floor. It did have eighteen-foot ceilings with fans slowly turning. Amos studied the interior through the window from across the street. All three barbers' chairs were occupied by customers. Two more men were sitting along the opposite wall. Even from this distance he could see that an animated conversation was underway. What really caught his eye was the customer in the middle chair. Each time the man spoke, everybody else stopped to listen. Might there be some clue here about the "African Blood Brotherhood" that Director Hoover had sent Agent Amos to investigate? At the very least these men would know what had everybody in town so agitated.

The instant he walked through the door Agent Amos knew that he had chosen the right place. There was surely something clandestine going on in this shop; all conversation stopped as he entered. Every head turned toward him. The barber nearest the door asked, "How can we help you today?" He must be Mr. C.L. Netherland of the sign, and there was something hidden in the question, something in his tone.

"I could sure use a shave," answered Amos.

The barber nodded. "First empty chair. That'll probably be Jake's," continued the owner. So, either the other men in the shop were not waiting for cuts, or everybody was anxious to get him out. The barber next to Netherland – "Jake?" – raised the corners of his mouth in a slight smile that never quite made it to his eyes, then returned to sharpening his razor on his wide leather strop.

"Meanwhile, you can wait right there," and Netherland gestured with his head to an empty wooden armchair next to the two men who were, perhaps, just visiting.

The barbers all returned immediately to their work while their customers kept their eyes on Special Agent Amos in the big mirror. Amos did a quick inventory of the men in the room. The barbers were lighter-skinned than the customers, but indoor life would account for that difference. They were also better dressed: stylish shirts and shoes. The lead barber had something in his vest pocket: probably a small pistol, although most barbers Amos knew preferred their razors for self-defense. Unlike the crowd in Carter's, the customers here in Netherland's barbershop all looked like workingmen. No paunches. No soft hands. The man in the third chair had something else about him, but Amos couldn't immediately put a finger on it.

The man who interested him, though, was that customer in the middle chair, getting his back and sides shaved by Jake. About fifty. From across the street, Amos had seen everyone listening to him, barbers and customers alike. Now, with a stranger in the shop, he was silent while the other men discussed an oil strike. But the others kept glancing at him.

"They got the blow-out under control Tuesday," said the man sitting next to Amos. Amos had decided to call him "blue shirt" until he had something more to remember him by. "Say it'll be bigger than Glen Pool." Special Agent Amos picked up a newspaper sitting on a table next to him. It was a way to look as though he wasn't clocking the conversation.

"Somebody's going to be rich," laughed the owner's customer, the man in the first chair. With the barber's cape covering him it was hard to determine much more about him than his age. Early twenties. "Do you know who, C.L.?" he asked.

His barber shook his head no. So, yes, the owner, C.L. Netherland. "I heard it was an Indian, though." And with that all the men looked at the customer in the third barber's chair, the one Amos had marked in his mind as being in some way unusual. Indian, then? But this man just looked like a dark-skinned Negro. "Did you hear that, Azell?" the first barber, "C.L." asked the man.

"Gus Captain," answered the man called Azell. "He's an Osage, not a Creek. And if that's true, he's the richest Indian in the world."

"Why can't you find oil on your land, Azell?" asked blue shirt, the man next to Amos.

239

"Because I won't let them look," answered the Indian, Azell, seriously. He still looked like a Black man to Agent Amos. "Oil? That's another trick to lose your land to the…" and here he said something Amos didn't get. "Machiner"? "Casino"? Was it another language? Indian language? If it was, nobody in the shop except him had any trouble understanding what the man said. And Amos must have unwittingly revealed how closely he was listening, because the silent middle customer was now calmly appraising him in the mirror.

The moment of eye contact broke when Jake took his barber's cape off the man and shook it out, interrupting the reflections. Jake rubbed some talc into the man's neck and then whisked it away with a soft brush. As the man rose he revealed a slim frame, a height about five-eleven, undistinguished workingman's clothes, and what Special Agent Amos had been looking for: the holster on his belt held a .45 caliber Army Colt automatic. That was a lot of gun for personal protection.

"Next," said the middle barber, looking at Amos. While Special Agent Amos stood and moved to the barber's chair, the silent man pulled a dime from his pocket for Jake and then went and occupied the seat Amos had just vacated. *Who was studying whom?* wondered Amos.

The barber put his cape and neck strip on Amos and reset the barber's chair so that he was reclining. The conversation resumed. "You don't want to be rich, Azell?" asked the young man in the first seat. He laughed again. Amos was starting to think of him as laughing man.

There was no answer from Azell. One of the men in the waiting area – Amos wasn't sure which because his face was now looking at the ceiling – chuckled and said, "I think Azell has his own business."

Amos's barber, Jake, had been taking a hot towel from the brass dispenser with wooden tongs. As he put it on the agent's face, completely obstructing his view, a man behind him spoke sharply, and this time Amos was certain it was some language he didn't know. "A he lay chee" it sounded like. And it must have been a warning, because the conversation ceased completely. While the towel was on his face, Amos heard the shop door open and close. He avoided looking around when the towel was removed and Jake, started lathering his whiskers, but when he did check it became clear that blue shirt and his companion from the waiting seats had left. Azell soon paid and he immediately left the shop, too. The third barber sat down in his chair and turned to study Amos.

Who had not left was the middle-aged workman who caught Amos's eye before he even entered the shop. "Ezekiel Payne," said the man, by way of introduction and a not-too subtle way of requesting information. "I farm a spread outside Boley."

Special Agent James Amos was well prepared for this. You don't gather information if you seem stingy with your own. "Henry Washington," he smiled. "Just got into town from New York City. I heard there are plenty of opportunities for an enterprising colored man here in Oklahoma."

"All kinds of opportunities," answered "Payne" without a return smile. Was that his real name? Like anybody in the habit of lying, Agent Amos suspected everybody he met of the same thing. And had there been some extra meaning in Payne's answer? Why say "all kinds of opportunities" unless he was hinting at something?

This was a peculiar dance they were doing. Amos was looking for armed radicals, but he was certain that radicals weren't the only ones going armed out here. If he offered himself as bait to the wrong persons he might find they were confidence men shaking down gullible investors. He might even discover a gang of highwaymen who would try to hold him up at gunpoint, or – more likely – to shoot him dead from ambush and then empty his pockets. Amos was utterly confident that neither type could actually take advantage of him, but wasting time with them wouldn't help him find radicals. Director Hoover had not sent him to this frontier city to arrest swindlers or bandits. So he calibrated his response and said, "I am just looking for the opportunity to work hard and build something without some ofay turning around and stealing it from me."

"Aren't we all," responded the man who called himself Payne. Nothing about his manner suggested that he had relaxed his vigilance.

Agent Amos wasn't giving up. "I read an article about Boley in the *Amsterdam News*," he said. "I think it was Booker T. Washington and he was praising it even above Tulsa. How far is it from here?" he asked, although he had studied that information in the files Director Hoover had given him.

"Sixty miles southwest, give or take," answered Payne, still studying him in the mirror.

"So what brings you so far from home? There must be a barbershop in Boley," smiled Amos.

It was a mistake. Too prying. He noticed the look in Payne's eyes immediately. Payne remained silent just long enough to make Amos uncomfortable with his delay, and then said only, "Yes, we have two."

Time for Special Agent Amos to assess what he actually had. This man Payne was definitely acting like he had secrets. A bootlegger? That would be a reason for a farm in the country and furtive business in the city. But so would a plan to arrange oil exploration on his land without arousing the notice of his neighbors. Only one of these was illegal, and neither was what Agent Amos had been sent to investigate. Since Payne's initial warning – Amos was now certain that it was he who had put out that non-English alert – none of the barbers had said a word. Neither had the remaining customer, laughing man. He quickly paid and exited when his haircut was done. Now Amos was alone with Payne and the three barbers. Several passersby had put their hands on the barbershop door as if to enter and then received some silent signal – maybe from Payne, maybe from the proprietor, Netherland – and walked on. Amos had done too much to make himself suspect and there was no reason to think that whatever was going on here was what he was looking for. Time to cut bait.

Jake finished with Agent Amos's shave and splashed some witch hazel on his face. When he removed his barber's cape, Amos stood and gave him a nickel. He turned to Payne and said simply, "Mr. Payne," then addressing the others added, "Gentlemen," and headed for the shop door.

The barbers said nothing, but as Amos was leaving Payne said, "Mr. Washington, I expect we will be seeing each other again." That was puzzling. A threat? An acknowledgement of Agent Amos's excessive curiosity? Amos was reassured to feel the familiar weight of his snub-nosed revolver on his belt. There was no evidence that he had found what he was looking for in C.L. Netherland's barbershop. There were plenty of other paths to pursue this investigation. There was every reason to remain vigilant. And he still hadn't discovered what was causing the anxiety he had observed in the street. Interesting city, Tulsa.

Linn-San Manuel, Texas
1965

I have written so much in the pages of this testimony about our people and about our troubles with the Rangers that I have barely even mentioned the river. They teach you children in their school that it is a border, but I ask you, what other great river do your teachers describe that way? They don't tell you that the Nile is a border; they tell you that it was a highway that watered a desert valley and allowed the creation of a great civilization. That is just how our ancestors saw this great river of the north when they arrived at its mouth from the court of King Felipe V, as a rival to the Yangtze and the Ganges, the Tigris and Euphrates. Even here, thirty miles away in San Manuel, we live in the Valley. All our farms depend on the Río Grande del Norte. So does the wildlife, the birds and animals that pass through here in such abundance that people from all over the world come here just to look at them!

You cannot remember the days when we used to take the ferry across for every saint's day, every baptism, every *quinceañera* on the other side. One time, we went to a wedding in Fresnos and my *abuelo* drove his Ford right through the river at *Las Cuevas* ford. We were all *mojados* that day! Nowadays we have to think carefully about the traffic and the humiliation of the border station and we have grown distant from your cousins across the river. I am so sorry they seem like strangers to you instead of family. When I was a girl it was nothing for people to cross for work or for business, especially once the bridges came and we could drive right over.

And let me explain a little history that I learned in Don Antonio's school about this "border." The Anglos like to say that the Río Grande has been the border since 1836, when they fought for their "freedom"... really the freedom to buy and sell Black people, which was illegal in Mexico. But this valley was never part of their "Republic of Texas." I have seen a copy of their own map, drawn in 1841, and it shows that all this land was Tamaulipas, all the way up to the Nueces River, one hundred miles north of us! This is how they invent and reinvent their own history. We didn't become a part of Texas until the Treaty of Guadalupe Hidalgo, but you can't tell them that; they don't want to hear.

Even in the worst moments of the *rinchada*, the Ranger terror, we could always seek shelter with family in Tamaulipas. And they with us! In the most violent days of the Revolution in Mexico we always had somebody's *tío* or *sobrina* staying at our house. It was horrible at the time; we became like vagabonds, running from one side of the river to the other depending on who was chasing us. I had no idea, though, that it could get much worse.

In 1917, when Congress declared war on Germany, the *gabachos* lost their minds completely. They all thought that Germany would magically transport an army from the trenches of France to the other side of our river and invade Texas. They really did! And, of course, they thought we would all join the Germans, because we have always haunted their nightmares. They murder us by the hundreds and then tell each other that we plan to kill them all! They steal our land and then call us bandits. They get fat from our work and then say we are lazy.

Let me return to that war, though. The truth is that we were very divided about what to do when the Anglos went to fight in France. Some of my classmates from Don Antonio's school moved across the river to stay with cousins in San Miguel de Camargo and Reynosa to avoid being drafted. They said they didn't want to die overseas fighting for *gabachos* who were trying to kill them here. Our state representative in Austin, Licenciado J.T. Canales, argued differently. He said that registering for the draft and enlisting was a good way to prove that we were really Americans and that the gringos should treat us with dignity. And there were lots of people who agreed with him.

David Cantú was one of those who signed up. He used an Anglo name so he wouldn't be stuck in a segregated unit digging holes in the ground for the *gabachos*. He won the Congressional Medal for – guess what? – swimming across a river!! He scouted the German army on the other side of the Meuse and swam back with the information.

Marcelino Serna joined the army even though he couldn't speak English. Today these *gabachos* would call him "illegal" because he was born on the other side. Like Cantú, he was a scout, working alone, ahead of his friends. One day he took out a machine gun by himself. He killed six Germans and captured eight. Another day they sent him after a sniper. He killed that sniper and 25 others with rifle and grenades and captured 24 Germans! They gave him a medal, too.

But J.T. was wrong about what this would mean for us at home. We could *all* have volunteered; we could *all* have been heroes… none of that would have stopped the Anglos from believing we were a bunch of German spies. Governor Ferguson even set up a special unit of Texas Rangers that they called "Loyalty" Rangers. Loyalty Rangers! Do you know what the real job of those "Loyalty" Rangers was? To keep our men from voting! I have thought about their irrational dread for many years. Here they were: grinding us into the dirt, robbing us of our land, assassinating us, reducing us to *peones* on our own ranches. But *at that exact moment* their heads were filled with nightmares about us coming with

German weapons and killing them in their sleep! And I wonder: Was it that they felt guilty for what they were doing to us? Or was it that they saw our starving cousins arriving every day from Nuevo León and Coahuila and Tamaulipas and they were afraid that they would never be able to murder enough of us? I still don't know. But I think we still keep them from sleeping.

After the war, Prohibition brought more armed gringos to the Valley. The Texas Rangers were joined by the Border Patrol, but I found it all very strange. The saloons closed and immediately reopened on the other side of the river. So every time they wanted a drink, all these upstanding Protestants, who said that liquor was a sin, crossed the border they pretended to enforce! And because they had to travel a little farther, they drank more. These hypocrites transformed Reynosa into a place for gringos to drink and fight and throw up in the streets. They created a new business opportunity for smugglers like Ignacia Gonzalez to bring tequila and whiskey across the river by the truckload. And let me tell you, when the Anglo politicians finally repealed Prohibition, she just switched to smuggling heroin. But that was later, let me stick to my point: by moving *their* bars and *their* whorehouses to the other side, the *gabachos* convinced themselves that it was *we* who were the source of all the vices of the world!

I think it was the flu epidemic after the war that convinced them that we were the source of all the germs, too. Congress actually passed a law barring idiots, imbeciles and epileptics from crossing the border. Those were their exact words. I don't know, maybe they thought *we* were the germs. And this – the idea that we were ourselves some kind of disease – is the story that I want to tell you.

It was early May and my cousin Concepción was getting married in San Juan at her parents' beautiful home on *Resaca Sardinas*, which my teacher Don Antonio taught us was a previous course of the Rio Grande. The gardens there were lush with palms and *encinos* and ebony trees. The *hierba negra* and the *heliotropo* were in full bloom. When we got there and started unloading food from my brother's truck every color of bird was around us: bright green *charas*, red *bolseros de Altamira*, yellow *chipes*. And the *mariposas*? Whose names only my murdered classmate Doroteo knew? They fluttered from flower to flower: giant black ones, tiny zebra-striped ones, bright blue ones, yellow ones. The sun was out, but it was not too hot. How could Concepción have had a more perfect day for her wedding?

We were laughing and talking and setting up food on tables in the garden while the priest was speaking to my *abuelo*. The bride and groom were in different parts of the house getting ready. Up on the porch the band was warming up. Around 1 pm the groom's brother Leocadio came out in the yard and asked whether I wanted to take a ride with him to the trolley station. Cousins of theirs were coming across from Majada and he was going to pick them up at the U.S. side of the bridge. I thought Leocadio might be a little sweet on me, but we would be family in about an hour so I said okay. As I put on my hat, the guitarist began to play a quick waltz on his big twelve-string *basso sexto*. The accordion joined in and the musicians began singing:

> *Trigueña hermosa, mi corazón se encuentra triste,*
> *porque no sabe si en algún día le correspondes;*
> *Yo te aseguro que en esta vida no hallas otro hombre*
> *que te quiera, trigueñita, como yo.*

Leocadio and I laughed and sang along as we walked around front. He opened the door of his Model T and gave me a low, courtly bow while I got in, which made me giggle. Then he cranked up the car, got in, and we drove to the river.

I don't remember what we talked about; it wasn't a long ride anyway. But I remember seeing the ominous flat brick building at the trolley station and the grim faces of our people lined up outside to go in. It seemed this building was only for us: Mexicans were going in and Mexicans were coming out but the *gabachos* were happily passing by outside, many of them visibly staggering with drunkenness. Remember, all the *borrachos* were drinking on the other side in those days. I had heard about this building, but I hadn't seen it yet and a part of me refused to accept that it could be real. But there it was. And there, all fashionably dressed for a wedding, came Leocadio's cousins from the other side. The women looked as colorful as the birds and butterflies and flowers in Concepción's garden. My heart sank.

The gringo mayor of McAllen had decided that Mexicans were bringing diseases across every day on the streetcar. He had ordered that before they could enter they must be sanitized and deloused. They had to strip naked, submit to being sprayed with a chemical bath, and have their clothing steamed.

Most of the crowd getting off the street car had obviously been through this before. They were lining up quietly and were wearing simple clothes that could survive the steam. Concepción's new in-laws, though, had either not heard about the delousing or they did not think it would apply to them. The Sauceda men were all wearing sharply pressed suits. Each of the ladies wore a highly starched, brightly colored dress and a stylish hat with a plume. They slowed as they saw the city police directing everybody into the line.

Leocadio's aunt, Doña Carlota Sauceda y Vela, did not slow; she froze. And then she demanded, loudly enough for us to hear up the block, "What is this line? Where are you directing us?"

Everybody knew Doña Carlota. She was the matriarch of a large *rancho*, the head of the Sauceda family. Many of the workingmen in the line turned and doffed their hats to her when they heard her voice and realized who it was. Her daughter Aurelia, though, became frightened, apparently uncertain which was worse, the gas chamber they were about to enter or the scene her mother was about to make. "*Mami*, please don't," she hissed.

"You!" shouted Doña Carlota at a U.S. Border Patrolman who was standing to the side. "What is this line?"

He pretended not to hear, but one of the city policemen - a skinny gringo, no more than twenty-five years old - walked over, twirling his wooden baton on its leather strap. "Is there a problem over here?" he asked irrelevantly.

Doña Carlota sighed heavily, which was her habit in dealing with subordinates who she considered mentally challenged. "I ask again: what is this line? And why am I being directed toward it while those people" (and here she gestured with a curled lip toward the *gabachos* strolling by) "are not?"

"This is the delousing line," answered the young white policeman. "And you are going through delousing because you are Mexican."

And here it became obvious that Doña Carlota knew exactly what this line was, what this building was, that she had known before she came, and had intended from the beginning to make the scene her daughter feared. She asked, even more loudly than before, "Little man, do I look like a cockroach to you?"

The policeman drew himself up with a smile, clearly ready to answer in the affirmative. But before he could, another policeman took him by the arm. This second officer had been watching the crowd in the line and he saw trouble brewing. Perhaps all these working people, who depended for their livelihoods on their jobs on the U.S. side, would submit quietly to this humiliation. Perhaps, though, they were not prepared to see Doña Carlota treated with the same disrespect.

But Doña Carlota was not finished. "My family has owned land on both sides of this river since 1750. It was granted to us by King Fernando *el Justo*. Where was your family when we were here? Living in a tree? In a hole in the ground

247

somewhere? Now you arrive in our Valley yesterday, they give you a gun and a stick and no manners, and this gives you the right to treat your betters like this?" She waved her hand from left to right, her contempt encompassing the entire scene.

Aurelia was crying now. "*Mami*, I want to go to the wedding."

The formerly deaf Border Patrolman was now moving toward the Saucedo family, his hand on the butt of his pistol. Aurelia's brother Eginio separated himself from his mother and approached the man. I could see Eginio pleading with him, but he spoke too quietly for me to hear.

Doña Carlota was still loudly challenging the city police. "Will you persist in your discourtesy?"

The Border Patrolman now said to Eginio, loudly enough for everyone to hear, "Get your mother under control."

That got Doña Carlota's attention. "I know you!" she shouted, pointing a finger at him. "I fed you a pie from my kitchen window when you were a filthy little child begging for food! I let you stay in our barn when you had no place else to go! Is this the shameless way you repay our generosity?"

Aurelia wept loudly, "Mother, they will lock you in their jail."

Doña Carlota stood up even straighter at this and spoke even more strongly, "If this is what we have come to in our Valley then perhaps I belong with the *putas* in the McAllen jail. They are my sisters. Who are all of you?" This last was clearly addressed to the other Mexicans in line for the gas chamber.

And with that challenge, the people, who had been waiting for disinfection as if this exchange had nothing to do with them, suddenly turned angrily on the police and the Border Patrol.

"*¡Desgraciados!*"

"*¡Sinvergüenzas¡*"

"*¿Cómo se atreve tratar a la doña de esa manera?*"

The policemen looked uncertainly at one another, but to a man they drew their revolvers from their holsters. This only infuriated the crowd more.

248

"¿Van a disparar la doña?"

"¿Cuántas pistolas necesitan para una sola dama?

I looked to Leocadio, but he was already speaking to another McAllen city policeman, begging him to defuse the dangerous situation.

Instead, Leocadio was arrested. They said he was "disturbing the peace." The police also arrested Aurelia and Eginio. At least they were smart enough not to arrest Doña Carlota. I cannot imagine what the angry crowd might have done if they had put their hands on her.

After the arrests it took a good hour for the crowd to disperse. Doña Carlota herself got back on the trolley with her remaining nieces and nephews and returned to Reynosa. I phoned Concepción's house to warn them not to expect the guests from Majada. Then I spent the rest of the afternoon and well into the night at the police station trying to secure the release of Aurelia, Eginio and Leocadio. After the wedding ceremony was over my *abuelo* joined me, but I never made it back in time for the reception.

This incident got a big write-up in the *gabacho* press. They reported it as a "riot" despite the fact that there was no fighting, no stone throwing, and no looting. They said Doña Carlota was worried about false rumors that the police were photographing women naked in the delousing room. None of us had ever heard those rumors, which told me that they were true and that every Anglo working in the city government and every reporter on the newspaper staff had seen such pictures.

Did this stop them from gassing people at their border? No, it did not. They went on doing this for years, long after the epidemics they said they feared had been forgotten. I do remember being surprised after the Second World War when the magazines reported on the gas chambers that Hitler built to exterminate the Jews. They looked exactly the same as the gas chambers of the *gabachos* on this side of the river. And the gas the Nazis used in those chambers? Zyklon B, the same gas the *gabachos* sprayed on us.

In that second war our men had to decide again whether to fight. Most of them went and many were heroes. I am sure the *gabachos* teach you children in their schools about Hitler. But I doubt that they teach you who he learned from. I doubt that they teach you how the gringos gave Sergeant Marcario García their Medal of Honor, then beat him with a baseball bat because he wanted to eat in one of their cafés. I doubt that they teach you how they refused to bury Private Felix Longoria because he was Mexican. I doubt that they teach you who invented Hitler's gas chambers.

This is why I must put my testimony on paper for you, my beloved grandchildren. You must learn these stories. You must know the truth. You must know our history before it is completely erased.

Globe, Arizona
1917

"Bisbee is a white man's camp. What do you think *you* can accomplish there that the rest of us haven't?"

Joey Quintana took a deep breath and said nothing. This was Frank Little, one of the most radical, respected, and experienced organizers in the IWW. Joey was going to Bisbee regardless of what Frank said; his orders were from Big Bill Haywood himself, the union's secretary-treasurer. But he could learn more about the situation by listening to Frank than by arguing with him… even if he was pretty sure what Frank meant by "the rest of us," and even if he didn't like it. People said Frank was half Indian, but right now he sounded like a garden-variety white man. Joey wondered momentarily, and not for the first time, why so many white Oklahomans liked to claim Cherokee heritage.

He was also concerned about who might be listening. Spies could be anywhere. He and Frank were union men in a company town in the midst of a class war. Copper prices had doubled because of the bosses' war in Europe and the owners' profits were soaring, but they weren't interested in sharing their windfall with anybody. So the workers were walking out in every copper camp from the Canadian border down to Mexico demanding union contracts and higher wages. The bosses were willing to part with their money for only one thing: detectives. They wouldn't pay to provide a decent life for their employees, but they would pay happily to spy on the miners and to beat up the union organizers. This café was in the monster's heart, on the corner of Bailey and North Broad Street in Globe, Arizona. Joey looked around at the other tables to see who might be a Pinkerton.

Frank, though, seemed totally unconcerned with who could be listening. "I have been there myself *many* times in the last ten years." He said. "So has Mother Jones. So has Big Bill. It's not a camp like here in Globe. The workers there think they have it good: affordable homes, YMCA, better wages than other camps, eight-hour day. What do you think has changed?"

Joey waited again. Frank said the word "workers" but he meant the skilled miners, mostly Cornishmen, who held all the underground jobs. Sure, they did have it good, at least compared to the miners in other camps. But what about the less-skilled men? Weren't they workers? What about the men doing above-ground work, mostly Italians and Finns? What about the workers whose job title was "Mexican," a category that the company gave to men from both sides of the border? Did they "have it good"? So, when Frank Little said "worker," did he mean a class? Or did he mean a skin color?

Frank wasn't done. "Let me tell you about Bisbee," he said. "It's not really a company town. If it were, Phelps, Dodge would own everything. The only things they really own are the mines and the YMCA. The YMCA "decency campaign" managed to shut a few saloons and a lot of the whorehouses, but all the barkeeps and all the madams are still there, and they're all still in business. Some of the local businessmen are even sympathetic to us, like Medigovich and Caretto. There is never a problem finding a place for a union meeting."

Joey was having trouble staying quiet now. He may never have been to Bisbee, but that didn't mean he knew nothing about it. Ten years earlier, when he was organizing across the border, it was the townsfolk of Bisbee who came to crush the strike. At the exact moment that Colonel Greene's Anglo clerical staff was gunning down his workers in Cananea, a hysterical telegram arrived in Bisbee describing insane Mexicans massacring "hundreds of white people." An armed posse of white basketball players from the Bisbee YMCA immediately mounted up and rode south, eager to demonstrate their "muscular Christianity" by shooting some Mexicans. They were followed by Captain Thomas Rynning of the Arizona Rangers, leading a troop of Bisbee volunteers who emptied the saloons of liquor and the hardware stores of guns before boarding the train. Joey knew he could learn more by listening than talking but Frank Little was making it really hard.

At that moment their server appeared with a percolator pot. "Coffee?" the man offered.

"Sam!" responded Frank in a reproving tone. "This is my friend, Joey Quintana. Joey, Sam Bishara. Please take that away and bring us some of *your* coffee, Sam." The server nodded and retreated and a young boy came and took the cups off the table. Joey looked at Frank curiously. "Wait," said Frank. "You'll see."

In a minute, Sam reappeared with a brass pitcher shaped like a Coca Cola bottle – narrow waist, wide above and below – and a long handle. The boy followed him and put a small bowl of raisins on the table. Sam set a tiny cup in front of Joey, then poured him an even tinier serving from the brass pitcher, which Joey now realized was a coffee pot of some kind. "*Tafaddal*," said Sam, or something like that. He repeated the gestures and the word with Frank.

"Thank you, Sam," said Frank, and gave Joey a look.

Joey realized he had been eyeing this *cafecito* with suspicion. Where were his manners? "Yes, thank you," he said. He lifted the cup, inhaled its strong aroma and – in that way that scents can revive memories – immediately recalled a cold morning from his childhood in Cañada de los Álamos. There was still snow on the hillsides and ice in the river. The men were preparing to clean the irrigation ditches and they were passing around a pot of Arbuckle's coffee that they had brewed on a crackling piñon fire near the mother ditch. The coffee was for everybody, as was the work. The *acequias* could never be cleaned if they didn't all do it together, so personal feuds and vendettas had to be forgotten during ditch cleaning season. The smell of Sam's coffee brought back the cold and the feeling of village men working together. It had been a long time since Joey had helped with that work.

Shaking off the thought, Joey sipped the small serving. It was bitter, yes, but somehow it did not need sugar or milk. The flavor of coffee was there, only more so. And there was something else, too. "This is the best coffee I have ever tasted," he said to Sam, and it was the truth. "Thank you!"

No sooner had he returned the tiny cup to the table than Sam poured another few drops into it. "*Taffadal*," he said again.

Frank showed him how to put a raisin between his teeth to sweeten the coffee as he was sipping it. Then he asked, "Worth trying?"

"Absolutely!" answered Joey enthusiastically. He slowly sipped this new serving and realized he was no longer irritated with Frank Little's dense inability to see his own prejudice. Frank was a comrade and they would make it work. This was *really* good coffee!

After a couple more pourings, which probably still didn't total a normal cup, Sam stepped away from their table to take care of other customers. Frank's mood had changed, too. "I'm optimistic about what you can do in Bisbee," he said. "We're demanding a $6 day for underground work and $5.75 for top work. That would totally do away with the Mexican wage. I think you're going to be able to organize around that!"

So did Joey. He and Frank continued to discuss the details of the work with enthusiasm. It was settled. Frank would head north to Butte and Joey would go south to Bisbee. This was really good coffee!

Bisbee, Arizona
1917

Joey spent his first few days in Bisbee getting the lay of the land. He couldn't be anonymous, not with so many people around who knew him, but he could meet with them separately and he could certainly do more listening than talking.

Some conversations were in people's homes and boarding houses, but a lot were at Caretto's Saloon on OK Street. It was right next door to the Bisbee jailhouse, which did not make Joey comfortable, but Baptiste Caretto had at one time been a union miner and he still made cash contributions to the union. It was as safe a meeting place as any.

A sign over the bar read "A Quiet and Orderly Resort." That was not the reputation the place had among the white men of Arizona. Caretto's didn't need shooting affrays to get its "bad name." Serving beer wasn't the problem, either. The bad name came from the Italian ownership. The bad name came from the colored soldiers who drank here when they had day leave from Fort Naco twelve miles away on the border with Mexico. The bad name came from the Mexicans and Mexican Americans who lived up the steps on Chihuahua Hill and who stopped in to quench a thirst before the steep walk home from the long shifts at the Copper Queen. Here in Bisbee the "good people", the YMCA element, had only recently passed an ordinance requiring every gun in town to be registered: by the owner's name, address and *nationality*. They saw everything through that lens.

It took time to prepare for a larger meeting. He had to talk first with leading men from both sides of the border. He had to talk first with men from different organizations and political tendencies. But because Joey already knew so many of them, he was ready in a week. He called the meeting for Carretto's Saloon. He called it for a weekday evening, right after the day shift. That way there would be plenty of workers there, even those who had not heard about it.

The bar began filling up shortly after the whistle blew at the mill. Joey waited patiently before beginning. Eventually, the crowd quieted as those who had just stepped in for a beer realized that something was about to happen.

"Why don't you tell us what brings you here." It was Elipio Mondragón. He was the son of Don Celedonio Mondragón, founder of the SPMDTU, a mutual aid and burial society with chapters all over southern Colorado and northern New Mexico. Joey had already discussed this with the *mutualistas*, but the invitation to speak, from a well-known *non*-union man, was a good way to open the meeting.

Before Joey could say a word though, up spoke a voice from the rear of the barroom. "This *angringado* wants us to join his *gabacho* union." Joey looked around and saw a man in a suit, seated at one of the tables. He should have noticed Faustino Escobosa when he first walked in. He was a sales rep for the *Alianza Hispano Americana*, a life insurance company.

The insult to him and the IWW might have seemed an inauspicious start to a novice organizer, but Joey was anything but a novice. He *wanted* the conflicting views to be aired. In any case, he didn't even have to speak up in his own behalf. "José Quintana has always stood for the rights of *all*, regardless of nationality," answered Bernardo Gallardo, his childhood friend from Cañada de los Álamos. Bernardo was there with a crowd of his *cuates* from *río arriba* and the Pecos valley. "Am I right?" he asked his friends.

"*Sí, sí, es la verdad,*" answered several men. Many of them had been with him in Los Cerrillos when Joey first brought Mexicans together with Serbs, Chinese, Italians, Anglos, and Indians to stand up to the copper bosses.

Abrán Salcido was in the room, and he was not going to be outdone in defending Joey. Abrán was an important leader in *Unión Minero*. Joey last worked with him in the big Cananea strike on the other side back in 1906. "There is no Mexican working class and no Anglo working class," said Abrán. "There is only an international proletariat."

This elicited gales of laughter from all sides. "Somebody needs to explain that to these white miners here in Bisbee," chuckled Elipio Mondragón.

Faustino Escobosa wasn't happy even with this. "You people need to stop thinking of yourselves as workers at all. The gringos have poisoned your minds. Stop begging for crumbs from their table. The opportunities for you to advance yourselves as businessmen are everywhere."

Elipio stopped laughing. "Do you even listen to yourself? The gringos haven't poisoned our minds. Yes, they stole our land. Yes, they stole our legislatures. But our minds are still free. And we know that if we are going to accomplish anything, it won't be one by one, it will be together, as it always has been."

There was general and loud assent to this. But Faustino was undeterred. "Together? Together with whom? Together with these *gabachos*? Their unions have never served any purpose but to exclude you. That's what they organized them for."

Joey had still said nothing. It was too important to let all the differences be aired. An outsider might look in this barroom and say that all the men were Mexican. Whether that outsider was a union man like IWW organizer Frank Little or a company man like Phelps, Dodge chairman James Douglas, that was all they could see. Joey, though, knew that the men in this room were not all anything. Some were native-born US citizens, some immigrants from Mexico. Some were *magonistas,* some *carrancistas*, but many were apolitical. They were divided by village, divided by an international border, divided by political ideology, and divided by old personal quarrels. If he were to have any chance of uniting them, it would not be by agreeing with one of their leaders against another. It did not matter how much he loved some of them. It did not matter how little he respected others.

"Faustino is right, Joey," said his friend Bernardo. A lot of the men were nodding agreement. "The Anglos in the mine are talking strike. But they have never treated us with respect. Are you here to suggest that we join them?" Every man in the bar now turned their attention to Joey.

It was time to speak. "No," said Joey. "I am not suggesting that we join *them*. I am here to propose that *we* join together. Us. I am suggesting that we make the company pay wages on a single scale. I am suggesting that we end this 'Mexican' wage. I am suggesting that we open up all jobs – above ground and below – to all workers. I am suggesting that we end the 'Mexican' job. And I am suggesting that *we* do this. If the Anglos want to join us, we should make them welcome, but we are the majority of workers here in Bisbee and we do not have to beg anyone for anything."

There was a long silence as he said this. It was not immediately broken when he stopped talking, either.

And then, pandemonium. People attempted to think through what he had said... out loud. What Joey suggested would immediately double the wage of every man there. That was undeniable. Double. But was it possible? This was the gist of every conversation in the room, if any of it could be described as conversation. Everyone was talking. Simultaneously. Joey did not attempt to restore order. He let the bedlam go. There was no chance of shouting above a commotion like this, and why would he want to? Nobody needed to be convinced by him. They all needed to convince themselves.

It was a long few minutes before the hubbub receded even to levels normally associated with a crowded saloon. And then, to Joey's relief, it was Elipio Mondragón – a young man with whom he had no particular alliance nor enmity – who asked, "What makes you think the mine operators will ever agree to that?"

The question brought even more quiet, because it was the question on everyone's mind. "Phelps, Dodge will *never* agree to that," said Joey. "Why should they?"

He heard surprised murmuring around the room: "What?" "*¿Qué dice él?*"

But Joey kept right on talking: "They profit every day we remain divided, profit by treating us like *burros*. They have no need to *agree* to anything. They will only treat us as men when they have no other choice, not because they agree, but because we give them no other choice, when we stand together and act as men." It was no great oratory, and Joey said it without drama, as the simple truth that it was.

Joey pulled out a stack of Local 800 membership cards. He gave some to Elipio and the *mutualistas*. He gave some to Abrán and the *sindicalistas*. He gave some to Bernardo. He gave some to the *magonistas* and to the *carrancistas* and to the *villistas*. He even gave some to Don Faustino, because – regardless of Escobosa's personal opinion of this – he would never jeopardize his insurance sales by opposing what his customers clearly wanted. And it was clear now, oh, it was transparent. The men were ready.

In that crowded, sweaty barroom there wasn't even a hint of a breeze, but the hair on Joey's arms stood up as if a wind was blowing unobstructed from Saskatchewan. Joey smelled the aroma of beer, and – in that way that scents can revive memories – he recalled an afternoon encounter with his friend Bernardo and with Bernardo's friend Jesús Vega in Doña Rosa's *cantina* in Los Cerrillos when the hair on his arms stood up. There had been no breeze in Doña Rosa's either. There had just been the smell of spilled beer... spilled beer and joy: the joy of unity over division, of purpose over anonymity, and of resistance over oppression.

**Johns Island, South Carolina
1918**

October 15

This evening when I returned from school to my room at the Bishops there was a letter addressed to Miss Septima Poinsette waiting for me on my desk. Mr. A. C. Dayson, the postmaster, originally came to the island as a teacher. He is sensitive to the demands of our work, so he always sends my mail directly to the house instead of making me walk the whole twelve miles to his post office. I knew who the letter was from before I even saw the return address. The postmark said U.S. Army, there was no postage stamp and it was a YMCA envelope: Lieutenant Osceola McKain.

No, not "lieutenant." The first news he shared with me was his promotion to Captain! In some ways I don't know what this means: How many men does he command? What are his responsibilities? And – so important to me now – does this put him in more or less danger? What I do know is that the Army recognizes him, sees his goodness and his leadership. I am still here at Promise Land after all this time, so it is good to see somebody I care for receive recognition, even if I am passed by. Most of the letter was devoted to the quotidian details of his life in France. I would love to read something about me, or – more honestly – about *us*, but the mere fact of his letters tells me that the possibility of an "us" exists.

Regarding today's work with the children I am afraid I must depart from my earnest efforts at observation and take some time to crow. Some teachers think the children should do all the listening: they are quick with the switch or the paddle if they see a distracted child. I believe that you have to let the children talk to you. I believe that they need a chance to say what they want to say. When you get through listening, you let them know they're right... according to what they have in mind. But you also let them know that – in this world – there is always more that they need to know. And then you ask if they're willing to listen to you.

I have written a great deal in this journal about the special challenges presented by Blue Gamble. Two days ago I spoke to him about his unwillingness to read aloud in class. I told him that he is a learner, and that learners need not be perfect. He seemed to consider that. This morning before class I mentioned to him that he allows no invitation. When I ask him to read, he averts his eyes and shakes his head. When I do not ask him, he looks hurt and excluded. He seemed to think this over, too. Later on, when I asked for volunteers to read the story I posted on a dry cleaning bag, he raised his hand. Then he stood and read...

almost without error! I am elated. I cannot claim to have hit on the magic, correct approach to this child, but I think that our growing personal trust may finally be extended to the classroom.

On the other hand… Today Kissy Fields surprised me with the vehemence of her rejection of any compliment for her work. The children have been exploring the economy of John's Island and Kissy – along with Etta, Robert and Prince – have been drawing pictures and writing descriptions of shrimping. Kissy made certain that their work included *everything*, starting with her Uncle Seribus making a cast net, and finishing with her Grandma Lovina seasoning the shrimp boil, not missing the boating and cleaning along the way. When she got up and showed her work to the class she even included the songs! She sang "Row Michael" when she showed her picture of cast netting. She sang "Talking About a Good Time" when she described people dancing at the shrimp boil.

This all went far beyond what I had asked for, so after school I told Kissy that her work was exceptional. She frowned and said I was just sweet mouthing her. When I insisted, she became angry. I asked why my compliments were so unacceptable. She did not answer. But when I asked when was the last time she *was* exceptional, she answered immediately (and surprisingly) that she was a very good girl until she was ten and then turned into a droll. I wonder what happened to her when she was ten. Perhaps I should ask Mrs. Melvina Bishop.

On another note: March Simmons informed me today that he is leaving school to work on a farm on the other side of the island.

October 17

After school today I went to March's home to speak with his mother, Mrs. Florine Simmons. She told me that March is indeed leaving school to work on Mr. Leo Parlor's farm. I listened very carefully to what she said about feeding her younger children and her need for March to contribute to that. I said my piece about the importance of learning, but I do not think she wanted to hear that today.

I also stopped by Mrs. Elvina Singleton's today to discuss how Celia is doing. During our conversation she mentioned that March Simmons had witnessed a young woman shot to death by an itinerant laborer from off-island. This happened two years ago. Now that man – who has never been charged or arrested – is back, and both Mrs. Simmons and March are afraid of him. No wonder she wants to get her son out of the neighborhood!

These mothers know so much about all the children. I could be a better teacher if I knew even half of what they know. If only they would treat me as a neighbor, a "been-here," instead of a visitor, a "come-here!" I suppose it will take a lot longer. Teachers do come and go from this island, so it may be a good idea for them to hold us all at arms' length instead of admitting us into the circle of community. And, truly, I was just confiding in this journal two days ago my desire to be promoted to another school. Perhaps I am the one who must begin acting as a neighbor if I want them to treat me as one.

October 21, 1918

After all this time I continue to shame myself with my quickness to find fault in others and my inability to see myself in the same critical light. Thursday I learned of an unpunished murder here on the island and how the return of the perpetrator was frightening March Simmons into quitting school so he could get as far away from the killer as possible. What was my reaction? Disappointment that nobody tells me anything. I was more concerned with the fact that the women don't treat me as one of them than I was about March's terror that he would be the killer's next victim. This is my third year teaching and I truly thought that I had learned to put the children before myself. Apparently that will take a little longer.

These were my thoughts on Saturday. So I tried to take stock of myself and to think of what I do to remain apart from the mothers, to ensure that they do not entrust me with the confidences that would deepen my work with their children. And that is when I had my moment of epiphany.

For almost two years I have been conducting classes in reading for the men of Promise Land. Mr. Flood Wilson suggested this and we have been making great strides in literacy for the dozen or so who attend. Why did it never occur to me to offer classes for the ladies? Why did it never occur to me to wonder what they must think about being excluded so? And why, oh, why have I never asked myself what they must think of me meeting so regularly with their husbands and not with them? My very first moment on this island I was roundly cursed by Mrs. Janey Blake who thought that Charlotte and I were hussies trying to steal Mr. Blake from her. The only way I could fail to see this is because I consider myself so far above the island folks that I would never consider one of the men as a beau, and that is almost worse than trying to steal a man from one of my pupil's mothers! I remain critical of Mother for her airs of superiority and I myself am equally bad.

But recognizing this distasteful quality in myself is nothing if I do not move to correct it and the first step was obvious. Saturday afternoon I went calling on Mrs. Emmaline Brown, the mother of Hamilton. She is a few years older than some of the other mothers and I have noticed that hers is a leading voice in the church. I found her working in her garden with Hamilton, harvesting some late squash. He took one look at me and ran off without a word.

Mrs. Brown chuckled and said, "Good morning to you, Miss Seppy. What Bubba do wrong on a day with no school?"

I smiled and answered, "It is a beautiful morning, Mrs. Brown. And I am not here to report on Bubba. I wish to speak with you on another matter."

Mrs. Brown's eyes narrowed and the smile left her lips. But, always gracious, she asked, "How may I help you, Miss Seppy?"

I had tried to rehearse what I wanted to say. I had tried to imagine how my invitation would be received. I had failed. Now all I could do was make the offer as directly as possible. "Mrs. Brown, do you suppose that you and some of the other ladies would be interested in getting together regularly for adult education classes?"

Mrs. Brown's ease of conversation seemed to fail her for a moment. She looked at me and sighed audibly and deeply. She hesitated. Now my imagination returned in force and in my mind I heard her ask, "It took you two years to think of this?" and "What in the world could a young girl like you have to teach grown folks?" and "Why would we choose to spend our free time with a seditty 'come-here' who thinks she's better than us?"

But her customary grace had not left her and she said none of these things. Instead, she said, "Several of the ladies would like such a class. Right off the top of my head I can think of Mrs. Mozelle Wright, Mrs. Carrie LaBoard, Mrs. Pearl Fields, Mrs. Elvina Singleton, Mrs. Florine Simmons..." And she looked at me searchingly to see if I understood.

I did. The fact that she could rattle off these names so quickly meant that the women had been stewing on this for a good long time. I briefly considered asking why they hadn't just asked me, instead of waiting for me to think of it, and judging me. But I kept that question to myself. I am twenty years old now and have learned to think before speaking. Instead I nodded and said, "I am so happy that you would consider trusting me with such an important role in the community."

Mrs. Brown smiled and nodded. She said loudly, "Bubba! Come fetch Miss Seppy a cool drink of water!" When Bubba reappeared – cautiously – from behind their home, she asked me, "Won't you set a spell so we can talk?" She gestured toward two wooden chairs in the shade of a live oak and we walked together out of the sunlight of her garden and into the cool spot under the tree.

We were quiet for a moment, enjoying a little breeze from Bohicket Creek. Bubba brought us each a Ball jar with water from the spring. Then Mrs. Brown said, "You know, grown folks here on the island used to be educated. My grandma, Queen Esther Bonneau, went to school all the way through eighth grade."

No, I did not know. "What happened?" I asked.

She turned and looked at me. I knew immediately that I shouldn't have asked such an obvious question. "Buckra put a stop to it," she snorted.

She was silent again for a good long time, then she seemed to decide she had to tell me what I needed to know. "Forty years ago," she said, "before I was born and before you were a thought, our families owned all this island. The Yankees landed in Legareville during the Lincoln war, but they couldn't hold it. They sailed away. So did the old masters, because they were afraid of the fighting. Our great-grandpas and great-grandmas returned this land to themselves; just a little bit of backpay for 150 years of work and whippings. They planted whatever crops they wanted to feed the children. They brought in teachers to teach the children. And all the men registered to vote."

I knew some of this, but I decided I could learn more by listening than by showing off my little bit of information. So I just said, "Yes?" to show I was paying attention.

Mrs. Brown nodded and went on. "Buckra took the land back first. They came with deeds and lawsuits and bank loans and they got a parcel here and a parcel there until all we had was the ground under our houses."

I looked around and imagined that everything I saw was the property of the families living there, that they didn't all work for white folks who we rarely saw. It put a different light on everything.

"The vote took them longer. Up there in Columbia and Spartanburg and Florence they murdered our leaders and put armed patrols on the road on election day to keep our people from voting. Here in the Low Country, though, there were too many of us and they didn't have the numbers to hold us away from the polls, guns or no guns. So they just redrew the election districts. We could keep sending Robert Smalls to Congress from here in the Low Country, but it didn't matter because they were going to control the rest of the state. There were more Black folks than white in South Carolina then, just like there are now, so they used both - shootings and those district lines - to keep themselves in control. And they used that control to cut off our school funds. My grandma tried to teach me, but I had to work, and she had to work and there wasn't any school for us. Congressman Smalls spoke up about it, but by that time there wasn't but five Negroes in the statehouse: from around here down to Hilton Head and from up around Georgetown. Buckra's voting majorities everywhere else in the state might be only slim, but he kept those majorities with shootings, beatings and burnings.

"The white ladies said that *they* needed to get the vote so that *we* could lose it. They kept saying that their men couldn't protect 'white supremacy' without the help of the ladies. That's what they called it, 'white supremacy,' and they said white ladies voting was the only way to hold down the Negro, to hold us down. White ladies can't vote yet in South Carolina, but I believe they're still saying that today.

"Then, twenty some years ago, they decided that as long as we Black folks were the majority in South Carolina, violence and districting might not be enough for them to control the state and keep us under their thumbs. They had a convention and they wrote a new state constitution with new voting rules. Under the new constitution it wasn't enough just to know how to read. They wanted you to read to the satisfaction of a white man... and there was no satisfying that white man."

Again, this was mostly familiar to me. I still stayed quiet for the same reason: I didn't want to act like a show-off and say so. I also didn't want to act like I was surprised that an island woman was familiar with so much history; I was trying to keep myself from acting superior. And I really wanted to know why Mrs. Brown was telling me this now. So I nodded all through it and waited.

So did she. She looked at me and waited some more. Then she sighed again and asked, "Miss Seppy, don't you see what I'm saying?"

I did not. I shook my head "no." And then... I did. It was as if I had stepped out of a dark cellar and into the daylight, I was that blinded by the revelation. Who does God bless with two astonishing epiphanies in one day? Apparently, me. I looked at Mrs. Brown with wide eyes and said, "Not literacy classes; *citizenship* classes!"

And Mrs. Brown smiled at me, like a teacher who has had a breakthrough with her slowest pupil. "Yes, child: citizenship."

"The state constitution!" I said.

"That's what that white man tests you on when you try to register to vote," said Mrs. Brown.

When Mr. Flood Wilson asked me to start classes for the men, they were most interested in learning to read the contracts they signed every year with their white employers. They wanted to stop the endless cheating by the white landowners and to get their fair share. But Mrs. Emmaline Brown has a much larger goal in mind. She wants to bring an end to the entire system of white power that holds them down. And not just them. Not just the people of Johns Island. All the colored people of South Carolina, including me and Mama and Father. All the colored people in America!

I asked Mrs. Brown to let the other ladies know so that we can start immediately. I am burning to begin this. Because I will not be the only teacher in that class. We will all teach each other. Mrs. Brown already showed me how much I still have to learn from her and the other ladies. And as for what I *do* have to teach? Well, it's not just reading. I have to teach *them* how to teach, too. Because even if I were to live to ninety, I could only teach but so many people. But if everyone I teach were to teach some others? And them? Well, I think nobody will be able to hold us back.

Saint-Rémy-sur-Bussy, Marne, France
1918

The sun was peeking through the clouds but there was already a little hint of fall in the late afternoon air. Sgt. Rector Beauchamp took a big breath of it as he strolled down Rue de la Croissette, ignoring the parade of wagons on the cobblestones bringing supplies to the front. He knew that Saint-Rémy-sur-Bussy was a village, smaller in fact than Haven, Oklahoma, back home, but something about being in France made him feel like a boulevardier, as if this little place were Paris. He rounded the corner onto Rue de la Damon and here was a sidewalk café! His fantasy was complete. Beauchamp seated himself at one of the three little tables in the street. Out popped a thin, balding man, maybe seventy, in a white shirt and black trousers.

"Bonjour! Puis-je prendre votre commande?" the man asked.

"Bonjour à vous," replied Sgt. Beauchamp. *"Je prendrai un bière s'il vous plait."*

The man – owner, guessed Rector – nodded and returned inside. Perfect, just perfect. Oklahoma had been dry since statehood; the Indian Territory, long before that. You could get a beer, of course, but the places were rough and hard liquor was more readily available. By alcoholic content whiskey was cheaper to transport and, therefore, more economical to serve. Beauchamp had read about the cafés of France in a book assigned by his French professor back at Creek Seminole College. Who knew that in a few years he would be sitting in front of one and ordering a hand-brewed beer? Hell, forget the beer. He had just ordered from a white man at a white establishment without being called a Black bastard and ordered to leave. France was a daily revelation!

The side street he was sitting in had very little traffic. Down the block, on Rue de la Croissette, the steady clatter of horseshoes and iron-tired wagon wheels reminded Sgt. Beauchamp that the war was still going on just a few kilometers away, and that he would be back in it, soon enough. He tuned out the racket and pretended that he was an urban sophisticate having a quiet afternoon before a night at the salon, or the opera, or whatever it was that sparkling cosmopolitan folk did with their evenings.

When the beer came it, too, was a revelation. Perhaps Rector was in an elevated mood, but he was quite certain that he had never tasted anything better. For several months Sgt. Beauchamp and his fellow troopers had been eating a stew made from salt cod, lard, rice and beans. The unfamiliar combination was wearing on him, and he was really craving his mama's *safke*. To drink, the soldiers got a cheap wine that everyone called "pinard." So perhaps this break from his routine – and unfamiliar – diet also contributed to his appreciation of the local beer.

When the village work day ended, a few locals came by and sat at the other tables. None was younger than sixty. The war had emptied all these towns of their young men. The newcomers didn't insist on conversing with him, but they did smile, say their "*bonjours*," and raise their beer glasses toward him as they were served. The shadows lengthened. Sgt. Beauchamp ordered a second beer, reluctant to end his idyll.

A girl – fifteen? sixteen? – walked into the street from a nearby alley just as two white American soldiers with the red, white, and black shoulder patch of the First Army and gold second lieutenant's bars turned in from the main road. What were they doing this far west? The First Army's zone was 26 kilometers away in Ste. Menehould. Why did they want to be so far from their comrades? The question made him uneasy.

To Sgt. Rector Beauchamp's surprise, neither man noticed him at his table in front of the little café. Instead, their eyes locked onto the girl. "I musta died and went to heaven," said one, grabbing the other's coat sleeve. "It's a fuckin' angel."

Rector had grown accustomed to the casual vulgarity of the army, but speaking this way in front of a girl froze him. The sun disappeared behind the house across the street and the temperature seemed to drop suddenly. He thought of a train station in Weleetka, Oklahoma.

The girl had not yet noticed the two white men. He couldn't help but think of them that way, although she, too, had white skin. It was something about their coarse manner, and the fact that it was directed at her. She continued toward them, oblivious. As she drew alongside, the first soldier hailed her. "Howdy, madamazel," he said, mangling the French word. "Howzabout we show you a good time?"

Sgt. Beauchamp, still apparently invisible, shivered. The girl looked up from her errand, confused. "*Excusez-mois*," she said, "*je ne parle pas anglais.*"

"You see that?" said Soldier 1 to his buddy. "She loves me, too." And he grabbed her by the elbow.

Now the girl's eyes opened wide in fear. *"Laissez moi partir, monsieur, s'il vous plait."* The soldier only laughed.

Time slowed. Once again Rector Beauchamp saw a train station in Weleetka. This time he saw a white cowhand named Johnny Cade. Cade was speaking, and had an ugly expression on his face, but a younger Rector couldn't hear the words over the sound of a girl weeping, out of sight, but right at hand. Nessa? No, it was this French girl, right here. He saw the white soldiers again, both officers, each with a big Army Colt on his hip. He heard the old men at the other tables ask what was going on. He saw the white soldiers draw their automatic pistols. And then he heard his own voice.

"Je peux vous aider, mademoiselle?"

He had reemerged from invisibility. The second white man, who had been silent until now, looked directly at him, but spoke to his comrade, who now had the girl by her waist. "Oh, look, Les! This monkey speaks French."

South Carolina. Beauchamp recognized both accent and attitude. The regiment had trained in Spartanburg for a few weeks before shipping out until mutual dislike between soldiers and townsfolk had required a redeployment to the east end of Long Island.

The man now addressed him directly: "Son, this is white man's business. I advise you to stay out of it."

"À l'aide! À l'aide!" shouted the girl, struggling to escape the first man's grip. An angry crowd was gathering in the little street. The white soldiers held their guns on them.

The first soldier, "Les," now addressed himself to Beauchamp, too. "We have a prior arrangement with this whore," he said. "We already paid her for two fucks apiece." And he repeated his friend's warning, "Stay out of it, nigger."

"Sgt. Rector Beauchamp!" Rector jumped to his feet, stood to attention, and snapped off a parade-ground salute. "369th Regiment, United States Army!" He wondered if what they said was true. Would he see his whole life flash by, or just those few moments in the Weleetka train station with Nessa Payne? "Begging your pardon, sirs, but I feel this is a case of mistaken identity!" He was still shouting, as if this were some weird parade-ground drill.

267

"What the fuck are you talking about, nigger?" asked Soldier #1, his eyes and his gun still on the increasingly angry locals. It was as if Beauchamp had not just introduced himself by name, rank and unit; as if he were not wearing his full uniform, stripes on his sleeve; as if his unit, rank and name were all "nigger."

"Sir!" Sgt. Beauchamp went on, "I saw a professional woman go by five minutes ago with the same color hair and same color frock." He was making every bit of this up as he was speaking. If any woman at all had gone by, he hadn't noticed. And "professional woman"? There was no insignia or uniform that identified women desperate enough to sell themselves. But he bravely pressed on, "This isn't the girl you're looking for."

By now the two white men were surrounded. A stocky woman in a bloody apron from the butcher shop next door menaced them with a cleaver. The owner of the café stood alongside his elderly customers with a knife in his hand. Six women and three men had joined them from the nearby houses. They were holding brooms, skillets, and fireplace tools.

The second officer, the one from South Carolina, took stock of the situation. "Leave it," he said quietly to his companion, who, after a moment, let the girl go. She ran, sobbing, to the woman with the iron skillet. That woman embraced her, comforted her, but did not take her eyes off the three soldiers, Rector included.

The second soldier now addressed the small crowd of villagers: "We are very sorry for the misunderstanding. We appreciate your hospitality and will now be on our way." Turning to Beauchamp he added in a softer voice, "Get your affairs in order, boy. We'll see you sooner than you think." Then he took the first soldier by the arm and they went quickly back down the street toward Rue de la Croissette.

The villagers were now frozen, uncertain what had been said in English. The butcher, the woman with the cleaver, asked "*Qu'ont-ils dit?*"

"*Ils ont présenté leurs excuses,*" answered Sgt. Beauchamp.

The mention of an apology enraged the people in the street all over again. Suddenly everybody was shouting threats and describing what they would do to the "*soldats Américains.*" Rector was glad, for once, that he, like all the men of the 369th, wore the uniform of the French Army.

After each bystander had repeated everything that happened three times, with special emphasis on their own role; after everybody had told everybody else what they should have done and said; and after all of them had made perfectly clear what they would do to the Americans if they came back; then, and only then, did they return their attention to Sgt. Beauchamp. He had seen the crying girl gather herself and listen to her neighbors shouting. Now she pointed to him and told everyone, "*Cet homme à sauvé ma vie.*"

There was another round of enthusiastic discussion. They all agreed, yes, he had saved the girl's life. Rector thought he had saved something else, but, yes, perhaps he had saved her life, too. The woman holding the girl, who he was now certain was her mother, stepped toward him. "*Merci, monsieur, pour tout ce que vous avez fait. Nous serons honorés de vous avoir comme notre invité pour le dîner.*"

A dinner invitation? He didn't have to be back before tomorrow. Why not? First, though, everybody wanted to know: Who was he? Where did the hero who had saved the life of the "*jeune fille*" come from? "*Êtes-vous un tirailleur sénégalais?*" asked the owner of the café.

Rector smiled. He didn't know what a "*tirailleur*" was, but he knew he wasn't from Senegal. He had met the African troops, been impressed with them. But it was time to admit that he, too, like the would-be abusers, was an American. "*Non, je suis un Américain. Je suis un Indien Seminole de l'Oklahoma.*"

He might have gone a little far with identifying his tribe and his home state. But, no, everybody was smiling about this. "*Oui, oui. Les Américains blancs détestent les Indiens rouges,*" happily explained the woman in the butcher's apron. They had come up with a convincing reason for the conflict among the Americans and they all clearly identified with Sitting Bull against Custer. Had they seen Buffalo Bill's Wild West? He decided against explaining that, to the two white men, he was just another Negro. The crowd seemed pleased with the explanation they had.

And so Sgt. Rector Beauchamp returned to his French idyll, walking up *Allée de Tilleuls,* to the home of Mme. Gautier and her beloved daughter Corette for a typical country meal of the Champagne region, or at least a meal of what people still had after four years of war. He was so delighted with them, and they with him, that he forgot the ugly threat the white men had left him with.

January 27, 1919
Pacific Palisades, California

Dear Nicholas Black Elk,

Háu tȟaŋháŋši!

Greetings to you and your relations! Greetings to whoever is reading this to you and - I hope - writing your reply. I am writing you from a great distance seeking your counsel. I am Ota K'te, also known as Luther Standing Bear, son of George Standing Bear and Pretty Face. When we last crossed paths you were a holy man, *wičháša wakȟáŋ*, with an enviable reputation both for success in healing the sick and for your powerful connection with the *wakíŋyaŋ* thunder spirits. I was a teacher then, at the Allen school, and a recent graduate of the Carlisle Indian School in Pennsylvania. I traveled hours to hear you speak about the prophecies of Wíyatke in the days of our grandfather's fathers.

Here is what I remember of Wíyatke's vision as you told it: A people will come from the east who will tie up the world in a spider's web of iron. They will fill up this world. They will make war on us and we will never live in the sacred hoop again. Our people will live in square houses.

This prophecy seems to have come true in every detail. I have been trying to remember what his instructions were to us. Wíyatke said we could not defeat the *wašíču* in war, but that still leaves the question of how we remain Lakota. How do we feed and clothe ourselves now that the great herds, the *pteóptaye*, are gone? How do boys become men without testing themselves in battle or the hunt? How are we Lakota if we cannot travel when and where we please without permission from the *wašíču*?

Look at me now, writing you a letter asking for your counsel instead of bringing you gifts in person! They tell me that you, too, have transformed yourself to be a part of this new world. They tell me you are no longer *wičháša wakȟáŋ*, that you have become a Catholic and that you minister to the baptized. This is hard for me to reconcile. You had power in the old ways, and a great following, too. When I was last at Pine Ridge, many, many people came to you for healing. What brought about your conversion? I am baptized in the Episcopalian Church, but over the years it feels to me less and less like something that belongs to us. I feel that my church membership is like a fence, built in the spirit world, to bar me from our old free life. Clearly, you have found something different. Please explain it to me.

Around the same time I left Pine Ridge, the agent also fired the doctor, a Santee relation from Minnesota who used the name Charles Eastman. He has now written books about growing up Dakota. He explains the Sun Dance, the sweat lodge, the Sacred Pipe. I don't know what to think about this. Is he a missionary, trying to convert the *wašíčus* to our beliefs? Does he think they will take us more seriously if they know us better? I am afraid he is turning the most sacred parts of our lives and thoughts into cheap entertainment for our enemies. I traveled with the Wild West shows, just like you did, so I worry about what it means for us to feed their fantasies about us.

I also worry when those adversaries are the very ones pretending expertise about our lives and our rituals. I recently discovered a book explaining *Wiwáŋyaŋg Wačhípi*, the sacred Sun Dance, written by James Walker! I don't know how to explain how disturbing this was to me. This is the same *wašíču* doctor that the Pine Ridge agent hired when he *fired* Eastman because he didn't want an Indian in that position! Now *wašíču* Walker gets to explain the holiest of our ceremonies to some New York City professors?

I looked at the book to see what he said. Imagine my surprise to discover that Walker got most of his information from George Sword. I don't like to speak badly of those who have walked on, but Sword was already *wágluȟe*, hanging around the fort, when I was just a little boy. Years before the Custer battle, he was the personal bodyguard for Agent J.J. Saville at Red Cloud. When I came back from school he was chief of police for the *wašíčus*. My uncle tells me that Sword took that name, *Mílahaŋska,* when he was 19 to show his allegiance to the white people! My relatives say he gave up his medicine bundle forty years ago.

That's why I find some of the claims Sword made in Walker's book impossible to believe. He claimed to have been a *leader* of war parties. At 19? Who would have followed him? He said he was a *counselor* for others on vision quest. That was a responsibility for a mature *wičháša wakȟáŋ*, not for an unproven young person. He claimed to have treated people with Bear Medicine. As an apprentice, perhaps, but I am skeptical that a man that young was a full *phežúta wičháša*. He even claimed to have been a guide, teaching participants how to do Sun Dance! All of this is too much for me to accept.

And they are not the only strange claims I found in Dr. Walker's book. Sword also told him that the holy men had their own secret society, that there were only five members left at the time he "discovered" it, and that only a member could induct a new holy man. So Walker sponsored several feasts at some personal expense in order to become, in his word, a "shaman."

This was the part where I stopped shaking my head at Sword and started wondering about Dr. Walker instead. What could he have been thinking? When Sword and his friends started asking him for money, didn't that send up some kind of warning flag for him? Didn't he have doubts when they told him they had a private language that no other Lakota understood? I had to laugh out loud when I read that they told him he needed a vision, but was unqualified to seek one. Every little boy whose voice dropped was qualified for that, but not him? Not the great medicine man who they were preparing to admit into their esoteric society? Anyway, they *gave* him a spirit animal, instead, and charged him money for that, too.

But then I realized: Why wouldn't he fall for all of this? This is the true way of the white men. The *wašíču* tell us that our religion is contemptible, but in their hearts they believe we hold the secrets of the universe. They think that only a handful of elders have mastered those secrets, they see that it took them a lifetime to do it, but they trust in their own ability to acquire them quickly, and they are determined to utilize some shortcut. And, of course, the key to that shortcut is cash, because that is what they all really worship.

Sword wasn't the only one telling stories to Dr. Walker. Left Heron and Bad Wound and a few of those other old timers from around Bear-in-the-Lodge Creek were talking to him, too. I knew those families thirty years ago when I was teaching school in that part of the reservation. Then my father moved up there with his third wife, Lena. My brothers Ellis and Willard still live there now. I can say for sure that Old Left Heron keeps a winter count and that he knows our history going back centuries. I know Bad Wound keeps the traditions. But I never heard that either of them are *wičháša wakháŋ*. Maybe you know different. And I guess there's no harm in them getting paid to tell our stories.

But what I really want to know is: What is *your* thinking on putting our stories and beliefs into print like this? There cannot be anybody still alive who is more qualified to prepare a book on Sun Dance, on Bear Medicine, or on all that is sacred than you. Would you consider it? I have been thinking about writing about my own boyhood, or perhaps about our customs, but my book would be the reminiscences of an ordinary child. A book written by you would contain knowledge and insights that are so much deeper. I just wonder who we would be writing *for*. You and I have already played Indian for the *wašíču* in the Wild West shows. For any book to be truly worthwhile, it would have to serve our own people and not a bunch of white folks searching for some novelty in their spiritual lives.

James Walker says in his foreword that he promised not to reveal any of the "shamans'" secrets during their lifetimes. He writes that he is now the only *wičháša wakȟáŋ* still alive! I don't know whether to laugh at his presumption or cry at our losses. Either way, the entire tone of his Sun Dance book is the description of a lost ritual of a vanished people. It is a souvenir of conquest. There is no doubt that we lost some battles, but we are still here. And I, for one, am not yet prepared to surrender our existence. Perhaps we can continue passing on our traditions from mouth to mouth as we used to. Perhaps the time has come for us to write books for one another. Either way, I ask you to consider sharing what the spirits taught you with a new generation.

There is a special irony these days in the *wašíčus'* hope that we would already have disappeared. It turns out that they really needed us in their Army during this World War. I heard a story about this from Edgar Fire Thunder, who was a classmate of mine at the Carlisle Indian School. Like my brother Ellis, he became a Pine Ridge policeman. In fact, he was a close friend of George Sword and succeeded him as police captain when Sword retired. Now, Fire Thunder is retired, too, and lives up near Bear-in-the-Lodge Creek with all those traditionals. His son William was in Europe fighting the Germans in this last war. So was Bad Wound's son, Vincent, and Left Heron's son, Oliver.

I don't know what I think of our young men fighting under the American flag. My brother Henry and his friends all think that the sooner we can become U.S. citizens, the better. And it certainly gives the young people an opportunity to become warriors and to count coup. But I still remember soldiers in those uniforms massacring our relations while flying that flag. I worried aloud to Edgar that serving in the *wašíču* Army may be one more way for us to lose sight of who we are.

But Fire Thunder, who is very proud of his son William's service, told me this story: All over the Western Front the Germans were tapping into our telephone lines to listen to our communications. When the officers realized, they were stuck with a puzzle. They could write in code, but paper messages take time to deliver and the Germans might have uncovered the secret to the code. They could continue to talk on the phone and the message would arrive instantly, but lots of Germans speak English and there would be no secrets at all. That's when they realized that the solution was right in front of them. There were William and Vincent and Oliver, all speaking Lakota!

It wasn't just Lakota, either. They had soldiers speaking Choctaw and Navajo and Cherokee, too. All the Army needed was two men with the same language on either end of the phone. They didn't have to have a code, all they had to do was talk, because the Germans couldn't understand any of it. Imagine if the Army had succeeded in wiping out our languages, which they certainly tried to do. They would have had no way of keeping secrets from the enemy. So our insistence on being ourselves worked out for them, too, and in a way that they never could have predicted. I know that young people from the "progressive" families around Pine Ridge got drafted into the Army. But their parents were careful to keep our language away from the children, so they weren't able to help with this. It certainly makes me think. And it makes me remember how the teachers at Carlisle used to wash our mouths out with soap when we spoke to each other in our Lakota language.

Well, that is about all. All those years ago, when I went to hear you preach, you kept talking about *Čhaŋgléška Wakȟáŋ*. You said that the sacred hoop is the whole earth. You said that our camps used to be set up in the form of the hoop. But you also said that the seven fires – *Očhéthi Šakówiŋ* – of our Lakota people are the sacred hoop. And I saw that you were wearing a hoop as an ornament. So I suppose one way of asking my question to you is: How do we repair *Čhaŋgléška Wakȟáŋ*? How do we heal ourselves?

I am sure you have been thinking about these questions, too. I wish to know your thoughts. Thank you for taking the time to listen to my words. Please give yours to whomever you get to read this letter so that they can send them to me. I await your answer.

Yours truly,
Luther Standing Bear

Tulsa, Oklahoma
5 April 1921
Confidential Report from Henry O. Flipper
To: Secretary of the Interior Albert Fall

Dear Secretary Fall:

In preparation for your visit to Oklahoma and at your request I have been investigating both the geological and political ramifications of petroleum investment in that state. A more complete report awaits your return to Washington but I submit this précis in case you have a need for immediate action while you are there.

1) The Miller Brothers are currently drilling below 1000 feet in the Anadarko Shelf near Tonkawa. This is a zone of rich marine sediment and is very promising. Despite their history of dry holes I have good reason to believe they will have success at about the 2000-foot horizon.
2) Overall, the state of Oklahoma is producing approximately 1 million barrels of oil *per day*! That means the most important factor in actually profiting from a successful well is proximity to rail transportation. The Miller Brothers have that, in large part due to the tourist operations of their 101 Ranch.
3) The biggest question mark surrounding the Miller Brothers' oil operations is the legality of the leases they hold from various Indian nations and individuals. The Justice Department currently has them in Federal Court and successful clearance of that suit is vital to the actual profitability of any productive well.
4) Oklahoma has given a dramatically different legal status to its Indians than you are familiar with from your dealings in New Mexico. For purposes of franchise and public accommodations they are treated as white men. This has not given them any significant political influence in the state. Also, our party's control of the lower house of the state legislature will neuter the Democratic governor.
5) People of my race represent one-quarter to one-third of all people in the eastern counties, particularly those of the former Creek Nation. These Negroes are prosperous and well organized and all brands of white Oklahomans denominate them a threat.
6) I have no intelligence regarding an "African Blood Brotherhood." I have heard that the Bureau of Investigation is looking into such a thing. Attorney General Daugherty may have more information.

7) I met Captain McKaine when he was a non-commissioned officer with the Punitive Expedition in Mexico. I was unimpressed with his leadership. I do not know his current whereabouts.

This should be sufficient information to approach the Millers. They are vulnerable to fears regarding the legality of their leases. They are also in a precarious position regarding their oil exploration. That window will close, though, if their Tonkawa well is successful, as I believe it soon will be. Any approach to them regarding contracting for the Naval Reserve at the Teapot Dome should be made soon.

Your obedient servant,
Henry Ossian Flipper

Marland, Oklahoma
1921

Hank Yarholar hated meeting dudes at the railroad station in Bliss. He had no interest in the Wild West shows that were such a big part of the 101 Ranch's income. The wild Indians in the cast were nice enough personally, but Hank found their costumes and their dances and their songs embarrassing. His *Mvskoke* language stayed at home with his family; he would not allow his private life to become a tourist attraction. He participated in the *posketv* with other Creeks at Thlopthlocco Town's dance ground; he would never dream of performing it in the Miller brothers' show. But when Hank was assigned to pick up visiting dignitaries from the train, the old Colonel's son, Junior Miller, insisted that Hank "dress like an Indian." It was as if Hank had to join the cast of the show every time he chauffeured visitors from the depot to the house.

These guests expected a "wild Indian." Hank's own ribbon shirt was out of the question, of course. First, he was not sharing anything of his own culture with these *wvcenvs...* that was a given. But, second, it wasn't what the audience pictured, either. They all expected buckskin and fringe. Hank was pretty certain that they would actually prefer bloody human scalps to fringe. He knew some performers in the show who did decorate their costumes with fake scalps made of horsehair. They earned tips before the show by telling audience members wildly fanciful stories about each one, as if all these young Sioux could have killed Custer at a battle that occurred twenty-five years before they were born!

So here he was, behind the wheel of one of the ranch's brand new closed-carriage Buicks, painted with the 101 brand and the show's logo. But instead of a clean suit and a tie, like a respectable chauffeur, he was wearing a buckskin jacket provided by the show's wardrobe mistress. On his feet were a pair of calf-high, beaded moccasins that were a gift from the Cheyenne actor Richard Thunderbird. Chief Thunderbird's Pawnee wife Nannie, who did beautiful handwork, made them for Hank just before the World War, as a good-bye gift when she and Thunderbird left Oklahoma for Hollywood. His gloves were also fringed buckskin, and they had beadwork done by a Sioux actor named Standing Bear, a friend of Thunderbird who was also now in the moving picture industry in California. Neither the gloves nor the designs on the moccasins were anything that a traditional *Mvskoke* man would wear. Hank was embarrassed the one time his father caught him wearing them. But old Tustenugge kept his silence and never brought it up again.

Still, they were boots and gloves and Hank wore boots and gloves everyday to work the range. The crowning piece of his chauffeur's costume was the part he really resented. It was a beaded headband, cranked out in the Miller Brother's sweatshop by impoverished Ponca and Otoe factory workers. All the audience members had the opportunity to buy them in the ranch's souvenir stores and they were sold at Coney Island and Madison Square Garden during the show's winter traveling season, too. The 101 Ranch was still cashing in on Geronimo's visit years before, by claiming that this was the exact headband he wore when he killed a buffalo as part of the show.

That had been an exceptionally ugly performance. There were *sixty-five thousand* guests at the show that day. For many weeks, the Boy Scouts of America had been demanding that President Roosevelt send troops to prevent what they believed would be a wholesale slaughter of buffalo. The Miller Brothers were happy to have all that free publicity. The soldiers were an added bonus, because they provided crowd control – at no cost! – for the gigantic audience. Junior advertised that Geronimo would kill his "last buffalo" at the show. The truth was Geronimo had never hunted buffalo before. It was his first. One of the Sioux actors drove the old Apache onto the show grounds in a 90-horsepower, luxury Locomobile. Instead of a bow and arrow, Geronimo fired a rifle. When the 80-year old man missed his first shot, Hank's crew drove the buffalo to point blank range. It went down on the next shot. Hank hated the memory of that day and hated the headband, yet here it was on his head as he sat in the Buick waiting for the train to pull into the ranch's Santa Fe Railroad station.

There was the whistle. In a few minutes the big 2-10-2 steam engine noisily stopped at the Miller Brothers' depot. Hank ignored the throngs of eager tourists disembarking from the excursion cars and the Pullman coaches. Toward the end of the train was a private car. That was where he would look for Junior's guests. He got out of the Buick and walked to the rather grand-looking train car. He quickly sized up the cluster of men climbing down, identified the two dignitaries, and addressed them. "Howdy," he said, extending his gloved hand. He had been instructed to keep the glove on so guests could admire the beadwork. "I'm Hank Yarholar, foreman of the 101 Ranch."

Both men ignored his hand and his words, preferring to look at the horizon. None of the other white men addressed him either. A Negro porter, though, handed him a steamer trunk, saying, "This is United States Attorney General Harry Daugherty and Secretary of the Interior Albert Fall. I have another three trunks for them."

Hank bit back his initial response, then said, "I have room in the automobile for Mr. Daugherty and Mr. Fall. These other men can take a hack with the luggage. I'll send somebody."

Everybody looked at him curiously. The man who had been introduced as the Secretary of the Interior said, "You speak English very well."

Hank supposed that this was intended as a compliment. "I was born here," he answered.

Both men seemed to find this amusing. In any case, they both smiled. The second man, Attorney General Daugherty, gestured with his hand. "Lead on, Chief!" he said.

Hank had heard this so many times that he almost didn't notice it... almost. He simply replied, "Please follow me," and led them back to the Buick. He held open each of the rear doors in turn, then got behind the wheel, started the engine, put it in gear, and drove past the ranch headquarters and out of town.

"Are we stopping at the house?" asked Secretary Fall.

"Later," Hank answered. "We are going to meet the Colonel first." Junior was a "colonel" now, too, courtesy of the Oklahoma governor. He drove to the airstrip, waved to the 101 mechanics and parked near the windsock. No sooner had he shut off the Buick than they could all hear the sound of another engine. The ranch's biplane flew into view, approached the strip as if about to land, and then performed a giant loop-the-loop before actually touching the ground and rolling to a stop. Junior just loved a grand entrance.

Attorney General Daugherty turned to Hank. "Does the Colonel often travel by airplane?" he asked.

"It's a very big ranch," Hank replied, giving the scripted answer all the hands had been drilled in regarding the Miller Brothers' use of that airplane. It made the 101 sound like a country and the brothers like heads of state. It was working on these two. They were both nodding sagely, as if to say, "of course." But Daugherty was studying the airplane with special interest.

Junior jumped down and gave the thumbs up when he was clear of the airplane. The pilot taxied back to the long, low barn they used as a hangar, awaited by the ground crew. Junior joined his guests with a big smile. "Harry! Albert!" he practically yelled. The airplane engine was loud. Everybody riding in it shouted for an hour or two when they got back on the ground. "Can I arrange an airborne tour of the 101 for you fellows?"

The men looked at one another. Daugherty answered for both of them: "I think we'll leave that kind of adventure for the younger men."

Junior laughed appreciatively, as if this was some great compliment for his courage. "As you wish!" he shouted. "Hank, take us to the White House!" That was the Miller Brothers' semi-humorous name for ranch headquarters. Hank was happy to do it. The itinerary called for cocktails, dinner and a viewing of the 101 Ranch Wild West Show. Hank had no part in any of that. He dropped the men off and returned the Buick to the garage. He would be free until tomorrow. He could worry about those new horrors then.

Early the next day Hank headed back to the White House to pick up the men. The sky was clear and the temperature was cooler than normal for a mid-April morning, which was a good thing considering the planned activity. A crew of hostlers was out front with some docile horses that were kept for dudes like these who might be uncomfortable on more-spirited stock. Hank's cousin, Archie Bruner, was supervising the preparation. Archie was dressed – again, courtesy of the wardrobe mistress - in the costume of a Cheyenne chief of the previous century, including leggings, a breechcloth, a scalpshirt, and an eagle-feather headdress with a train that fell to his knees! From Hank's standpoint it was a preposterous getup, but he was in no position to comment, given that he was – again – attired in his fringed buckskin and beaded headband.

"Hank," said Archie laconically.

"Morning," responded Hank. "We all set here?"

"Yeah. Where we headed?"

"I got the fellas to hobble the buffalo over to Horseshoe Lake. They're in the wash under the hill on the west end."

This was Hank's new shame. They had staked out five buffalos for these idiots to "hunt": two cows and three calves.

"What's that, ten miles?" asked Archie. His role in this little drama was "Indian hunting guide." He was going to have to put on a show of "tracking the herd," relying mostly on made-up Indian lore in order to keep the dudes entertained until they got there.

"A little less," answered Hank. "If you can amuse them with fording Bird's Nest Creek and then come up the south side of the Salt Fork to opposite the lake I think the timing will work out. We can unhobble the buffalo and let you surprise them with the sun at your back but the afternoon breeze in your face. The guests will have a good view without spooking the animals. We'll still have plenty of time to butcher a calf and prepare it for dinner while there's daylight."

"Sounds about right," agreed Archie.

"Please don't let these idiots shoot you," said Hank.

"I'm tempted not to let them have live rounds," smiled Archie. "I'm never certain what – or who – they think they're hunting."

Hank chuckled. Now he had to make arrangements for this outing with the cooking staff. They would take a direct route to the site, prep the meal – including the buffalo steaks, from a previously slaughtered and butchered bull – and then pretend to bring their wagon up behind the "hunters," as if they had been tailing the guests all day. When all was in motion, Hank rode up to the lake to supervise the final arrangements for the "hunt" and to prepare the campsite. This meant erecting canvas tipis from the 101 Ranch Wild West show in the trees by the lake. It was a big job. They would pretend to do it while the staff photographer was taking souvenir pictures of the guests with their trophies, but it was better to have as much as possible set up early. Hank had a lot of people to supervise and a lot of work to complete.

Much later, Hank passed Archie a bag of tobacco and the two men rolled cigarettes in the dark under some *cvhahtv* trees not far from the campfire where Junior was entertaining the men from Washington. They were unwinding from the difficult day. President Harding's men were poor riders and took longer than expected to get to the lake. They also had trouble killing the hobbled buffalo. Now that they were done serving the meal, Hank and Archie were hoping that their services were done for the day. But, as it happened, the Attorney General and the Secretary of the Interior wanted them to play Indian a little longer.

"Chief Stalking Horse?" called Junior. This was Archie's stage name for hunting trips. "Could you join us by the fire?" Archie stood. For perhaps the thousandth time, Hank wondered why *wvcenv* liked framing their orders as inquiries. "You, too, Hank," added Junior. Hank groaned, but only inwardly, as he and Archie walked over and sat down on a felled tree at the center of the circle of tipis.

"Chief," started Attorney General Daugherty, "I am charged with prosecuting a lawsuit instituted by our predecessors against your boss. What do you know about the Ponca case?"

"Me not follow white man's court," said Archie. He had been speaking this ridiculous argot all day, and he found it exhausting, but it was his job to remain in character. "Me Cheyenne. Not know Ponca." This was all a grotesque lie. Archie was – like Hank – *Mvskoke* Creek. He was also well acquainted with most of the Ponca Indians in the case initiated by the Woodrow Wilson administration. Both Archie and Hank knew exactly how old Colonel Miller and his sons had been scamming the Oklahoma tribes out of their grazing rights, mineral rights, and – lately – land titles. Archie knew how Colonel Miller had cheated him out of *his* land. That was why he was here playing Indian instead of at home farming with his family. What kind of clown was this Attorney General, asking this question about land theft *in front of the thief himself*? Especially since Daugherty and Junior had been acting like best buddies all day: literally as thick as thieves.

Now Secretary Fall added his two cents: "It is my obligation to act as the trustee for the Indian and to ensure that the leases they put the pen to are in their best interests and that they are not taken in by the siren song of unscrupulous white men."

Hank was thunderstruck by this. He read the papers. He knew how Albert Fall had used his political positions in New Mexico to steal mineral and grazing lands from Indians… and Mexican Americans, too. And to whom did he think he was delivering this preposterous oration?

The moment Secretary Fall used the phrase "siren song," Archie smiled. Hank gave him a warning look that he hoped the *wvcenv* didn't notice. But Archie was not going to stop. "Me hear Few Leases stop up ears with beeswax to quiet siren," he said with an air of great seriousness.

Oh, no. Thankfully, Secretary Fall missed this joke entirely and Junior wouldn't understand the classical reference anyway, having had less than a year of high school. The Attorney General, though, tilted his head quizzically. Hank gave Archie another sharp look. Allusions to Homer's Odyssey were definitely out of character for "Chief Stalking Horse." Fortunately, the deeply rooted *wvcenv* belief in white superiority kicked in again and Daugherty shook off the momentary puzzle.

"How about you, Hank?" asked Daugherty. "Any experience with leases?"

Hank paused. He didn't see how he would be able be able to answer this without sharing an actual opinion... one that Junior wouldn't like. Archie came to his rescue: "Man give Hank $5 last Christmas. Santa only give *sofke*."

To any *mvskoke*, this was sharp social commentary about the ridiculously low payments white swindlers were making for leases of allotted lands and the willingness of some cash-strapped tribe members to accept them because they provided money at holiday time. The *wvcenv* all laughed at the idea of Indian cornmeal mush as a holiday treat. Either they were unperturbed by the "Chief's" sudden familiarity with lease payments or the meaning of the joke escaped them completely. Whichever it was, they began speaking among themselves again, so – after a minute – Archie and Hank moved away from the fire.

"Well done," Hank said. "You may be the funniest Indian in Oklahoma."

"Oh, I'm more modest in my claims," replied Archie, waving a hand dismissively. "I believe I'm only the funniest Indian in the world."

Both men chuckled. "It's your Cherokee friend Will that's making all the money, though. And he steals your material, too."

"Will says he never met a man he didn't like," answered Archie. "I am quite certain he never met these two."

That reminder of the presence of the *wvcenv* politicians nearby quieted them. Which is why they heard the negotiations taking place at the campfire... the negotiations which were the real reason for this visit to the 101 Ranch.

"The Poncas' case against you has a *great* deal of legal merit," the Attorney General was saying. "It was *not* just a partisan attack by my predecessor and the Democrats. It would be *very costly* to dismiss that prosecution." He put strong emphasis on the words "very costly," which got Hank's attention immediately. His eyes opened wide and he looked at Archie. Daugherty was not being very subtle. This was a transparent effort at a shakedown to make the suit against the Colonel go away.

The Attorney General's hint was apparently too cryptic for Junior, though. He seemed not to understand the significance of the words "very costly." "How am I supposed to do business out here without Indian lands?" he demanded. "The whole state of Oklahoma is Indian land!"

"How, indeed?" repeated the Secretary of the Interior, clearly implying that the two cabinet members had a solution to Junior's dilemma in mind – at least it was clear to Hank and Archie, who were staring at one another in astonishment. "I should think it would be damned near impossible," continued Fall.

Junior, though, was still missing the point they were trying to direct him toward. He was sputtering wordlessly now, so frustrated that he was unable to speak. Secretary Fall tried dropping a different hint about another piece of business. "You know, I have been charged with guaranteeing a reserve supply of fuel for the Navy, to ensure that we have sufficient petroleum for our battleships."

"Are you hearing this?" Hank whispered to his cousin. Archie nodded. Junior, however, still wasn't.

"A savvy, experienced oil driller might be happy to be awarded the contract for exploration in a place where a productive well is *completely assured*," prodded Secretary Fall.

Junior and his brothers had been trying to get in on the Oklahoma oil boom for several years but their holes kept turning up dry. "How would a driller be able to get such a contract?" he asked.

Daugherty chuckled. Secretary Fall said – again! – "How indeed?"

And that was when Junior finally got it. "We are facing real jail time for those Ponca leases. You can make that go away? You know it's all political!"

Harry Daugherty said, "As I said, it would be very costly to make it go away. It is my advice – I am speaking as your friend here, understand, not as the Attorney General – that you simply plead guilty."

"What?" shouted Junior.

"Okay, okay," placated Secretary Fall, apparently realizing that everything would need to be spelled out for this idiot. "It seems that Colonel Miller is a plain-spoken man, so let's speak plainly. What if you were to plead guilty to all those charges but could keep the land and only have to pay a nominal fine, say $10,000 total, for you and your brothers?"

Both Archie and Hank gasped. The stolen Ponca lands alone were worth at least a hundred times that. And that didn't include what the Millers had taken from other tribes, including the Creek. "What would I have to do to make that happen?" asked Junior.

"Let's keep it simple," said Secretary Fall to A.G. Daugherty. He left the rest of the sentence - "for this simpleton" - unspoken.

Daugherty nodded in agreement. He said, "You write a personal check, tomorrow when we return to your office, for that same amount, $10,000, payable to me."

"That's a lot of money," complained Junior.

"I hardly need to remind you of the alternative," Daugherty said. He sighed. Did he have to threaten Junior out loud with imprisonment and the confiscation of his 110,000-acre ranch, all stolen from the Oklahoma tribes?

He did not. Junior asked, "What about that Navy oil drilling contract?"

"Oh," said Fall, "that check is for me. Same amount."

And that was it. It was all settled. The *wvcenv* men's conversation soon turned back to bragging about the day's "hunt." The two politicians evidently considered it a great success. Archie and Hank though were mute, still astonished about the magnitude of what they had just heard.

Archie finally broke the silence. "Hank," he asked, "do you know the difference between death and taxes?"

Hank just looked at him, so Archie answered his own question: "Death does not get worse every time Congress is in session."

Over at the campfire Attorney General Daugherty was asking Junior a lot of very detailed questions about the Miller brothers' airplane. *That can't be good*, thought Hank. *What did this deeply corrupt man want an airplane for?*

**Bisbee, Arizona
1917**

The telegram about the lynching of Frank Little arrived on the third day of the strike. On the same day that Joey came here to organize the Phelps, Dodge workers in Bisbee, Frank had gone to assist the Anaconda Copper miners, 1300 miles away in Butte, Montana. Now Frank had been abducted from his rooming house, tortured, dragged behind a car, and killed by a gang of masked men. They left his body hanging from a railroad trestle outside of town. Had it even been a month since Joey's meeting with Frank Little at Bishara's Café in Globe?

Joey Quintana knew the war was going to change things. At the union convention in November, they were still just saying, "Rich man's war; poor man's fight." Most IWWs didn't want to get distracted from the class struggle by news about a war in Europe. But that was before the newspapers got everybody worked up about the Germans again. That was before they reported German submarines sinking American ships again. That was before they reported that Germany asked Mexico to ally with them and invade Texas, New Mexico and Arizona.

At first Joey was sure this "Zimmerman Note" story about a German alliance with Mexico was just capitalist propaganda, playing on white people's prejudice against Mexicans and Mexico. But at the end of March the Germans admitted that that they actually had proposed such an alliance and – even though Mexico rejected the proposal – all these border whites started to act as if their worst nightmares were now coming true. Maybe they forgot that it was they who had been lynching Mexicans by the hundreds, and not the other way around. Or maybe they hadn't forgotten. Maybe they feared Mexicans because in their hearts the Anglos didn't believe that they could get away with such atrocities in any just universe. Whichever of these explanations was true, suddenly the newspapers of the southwest were filled with fictitious stories of imaginary Mexican invaders and saboteurs, pockets full of German gold, intent on carnage against white people.

Congress declared war on Germany only four days after the Germans acknowledged that they had, in fact, tried unsuccessfully to get Mexico to invade the United States. Most IWWs didn't think this should change their strategy or tactics at all: the only war was the class war, and they would keep right on organizing for the union. Big Bill, the union's secretary-treasurer, didn't really want to take a position on the war at all. He thought everybody should make up their own minds about registering for the draft. Others in the IWW leadership actively opposed making alliances with the pacifists who, after all, could be members of any class. The radicals, though, were determined to make a stand against an imperialist war. Frank Little gave speeches up and down the west coast and the northern Rockies saying that any worker who joined up was just a scab in a uniform. For two months he said this, anyway. Now he was dead. Murdered, according to the police, by "parties unknown."

The official line of the IWW was that the copper bosses assassinated Frank for organizing the miners. And Joey was sure this was true. But how much did thoughtless public war fever give the companies political cover for Frank's killing? How much did Frank's antiwar militancy give the middle class an excuse to look the other way and ignore his lynching? And how would this puffed-up patriotism effect Joey's own work here in Bisbee, only thirteen miles from the Mexican border? How would it effect a strike of predominantly Mexican and Mexican-American workers in the "white man's camp" at the Copper Queen?

Joey got up shortly after sunrise to take advantage of the relative cool. On any normal morning, the dirt paths and step streets of Chihuahua Hill would already be bustling with workers on their way to the smelter across Naco Road. But the strike had idled both the mine and the mill. The strikers were luxuriating in an extra hour or so of sleep. They had all been at a mass meeting the night before. And with every speech translated into English, Spanish, Serbian, Finnish, and German, the meeting ran late. Today, Joey seemed to have the neighborhood to himself.

This side of the hill was still in morning shade. Without the noise of the machinery Joey could actually hear the buzzing cicadas. What did the *vecinos* back in Cañada de los Álamos call them? *Jurundunes*! He had not thought of them in a long time. Even the sky was showing the effects of this strike: astonishingly blue. A few days of idle smelters had cleared off the usual haze and suddenly Bisbee was a mile-high mountain valley instead of an industrial cesspool of gambling dens, whorehouses and gin mills... at least if you looked up instead of down. And that is what Joey did. He looked up, took a deep breath, and savored this moment of respite from the class struggle.

It didn't last long. The sound of an automobile engine interrupted Joey's reverie and he looked down again to see Cochise County Sheriff H.C. Wheeler's Oldsmobile, top down, driving up OK Street. One of his deputies was behind the wheel and Wheeler sat in the passenger seat wearing his white Stetson and trademark bow tie. But what caught Joey's eye was the big belt-fed machine gun somehow bolted across the back seat of the open touring car with another deputy at the trigger. Joey froze. He felt a chill on the back of his neck. In his mind's

287

eye he saw Frank Little, hanging from a railroad trestle in Montana. The deputies hadn't seen Joey yet. Should he duck? Walk away? Absolutely not. He gathered himself to face whatever was in store. Would Frank have left Butte if he knew what the class enemy had planned? Joey continued down the step street, directly toward Sheriff Wheeler.

Wheeler and his deputies were directing most of their attention behind them, and as Joey came down the steps he saw what they were looking at. Around the corner of OK and Brewery came men with shouldered rifles: a dozen, two dozen, fifty, a hundred… Joey stopped trying to count. There were a lot of them, and they weren't carrying their personal firearms, either. Each man had an identical, brand-new, bolt-action, military-style weapon. He didn't know what kind, but somebody clearly had funded this operation, and in Bisbee, that meant Phelps, Dodge. The men were all wearing freshly-pressed suits and ties as if they were on their way to a business meeting. Joey saw that there were more of them on Main Street and still more on the Naco Road. There were hundreds of them, all silent. He recognized only a few, but it looked like the entire middle class of Bisbee: lawyers, teachers, doctors, storekeepers, clergy, YMCA staff. It was time for him to let them know he was here before they began firing on him in panic.

"Good morning, Sheriff Wheeler," Joey called. He was standing on the steps above the angle of the machine gun, hands high to show that he had no weapon.

"José Quintana!" shouted the sheriff. How did he know Joey's name? Joey supposed it was a compliment that his reputation preceded him. "Keep your hands up, fingers fully extended. You are under arrest!"

Joey kept his hands in plain sight. But he asked, "For what? Has it become a crime to organize a union in Cochise County? When did you stop being sheriff and go to work for Phelps, Dodge?"

Wheeler shook his head. "You subversives are all the same. One word from me and I could have you cut in half." He gestured at the machine gun. "You're still giving speeches?"

"That's all true, Mr. Wheeler. But you didn't answer my questions. Are you the county sheriff, elected to protect everybody? Or are you working private security for Walter Douglas?"

Even at the distance he was still standing, Joey could see the sheriff bristle. Wheeler prided himself on his independence and on his personal courage. Now he just said, "Step down here. And keep your hands up."

Joey did both. When he got to the street, Wheeler told a deputy, "Check him for weapons."

The deputy, who held a pistol on Joey, hesitated. Wheeler turned on him angrily, "I told you to check this Red son of a bitch for weapons."

"What if he has a bomb?" whined the deputy. "Don't they all carry bombs? What if he blows us both up?"

"God damn it!" exploded Wheeler. "Do I have to do everything myself?" He quickly went over every inch of Joey's body, discovering only a small book in his pocket. He shook out the pages, to see if something was hidden inside, then held up the volume, displaying its red cover, and asked, "What the hell is this?"

"It's the Little Red Book," smiled Joey. "Songs of the Workers."

"A song book?"

"To fan the flames of discontent," explained Joey. "Now why am I under arrest?"

"For treason!" answered the sheriff. "For espionage. For sabotage. For being a goddamned agent of Imperial Germany!"

"Sheriff Wheeler," Joey said, with all the patience he could muster, "I am an American. I was born here. Both my parents were born here. All my grandparents were born here. Who told you that I'm a German? Was it the same people who paid for all these guns?"

But the sheriff had lost interest in the conversation. "March this enemy spy to Main Street and hold him while we round up the rest of these Red bastards. And don't let him get away." This extra emphasis was directed to the deputy who had failed to search Joey.

The sheriff immediately turned and began giving orders to his little army, pointing some directly up the step streets of Chihuahua Hill and others around the sides, presumably to prevent the escape of any other IWWs. Joey was marched at rifle point to the street in front of the post office.

A few hundred more armed merchants and professionals were guarding the street, all with the same military-style weapons that looked like they had just come out of the crate. There were also snipers on top of the Copper Queen Headquarters and the municipal building. He had seen this before, a large Eastern corporation enlisting the local middle class to act as gun thugs. It was cheaper than hiring cutthroats from the "detective" agencies, and it looked better to newspaper reporters, who were – after all – members of the same middle class. But Joey was stunned to see some business people who had been union supporters all along. There was Vladislav Medigovich. The union had been using his theater for all its mass rallies. He spotted Baptiste Caretto. His bar hosted Joey's first meeting in Bisbee. And he saw Morris Levin. His grocery store was providing food for indigent strikers. Why would these allies be here with guns now?

Joey tried unsuccessfully to catch the eye of Vladislav's son, George. After a few minutes he realized that George was intentionally ignoring him. So he said, loudly, "George Medigovich!" Some of the other armed guards gave George dirty looks, but he came over to Joey anyway.

The younger Medigovich stood close to Joey, but with his face turned away, as if his proximity was incidental, and rasped, "What do you want?"

Joey honored George's obvious discomfort by not facing him and said, "I want to know when you guys signed on with the copper bosses."

Out of the corner of his eye he saw George shake his head impatiently. "This has nothing to do with that. This isn't their Civic League. This has nothing to do with Phelps, Dodge at all. This is the *Loyalty* League," he said, emphasizing the word as if it made all the difference in the world.

"Loyalty?" repeated Joey.

"Loyalty," said George. "We're at war. We all need to band together to support our troops."

Now it was Joey's turn to shake his head. "Do you really think…" he began, but George had already stepped away. And, in any case, new prisoners were being marched down the street. And they were not strike leaders, or union organizers. Some were rank-and-file workers. Some weren't even employees of the company. He saw a man who made his living selling sandwiches. He saw a man who swept up in Caretto's bar. He saw a reporter for an Eastern newspaper who was in town covering the labor dispute. And he wasn't seeing a few prisoners; he was seeing *hundreds!* Sheriff Weaver's posse – whose numbers now seemed to be in the thousands – was rounding up what appeared to be every working person in Bisbee.

He saw plenty of Germans and Austrians, which might have made some sort of sick sense since their nations of origin were at war with the United States... might have unless you remembered that these people had *left* their homes to be American. But there were many, many more Serbs being held here in the street, and Serbia was *allied* with the United States! And – by far – the largest group of prisoners was Mexican, and Mexico remained neutral in the war. No, regardless of what the copper bosses had convinced the sheriff and the town burgers, this was a mass arrest of workers and their sympathizers.

As the hours passed, a photographer arrived with all his glass plates and equipment. Was he going to make picture postcards to sell as souvenirs? Joey guessed that there would be plenty of customers. The guards watching them seemed to think this was some kind of festival. *A festival of the plutocrats*, thought Joey.

The number of prisoners in the street was over a thousand now, and their armed guards must have been double that. The sun was overhead, and it was another extremely hot Arizona day. One by one the men who Joey knew personally – along with many who he only recognized by sight – came over to ask him what was going on. He didn't know. He considered sitting down in the dusty street. He considered asking if they would be fed. He was not the only man in this crowd to be captured before breakfast and he was starting to feel a little woozy.

That was when Sheriff Weaver, still in his improvised armored car with the machine gun, started giving new orders, and in a few minutes they were all marching down the Naco Road. Joey's suspicions about numbers were confirmed. The long line of prisoners in the middle of the road was matched on both sides by a line of armed "Loyalty Leaguers", each of them shouldering identical new rifles. He also noticed snipers in the hills. After an hour of walking, his fear that they were going to be marched all the way to the Mexican border was eased, though, when they turned off the main road and were led into the baseball stadium in the next town of Warren.

Joey and the other captured men – they were all men – were forced into the grandstand. When that was filled, the vigilantes put the overflow in the infield. There were guards in the outfield, guards at the gates, and guards in the

291

grandstands. Joey also noticed a machine gun on the roof of the Calumet and Arizona Copper Company office building across the street.

Women began lining up around the outfield fence, some supporting the vigilantes, some supporting their captives. Joey saw many wives and mothers of interned men begging for mercy. None seemed to be available. One white woman in her fifties, though, was yelling at her two captured sons, demanding that they hold firm and not surrender. She loudly denounced the Loyalty Leaguers as "dirty cowards" and threatened to smack them, despite the fact that she was walking with the aid of a crutch. The vigilantes finally brought her inside and imprisoned her with her boys.

The photographer arrived again, all his equipment in the back of a light truck. Once he set up his camera, the "Loyalty Leaguers" began striking heroic poses, with their weapons prominently figured, as if this were some sort of pageant, or comic opera. But it was all deadly serious. Nobody had been given any food or water. Those rifles were all loaded. Sheriff Weaver's army was deployed around the stadium so that there could be no escape. And Joey still had no idea what the sheriff's plan was. Make them all sign oaths? Hold kangaroo trials? Line them all up and shoot them?

After a few hours Joey heard, then saw, a train pull up on the track near the ballpark. Cattle cars. Maybe two dozen. They were going to be deported in cattle cars? Joey had heard stories about posses deporting union leaders. He had heard about the Cripple Creek strike a dozen years before, when the Colorado National Guard loaded union leaders, their attorneys, sympathetic newspaper reporters, and even local lawmen into freight cars and then dropped them in the middle of nowhere, across the state line in Kansas and in New Mexico. But that deportation amounted to about a hundred people total. There were over a thousand here at the Warren baseball park. Was Phelps, Dodge really planning to deport the entire blue-collar work force of Bisbee? And did these "Loyalty Leaguers" actually believe that every workingman in town was a German agent?

Apparently that is exactly what the copper bosses were planning. And apparently that is exactly what they had convinced the middle-class town folk. Because within the hour Joey and a thousand other men were ordered at gunpoint into the cattle cars, three inches deep in stinking manure, armed vigilantes on the roof. He hadn't eaten or had anything to drink since getting up that morning. The temperature was soaring now. It was hotter still inside the cattle car, crowded together with fifty other men. Yes, they were his class brothers, but it was truly rank in that car, and Joey knew that he wasn't smelling like roses, either. The cow manure was not an improvement. It was becoming

292

hard to breathe. As light-headed as he was, Joey chose to stand. Many of the other men no longer could, though.

The car clanked against its neighbors and the train crept into motion. That knocked Joey sprawling against his still-upright neighbors. He tripped over some of the men who were already sitting and fell headlong into the cow dung. So much for trying to stay out of it. At least he could no longer smell himself.

Now the train was headed downslope, out of the Mule Mountains and into the open saguaro and mesquite flats. And he still had no idea where they were going, or what would happen to them there. What new horrors did this day have in store?

Saint-Rémy-sur-Bussy, Marne, France
1918

"Aidez le! Aidez le! Ils vont l'assassiner!" shouted the woman, and she grabbed the hand of Captain Osceola McKaine.

"What?" asked his companion, Lieutenant Vernon Daly.

"Somebody is killing somebody," he said. *"Qui tue qui?"* he asked.

"Les soldats blancs vont tuer le soldat noir!" she cried.

"It's a lynching!" McKaine told Daly. "One of ours. Get the fellows!" He turned back to the woman and asked, *"Où?"*

She pointed and ran down the narrow street with McKaine alongside. Daly watched one moment to see where they were going, then sped in the other direction to round up some more men of the 367th.

McKaine turned the corner at speed and then froze. He shivered as if the temperature had dropped twenty degrees. His nightmares had suddenly appeared in front of his waking eyes.

The first detail he was able to focus on in this tableau of horror was the name of the bloody, semi-conscious colored soldier being dragged down the street: Rector Beauchamp, a platoon sergeant in another regiment. But what the hell? The soldiers who held him were all white. Seven of them. Five enlisted men, two officers, both lieutenants. Two of the enlisted men were carrying their Springfield rifles at port arms with fixed bayonets. The officers were walking with their M1911 Colts drawn. The other three men had their rifles slung behind their backs. Two supported the beaten man by the arms. The other, chillingly, carried a stout rope. A young woman, her hair loose, weeping and red-faced was behind them. She was crying something, but he had suddenly lost his ability to understand French. He was all too conscious of being alone in the face of all these murderous white men.

"Halt!" bellowed Captain Osceola McKaine in the command voice he had learned in combat in the Philippines. "Explain yourselves!"

The white enlisted men were brought up short by his peremptory tone. But the officers continued toward him, pistols ready. "This is none of your business, nigger," said one. "Get the fuck out of our way unless you want to join him."

"I am *Captain* Osceola McKaine, 92nd Infantry, United States Army," said McKaine, emphasizing his rank to the lieutenants in front of him. For the moment, the two silver bars on his uniform were the only card he had to play. Would they trump all those guns? "Identify yourselves!" he ordered.

"This man is under arrest," said the second officer, the one who had not yet spoken. He did not identify himself, but McKaine recognized his accent immediately. He might well be a neighbor from home. He was surely from South Carolina. "He raped this girl," continued the white officer, pointing to the crying young woman. "We weren't in time to save her, but we caught him. If you will just step aside we will bring him in for court martial."

McKaine stood his ground. "And the rope?" he asked.

"You are one inquisitive nigger, aren't you?" smirked the first white officer, now raising his pistol. "Do you want to be arrested, too?"

McKaine ignored this and continued speaking to the South Carolinian. "I direct you to turn your prisoner over to me, pursuant to the 1916 Articles of War. Sgt. Beauchamp will be held by his company captain for an immediate court martial. Identify yourselves so that you can be available as witnesses against him!"

The lieutenant hesitated, but his friend said, "Fuck this. Let's just shoot these two coons right here, right now. That's what Ben Cameron would do!" He put his pistol to McKaine's eye.

Ben Cameron? wondered Captain McKaine. As if the pistol in his face unstuffed his ears, he was suddenly able to understand the sobbing girl who was now clinging to the leg of Rector Beauchamp. *C'est mon ami! Il n'a rien fait de mal!* "He is my friend! He did nothing wrong!" she was saying.

Around the corner came Vernon with Lt. Hugh Page and Capt. Ed Walton, all three with side-arms drawn. Both white officers now turned their guns on the new arrivals. McKaine said loudly, "These men were just turning their prisoner over to me!"

"Come on, Reg," said the loudmouthed white lieutenant. "We still outnumber these bastards. Let's do it."

Reg, realized McKaine. Of course. What a ridiculous coincidence. Everybody in Sumter knew Reginald Manigault. He was the darling son of an old planter family, playboy, Princeton grad. But having been away for so long himself, in college and in the Army, Osceola hadn't immediately recognized him. He spoke up again, "Lieutenant Manigault, surrender your prisoner now or face court martial yourself!"

Hearing his name startled the white man. He turned back to Captain McKaine in puzzlement. And then he noticed what he had failed to see about the arrival of the additional colored officers: the white enlisted men behind him were now looking very uncertain about what to do. The two riflemen had lowered their weapons. The man with the rope dropped it and kicked it aside as if nobody would notice he had it. And the men holding the bloody sergeant looked as though they might turn and run at any moment. "Lester," he said to his companion quietly and gestured with his eyes toward the irresolute soldiers who were supposed to be backing them up. He lowered his pistol, and – after looking behind him – so did "Lester."

McKaine continued, "Understand that I will be making a full report of this incident. I will take a witness statement from this young woman as well. Again, identify yourselves."

"Fuck you," said "Lester."

"Do what you think you must," said Lt. Reginald Manigault. "Who do you think they will believe?" He holstered his pistol and, motioning with his left hand, led the white men away.

Daly, Page and Walton cautiously kept their sidearms raised even then.

The story McKaine got from the girl, whose name was Corette, was the same Sgt. Beauchamp provided once he had recovered enough to speak. It was worse than McKaine imagined. The white officers hadn't accidentally stumbled upon a colored soldier arm in arm with a French girl. Not at all. They had attempted to *rape* Corette the previous day and were only prevented by Rector Beauchamp's intervention. So this lynch attack was premeditated payback for Sgt. Beauchamp's courage and humanity. Now Corette's mother offered lunch to all the men, but McKaine was anxious to get back and provide a written report to Major General Ballou. And he was very anxious to see that Sgt. Beauchamp received medical attention. He thanked her and left.

As they walked back to their regimental area, McKaine went over in his mind everything that had happened. There was one thing he didn't understand at all. "Who the hell is Ben Cameron?" he asked.

Hugh Page and Ed Walton looked at him vacantly and shrugged their shoulders. But Vernon Daly asked, "Why?"

"That cracker put his gun in my face and threatened to kill me because he said that's what Ben Cameron would do," explained McKaine. "It was just before you fellows showed up."

"My God," said Daly, shaking his head. "Jesus save us."

"What?" asked Osceola McKaine.

"You were part of the NAACP protests against that moving picture, *Birth of a Nation*," answered Daly.

They both had been. The hate film was playing in New York City when they were on leave from training in Long Island. They joined the picket lines protesting its showing at the Liberty Theater in Times Square. Osceola had a good idea what its vicious plot was, but he certainly hadn't seen it and still had no idea who "Ben Cameron" might be. "So?" he asked.

"Ben Cameron is the 'hero' of the story," explained Vernon. "He founds the Ku Klux Klan, he lynches a Negro who rapes his sister, he... It's all just too unbelievable."

"Except to a cracker," muttered Hugh Page. "They all believe that shit. And now, with that filthy moving picture, they all think they saw it with their own eyes."

That silenced them for a good long time. As they caught sight of their regimental area Osceola McKaine spoke again. "We have a lot of work to do when we get back to the States," he said.

"Work?" repeated Vernon Daly with a raised eyebrow. "We are going to have to fight. When we get done with this war, our fight will just be starting."

Osceola started to respond to this. And then he didn't. He just nodded his agreement.

Charleville-Mézières, France
1918

To: Maj. Nicholas Biddle
Military Intelligence Branch
From: Confidential Agent Maj. Walter Loving

I write from the headquarters of the French Fourth Army (General Henri Gouraud commanding) where the 93rd colored infantry is attached by order of General Pershing because he foresaw problems with colored troops serving alongside white American troops.

The 93rd performed heroically in the offensive against the Germans in the Meuse-Argonne region and in the Second Battle of the Marne. 171 members of the 369th Regiment were awarded the Croix de Guerre by their French generals. Privates Henry Johnson and Needham Roberts in particular were cited for fighting off 24 Germans with only knives and rifle butts. You may have read that story in the *Saturday Evening Post*.

There are morale problems nonetheless. General Pershing's headquarters issued a warning to French civilians against fraternizing with our colored soldiers because of our supposed propensity to rape and sexual assault. The soldiers of the 92nd and 93rd Divisions took this as an insult, which it is.

I also found that white troops of the American First Army attempted to lynch a colored sergeant of the 93rd Division. The lynching was only prevented by the quick thinking of Capt. Osceola McKaine. Capt. McKaine submitted a detailed report of this incident, but no disciplinary action has been taken against the white soldiers. It seems that every Negro soldier in France in both combat and labor battalions has heard this story.

I have mentioned Capt. McKaine several times in these reports. He is a leader who always argued that exemplary military service by colored troops and officers will make a difference in their treatment when they return home. I no longer hear this in his conversations.

Two nights ago I accompanied him to a *brasserie* along with First Lieutenant Edgar Love, an army chaplain. While we were dining a group of Senegalese soldiers entered and, invited by Captain McKaine, joined us at our table. The Africans complained about the bigotry of their white French officers. They described the abuses they experience at the hands of the French who rule their homeland, and how they are made to feel like children in their own villages.

Captain McKaine said very little, but he listened attentively. After dinner the assistant to the chef, a Vietnamese from French Indo-China who called himself Ho Chi Minh, sat down with us, too. This cook spoke passionately about the oppression of the world's colored peoples. He claimed intimate knowledge of the race question in the United States, having worked in a New York City bakery before the war, and he said that American Negroes are colonial subjects, too. The Osceola McKaine of last year would have argued with him, insisting on our opportunities and on the possibilities for achievement. But on this night he was silent, which disquieted me. If Osceola McKaine were to join the ranks of our colored radicals he would be a formidable opponent.

I will remain in France another few weeks. My next visit is to the 805th Pioneers. You will receive my formal report forthwith.

Columbus, New Mexico
1917

It had been a month now since Joey Quintana's deportation from Arizona. The so-called "loyalty league" of Bisbee captured – kidnapped, really – over a thousand striking mine workers, along with members of other unions, strike sympathizers, and an assortment of people who just got caught in the roundup. The vigilante mob shipped their captives across the state line to New Mexico in cattle cars and kicked them off the train in the middle of the desert with no food and no water. Now all the Bisbee deportees were staying in a tent city at a U.S. Army base in Columbus, New Mexico.

The tents that Joey and the others slept in were originally put there to house Mexicans of Chinese descent. The Chinese-Mexicans fled across the border when Pancho Villa threatened to kill them for cooperating with the American invasion the year before. Those refugees were interned in the camp because – despite the assistance many of them had given to the U.S. Army – it was illegal for any Chinese person to enter the United States. In one respect, the Bisbee deportees were just like the Chinese-Mexicans: nobody knew exactly what to do with them.

At first, the national press paid a lot of attention to the internees in the camp. Their readers were astonished by the Bisbee mob's disruption of telegraph lines, their seizure of a railroad across state lines, and their gross violations of the civil liberties of the copper miners. President Wilson alerted the War Department and sent the Judge Advocate General of the United States to investigate. Former Governor Hunt came from Arizona to express solidarity. The internees all agreed that none of them would return to Bisbee unless they could all return to Bisbee. They were standing together as union men and they were standing strong.

But then the president's investigators returned to Washington. Governor Hunt went back to suing his opponent over the outcome of the last election. The newspaper reporters went on to other stories: forest fires in the Pacific Northwest, an amnesia victim in New Jersey, a World Series between the New York Giants and the Chicago White Sox, and – day after day – news of the war in Europe. Most days, war news filled the entire front page. A thousand men remained in this camp, standing strong and trying to find ways to fill their days, while nobody outside paid any attention.

The camp was garrisoned by the 24th Infantry Regiment. Joey had encountered them before; colored troops were often sent to break mine strikes in the Northern Rockies. Sometimes he thought they were here now because of their experience fighting the workers. Other times he thought that President Wilson just didn't want to let Negro soldiers go to Europe. In either case, he thought it was strange that combat veterans were sitting here babysitting him while draftees with only six weeks of training were being sent to fight the Germans.

The 24th unintentionally provided some entertainment to the deportees in the camp, mostly because the soldiers needed to amuse themselves. The regiment had a celebrated dance band, and their morning rehearsals were a highlight of everybody's day. They had several outstanding boxers, too. A young soldier named Hayden knocked out a professional fighter from the white 7th Cavalry in a match that was attended by traincar-loads of visitors from as far away as El Paso, Texas. The deportees from Bisbee all rooted for "Speedball" Hayden as if he were one of them. But mostly there was nothing for the strikers and their supporters to do but wait to hear whether they could all return to Arizona together. Joey did not like the sitting around. There was no work for him, no organizing to do. All they did was talk, sing, and talk some more. As the weeks went by, Joey felt as though he had heard every story, every joke, every song that each of the thousand deportees knew. Twice. If he heard "Banks of the Rhondda" or "O Sole Mio" one more time...

That is why he found himself outside the enlisted men's club one afternoon, thinking that maybe it was time to make some new acquaintances. He didn't know whether he would be welcome, so he took a deep breath before stepping through the open door.

Inside he saw four soldiers sitting around a table, looking at piles of playing cards. Two of the men – older, lighter, with sergeant's stripes on their uniforms – were laughing. Unpleasantly, Joey thought. Whatever the source of their mirth, the two younger, darker-skinned men were clearly not amused.

"You always have a warn for your partner when we're bidding," complained one of those younger soldiers. "Then a which and a why when somebody calls you on it."

"Do you speak English at all?" asked one of the sergeants with a smirk. Now that Joey was looking at him more closely, he wondered if the man was colored at all. But, no, he had to be. Only the officers of the 24th were white. The sergeant picked up the cards from the table. As he cut the deck, preparing to shuffle for another hand, the other private, who hadn't spoken yet, noticed Joey. He sat up straight, which caught the attention of the other three card players. They all turned to look at him, and not in a friendly way.

"You lost?" asked the young soldier who spotted Joey.

Joey didn't answer right away. He took a moment instead to look first at the cards and then, one at a time, at the faces of the soldiers.

The young private tried again, a little louder, and this time in border Spanish: "*¿Habla inglés, Paco?*"

Joey ignored this, too. After another silence, though, he asked, "Bid whist? How does a fellow get into this game?"

None of them looked happy about this question, but the white-looking sergeant, slammed the cards down on the table in irritation. He turned in his chair and said, "You speak English real good, Paco, so hear me. Get back on the other side of camp with the rest of the IWWs and greasers."

Joey remained unruffled. He just asked, "Am I a prisoner?"

Nobody really knew the answer to this question. The War Department had issued orders to the soldiers of the 24th to house and feed all these people, but, otherwise, their status was unclear. So there was another long silence. Finally the angry sergeant said, "We're soldiers. We don't like German spies. Take a walk, Fritz."

Joey chose to treat this new insult as a joke and an invitation to continue talking. "Paco. Fritz. You're a funny man. Why don't you call me Joey? That has the advantage of being my name." He extended his hand to the hostile soldier. "And your name?" he asked. The man stared pointedly at Joey's hand without taking it and without answering.

But his partner evidently had a new thought. Because he suddenly gave Joey a predatory smile that never reached his eyes and took Joey's hand. "Sergeant Grant Mims," he said, "24th U.S. Infantry. It's a pleasure to make your acquaintance." He looked like a man who didn't smile unless he was about to eat. Joey wondered if he was the meal.

Apparently his partner, the white-looking sergeant, knew the answer to that question, because he suddenly lost his glare. He, too, now smiled and extended his hand. "First Sergeant William Nesbit." The two younger men looked utterly baffled by the sudden reversal of attitude. Nesbit spoke for them. "And our friends are Private Luther Rucker and Private Gabriel Joyner."

Friends? Joey thought. Rucker was the man who suggested Nesbit was a cheater, the man who Nesbit was mocking as Joey was walking in. But Privates Rucker and Joyner followed Nesbit's lead and shook Joey's hand, even if they were still too puzzled to speak.

Joey filled out his own introduction. "Joey Quintana," he said. "Industrial Workers of the World."

This had precisely the shocking effect that he expected. "You're an IWW?" asked Gabriel Joyner, the soldier who first noticed Joey's entrance into the club. His mouth was hanging open, as though he expected Joey to sprout horns and a forked tail.

"One Big Union," smiled Joey Quintana.

Sergeant Mims was still smiling. "I heard you're all paid German agents," he said.

Ah, thought Joey. He smiled back. *That was his angle.* He had met men like Mims before, in every copper camp, every ranch, every hobo jungle. They were tireless hustlers. Mims must be calculating in his head: a thousand men multiplied by the imaginary German gold in their pockets? It was an awful lot of hypothetical money. He must be hoping Joey could induce his comrades into some gentlemen's games of chance. And he obviously believed this nonsensical anti-union propaganda.

Sergeant Mims's smile lost some of its luster. Joey's look of recognition must have told him that he overplayed his hand. "I heard all you IWWs carry bombs," Mims added quickly, as if to disguise the comment about German gold, although with another lie that he probably also believed.

If these had been workingmen instead of soldiers, Joey would have laughed these comments off with an observation about the bosses' lies. Instead he snorted, "I bet a white man told you that."

This got a good laugh from all the card players. "True," said Private Joyner, "that's true. But why would the white man lie about that?"

"Who knows why buckra say what buckra say?" replied his partner Private Rucker.

Another round of laughter. "You know how to tell when ofay is lying?" asked Sgt. Nesbit. More chuckles. They all did.

But Gabriel Joyner was curious now and not to be deflected. "So what *do* you IWWs stand for?"

"Like I said," Joey smiled, "one big union of all the workers."

Sgt. Nesbit's expression turned again. He balled his right hand into a fist and said, with ice in his voice, "Boy, you have a lot of heart talking to a group of Black men about a union."

Now it was Joey's turn to be surprised, speechless in fact. But his wide eyes and his open mouth begged clarification.

"Boy, don't you know a union is just a white man's way to keep the jobs for themselves? Keep colored men from working?" asked the white-looking sergeant.

Joey did not, and shook his head to indicate it, so Nesbit continued. "When the unions control a town, they keep us out. Cripple Creek, Colorado? That was a union town. And it was a sundown town. I know, I was there. Unions there made sure even the barbers were white. Coeur d'Alene, Idaho? Same thing. Every time they call us to make peace in those towns it's the union men yelling, 'Nigger, get out.'"

Joey was silent. He knew that the color prejudice that poisoned America hadn't skipped over the worker's movement. He was quite certain that the reason the bosses kept sending the 24th and other colored units in to break the unions was to keep the races separate. But Joey was a good organizer, so he wanted to listen a little longer before speaking. It helped to find areas of agreement before exploring what divided you.

Sgt. Nesbit wasn't done. "Let me ask you something, Paco. You read the newspapers? We do. Your unions just burned down the colored section of East St. Louis. Burned it down. Killed 200 Black folks. Killed them dead. And why? Because they think every job except picking cotton belongs to white men. You come in here talking about union? Maybe you got big balls. Maybe you got no brain. Maybe both."

Joey had heard that the American Federation of Labor was involved with the mass murder in East St. Louis; it had definitely not been the IWW. But to anybody outside the labor movement this distinction was not likely to make a difference. He remained quiet.

Sgt. Mims had momentarily forgotten the German gold he imagined in Joey's pockets. "You know, as long as the ofay's away, you Mexicans act like we're all amigos. But when it's just you and them? Well then you want to play white and downgrade us colored men. Which side are you really on?"

This was really too much for Joey. "First of all, you call me a Mexican, like I came across some border. I was born and raised four hundred miles *north* of here. So were my parents. So were my grandparents and great-grandparents."

Now it was Mims's turn to be mystified. "So?" he asked. "Are you a Mexican or not?"

Quicksand. He had stepped right in it. Instead of responding Joey went on. "Second of all, you're right." He looked directly at Sgt. Nesbit. "Lots of white men can't see us as men or as workers, so they form unions and keep us out. That's how the bosses play us. American-born men form a union, just for Americans? The bosses bring in Italians and Bohemians to break it. Organize them, too, because they're white? Bosses bring in the Mexicans. Organize the Mexicans, like we did in Arizona? Well, then they tell everybody that we're agents of the Germans."

"What about us?" asked Joyner.

"You are the U.S. Army," answered Joey. "The companies own the government and they own the Army, too. That's why they use you to break our strikes." He had to stop talking here. Memories were threatening to incapacitate him again. In front of him were uniformed U.S. infantrymen. But in his mind were gunmen, in the pay of the Rockefellers, in the uniform of the Colorado National Guard. In his mind were men and women and children being pulled from a pit under a tent in Ludlow. In his mind was the lifeless body of his sister Piedad. His vision blurred and he looked away.

Gabriel Joyner was still asking his question. "No, I meant what about us Black folk," he clarified.

Joey blinked and returned to the present. "One big union of all the workers. That means everybody."

Nesbit was skeptical. "You got colored IWWs?" he asked.

"Yes," answered Joey. "Yes, of course there are. The longshoremen in Philadelphia are all IWWs and half of them are colored. Black and white, all organized together in one union."

"White union president, though, right?" asked Joyner. He was thinking about the officers in the 24th Infantry. All of them were white, despite the fact that it was an all-Black outfit.

"No," Joey shook his head. "Ben Fletcher is the president of that local and he's a colored man. And he's not the only Negro leader in the IWW, either."

This didn't sit well with either Mims or Underwood, but they said nothing. Nesbit, though, was unimpressed and said so. "I didn't see any colored in those unions in Idaho or Colorado. No Mexicans, either, come to think of it."

Joey nodded. He was still not going to get into the fine points of the AFL vs. the IWW or into the internal politics of the Western Federation of Miners, either. He just said, "You're right. Unions are not all that they should be. I have to fight prejudice in our union every day. And yet, you're prepared to sit there in the uniform of the United States Army and criticize *us* for separation by race? I saw Black troopers from Fort Huachuca in Brewery Gulch in Bisbee, but they weren't allowed in the white bars, and I think you know it. How long before the white folks there decide that's a sundown town, too?"

That was more criticism than any soldier was prepared to hear from a civilian. It was more criticism than they were prepared to hear from a Mexican. Joey knew it. He also knew that even if one or more of them was prepared to consider what he had said, they would never give him the satisfaction of agreeing with him while he was still in the room. So he stood. "Gentlemen, it has been a pleasure chatting with you. Maybe I'll have the chance to play some cards with you one day soon."

"I look forward to that!" replied Sgt. Mims quickly. The others gave Mims angry looks and then nodded their acknowledgements to Joey.

¡Hasta entonces!" smiled Joey as he left their tent.

"What do you think of that?" asked Gabriel.

"I think it's bullshit," answered Nesbit. He picked up the cards again and began to shuffle.

"You didn't have to make him leave so soon, though, did you?" asked Mims. He was still wondering about the Kaiser's gold and wondering how much of it he could take from this Mexican IWW.

Transcript of an oral history tape recording of John Howat Walker, April 13

Yes, I am happy to see you here again. I am afraid that our stories will never get told, you know? That even the growth of the labor movement gets turned into one big happy triumph of American business. As if they didn't try to choke our unions to death in the crib when they were babies.

Blair Mountain? Sure, I remember it real well. I wasn't there every minute, like Mother Jones was, but I was there for enough.

You read the newspaper accounts? Then you may know less than if you never heard anything about it at all! That's right. I heard you historians like to read old newspapers. You think because they came out at the time that means they have the inside dope. They're worse than any book for the operators' lies. Them papers said us miners were a bunch of inbred hillbillies. They said we looted the towns. They said we ignored the President. They said we spread propaganda. What are their stories if not propaganda? You want to know what happened, you ask me or any other union man who was there. Or if you want to read, then read the articles in the *UMW Journal*. Because we covered the story, too. Only we had to tell the truth. Because our readers were there and they knew better. We called a gun thug a gun thug. The bosses' papers called them "citizens." As if we weren't. Ever since I was a little boy I knew that all those shopkeepers and lawyers and teachers and doctors thought we were animals. They wouldn't have jobs or warm homes without us. But they thought we were animals because we went underground. We knew better. We knew that we were people with thoughts and feelings. But we knew what they thought of us, too.

Mother Jones, right. So this was after the World War, see?

The first one, that's right. We thought things would get better. So many workers left their jobs and their wives and their families to fight for democracy in Europe. We were fighting against feudal autocrats over there. Why should we come back to the same thing in West Virginia? We knew that if West Virginia was allowed to stay like tsarist Russia then pretty soon the operators everywhere else were going to get ideas. So Mother Jones went back to West Virginia again. Them Baldwin-Felts weren't so quick to shoot an old lady down in the street like they would one of us. That's the God's honest truth.

.She got to signing up members quick. The miners heard Mother Jones ask whether they were men or not. They wanted a living wage like anybody else. The operators tried their usual tricks. They evicted people from their company houses. They cut off their accounts at the company stores. They tried to split up the miners by whether they were from the hills or the hollows. Whether they were Italians or Hunkies or colored.

That's right, there were a lot of colored in the union there in West Virginia. They were good union men. As good as any white man.

I know what I told you last week. Do you want to argue with me about it or do you want to hear this story?

Yes, Mother Jones spoke to the colored, too. They listened to her like everybody else.

Well most of them towns didn't have no mayor or police, only Baldwin-Felts. But see, in Mingo County, right up on the Tug River, across from Kentucky, was a town with its own mayor and police: Matewan. They were elected by the miners. They stood for the law, not just whatever the operators said. Them Baldwin-Felts tried to evict the men from their homes there, too. But the chief of police, old Sid Hatfield? He told them their eviction notices weren't legal. The Baldwin-Felts tried to shoot it out with Sid. But they hadn't counted on Sid, nor his posse, neither. Seven of them Baldwin-Felts died that day, including Lee and Albert Felts themselves. Now this didn't have nothing to do with the union until later, but you see what the situation was.

The organizing went right on but the coal operators wouldn't talk to us. Nice and pretty, they all wrote us the same letter, every different company, like it was only one lawyer worked for all of them, and he just copied that letter out again and again. Or anyway he had his typist do it for him, all on the different stationeries of the different coal operators. They all said they wouldn't talk to us. They all said they wouldn't negotiate. So after that the men went on strike and the shooting started right away.

Mother Jones was there. I was there with her. I saw it. The union bought tents for the families that got evicted from company houses and we set them up on the bottomlands between Little Blackberry Creek and Sulphur Creek. They call that Blackberry City. This story I want to tell you happened on a Monday, the fifth of July. We hadn't organized an Independence Day celebration the day before because a lot of the families in that camp spent their Sundays in worship. So it was a Monday. Not too hot. We had mutton barbecuing in a pit in the open meadow. There was a little breeze coming through the ash and maple trees. They had a local dance band there, too: fiddle, guitar and mandolin. They called themselves the Mate Creek Boys. They were all union miners, all living in that tent camp at Blackberry City. So the boys were playing and people were dancing. Just having a good time, you know. I can still see all the happy faces. I can smell the barbecue. I can hear that band right now. They were playing "The Wreck of the Old 97." But I can't hear the rifle shot. Never did hear it. I just saw little Lucille Mae Skeens drop to the ground. She was dancing with her daddy, Leander. He tried to pick her up, like that would bring her back. Her mommy, Jane, was screaming. Her little brothers, Woodrow and Corbet were trying to comfort their mommy. The band stopped playing. Men ran to their tents to get their old bird guns and squirrel guns and find the shooter.

But it weren't no use. It was snipers with high-powered rifles. Never found out who they were. We just know they were paid by the coal operators. They were up in the hills across the Tug Fork on the Kentucky side. That weren't the first time they shot at us. It wouldn't be the last. It was just that was the day they killed little Lucille Mae. They killed her while she was dancing with her daddy.

Yes, there were snipers up on our side, too, but that weren't the doing of the union, just some angry men, and who could blame them for being angry? Their families were getting shot at.

Mother Jones was everywhere. See, she had no trouble arranging meetings in that town of Matewan. It was an elected government there and not no Baldwin-Felts government. She told the men that they were her boys and that she was proud that they were finally standing up for themselves. She told them that they were the ones who took the coal out of the ground. The whole nation depended on them for that. They deserved to be able to come up out of the ground and have a weekend and an afternoon and see the daylight sometimes. She told them that the operators were stealing their children's childhood, and that was true. They loved hearing her talk about all that. We were pretty sure we had 100% membership there in Mingo County and we were feeling good about our chances of winning that strike and winning union recognition and a union contract for the men. But them operators had a few new tricks up their sleeves, tricks we hadn't seen before.

One thing was that they wanted to paint old Sheriff Sid Hatfield as a murderer and a reckless, trigger-happy hillbilly because he was a Tug Creek Hatfield. That's right, like a Hatfields-and-McCoys Hatfield. The national newspapers were full of stories about the strike, but they called it a "feud." Everybody was quoted with colorful dialect spelling. They spelled the word "foreigner" as "furriner" and "fer" instead of "for" because it made the workers look stupid. And who doesn't pronounce "interested" as "int'rested"? They never published a story without including something about moonshine. As if coal miners don't care about safety or wages or hours unless we get drunk.

The operators put Sid Hatfield on trial for murder, even though it was them Baldwin-Felts that started the shooting and even though it was them Baldwin-Felts that were illegally evicting families with their phony-baloney court orders that no judge ever signed or even saw. That trial didn't end the way they wanted it to, though, because the jury saw right through all their lies and they acquitted Sid. They acquitted him and his whole posse, too.

The other trick? Well it doesn't seem new anymore now, does it? That Taft-Hartley Slave Labor Act turned it into U.S. law. I know that law violates the Constitution. Every union man knows that. Taft-Hartley makes us all swear an oath that we're not commies. It makes it look like we are all a bunch of Bolsheviks. Or maybe spies like those Rosenbergs. Well, them coal operators told all the respectable people in West Virginia, and everywhere else, too, that we *were* a bunch of commies and that if they didn't stop us we would turn America into Russia. Imagine that? West Virginia was already Russia with their Baldwin-Felts and their company towns.

So you see the organizing was going well and the strike was going well but the operators were planning to get a civil war going in West Virginia. All they had to do was light a spark because the coal miners were sticking together and it was scaring them respectable town folk. This was an old trick, and I have to tell you, I didn't see this as clearly as Mother Jones did. She saw that our enemies can commit an atrocity against us *on purpose.* It's a way to make us forget our plans, forget our strategy, and forget our tactics. It's a way to get us into revenge thinking instead of working-class thinking.

Okay, okay, I'll tell the story, but do you know the song "Gospel Plow?" You don't? That's all right, it doesn't matter.

So after Sid Hatfield was acquitted of the shootings in Matewan, the operators charged him with blowing up a mine tipple in McDowell County. Sid was really confident about this new trial. He didn't know nothing at all about that tipple. He hadn't been nowhere near there at the time. How could they even have witnesses against him? The day of the trial he took the train to Welch, had breakfast in the hotel there and then went to the courthouse. At the top of the courthouse steps was a bunch of Baldwin-Felts. Sid smiled real big at them. And just as he raised his hand to say "Howdy," every one of them pulled out their pistols and shot him down those steps. See, that wasn't no trial they were planning there in Welch. That was just a way to bring him there for a public assassination. The McDowell County sheriff wasn't nowhere to be seen that day, nor any of his deputies. He was off at a spa in Virginia, probably paid for by Baldwin-Felts.

Sid was about the only law enforcement man in all of West Virginia who wasn't on the coal operators' payroll, so he was a big hero to the miners. Maybe them Baldwin-Felts was just trying to get payback for Lee and Albert and the others. But the operators had a plan. Them operators knew if they killed Sid Hatfield the miners would get distracted from striking for a union and want revenge for Sid.

I didn't see it so clear at the time, I'll admit it. But Mother Jones saw. She saw it plain as day. All them District 17 officers – Keeney, Blizzard, Munsey, Mooney, all of them – got up at a mass meeting in the state capital and told the miners to arm themselves. Mother Jones was the only one saying any different. She said no bullets were going to bring back Sid. She kept talking about an eight-hour day and checkweighmen and a grievance committee. But everybody else was hot to avenge Sid Hatfield.

Now I know you saw the movie Flamingo Road with Joan Crawford. Sure, everybody saw that. Do you remember Sydney Greenstreet played a sheriff in that movie? That's right, Titus Semple. He ruled the whole county for his own profit and he could ruin Joan Crawford just because he felt like it? Well, old Sheriff Semple didn't have nothing on Boss Don Chafin, the Sheriff of Logan County. Chafin had been ruling Logan County with the coal operators and his gun and badge since he was 22 years old. He might still be today, after all these years, I don't know. I haven't been there since… well, since back then after the First War. Somehow his $65-a-week salary had made him a millionaire in ten years. You see what I'm saying? We figured out he was taking $50,000 a year in bribes alone, from the coal operators, from the moonshiners, from the pimps and madams, from the gambling houses, from anybody with a dollar. That doesn't include whatever he was robbing from regular people. Now this was southern West Virginia and somehow or other he also had an armory with thousands of rifles, machine guns, and airplanes, too. Now you tell me what a rural county in southern West Virginia needs with enough weapons to invade a country! And he just dared all them miners to cross Logan County on their way to Mingo County. He dared them. So, of course, that's what everybody decided to do.

Mother Jones, I haven't forgotten. Thousands of armed miners were coming in to Kanawha County by car, train and on foot. They came from all over the state of West Virginia. They were going to avenge Smilin' Sid Hatfield's death. They were gathering and they were going to march through Logan County on their way to Mingo County, Don Chafin be damned! The union leaders were there, too. Mother Jones, she went to stop them. She told them the march wasn't no good and that it wouldn't help. She got up in front of the whole crowd waving a piece of paper that she said was a telegram from Mr. Warren G. Harding. She said President Harding had promised to end gunman rule in West Virginia. Well, I told you them miners loved Mother Jones. But they didn't like this one bit. Keeney asked her to see that telegram, but she wouldn't show him, so he said it was a lie. She told him to go to hell. Bill Blizzard, who was another District 17 officer, he asked the men whether they were going to be ruled by an old woman, but the truth was they loved Mother Jones, so now they weren't sure. Frank Keeney telegraphed the White House to find out if Harding had really promised all that to Mother Jones. And Keeney found out that Mary hadn't even been in touch with the president. That paper she showed everybody was a lie and Mother Jones got caught in it and so the miners were all set to march on Logan and Mingo County again. At the time this was really exciting news and I couldn't understand why Mother Jones had tried to stop it and I really couldn't understand why she lied about it. But I have been thinking about this all these thirty years since then and I think I understand it now.

I won't tell you about the Battle of Blair Mountain because Mother Jones left the state after Keeney and Blizzard called her a liar and went ahead and proved it to the men, too. But I will tell you this, because it shows why she was right. The very next day Keeney and Mooney were called to Charleston to meet with Major General Harry Bandholtz of the United States Army. He told them what President Harding *had* done and that Harding had ordered the army to *stop* their march, *by any means*. The Air Corps had flown their big bombers in, loaded up with explosives and gas. Those miners were all ready to fight Boss Chafin, they were, but they were not going to take up arms against the United States of America. So Keeney and Mooney got up in front of everybody and told the marchers that the army was coming and told them to go home. They didn't like it a bit, but that's what they told them. And that's what them miners decided to do, too.

Right about now you should be wondering, "Well, if they decided to go home, why was there a battle at Blair Mountain at all?" And I'll tell you. *Because the operators wanted it!* The operators *wanted* to provoke it. As soon as the miners turned around to go home, Boss Chafin and the West Virginia State Police led a couple hundred of those "Citizens Alliance" fellows, who were just middle-class gun thugs, down Beech Creek to Sharples in the dark, going from camp to camp, arresting and murdering miners. And when the word spread what they were doing, by God, the march was on again!

They fought up there in the hills for days. Boss Chafin's planes were dropping dynamite bombs on our boys. General Billy Mitchell still had his Army bombers in Charleston and he was threatening to drop gas on us, just like in the First War, and to drop explosives on us, too, if the gas didn't stop us. But the main thing was they had us all caught up in you-did-this-and-we'll-do-that and retaliating for murders instead of standing together for a union contract and eight hours and no company stores. And when Warren Harding sent in the U.S. Army, well, by then it really was to restore order. They could say they were there to stop all the fighting. They could say they weren't there to break our strike. It was another ten years before we got a union contract in them hills and we lost members in all our other districts, too.

No, I don't blame the men. I don't blame their officers neither. Sometimes it all just gets to be more than a man can bear. This class war can sometimes feel mighty one-sided when the bosses can cut our wages and murder our organizers and use court injunctions to take away our rights to speak and assemble. I wasn't mad at Frank Keeney and Bill Blizzard then. I'm sure not going to get mad at them now when I was so fired up and supporting them myself when it was all happening. I'm just explaining this because you're so interested in Mother Jones. She was the one who seen it so clearly, even in the heat of the moment. We all just felt she was a woman and a mother and she didn't understand how a man can feel. I think she did understand that. I think she understood that real well, better than us, even. That's why she lied and tried to stop the march. But then seeing how the bosses got the march going again the next day after Keeney and Blizzard stopped it you know they probably would have done the same thing if Mother Jones had got away with her little lie.

No, you see, she was not in with them other ladies that you're talking about, because the truth was, they were on the other side of the class war.

What do I mean? Look at the movement that those ladies led at that time, the one that was successful even before the women's suffrage.

Sure, I'm talking about the Eighteenth Amendment, prohibition. What was that all about? It was a class issue. They didn't care about their own husbands having a little cocktail at one of their high-class parties. But they were always complaining about a workingman stopping off at a bar for a quick beer with his fellows before going home. They were always complaining about a Hunkie or an Italian having a drink, as if there was something un-American about that.

314

Mother Jones used to say that the businessmen threw fits when they saw a worker enjoy a beer as if that would make him work less, or maybe give less to his family, but they didn't notice that same worker's children and wife toiling in the mine or the mill for next to nothing.

And then there was the vote. Sure, the Nineteenth Amendment gave ladies the vote everywhere in 1920. But ladies already had the vote in some places before that. Mother Jones used to remind them suffragists that ladies voted in Colorado all through the mine wars, including the Ludlow Massacre. How did that help the workers? Were those ladies voting for human rights? No. Hell, no. Those ladies were electing the men who put Baldwin-Felts gun thugs in Colorado National Guard uniforms. They were letting them machine-gun and burn the women and children in the tents at Ludlow! Mother Jones said many times that she actually heard a coal operator say if the women in Colorado hadn't had the vote the miners would have won a union a long time ago!

No, she only lived a few more years after that, but she raised hell the whole time. And she missed our successes. I told you, we still had to fight like hell, but we finally got a million coal miners organized. And the coal industry wasn't all, neither. It was *our* organizers, UMW men, who got the unions started in steel and in auto and in rubber, too. But Mother Jones was there when we needed her most. Looking back over my life is like looking back over a long war. The operators had machine guns and planes. They had newspapers and detectives. They had governors and state police and judges and presidents. All we had was each other. Johnny da Mitch sold out to the bosses. Bill Green sold out to the bosses. But we had Mary Jones. We had our Mother Jones. And she reminded us that it didn't matter how many battles we lost. Our victory was in the struggle. Yes. Our victory was in standing up. Every time the operators tried to convince us that we weren't human, we stood up. We let them know that we were. We are human beings and we stand up. And that was the gift of Mother Jones.

[Recording ends here.]

Five

It was a long trip from Boley to Crowder in the segregated train car, riding with the luggage and the mail. Once he got there, Ezekiel Payne would still have to transfer to the MKT for the ride north to Rentiesville. Sure, he could have driven directly in his T-Model Ford in about two hours, but today he was trying to keep his movements quiet. Route 12 went through Okemah and Henryetta and these days he never went to either without at least one passenger prominently displaying a short-barreled shotgun. They were sundown towns with a history of violence against Black people. A colored man driving his own car was a red flag to the white folks there under any circumstances, and Ezekiel did not want to call attention to this errand. The less the white folks knew about any meeting in Rentiesville, the better. On the train, Ezekiel was just an anonymous Negro with a .45 automatic concealed under his coat. That didn't eliminate the chance of trouble, but it did reduced it.

The three-hour ride on the Fort Smith and Western Railway gave Ezekiel a lot of time to worry and reflect. And – as always – his first worry was his daughter Nessa who he was leaving behind in Boley while he made this trip. He didn't like letting Nessa stay overnight at her friend Abby's house. The same dangers that demanded his attendance at the meeting in Rentiesville made it harder than ever to trust anybody other than himself to look out for his daughter, even the Walker family.

He *had* learned to trust the Beauchamp boy. Since Rector Beauchamp's return from France, he and Nessa had been keeping company. It was clear that Rector was making plans to marry her. It was also clear that Rector and Nessa had discussed it, and that the only thing keeping Rector from formally asking Ezekiel for his daughter's hand was the search for more lucrative employment than teaching at the little school in Haven that Rector himself had attended. Ezekiel was inclined to just tell them to go ahead and get married, but he respected Rector's seriousness and his need to proceed according to his own rules. Rector would speak to Ezekiel about marrying Nessa when he was ready.

Rector impressed Ezekiel the very first time he met him. Before his Army service in France, Nessa and Rector went with a group of boys and girls to a dance over at Weleetka Colored School. On their way home there was some trouble with a crowd of white cowhands at the Fort Smith and Western Railway station. None of the parents had ever gotten the exact details out of the young people. But Rector had gotten them all home safely and what impressed Ezekiel was that he had managed this without drawing the big Navy Colt he carried back then and risking a shooting fracas. He suspected that Rector had let the white boys see that Colt, though, and that was fine. All these reckless ofays sported pistols. Sometimes all they needed was a reminder that the gun factory hadn't shut down after manufacturing theirs.

Another story he hadn't quite been able to pry out of anybody concerned a near lynching in France. Some of the young men were convinced that all they needed to do was step up and respond to Uncle Sam's call. They thought they would all come home from the army with their freedom and their equality. Ezekiel knew better because of his own experience in the old 9th Cavalry and after. Rector Beauchamp was not so naïve either. Whether Rector told Nessa exactly what happened to him over there or not, Ezekiel didn't know. He guessed, though, that whatever it was had been worse than Weleetka.

In any case, Rector Beauchamp's readiness to protect Nessa Payne was moot today, because Rector was going to the same meeting Ezekiel was. So were plenty of other young Black veterans of the Great War, including some from the elite families in Boley and Haven and Clearview, boys who Ezekiel had judged trifling before they went overseas. What was it DuBois had written in *The Crisis*? "We return from fighting. We return fighting." And that's what he saw in a lot of these young men. They had seen something beyond eastern Oklahoma, beyond Indian Territory. He was prepared to depend on many of them in a way that he would never have depended on their fathers. They were no longer boys.

These thoughts occupied Ezekiel's mind on the long ride southeast. The train crossed the Canadian River into the old Choctaw Nation, and he got off at the Crowder station to make the transfer. Forty minutes later he boarded a northbound Katy. They crossed the Canadian again, then the North Fork, and Ezekiel had the conductor stop the train in Rentiesville about forty-five minutes later. There was no real depot; Rentiesville was just a flag stop. And once Ezekiel got off the train on Gertrude Avenue, there was no hiding: Rentiesville was just too small. Just like in Boley, every Negro in town would clock his movements from the moment he left the tracks. But at maybe a quarter the size of Boley he hoped that the Oklahoma Klan would be paying less attention. They were unlikely to be watching every one of the forty or fifty Negro towns in the state.

He walked right past the First Baptist Church, the logical place for such a meeting, and went up to Buck Franklin's house. Buck was an enrolled Choctaw, a Black Indian, and a prominent Oklahoma lawyer. White Oklahoma carried on a permanent campaign to seize the land and other wealth of Indians and Negroes. Buck represented many of those Indians and Negroes in the endless avalanche of lawsuits that were the "legal" front in that campaign. His practice specialized in petroleum law because so much Oklahoma oil was underneath the allotments that tribal members received when the federal government dissolved the Nations. To be a people's lawyer in Oklahoma was to specialize in mineral leasing.

Buck's wife answered Ezekiel's knock, accompanied by the little boy, John Hope. "So John," said Ezekiel, after the initial formal greetings, "what's the word?"

The six-year old smiled brightly at him. "The word is, I am going to be president of the United States some day!"

Ezekiel smiled, but he didn't laugh. If any colored child in America could carry out that promise it was definitely little John Hope. He turned back to Mrs. Franklin. "I am really happy to see you, Molly, but why are we meeting in your home?"

Molly's lips turned up at the corners of her mouth, but with no accompanying smile in her eyes. "We are here because the church is not available to us. Reverend Robinson is angry because Buck won't attend his services on Sundays. Do you know we're getting anonymous death threats?"

"From *colored* folk?" asked Ezekiel. He never stopped being astonished at the pettiness of which some people were capable.

Mrs. Franklin just nodded. "Can I get you something to drink? Coffee? Something stronger?"

"Thank you, Molly," he answered. "A cup of coffee would be a blessing right now."

She nodded again and then showed him into the living room before continuing, still with the little boy in tow, to the back of the house.

"Hello, B.C." Ezekiel said to her husband as he entered the large living room. Buck Franklin – B.C. – was sitting behind his big desk on the side of the room.

Then Ezekiel turned and nodded at the other men, who were sitting on the settee and on dining room chairs and kitchen chairs and even on some crates that had been pulled into the room. He knew many of them by name, but the rule of this gathering was that there would be no names mentioned. It had started several years earlier as a safeguard against spies and eavesdroppers. It had become a ritual since, along with the rules against note-taking and formal minutes. Ezekiel pulled up a chair. He didn't give any special greeting to Nessa's young man, Rector, who was sitting on a wooden vegetable crate in front of a wall of books near B.C.'s desk.

"I think we'll get started now," said a small, dark man sitting to Ezekiel's left. This was Doc White from Seminole County. Doc was a socialist, a member of the Working Class Union. Four years earlier, when the U.S. first entered the European War, the members – white, Black and native – had taken up arms against the draft. Ezekiel didn't know all the details. What he did know was that they planned a march on Washington under the red flag. They hadn't gotten farther than Sasakwa, though. Hundreds of them had been arrested after a shoot-out with the sheriff's posse. Over a hundred were convicted, too, some of them for long prison sentences. Why Doc thought it was his meeting to call to order, especially here in B.C.'s house, was a mystery to Ezekiel.

B.C. didn't interrupt and Doc continued. "We have a guest with us today from New York City," he said, "and we should acknowledge him before we get into our agenda."

There was no "agenda," just as there were no minutes. Everybody knew why they were here right now, but – again – nobody interrupted Doc to say this. "Most of you are familiar with *The Messenger*…" Ezekiel stopped listening. He had read the magazine and was familiar with the ideas of Chandler Owen and Philip Randolph, and… really? Doc had brought in a New York Socialist? This meeting was *never* about some organization that this or that person might be a member of, whether it was a church or a political group. This was practical work and it was supposed to be apart from – or perhaps above – all that other stuff.

Ezekiel was not interested in hearing whatever it was that Doc was saying and was glad of the interruption when little John Hope walked in with a cup and saucer and handed him his coffee. He patted the boy on the shoulder and took a taste: warm and rich, not too sweet. The boy looked at the men and then left. Doc was still going on about this college and that fraternity – all his guest's bourgie credentials – and ignoring some loud and pointed throat clearing by the other men in the room. "He comes to us today as a representative of the League for Democracy…" That caught Ezekiel's attention. League for Democracy was an organization of veterans of the Great War. He glanced at Rector, who he knew was a member, but Rector was looking at Doc.

"It is my honor to introduce Captain Osce…"

Doc was immediately cut off with a sharp reproof by Kitt Samson. "No names, man! No names!" Doc was afraid of Kitt; a lot of the middle-class men present were intimidated by the former outlaw, and they looked at the floor to avoid catching his eye.

Ezekiel, though, was now staring quite frankly at his son-in-law to be. He hadn't heard much about Rector's near miss with a would-be lynch mob of white soldiers on the Western Front. One detail he *had* heard was the name Osceola McKaine, the Black captain who had confronted and halted the mob. Rector was steadfastly avoiding eye contact. He wasn't looking at the floor to avoid Kitt like the others: Ezekiel had made certain that the Samson brothers knew Nessa's friends and looked out for them. But he was definitely looking away from Ezekiel.

The visitor – Captain McKaine? – papered over the awkward silence by saying, "I deeply appreciate the confidence all of you have shown by allowing me to meet with you. I do not want to interrupt your work. I just want to assure you that Black veterans all over the country are banding together now just as you began to do before the war. I will not be taking notes or writing about any details of your work. I do want to share your spirit with those who are just beginning in this journey."

Kitt looked quizzically at Ezekiel. Ezekiel was a kind of surrogate father for Kitt and his brother Hap who had never known their own parents. It was Ezekiel who got them to give up cattle rustling and come to work for him. As wild as they were, he made them welcome in his home. They were never members of Nessa's social circle, which was mostly made up of Boley schoolboys and girls, but they treated her as if she were a protected younger sister. Now Kitt wanted to know if this stranger should be allowed to remain in the meeting. If Ezekiel said so, Kitt would shoot him dead where he sat… or embrace him as a friend.

Ezekiel raised an index finger to Kitt, asking for a moment to decide, and looked again at Rector. This time Rector acknowledged him with an almost imperceptible nod. Yes. This was Captain Osceola McKaine. Ezekiel turned back to Kitt and gave him a silent okay. None of these exchanges were noted by anybody except B.C. Franklin, who nodded his own thanks to Ezekiel. Then B.C. said, "Thank you for those words. You're welcome to sit in with us. Right now we need to hear a little update about Tulsa." And he turned to a well-dressed, light-skinned man who was sitting on the sofa.

C.L. Netherland put down his coffee. Netherland was a barber. Unlike most of the other men he wasn't sporting a pistol on his hip, but Ezekiel knew Netherland always carried a straight razor. Ezekiel wasn't the only one who knew it, either. There were no stories about men who tried C.L. and that said all anybody needed to know. Like Ezekiel, Netherland had no outside organizational affiliations. He was just a race man and he had been doing this practical work at least as long as Ezekiel.

Netherland looked around first to see that he had everybody's attention. "I don't know how many of you read the white newspapers," he began. "The afternoon paper, the *Tulsa Tribune*, is trying to boost up their sales so they've been running stories every day about a crime wave." Some of the men in the room looked puzzled. What did this have to do with Negroes? Like the rest of eastern Oklahoma, Tulsa was overrun with bootleggers, hijackers, drug dealers, casinos and whorehouses. The white folks were as corrupt as they could be and everybody knew that the politicians and policemen were all getting a taste.

Netherland saw their shrugs and shook his head impatiently. "You're not paying attention. The *Tribune* is blaming this on *us*!" The uncomprehending looks around the room did not change. Netherland got a little louder. "Today's story was about a tour of what the paper called 'vice spots.' The entire point of the story was that Negro hotel porters are pimping white women." Understanding began to dawn. "They're bringing up a lot of lynching stories," he went on.

"Isn't that a good thing?" asked Hank Cobb, a Garveyite from Okmulgee. "Isn't that what Ida Wells does?"

"She's not telling white folks that it's a good idea, is she?" replied Netherland sharply.

Ezekiel saw understanding slowly cross Cobb's face. All he said, though, was "Oh."

"The *Tribune* brought up the Atchison case, but they advocated *for* the lynching," said the barber.

Cobb said nothing to this at all. He was the one who had organized the armed defense of the Black community in his hometown when Joe Atchison, a railroad porter, was arrested for raping a white woman. Cobb raised a force of several

321

hundred armed men, including most of those who were in the room right now, and they were able to drive off the lynch mob without firing a shot. A good thing, too, because Atchison had nothing whatever to do with the crime and was released without charges a few days later.

"They're praising the Belton lynching, too. They also ran a new article about how Tate Brady and them horsewhipped those IWWs a few years ago."

"What does any of that have to do with us?" asked one of the young veterans. "That's all white folks business."

Ezekiel felt the muscles in his chest tighten. For how many years had he been engaged in this stupid argument? He was tired of it. But he spoke anyway: "Yes, Roy Belton was a white boy, and he was probably guilty of that hijacking, too. But this is Oklahoma and if those Klans will murder a white man, why do you think they won't do the same thing to any one of us as soon as they get the chance? Smitherman said that in the *Star*. You don't have to read the *Tribune*. Do you at least read the race press?"

He took a breath. "Let me tell you something about IWWs. You were back from France in time for the Phillips County riots. When that peckerwood mob ran up and down the Arkansas Delta murdering our people? Their excuse was that *we* were following IWWs. Black sharecroppers asking for a square deal and the white man can't even imagine that could happen unless we're following some IWWs. Did you know Doc Johnston from Coweta? He was there. He was on a hunting trip with his brothers, David and Leroy. David wasn't an IWW. He was a dentist. Leroy was a veteran, wounded in France. He wasn't an IWW either. Those Klans pulled the Johnston brothers off the train and shot all three of them to death. Left them in the road and wouldn't let their mama bury them. Anything the big white men don't like, they get their Klans to attack. You think the IWWs are your enemy because they didn't fight in your war? Fine. As long as you don't believe those Klans are your friends."

Nobody answered. Ezekiel Payne's voice was not often heard in these meetings, but people listened when he spoke. He had been doing this work for a long time. Kitt glared around to see if anybody had any smart remarks. It wasn't just his respect for Ezekiel, either. Ezekiel's words were his thoughts.

After a moment the guest, who Ezekiel now knew was Captain McKaine, tentatively lifted a hand. "May I add a word?" he asked. When nobody objected he continued, "This idea about a 'Negro crime wave' is one of their tricks. In Atlanta, in Charleston, in St. Louis, in Chicago… everywhere. You get some

322

newspaper trying to boost their circulation and they start whipping white folks up about Negro bars and Negro pimps. That is exactly how all those attacks on our communities started. Maybe the spark was boys swimming in the lake. Maybe it was some lie about a rape. But that was just the spark. The powder was weeks of stories about crime." And then he added, "Sorry if I spoke out of turn."

"Not at all," said B.C. He turned to Netherland. "Anything else?"

"Yes," answered the barber. "Tate Brady has been organizing private showings of *Birth of a Nation*." This revelation evoked grunts from around the room. Every man in the room had participated in the protests against this love letter to white supremacist terror when it began showing in the theaters before the war. Wherever the movie showed it was followed by attacks on Black people. "And they have some Baptist preacher from Atlanta doing an invocation. Caleb Ridley."

The visitor turned his face quickly toward Netherland when he heard this name. "You know him?" Netherland asked.

"Of him."

"Bad news?"

McKaine just nodded. He looked like he wanted to say more, but was conscious of not truly belonging here. B.C. noticed and made eye contact. "What?" he asked.

The visitor thought for a moment, then said, "He is traveling the country getting members for the new Ku Klux Klan. Everywhere he speaks there is a hanging."

The men considered this silently for a few minutes. B.C. looked back to Netherland and asked, "When do we need to move?"

"Now. This could be tomorrow."

Now in every part of B.C.'s living room men turned directly to their neighbors and began murmuring: people who needed to be contacted, travel arrangements, places to stay. The less said about this publicly the better. Security arrangements for this meeting didn't preclude the presence of agents. Confining this part of the conversation to people who knew each other personally was long-established practice. Now, though, up spoke one of the young men, presumably a veteran because he was wearing a wool service coat. Ezekiel didn't know him, but thought he was from Red Bird. "Who will be providing firearms and what type?" he asked. "We need to know."

Kitt jumped up in his place and pointed directly at the questioner: "Negro, who the fuck is you?" He took a step toward the man, but Ezekiel caught his eye. Ezekiel waved his fingers back and forth across his throat in a gesture of silence, then pointed toward the door. He looked at Rector, too, and pointed again toward the door. Without another word Kitt left, followed by his brother Hap, Rector, and several of Rector's comrades from the army.

The man in the coat seemed to consider their departure an admission of defeat, because he persisted. "If you are not willing to go on record with your commitment, then you're not serious. How can we make tactical plans if we don't know numbers and dispositions?"

B.C. looked at Ezekiel as if his age, his long experience with this work, or perhaps his service as a Buffalo Soldier in the previous century made him the person to respond to this. So did the barber, C.L. Netherland. So did several others, including Doc White. But Ezekiel would not speak: he did not publicly acknowledge clandestine work, ever, even to say that it could not be acknowledged. This, though, was what Doc White now said: "Son, work that is secret does not get discussed. Even in a meeting like this."

Army Coat was still not having it. "You see, that's the kind of cowardly statement made by a man who hides behind secrecy as an excuse for not actually doing what needs to be done."

And this is why Ezekiel would not engage with him. Doc White was a lot of things: He did like to hear himself speak. He did always believe that he was the smartest man in any room. But he was no coward. He had been doing this work for years. Ezekiel said to C.L. Netherland, "See you tomorrow." He nodded to the other men. And he left. Everything that needed to be done in that room had been done. He was not going to engage with Army Coat.

Kitt was sitting behind the wheel of his big Dodge behind the house. The 30-horse engine was already running. Hap, Rector and one of Rector's friends were in the back, leaving the front passenger seat for Ezekiel. "Who is that Negro?" asked Kitt.

"Either he's too inexperienced to represent anybody or he's exactly what you think he is," answered Ezekiel. "Do you know him?" he asked the men behind him, turning toward them.

Rector's friend just shook his head "no." Rector said, "I thought he was a Garveyite."

"He come with Cobb?" asked Kitt.

"No," said Rector. "But he had the red, black and green pin."

"What do we do with him?" asked Rector's friend.

"Not a thing," answered Ezekiel. "The Klan knows we can put together an armed defense quickly. If he *is* an informer, all they learned is that we're aware of what they're doing in Tulsa. Maybe they sent him in for intelligence. If so, they didn't get any. Maybe they sent him in for a provocation, to get us to beat him or torture him so they can prosecute us. They won't get that, either. Right now, our job is to get to Tulsa and prepare for whatever is coming." He looked at Rector. "You telephone the Walkers. Speak to Nessa."

Rector nodded. Kitt put the car in gear and pulled around and out into the street. Five of Rector's friends followed in a four-door Chevrolet. Tulsa was about seventy miles away via Muskogee. They had at least a three-hour drive in front of them. And days of hard and dangerous work.

Tulsa, Oklahoma
1921

Black folks in Tulsa got their news from the *Star*. They generally didn't bother reading white folks' newspapers. But that day, the editorial in the white paper, the *Tribune*, had everybody in Greenwood talking within an hour of its publication. "Negro to be Lynched!" That kind of headline was never a prediction. It was a call to arms for the Klans. No Negro had *ever* been lynched inside the Tulsa city limits but the editors of the *Tribune* were clearly planning on a first. Apparently a teenaged boy who worked downtown shining shoes had been arrested for assaulting a white girl. Other Black people who worked over there were returning to Greenwood and reporting that a growing mob of whites by the courthouse on Sixth and Boulder was demanding that Sheriff McCullough turn the boy over to them. Now a crowd of about fifty stood in front of the *Star* building listening to Editor Smitherman argue with his friend, hotel owner J.B. Stradford, about what immediate steps to take.

Stradford was all for sending every available man over to the courthouse to help Sheriff McCullough protect the boy. He reminded Editor Smitherman of the recent attempted lynchings in Okmulgee, Oktaha, and Hugo and the successful tactic of protecting the accused with large, organized groups of armed Black citizens. Smitherman said that this white mob's aims went well beyond one lynching. He pointed to the invasions of Black neighborhoods in Chicago, St. Louis, Omaha and other cities; and to the horrible memory of Philips County, Arkansas where white mobs had killed hundreds of Negroes. He argued that as many men as could be spared should be deployed along a line near the tracks of the San Francisco Railroad to protect the people and property of Greenwood.

There was a third point of view, too. O.W. Gurley, the Greenwood real estate tycoon, loudly urged everybody to calm down and go home. He said that he was in touch with the sheriff and that there was no danger of a white mob and that there was no danger of any lynching. The crowd responded to this claim with jeers. But the grocer, O.B. Mann, went beyond laughing at Hurley. Mann was an army veteran, six-foot-four, with a bullying manner and an angry disposition. He got right up close to Hurley – too close for any friendly conversation – and demanded, "How much do the ofays pay you to sell out your people, Negro?" When nobody spoke up in Hurley's defense, the tycoon left without a word. The people returned to considering whether to follow J.B. Stradford to the courthouse or help Editor Smitherman organize an armed defense of the neighborhood. In the end they compromised, sending five carloads of men with rifles, pistols, and scatterguns to volunteer with Sheriff McCullough. The rest got ready to protect their homes.

A similar conversation was taking place in C.L. Netherland's barbershop that afternoon. Small groups of young veterans were quietly arriving in Tulsa from Clearview, Langston, Redbird, Bookertee and every other Black settlement in eastern Oklahoma. They were arriving by train and by automobile and they were arriving armed. White mob violence had driven Black folks out of Okemah, Henryetta, and Broken Arrow and turned them into sundown towns. The young veterans were determined that this pattern would not be repeated anywhere in Oklahoma, but especially not in Tulsa with its thriving Black business and professional community. They were serious men and they needed serious coordination. That coordination was taking place in Netherland's barbershop.

It was really a perfect place because men could come and go without attracting undue attention. What else should be happening in a barbershop? Weren't people always sitting around talking, whether they were waiting for a cut or not? As long as they knew who was there with them, they could speak freely, too. As the day went on, as men came and went, C.L. passed information from one group to the next.

Ezekiel Payne walked up to the shop in the early afternoon with Kitt and Hap Samson flanking him, looked inside to see who was there, and then sent them on their way. Their errands did not require his presence. He went right in. Doc White, the socialist high school teacher from Taft, sat in Netherland's barber chair up front getting a touch up. Azell Carolina, a young rancher from a Creek Indian family with a place near the Canadian River was getting a cut from Netherland's nephew Harris in the third chair. In the waiting area were two vets of the 369th from Langston whose names escaped Ezekiel but who he knew to be officers in the Garveyite African Legion. Nobody was sitting in the middle chair, so Ezekiel sat right down and asked C.L.'s number two, Jake Jefferson, for a haircut.

C.L. got right to it. "What do you see?"

"White folks are getting their courage up. Not just oil roustabouts and cowboys, either. Lawyers, shopkeepers, teachers… all drinking heavy and talking reckless. I left Rector downtown with two carloads of his army buddies laying low and watching the streets. I want to be sure the Negroes who work down there can get back across the tracks to Greenwood safe. I'm worried about Buck Franklin, too. His law office is near the courthouse and the ofays know him. Rector has his eye on Buck's door."

C.L. nodded. "The neighborhood?"

"We have people in windows in buildings on our side of the railroad tracks covering Elgin, Detroit, Frankfort and Cincinnati Avenues. Curtains drawn, mattresses up on the walls. They see out but nobody sees in. It's covered. What about you?" The question was directed to the two Garveyites.

One of them – did he call himself Afari? – said, "We're working on a back-up plan, trying to secure a safe route for women and children on the Frisco tracks to Rentie, just in case things go wrong."

"Smart," said Ezekiel. "You?" he asked Azell.

The Indian paused, looked away, then answered, "My dad and them aren't coming. They don't want to leave the settlements uncovered."

Ezekiel had expected this decision. Azell's father, Mont, and the other former Creek Lighthorsemen felt an obligation to guard those settlements up the Canadian River. They couldn't leave their families unprotected to help out people who they still thought of as State Negroes in Tulsa. But Azell added, "They sent me here to help out, though."

"And we appreciate it," said Ezekiel.

Just then, the bell on the barbershop door rang and in walked a complete stranger. Nobody needed a reminder to change the subject. After a moment of scrutinizing the man they began talking about an oil strike that was going to make some Osage rich. The stranger pretended not to study all their faces. Jake Jefferson finished Ezekiel's haircut. When the newcomer took his seat in the barber chair and asked for a shave, Ezekiel sat down in the waiting area to assess him. As soon as Jake covered the man's face with hot towels, Doc and the two young Garveyites quietly slipped out the door. Azell left soon after. The Klan's conspiracy was clearly underway and each one of them had a crucial part in protecting the people. Ezekiel would deal with this intruder, whatever his business might be.

The newcomer had some kind of eastern accent that Ezekiel couldn't place. His jacket didn't quite hide a small revolver on his belt. Neither did his relaxed manner hide his curiosity about Ezekiel and C.L., or their business. He identified himself as Henry Washington, which didn't mean a thing. It probably wasn't his name, anyway. Who was this man? The local Klansmen wouldn't bring an out-of-state Negro to do their spying. They had their own employees and clients. It was a conundrum. Ezekiel remained all through the man's shave, hoping he would let slip some clue, but there was nothing.

When "Washington" left, C.L. Netherland asked Ezekiel, "What do you make of that?"

"I have no idea," answered Ezekiel. "But it doesn't matter. We have more important work to do."

"I forgot to ask where you are going to be," said Netherland.

"We can't forget this boy Rowland who they arrested," replied Ezekiel. "I'm guessing Stradford and Smitherman and them are going to volunteer to serve as deputies to help the sheriff protect him. I think I need to be there with them."

Netherland nodded his agreement. "Be careful, though. I don't think those two know what this is."

Ezekiel smiled for the first time. "Who are you telling?"

He lost his smile as soon as he got back out on the street. He recognized this tension. He had felt it before, back in the cavalry, in the Johnson County War, when you knew somebody was about to start shooting, but you didn't know who, or when, or even why.

Ezekiel walked down Elgin Avenue toward white Tulsa. As he approached the railroad tracks he kept his eyes off the windows where he had stationed riflemen: there was no sense in giving their positions away to watchers, even if he doubted that the drunken mob at the courthouse had posted any. Once he crossed the tracks, white folks on Sixth Avenue gave him curious looks as he walked the five blocks over to Boulder Avenue, as if to say "Doesn't this country nigger know what's happening today?" but they kept their distance and they didn't say a word. This was still Oklahoma and Ezekiel still had a cannon visible on his hip, a .45-caliber Colt M1911.

Rounding the corner onto Boulder, though, was another story. Earlier, he had seen a large crowd of white men – cowboys and oilhands, businessmen and professionals – working on whiskey courage, just what he told C.L. Now, though, the crowd had swelled considerably, both in size and in intoxication. Ezekiel really had no way of counting them; if he had to guess, he would say two thousand. The sheriff had positioned men on the courthouse roof, but they were armed with shotguns instead of rifles. Scatterguns needed to be in the street to be any use against a mob. Why were they hiding up there? Rector's men were sitting inside their cars, engines idling, weapons out of sight. Again, as he had with his men in the windows when he crossed the tracks from Greenwood, Ezekiel avoided acknowledging them.

Right in the middle of all these hundreds of wild white folks was J.B. Stradford, the Greenwood businessman, in his bespoke suit and custom shoes, looking sharp, looking rich, looking like everything the peckerwoods resented. He wasn't alone, true. He had about seventy-five Greenwood Negroes with him, all members of the professional and business classes, all armed. Again, thought Ezekiel, it was everything these peckerwoods resented. J.B. was talking to Sheriff McCullough, and he was talking loud enough for every white man on the street to hear him.

"Sheriff, we're here to help you protect the court house," he said.

"You hear the nerve of this nigger?" asked a nearby white man. Tate Brady, the Klansman.

Another man near him, wearing the turned-around collar of a preacher, demanded of the crowd, "Are you white men, or not? Are you waiting for them to outrage your daughters?"

"Pipe down!" said Sheriff McCullough to the pastor. "Nobody is outraging anybody's daughters. And you," he turned back to J.B., "can take your friends back to Greenwood. We have the situation completely under control. Don't you see that you're making things worse by being here?"

But the situation was far from "under control." The preacher – Caleb Ridley? – had already renewed his oration. "This political hack," he said loudly, pointing to the sheriff and exaggerating his enunciation of each syllable, "wants us to believe that nobody's daughter has been outraged. And yet the black devil rapist remains alive inside his office! Why is he protecting these niggers? Why does he allow them to walk armed among us?"

That question seemed to inflame the mob even more. A drunken white cowhand confronted Pell Skidds, the science teacher at Booker T. Washington High School. "Nigger!" he shouted, "Give me that gun!" And he reached for Pell's . 38.

Skidds pulled his gun away from the drunk without a word. Another man in J.B. Stradford's posse, though, the grocer, O.B. Mann, answered for him. "Fuck you,

330

ofay," he said, and he clubbed the cowboy to the ground with the butt of his Winchester repeater.

Then Ezekiel heard a single pistol shot. From where? Pell Skidds went down and people were running, it seemed like in all directions. The sheriff disappeared. "Up Boulder! Up Boulder!" ordered Ezekiel. Two thousand crazy white men against seventy or eighty Negroes wasn't bad odds, but only if he got J.B.'s posse organized really fast. More whites were shooting at them now, but the Greenwood men were returning fire, so most of the would-be lynch mob was scattering.

Rector's men were the real difference, though. The drivers immediately pulled their cars into the street to cover the posse's retreat to their own neighborhood. The steel vehicles blocked much of the white mob's gunfire from hitting any of the Greenwood men. On the roof of each car was a sharpshooter, firing from a prone position with a 1903 model Springfield rifle. More shooters stood on the running boards, also armed with rifles. The cars drove slowly up Boulder Avenue, side by side, allowing the posse an orderly return to the relative safety of Greenwood.

Ezekiel was now walking backward, between Kitt Samson's big Dodge, driven by Rector Beauchamp and a 490-Series Chevrolet driven by one of Rector's army buddies. He had his Army .45 in his hand and he was picking his shots carefully, looking to take down only those members of the mob who were shooting at them. There weren't many bold enough to come within pistol range. The young veterans near him, with their long guns, were a different story. Ezekiel counted at least ten Klansmen down. And there seemed to be fewer following them as they approached the railroad tracks and crossed back into Greenwood.

It was only then – safe under the eyes and guns of the snipers he had placed in the windows of the first buildings on their side of the tracks – that Ezekiel turned around to see how they had fared in escaping the mob. He was not terribly surprised to see that the only men still with him were the young Army veterans who had been with Rector in the cars. Not one of the six dozen or so businessmen and professionals in J.B. Stradford's posse was there. Apparently, while the young soldiers covered their retreat, the middle-class crowd fled to the relative safety of Greenwood. No, that wasn't quite true: there was the high school teacher, Pell Skidds – limping from a bullet in the calf – and there was the grocer, O.B. Mann. They had been with Stradford and here they still were. Oh, and Mann's friend, Horace Taylor! Amazing. Only one leg, walking with the help of a crutch, and still out here fighting against the Klan.

O.B. laughed, "It'll be a cold day in hell before those ofays try that again."

Ezekiel gave him a hard look, but before he could say anything Rector did. "Keep laughing. This is definitely not done. They'll be back before the day is over. They are not going to leave it like this."

O.B., always ready to argue, turned to say something, but his friend, Pegleg Taylor, quietly said, "Leave it be." And he did. Ezekiel walked back up to C.L. Netherland's barbershop. He didn't have to deploy the young veterans who had covered Stradford's retreat. Rector would do that. He had to prepare for what was to come. It would be worse than they imagined.

Tulsa, Oklahoma
Wednesday Morning

This situation was nothing like what Director Hoover outlined to him. Agent Amos saw no evidence of any clandestine armed organization in Black Tulsa. Instead, it seemed as though every colored man over the age of 17 was openly armed and trying to defend the neighborhood against what looked like the entire white population of the state of Oklahoma. He had been looking for a violent Negro conspiracy? The real conspiracy, the Klan conspiracy, had apparently been unfolding right in front of him.

There were certainly no white anarchists or IWWs leading the Negroes as Hoover suggested. Amos couldn't see any white man even trying to enter the district under these circumstances. Last night several large trucks – loaded with Klansmen and mounted with air-cooled, Colt .30-caliber M1914 machine guns – had attempted an assault on Greenwood. They were driven back by sustained rifle fire. Amos himself had returned from his boarding house to the relative safety of the brick Stradford Hotel and retrieved his big .45 and badge from the safe. He had no illusions whatsoever about the power of that federal badge in the face of the white mob. But under these circumstances he preferred his automatic and all the ammunition he could carry to the snub-nosed five-shot revolver he had been carrying for the last few days. And he was finished with trying to hide his identity from the Negro community. What for?

Now it was time to get back to the train station, telegraph a report if possible, and get out of this insane city before things deteriorated further. This had become a problem for the Oklahoma National Guard, not the Bureau of Investigation. After the last intense exchange of machine-gun and rifle fire at about 4 AM he had heard only sporadic shooting. The sun was up and he thought he should be able to walk eight blocks and cross the tracks to the Frisco Railway's depot. Yes, it was in white Tulsa, but only barely. If he timed his trip right he could arrive just as the train did, and not have to remain a target for long.

He left his valise at the desk. It wasn't worth his life and he might need both hands free for shooting. As he stepped out onto Archer Avenue he noticed columns of smoke towards Cincinnati Avenue. Maybe it was just that the fire company couldn't get through, but he doubted it. More likely, the Klan was trying to flush the defenders. He decided to try crossing the tracks on Greenwood, then walk down First to the station. It put him on the white side of town for a few more minutes, but those building fires concerned him. And now he was hearing an increased volume of gunfire in that direction, too. Mostly 30.06-caliber rifles from the sound, but other weapons as well.

And then there was another sound: an airplane, no, *two* airplanes. He looked up behind him and saw them approaching from the north. As they got closer he saw that each carried a pilot and a passenger. One was painted with big red letters saying "101 Ranch." The other was green with the name "Sinclair Oil" in black. He wondered briefly what they were doing here until he saw the dust of bullets hitting the street between him and the planes. A gunner was *shooting at him* from the 101 Ranch airplane! Amos quickly stepped into the cover of a doorway, raised his .45, and let off two rounds. He didn't think he had hit anything, but both airplanes now banked away to the west and stopped following him. And Amos had a realization: the Klan had planes! Were the Harlem radicals actually right about America? Had the white folks decided to exterminate every Negro in the country?

He quickly filed that thought for later examination. It was not going to get him through the next forty-five minutes. Right now he had to cross the railroad tracks, make it to the station and get out of this maelstrom. He stepped out of the temporary shelter of the doorway and saw one of the trucks from last night. It had a one-hundred pound, watercooled, Browning machine gun bolted onto its chassis. Amos had assessed those weapons in detail at Mr. Hoover's request. They fired 7 or 8 high-velocity rounds *per second*. He was not walking toward it; that would be suicide. As it set up in the intersection of First and Greenwood, though, the vehicle began taking rifle fire from windows above him on the Greenwood side of the tracks. The Klan gunner ducked down and the driver spun his tires and sped away. This was clearly not the best way to get to the train depot. He would have to take his chances crossing on a block nearer the smoke he still saw rising over to the west. Maybe Elgin Avenue. Maybe Detroit.

Agent Amos returned carefully up Greenwood Avenue, now watching for new attacks from the air as well as checking behind him for that machine gun. He could hear the aircraft again and they seemed to be close by, but the engine racket was soon drowned out by what sounded like hail on the rooftops. Hail? He had seen hail in the spring and summer before, but always associated with a thunderstorm. Except for the smoke from the fires, this morning's sky was clear. What could that rattling noise be?

Incendiaries. There was one of the airplanes again, the one with the Sinclair Oil markings. It was dropping balls of flame! As he drew closer he saw that they were little pieces of tar, and they were all on fire. The ones that fell in the street were burning harmlessly, but the ones that fell on the wood-framed buildings –

of which there were many – were igniting fires up and down the neighborhood. The Klan wasn't getting close enough to torch people's homes and stores from the ground so they were burning Black Tulsa from the air!

As he crossed Frankfort Avenue he encountered his first pedestrian since leaving the hotel. It was the one-legged veteran he met at the barbershop two days earlier, the one who was friends with the loud-mouthed grocer, the one the grocer called "Peg." The man was kneeling behind a news kiosk, looking down the sights of a long-barreled 8mm rifle, the kind that colored sharpshooters attached to the French army had been issued. When he realized that Amos was there he looked up briefly, then returned to scanning the street on the other side of the tracks.

"What the fuck is you doing here, detective?" asked "Peg."

So he had been made as a detective from the day he entered Tulsa. "I am Bureau of Investigation Agent James Amos." He took out his U.S. government badge.

"Pleased to meet you, James," answered the one-legged man without even glancing at Amos's identification. "I am Corporal Horace Taylor, Ninety-Third Infantry Division, United States Army."

A combat unit. When Amos first saw Horace Taylor and his ragged uniform coat at the barbershop he had made the assumption that Taylor – like most colored draftees – had been assigned to a labor battalion in France and never issued a weapon. This Corporal Taylor was definitely a revelation. Right now, though - with buildings on fire, aerial bombardment, and Klan machine gunners nearby - was not the time to learn more about him. Agent Amos needed to find an exit strategy; maybe Taylor could help. So Amos just said, "I'm trying to get out of this madhouse. Have all you people gone insane?"

"You people?" asked Taylor with a laugh. "I don't know about 'us people,' but these white folks have surely lost their minds." Agent Amos had already stopped thinking of him as "Peg." The man spoke with a great deal of pride and precision. How had he been so quick to write him off as a beggar?

"You are walking in the wrong direction, though," said Corporal Taylor. "You want to get out of here alive, you need to walk north, as far as you can. Maybe if you get to Vera you can catch a train out."

"I want to get a train from the Tulsa depot right there," pointed Agent Amos.

Taylor turned and looked at him again, this time with an expression of disbelief. "Are you and I in the same street right now?" he asked. "Klans are over there… with machine guns. They're dropping firebombs from the sky. You propose to walk *toward* them?"

He had a point. As Amos stopped to consider his options a Dodge truck sped around a corner across the tracks loaded with armed white men. Taylor immediately fired a single shot. The front right wheel of the truck exploded and flew completely off its axle. As the truck chassis fell to the street and skidded to a stop, the men on board leaped out and scattered back in the direction from which they had come. Reloading quickly, Taylor dropped two of them to the pavement. The veteran ejected the last spent case, seated a new round with the bolt, and waited for another target to enter his view. "How long do you intend remaining here?" asked Agent Amos.

"See those burning buildings?" asked Taylor.

How could Amos miss them? Pillars of fire reached skyward into the smoke. They were now fully engaged in flames. Even if the firemen were to come, there was no putting them out. But he answered, "I see them."

"Our men set up sandbagged positions in those windows there to defend the neighborhood. No more. They had to retreat up the street. I may be the remainder of our defense right now. I am here for the duration. I can't really run anyway." He pointed to his wooden leg.

"You have enough ammunition?" asked Amos.

Taylor laughed. "Enough ammunition? For what? Once these ofays work their way around behind me I'm not going to need any ammunition."

Amos wasn't certain what to say. What do you tell a man who is calmly prepared to leave this earth and to take as many enemies as he can with him?

"Tell you what," said Taylor. "Walk up this street two blocks. You'll come to a hardware store. Ask inside for a man named Ezekiel Payne. He'll tell you how to get out."

Ezekiel Payne. So that *had* been the farmer's real name. One thing was for certain: Amos had been right to mark him. If this one-legged veteran, who could hold off a mob by himself, acknowledged Payne, then Payne was the man to look for.

"Good luck," he said to Taylor and turned away. Even over the sound of burning buildings, even over the sound of nearby gunfire, even over the sound of the returning airplanes, Special Agent James Amos could hear Corporal Horace Taylor laughing. He supposed that Taylor was laughing at his good luck.

Tulsa, Oklahoma
1921

Black Zion? Smoke was rising from fires a few blocks south, east and west. There was small arms fire in those directions as well, and – occasionally – long bursts from Klan machine guns. Airplanes from Sinclair Oil and the Miller Brothers 101 Ranch flew overhead dropping incendiary pellets from the air. Reports from his spotters made it seem as if every white man in Oklahoma had taken up arms this morning to murder every soul in Black Tulsa. Black Zion? Maybe 35 years ago when he moved to the Creek Nation after his discharge from the army, but not today. No, not today.

Ezekiel Payne had been preparing for this war for so many years now. He had, in a lot of ways, been *fighting* this war for a decade and a half. When Oklahoma became a state the first act of the legislature defined who was Black and then banned integrated schools, integrated public transportation, and interracial marriages. Immediately after statehood, a white mob in Henryetta, only thirty miles from his home, lynched one Black man and then burned out the entire Black district. They expelled every colored person from that town with their ropes and their torches.

Then the war moved closer. A mob from the county seat took Laura Nelson and her son L.D., whose ranch was only six miles from Ezekiel's, out of the Okemah jail and hung them from the Canadian River bridge. They sold postcards of that hanging. They dynamited a hotel and drove all the Black residents and Black-owned businesses out of Okemah, too.

It was that second lynching that got Ezekiel thinking about organized self-defense. For ten years that organization had foiled countless lynchings. But since the war things had changed. He had read about it in the papers. The sheer scale of the violence unleashed by these white mobs – in Chicago, in Atlanta, in Charleston, in St. Louis, in rural Arkansas – went beyond even what the word lynching made one think.

The playbook, though, was always the same. It was as if these white mobs were acting out a script in some satanic traveling theater. First, the local newspaper would start reporting on a "crime wave." Ezekiel couldn't even remember hearing that phrase before statehood. But it was a code word. It didn't refer to cattle rustlers or highwaymen or even bank robbers. They had all been out here in the Territory when he first arrived, but they weren't the "crime wave." No, "crime wave" always referred to Negroes, and it was usually about saloons and brothels and the implication that they would poison decent white folk. He had seen this himself in the white press in Okemah and heard about it elsewhere.

Then the newspaper stories would be be followed by the killing of some criminal suspect. Like the Nelsons, this was always somebody that respectable colored folk were reluctant to defend or be identified with. According to the white papers, a group of "unknown" citizens would march "silently" and in an "orderly fashion" to the jail where they would seize the suspect from the deputy and execute him. These claims beggared belief. The condition of the bodies? The presence of a professional photographer? The sheriff knew who took the Nelsons out, he knew the plans in advance, and there was nothing "silent" or "orderly" about that mob.

The lynchings were always followed by panicked reports in the white press of armed Black men on the way to exact vengeance. Back in '07 the whites of Henryetta had nearly fled the town because they feared that the *1300 rounds of ammunition* they had stockpiled would not be enough to stop the 35 armed Black men they heard were coming for them: more than seven 5-round magazines for each imaginary invader! In the case of Okemah, they said it was the entire town of Boley, ten miles away, that was supposedly coming to kill the white people, and – Ezekiel supposed – outrage their women. Sheriff Dunnegan armed every white man in Okemah, prepared for an attack that – like the one expected in Henryetta – never came. From that day on, Okemah was a sundown town.

It was the consistency of this pattern, from town to town, from state to state, that made Ezekiel think that all these white folks were actually reading from the same secret script. But sometimes he had an even darker thought. Sometimes he imagined that white guilt and white fears were so strong – and so *uniform* – that it resulted in these common patterns of violence and blame. What if white folks were so filled with guilt and shame for their own crimes that they imagined an army of Black people retaliating against them because *it would have to be so in any just universe*? What if white folks had to bar Negroes from their towns because *they couldn't look them in the eye* after the atrocities they had committed against them? What if white folks imagined that colored folks were impervious to bullets because they knew *their own actions were demonic* and thought God himself was sending avenging Black angels to destroy them? And – finally – what if those loathsome postcards of their victims that they all kept as souvenirs were meant to reassure them that these Black angels were, in fact, mortal?

Things got even worse after the War. Chicago, St. Louis, Omaha... these weren't towns like Henryetta, they were big cities. Ezekiel and people like him had been thinking for a long time about defending the Black towns of Oklahoma, but after the War they began preparing for this invasion of Greenwood, of Black Tulsa. They prepared for the armed white mobs. They even prepared for the truck-mounted machine guns. But in their wildest nightmares they hadn't thought about preparing for aerial bombardment! And yet... the green biplane of Sinclair Oil flew overhead again, and again it was driven off by rifle fire from the roof across the street. Hap Samson.

Defending the neighborhood had ceased to be the plan. All morning long Ezekiel had been sending family groups north to safety, each accompanied by armed members of his network. He had no idea how many families were still sheltering in place. With each new column of flame and smoke, with each new burst of machine-gun fire, he worried about the future of those families. He had very few men left. Other than himself, so far as he knew, it was just his prospective son-in-law Rector Beauchamp and his other two surrogate sons, the Samson brothers. They had to think about getting out themselves.

As he thought about this, the door of the hardware store opened and in walked the suspicious man from the barbershop, "Henry Washington." Had it been only yesterday? It already felt like another lifetime. Behind him, and holding a 1903 model 30.06 on him, was Kitt Samson. "This spying-ass Negro came walking up the street like it was some other day. Called your name like he knew you. How you want him?"

"Horace Taylor told me to come find you," said the man. "He told me you could help me get out of town."

"Peg still living?" asked Kitt, without lowering his weapon.

"He was when I spoke to him," answered "Washington." "But that was ten minutes ago. He was exposed and short on rounds. I couldn't say how he is now."

"I told you my real name when we met at the barbershop," said Ezekiel after some thought. "How about you reciprocate now, stranger?"

The man did not hesitate. He handed Ezekiel a government badge and said, "My name is James Amos. I am a special agent of the United States Bureau of Investigation."

"What the fuck is that?" asked Kitt.

Indeed, wondered Ezekiel. What *was* that? And why did they have Negro agents?

"I don't mean to be rude," answered the detective, what was his name, Amos? "But is my answering your questions really the best use of our time now?"

"Shut the fuck up, special agent," said Kitt, sarcastically emphasizing the title. "I shoot you now, every white man in Washington, D.C. thinks you're just another nigger that died today in Tulsa."

"That's true," said Ezekiel. "Honestly, even if we just leave you now you're likely to end up another dead Black man in Tulsa before this day is out. Any of those white men impressed by your badge?" He gestured with his lips toward the door, toward the carnage out in the street.

Special Agent Amos paused to consider the truth of Ezekiel's words. Then he said, "I would like to be a live Black man when this day is over. I would like to be far from Tulsa. I would also like to report what I saw here today to President Harding. This is an outrage."

Kitt was unimpressed. "Why don't you start by telling us why you're spying on us?"

But Ezekiel had decided. "It doesn't matter. He's wearing the same skin as us today. He leaves with us. Get Hap. Get Rector. Let's move. I'm still worried about Doctor Jackson."

Kitt stepped outside and whistled sharply, three times. His brother and Rector were out as flankers. On this signal they would start moving north near the Midland Valley Railroad's tracks. That way they could all provide covering fire for each other if necessary.

"Is he still carrying that little .32?" Ezekiel asked Kitt. He nodded at Amos in case it wasn't clear who he was asking about.

"He was," answered Kitt, emphasizing the past tense. "Also this," he added. He held out a .45-caliber Colt automatic.

"Give them back," said Ezekiel. "We're going to need his help before this hour is through."

341

"Sure," said Kitt, and he handed the weapons to Special Agent Amos. But his tone said that he was anything but sure. And they began walking up Frankfort Avenue.

Before they had gone ten steps an open Dodge touring car sped from Sixth Street and into the intersection with five armed white men inside. Amos began firing immediately. The big .45 barked three times before the white men even registered their presence, then twice more. Ezekiel and Kitt each got off a shot of their own and the invaders were all dead. Their car slammed into the window of a funeral parlor.

"Good shooting," said Ezekiel.

"Who the fuck *are* you?" asked Kitt, impressed.

Amos just took out his magazine and filled it back to capacity.

They started to hear machine gun fire again, now to the east. "That's Detroit Avenue," said Kitt. "Doc Jackson's."

"Let's go," agreed Ezekiel, and the three men turned the corner and headed in that direction. After half a block they met Rector who had been paralleling them through the alleys.

Rector froze when he saw Special Agent Amos. He turned to Ezekiel, "This is the informer for the Klan?"

"Let it go for now," answered Ezekiel and kept walking, followed by Kitt Samson. Rector looked skeptically at Amos a moment more. Amos lowered his .45, but didn't continue walking until Rector looked away and went after the others.

Then they spotted something that froze all of them. Hanging from a utility pole at the corner of Greenwood Avenue was the body of a man. He had been stripped, beaten and shot. His body was mutilated, but his face and his size and the apron lying on the street identified him. It was the six-foot-four grocer O.B. Mann. Rector Beauchamp fell to his knees and vomited in the street. He had seen a lot in France that he wanted to forget. But the hemp rope? That was uncomfortably personal. The near lynching in Saint-Rémy-sur-Bussy still haunted his nightmares. He thought of Captain Osceola McKaine and hoped he was far from here by now. He also remembered who rescued him that day and wished McKaine was by his side. But Ezekiel Payne and the Samson brothers were the best comrades he knew, even if he had never told them of his close call in the Marne. So he shook off his nausea.

"You okay?" asked Kitt.

Rector nodded.

By the time they got to Detroit Avenue the firing there had stopped. Ezekiel signaled the others to hold back while he quickly looked around the corner to check things out. And it was a good thing he did. There were at least sixty, maybe seventy white men around A.C. Jackson's prosperous house, maybe half of them wearing the uniform of the Oklahoma National Guard. The rest looked like oil-rig workers, cowboys and saloon riffraff. The house itself was on fire. It was riddled with bullet holes and there was no glass left in any window. All Ezekiel could think about was Mrs. Jackson and the children. Then he saw something that made his stomach sink even more: Doctor Jackson himself standing out near the sidewalk with both hands in the air, a white linen napkin in his right hand.

Surrendering. That meant that the family was still inside. Jackson had fought to protect them, but this white flag showed that he must now believe that his only choice was to place himself at the mercy of the very assassins who had put his home to the torch and who had fired blindly through the walls at his wife and at his children. Ezekiel could not hear what Dr. Jackson was saying. He could not hear the argument that the white men surrounding the doctor were having.

But he could see. He could see the sneer on the face of the man who raised his revolver and – without looking Jackson in the eye – shot him in the chest. He could see the man spit a stream of tobacco in the face of this brilliant surgeon as he lay bleeding out at his feet. He could see the man put a second round in the doctor's stomach. And right then Ezekiel lost his tactical reserve. He raised his carbine and put a bullet in the head of the contemptible piece of trash who could snuff out the life of a man of medicine like that, who could destroy a doctor who had saved as many white Oklahomans' lives as Black, a man who the Mayo brothers considered their most able colleague.

"Niggers!" shouted a member of the white mob, pointing at him. But that was all he said, because he, too, immediately went to the ground. Kitt Samson ejected the spent shell, chambered a new round and pulled Ezekiel back around the corner.

"Now we're in it," Kitt said.

"You and the detective find some cover back down the block," ordered Ezekiel. "Rector and I will hold them here until we can get back to you." Rector was already firing from the limited shelter of a hedge. Ezekiel noticed that five or ten of the white men were moving toward the next block south to circle around and come up behind them from the parallel street.

He aimed carefully at a member of the mob who had been slow to take cover and fired. "Sorry, son," he told Rector. "I shouldn't have done that. I need you to get out of this alive. I need you to take care of Nessa."

Rector replied without taking his eyes off the cars and bushes that sheltered the mob. "Sir, Nessa was raised by a man. Nessa deserves a man for a husband."

What could Ezekiel say? What would he have thought of a son-in-law who was *not* at his side at this time, in this place? "You're right, son. You're right."

None of the mob was stirring from their hiding places down the block. The white men were taking a lot of wild shots in their general direction, making enough noise to make it unclear to them whether Ezekiel and Rector were even shooting back. "Knock out a window on that T-model down there so they know we're shooting at them," said Ezekiel. "Then we need to get back to Kitt before that other group gets up to this block." Rector blew out the windshield on the Ford and took off. Then Ezekiel shot up the radiator on a Chevrolet flatbed. That raised enough steam to help cover his own exit and he followed Rector.

Agent Amos and Kitt Samson had taken a position behind the low brick wall in front of a bungalow three-quarters of the way up the block. As Ezekiel arrived a white man in stained coveralls ran heedlessly around the corner. Amos immediately dropped him with a shot from his .45. That would slow this new group, but not for long. And they would soon be joined by fifty more from the other corner that Ezekiel and Rector just left.

"Kitt," asked Ezekiel, "where will Hap be right now?"

"He would be right where the Midland Valley tracks split off from the Santa Fe," answered Kitt. "He wouldn't go on from there without us. That's where I hid my car."

"Good," said Ezekiel. "Get this man to Hap and get him out of the state." He gestured toward Agent Amos.

"Why would I want to do anything for this informant?" objected Kitt.

"Because he *is* an informant," answered Ezekiel. "Let him inform his bosses in Washington what's going on here."

Kitt shook his head, unconvinced. But Ezekiel added, "Please trust me on this."

"How are we getting out?" asked Amos.

"Through the alleys and yards," answered Ezekiel. "You're going to have to trust me, too. This man can get in and out of anywhere without being seen. Just don't ask why."

"Covering fire?" asked Rector.

"Yes. They're going to need that. Kitt leads, the detective follows, you cover their backs."

"What about you?" asked Amos.

"I am going to divert this entire group," said Ezekiel. He fired one shot to the west and another to the east, then set down his Springfield. "You still have that . 32?" he asked.

Amos shook his head. "I can't give you that. That was a personal gift to me from Theodore Roosevelt." That got the immediate attention of all the other men.

"Who the fuck are you?" asked Kitt again.

"A story for another day," reminded Ezekiel. "We don't have much time here."

"Take this," said Agent Amos, and he handed Ezekiel his Army .45.

Ezekiel nodded, checked its weight, and put it in his left hand. Then he took his own Colt from its holster with his right hand. "Ready?" he asked the other men. "Go when I start firing."

And then Ezekiel Payne walked from behind that brick half-wall and stepped into the middle of the street with both guns raised, one pointed at the corner of Detroit Avenue, the other at the corner of Greenwood. He took fire from both directions, wild and unaimed at first, as the members of the mob were afraid to

345

expose themselves to this intimidating vision. He held his own fire until targets presented themselves. As the others broke around the side of the building, they got a glimpse of him standing in the street like… well, like nothing any of them had ever seen before.

Agent Amos's first thought was, "There is no way in hell that he's going to be able to hit *anybody* that way," but he quickly realized that this was not Ezekiel's intention. And then he knew that he had been right to notice Ezekiel from that first moment in the barbershop. He said a silent "thank-you" to this man who was stepping into the bullets of five or six dozen guns to cover his flight.

Kitt shouted, "Pops, what are you doing?" but Rector grabbed him and pulled him away.

"Don't make this be for nothing," said Rector to Kitt, driving back an incautious member of the white mob by blasting a fragment of brick from the side of the house on the corner to the left with his rifle, and then Kitt took off. Rector's last sight of Nessa's father – arms raised level with his head, pistol in each hand – burned itself into his memory where it remained until the day he died, living even afterward in the memories of his children and grandchildren, each of whom could see it in their mind's eye as if he or she had been there themselves, so vivid was Rector's description.

Agent Amos was right; Ezekiel hit nobody. But he took his time with his shots and so the others were already two blocks north by the time the rioters were certain he had used all his remaining rounds. Those who got a glimpse of him while he remained standing were confirmed in their worst fears: an avenging Black angel, impervious to their panicked, wild shooting, sent by an angry God to punish them for their sins.

Ezekiel, was – of course – a man, and neither bulletproof nor immortal. Once they realized he had no ammunition left they ran at him and riddled his body with bullets. They continued shooting him long after it was obvious that he was dead. Men who hadn't dared so much as look at him while he stood alive in the street shot at him now. They didn't display him from a utility pole as they had with the loud-mouthed grocer. They didn't burn his body as others like them had done with the grocer's one-legged friend. No, they wanted every Negro in Tulsa to see their triumph over this man who had shown himself fearless; they wanted every white man in Oklahoma to see how they brought down this man who defied them; they wanted to be able to look again and again at his body themselves and to convince themselves that they had not been frightened of him, that sixty of them had not hid themselves from one Ezekiel Payne as if he could have destroyed all of them with a look or a gesture.

So they strapped his body up on the bed of a Ford truck. They drove it up and down the streets, displaying their trophy like a parade float. They brought him downtown to the armory, where the Oklahoma National Guard was imprisoning Negroes for the crime of their color, and they parked it there so that every new captive could see him as they were brought inside. They took photos of Ezekiel's body on that truck and they sold postcards as souvenirs to the white people of eastern Oklahoma.

Buck Franklin, the lawyer, was marched down the block at gunpoint, hands in the air, along with dozens of other Black detainees. Buck had seen the incendiaries dropped from airplanes. He had even been fired at by a gunman in the sky. In his mind, as he walked, he was already preparing lawsuits on behalf of the Negroes of Tulsa. But his strongest memory of that day, the one he passed to his little boy John Hope, was of the body of his friend, Ezekiel Payne, exhibited like some demonic hunting trophy. Like the grandchildren of Rector Beauchamp, John Hope Franklin never forgot.

Six

Oh, grandchildren, there were so many reasons I did not want to make that trip to St. Louis, but I cannot claim to have had foreknowledge of the calamity to come; it wasn't as if I had a bad feeling about it. If anything, I felt that perhaps the disasters of my life were now over! Chicho and I were in love. We moved to a handsome house near 8th Street and Kruttschnitt in Edinburg, a short walk from the Hidalgo County Courthouse. Chicho was still working out of a room in our home, but he was looking at space for a real law office, near 12th Street. And there was talk in our community of running him for state legislature. For all those good things, I wanted to stay at home in the Valley. Why would I want to interrupt our promising life with a trip out of state?

Then there was my good news. Nowadays I think you young people speak of this more openly – and that is a good thing! – but in those days it was private, maybe "secret" is the better word. Back then the men knew nothing about it and considered it a mystery of women. Anyway, I am a modern woman, so I will discuss it here with you, my grandchildren. *Mi regla* had been a consistent visitor since around my 13th birthday. It had now been absent for two straight months, and – although I had not yet felt ill on awakening – I suspected that Chicho and I would soon have a little family. This was long before the days of pregnancy testing and I didn't want to tell him until I was certain. But I also had no desire to travel so far from my mother, my *abuela* and my *tías* in that condition.

I also didn't much like Chicho's reason for the trip. Before the Revolution on the other side, St. Louis had been the headquarters for the Mexican Liberal Party. Their newspaper, *Regeneración*, was published there until the secret police of Porfirio Díaz tried to assassinate the editorial board. Chicho had gotten it into his mind that if his political career was to serve more than just his personal ambition, if it was to further the larger needs of our people, then he had to meet with the leading Mexican progressives in the United States. He convinced himself that he would find them not in Los Angeles, not in Brownsville, but in... St. Louis. I didn't disagree with him about where they were. I had no idea where the *magonistas* might have gotten themselves to. I simply had no desire to meet them, nor to have my husband meet them, either.

For me, *magonismo* was dead. When Narciso and I first met at the meeting in Laguna Seca I was already speaking about a new strategy. I thought we should embrace our rights as citizens of the United States instead of being torn between the two sides of the river. Here in Texas, Don Aniceto's raids had not brought our liberation, only the *rinchada* terror. Thousands died at the hands of the Rangers and the posses. And what did the Magón brothers say about this? They criticized Don Aniceto for not doing enough! On the other side it was not thousands who died, it was hundreds of thousands! And did all that death bring justice and land to the people? Could I honestly say today as I write this testimony that an Alemán Valdés or a Ruiz Cortines is so different than Porfirio Díaz? I already knew back then, when Chicho was planning this trip, that President Carranza had used the workers' Magonist unions to defeat the *campesinos* who followed Zapata and Villa. Then he turned around and used the Army to break those unions! I felt that the Magón brothers' anarchism led to chaos and murder. I was not interested in pursuing it any longer.

Chicho won me over by saying that the trip could be our honeymoon, our opportunity to explore a wider world. Remember that for all my reading I had never been more than seventy-five miles from home, on either side of the river. Chicho had been south to Monterrey and north to Detroit. He went to France when he was in the army. He told me about the Palace of Fine Arts we would visit in St. Louis. He told me about the St. Louis Zoo with its spectacular walk-through birdcage. He told me about the miracle of a city illuminated by electricity. And we did, indeed, see all those sights before things went so terribly wrong. Moreover, Narciso promised that we would visit New Orleans on our way home. I was mad for all things French. I wanted so much to taste the famous French cuisine and to see the French architecture.

Of course, we would never make it to New Orleans, but I didn't know that then. I convinced myself that it was early enough in my pregnancy not to worry. Wasn't cosmopolitan travel a reason for marrying a highly educated man like my husband?

I swallowed my objections and Narciso booked the trip. Rail travel in those days could still be quite an adventure. The Gulf Coast Line carried us only the first few hundred miles, from our home in Edinburg to Houston. It was late September, so the summer heat wasn't at its worst, but oh, my! Smoke and cinders from the locomotive streamed through the open windows all day long, ruining my clothes and making it hard to breathe. That evening, though, we switched to a Pullman sleeper car on the International and Great Northern Railroad, and that was a whole different world. The porters were beautifully uniformed and thoughtful. They handled our luggage with care and they took food orders, too. I felt so fancy! In the morning we awakened in Texarkana. The Pullman porters served us breakfast and transferred us again, this time to the Iron Mountain Railroad. We rode that all day to St. Louis.

I had never seen anything like it. We thought of Brownsville as a big city, but St. Louis seemed to be a hundred Brownsvilles! Only New York, Chicago and Philadelphia were bigger, and of course I still thought that some day I was going to visit them all, too, along with Madrid, Paris, London, and Tokyo.

We stayed at the Planter's House, which was ten stories high and had iron columns and an immense balcony over the Broadway entrance. To this day I have never again been in a dining room as grand. They said it was designed in the style of the French Empire. The waiters were dressed as formally as the diners, and they were equally haughty! I was so proud of Chicho, reading the menu and ordering in French. I never doubted that we, the Spanish aristocracy of the Valley belonged right there with all those other fine people. I felt once again that perhaps all the horror that the low-class Texans had visited upon us was now over.

I will not share the details of our night in that airy room on the second floor. I will tell you that I woke up the next morning dizzy and nauseous and that this confirmation filled me with optimism for our life together. I had a light breakfast – I could barely stomach even that – and we went out to tour all the sights of the great city. It was not until the following day that, this time after skipping breakfast completely, we went to look for the *magonistas*.

Chicho had an address. I have no idea where he got it. The concierge in the hotel lobby looked askance at it, but it turned out to be practically around the corner. We didn't even need a carriage. There was a garish sign over the front door reading "The National Rip-Saw: Blind As a Bat to Everything But Right." This did not strike me as especially promising, but we went in anyway.

Narciso began speaking to the people, but my nausea was back. This time I didn't think it had anything to do with expecting a baby. For on the counter was a stack of leaflets with a bold headline denouncing "Nigger Equality." I looked more closely and saw, again in bold letters, the words "SOCIALISTS WANT TO PUT THE NEGRO WHERE HE BELONGS SO HE CAN'T COMPETE WITH THE WHITE MAN." What kind of people were these that Chicho wanted to meet? Had he not heard me when I criticized this race hatred? I knew that any *malcriado* who thought this about *morenos* believed the same thing about us. But my husband was chuckling away with these people, folding up a piece of paper they gave him, and gesturing to me that it was time to go. It certainly was!

"What a great bunch!" he enthused as we returned to the street.

I remained silent.

"We have a name and an address," he continued, apparently unaware that I had an entirely different opinion about these "rip saws."

"We are going to meet a José Quintana." He raised his arm to hail a cab. Instead of a taxi, though, a big Buick pulled up. While the driver remained behind the wheel, a second man jumped out and showed us some kind of a badge.

"United States Department of Justice," he announced, "Bureau of Investigation. Would you folks help us out by answering some questions?"

I turned to walk back to the hotel. It had been many years since I trusted a man with a badge. Chicho, though, was eager to assist. "Certainly!" he answered. "We would be honored."

The government man, who had never offered us a name, invited us to get in the back of his car. My husband, always the gentleman, held the door for me. Despite my reluctance, I got in and Narciso followed. Our "host" climbed back in the front and his partner wordlessly drove away from the curb.

We rode only five blocks and pulled up in front of an absolutely monumental granite building with an immense dome. Carved in stone were the words "U.S. Customs House and Post Office." It was a far cry from the post office back in Edinburg! The men wordlessly led us to a second-story office with gilt letters on the door's frosted glass window. The sign said "Bureau of Investigation."

Inside we were invited to sit in two uncomfortable wooden chairs in front of a large but still unimpressive desk. One man – our "host" from the street – sat behind the desk in a leather chair that gasped as he sank into it. His driver remained standing between us and the door.

"Name?" demanded our "host."

For the first time Narciso looked as though he understood all this to be incredibly rude. "I am Narciso Garza de Pérez y Cotto, Esquire. Former

351

Lieutenant in the US Army. At your service. My wife is Mrs. Timotea Garza. May I ask for *your* names?"

The man ignored this. He asked instead, "What is the nature of your business at the offices of a disloyal newspaper?"

Chicho was now in courtroom mode. His voice deepened and his volume increased. "I am an attorney, licensed to plea before the bar in the states of Texas and Michigan. To whom am I speaking?"

This was apparently a surprise to our "host," but he did not apologize. He did, however, finally introduce himself. "I am Special Agent Frank Willey. This," he gestured to the man behind us, "is Special Agent Ian McCloud."

"It is our great pleasure to make your acquaintance," replied Chicho. It was not, for me at least, any kind of pleasure, but so far nobody had addressed me.

"We have been conducting surveillance of that office for disloyal activity," explained Agent Willey, if that was, indeed, his name. "Could you explain your business there?"

Instead of answering that, Chicho questioned him. "I am a veteran of the War in France. I served in the 23rd Infantry and was wounded in combat at Belleau Wood. May I ask where you served?"

Chicho wasn't answering Agent Willey's questions and Agent Willey wasn't answering Chicho's questions. "I am sure you understand the importance of our rooting out disloyal elements," he said. "Were you aware that the people you met in that office are IWWs?"

You, my grandchildren reading this account, will have never heard of the IWW. But just as today the mere mention of the word "communist" has people searching in closets and under floors for terrifying and vicious enemies of our freedom, so the IWW were the reds of those days. I had heard of them, but I had certainly never met one. Were the people at the "National Rip-Saw" really IWWs?

"I spoke to St. Louis Alderman Hoehn and to Board of Education member O'Hare," said Chicho. "These people are elected officials in this city. I hardly think they are bomb throwers. Are you planning on arresting them?"

Agent Willey said nothing about this, but behind us McCloud chuckled. When I turned around to look at him he stopped laughing and rearranged the bland expression on his face.

The interview was winding down, but Willey had one more question for us, or rather, for Narciso, since he hadn't even looked at me since we arrived in this office. "Do you plan on meeting any more IWWs while you are here in St. Louis?"

Chicho was quick to reply. "To my knowledge we have not met with *any* IWWs, here or elsewhere. We have no plans to meet with any IWWs, either."

With that, we were dismissed. I thought of asking the agents for a ride back to our hotel, but changed my mind. It wasn't worth taunting them over a six-block walk. On the way back down Olive Street, though, I did ask Chicho about what was really bothering me. "What did you think of those Ripsaw people?"

"They seemed nice enough," he answered. "They have nothing to do with the Magón brothers, but they know people who do."

"They were selling race hatred there," I persisted.

Narciso seemed preoccupied and didn't ask me to clarify. Instead he gestured as if to wave off my unwelcome observation. "I would still like to find this José Quintana," he said, "but I don't want to bring federal agents to his door and I certainly don't want to endanger you."

I wasn't dropping my objection: "Chicho, they were selling a pamphlet opposing racial equality."

"So?" he asked. "We're white, just like them. What difference does it make?"

Given what happened the next day I will forever regret my response. Perhaps I should have been a good wife and accepted what he said. Perhaps I should have argued, saying that any *gabacho* who used the word "nigger" for Black people didn't consider us white either. But what I did was storm off down the street. Events were soon enough going to prove me right, but not in any way that would give me satisfaction.

I ignored Narciso's efforts at conversation that day, returning to bed and allowing him to pursue whatever business he had in the city without me. I have no idea whether he went sightseeing or to the theater or to meet this Quintana person. I only know that the next day he decided to cut short our visit to St. Louis and head immediately to New Orleans. We returned to the Iron Mountain Railroad station and boarded a train for Arkansas.

I suppose some part of me still secretly believed Narciso's claims of our whiteness, because I failed to interpret the disturbing headlines in the newspapers that day as dangerous to us personally. "Negroes Plan to Kill all Whites!" they screamed in large letters. "IWWs incite ignorant Blacks!" I saw in this an exact parallel to the way the Texas newspapers reported on the mass murders of my family and friends by acting as if *we* were at fault. The Rangers and their posses hunted us down and killed us, then acted as if they were afraid that *we* were going to kill *them*! To me it proved my point from the previous day: the same people who hated Negroes hated us. But I still failed to see how *we* were in jeopardy here, a thousand miles from our Valley and far from any Texas Rangers.

We got off the train at its final stop in Helena, Arkansas. We intended to cross the Mississippi River by ferry and then continue to New Orleans on the Illinois Central. The Helena station was a small one, but then, the town of Helena wasn't even as big as Brownsville, Texas. The size of the station wasn't what struck me as we got off, though; it was the sheer number of people packed inside. There were dozens of overly excited *gabachos*, and they seemed to be of the same low class that made up the murderous posses in Texas. I remembered the newspaper story from that morning and feared for the life of any Negro who might have been traveling with us on our train.

To my terror, they immediately turned their attention instead to Narciso! "Are you an IWW?" one man demanded. What was it with these people and their IWWs?

"No, I am not," replied Narciso, with a courteous tone that I thought was entirely unwarranted given the rudeness of his questioner. "I am an attorney at law."

That silenced all of them, but only momentarily. "This is the nigger we've been looking for!" shouted the man.

And then they were all shouting. I heard the phrases "Nigger lawyer!" "Light-skin nigger!" and "Passing for white!" as they surrounded my husband, punching and kicking, and finally taking him by his hands and feet and running from the station. I fell to my knees, howling without words as the train station emptied and I lost sight of Chicho. I could hear shotgun blasts and I saw my teacher, Don Antonio, drop from his saddle while Ranger Captain Henry Ransom drove away. I could hear hundreds of rifle rounds and see my father's body cut to pieces by the cowardly Texas Rangers. I could hear the pistol shots and see little Doroteo, the boy who knew every butterfly, murdered by the *gabachos*. And then I could hear only my own wordless screams. I could see nothing through the oceans of tears. Chicho! My Chicho!

I do not know whether there is a heaven. I do not know whether I will merit admission when my days are over. I do not know whether I will meet your grandfather again in the next life. I do know that I never again laid eyes on Narciso Garza in this one. If he had survived that mob, there is nothing that could have stopped him from finding his way back to me and to your mother who was born six months later. That is how I know they killed him. But I never saw his body. There is no grave for him here in San Manuel or anywhere in Hidalgo County. He must lie, unknown and unmarked, somewhere back there in Arkansas, beside a strange river, far from family and friends.

The newspapers said nothing of his death. They reported the murders of dozens of Negroes by that mob. They reported dozens more sentenced to hang afterward by white juries. Why? The papers said it was because they planned to "kill all the white people."

Just a few years ago I read a story about a Negro civil rights leader who was there in Arkansas at that time, helping Black tenant farmers organize a lawsuit to defend their rights. Of course. In the minds of the *gabachos*, organizing a lawsuit is the same as killing all the white people. That must have been what set off the mob, what triggered all those murders, including Narciso's. These *gabachos* truly believe that they will all die if any of us is treated fairly. That man, that colored lawyer who was there, said that he escaped with his life only because a train conductor, thinking he was white, told him that there was a "damned yellow nigger passing for white" and that "the boys" were going to get him. I cried all over again when I read this. That's who the mob had been looking for. That man may have escaped "the boys" but my Chicho had not.

I have no recollection at all of how I got home. I remember getting off a train in Brownsville without any luggage. I have a few memories of the following months here in San Manuel. To this day I have no idea who sold our home in Edinburg; I have no idea where the money went. I grieved when I lost my father and my friends and my beloved teacher Don Antonio at the hands of the Rangers, but nothing unhinged me like the loss of my husband Narciso at the hands of that mob. They were bent on killing Negroes. They killed your grandfather. Losing him very nearly killed me.

355

The birth of our daughter brought me back to life. I had no choice but to name her Dolores. Really, what other name could I possibly have given her? I live now in the knowledge that I spent my last hours with Narciso in silence and in anger. I cannot undo that. It is only one of my *dolores*. My baby Dolores – your mother! – is now a grown woman of forty-five with children of her own and I still see Narciso's face in hers. I see his face in your faces, too.

Before I was even born we had lost the grant stretching back forty miles from the river. We still had our ranch in San Manuel. We still had our family. We had our fathers and grandfathers. Spanish was still the language of our Valley. The Kings and the Kenedys and all the other Anglos who came to steal our land had to learn Spanish to do it!

As a young girl I lost my teacher and my father. I even lost the sense that our lives were our own, and not something to be casually snuffed out by a *gabacho* who got here yesterday, the way he would step on an ant. But I still had the belief that our education mattered, that nobody could steal a degree the way they stole a deed.

When they stole my Narciso they took all of that. I didn't just lose the house in Edinburg; I lost the belief that I could get it back. Everything I gave your mother, *mi pobrecita* Dolores, had to be earned in the little garden I still had in San Manuel: selling vegetables, selling eggs, taking in washing. Dolores was denied even the eighth-grade education I had. Don't even mention her father's college and law degrees!

We live in what is now no more than a *colonia*, surrounded by landless refugees from Zacatecas and Tamaulipas. But though I claim ancestry in a direct line to the lords of this Valley, granted to them by King Carlos III, though I live in the birthplace of my parents and grandparents, back to my four-times great-grandparents, I am like my neighbors. I am exactly like my neighbors. *Como dijo Moisés: Peregrino soy en tierra extraña.* I am a stranger in a foreign land.

Harlem, NY
1921

To: Director John Hoover
Bureau of Investigation
From: Special Agent James Amos

As you directed I am following up the Tulsa investigation by looking into the African Blood Brotherhood in New York City. I attended their public meeting at the Church of St. Mark the Evangelist on 138th Street. The priest here has made it a home for every West Indian radical and you will find it mentioned in my previous reports on Marcus Garvey. I have seen no evidence that Father Christopher is himself a subversive, only that he is undiscriminating in his efforts to convert the neighbors to Roman Catholicism and so welcomes all sorts in the hope that they will stay for mass.

This meeting was on a Thursday night and there were 22 people in attendance, all Negro, all male, mostly West Indian. Among the few who were not, I recognized Agent 800. He sat with other veterans of the late war and we avoided contact with one another to maintain security. I was not able to identify the Captain McKaine you asked about. According to my contact in Military Intelligence Division, Agent 800 attended Officer's Candidate School with McKaine in Des Moines and served with him in France. He may know whether McKaine is in New York. He may also know whether he was in Oklahoma or not.

Among the West Indians present, I recognized Otto Huiswood (Surinam), Richard Moore (Barbados), Wilfred Domingo (Jamaica), and Hubert Harrison (St. Croix). None of these nations were included in Attorney General Palmer's deportation of radicals, but, as you requested, I will continue to explore the possibility that much of the leadership of the Brotherhood – like that of Garvey's organization – is made up of subversive foreign nationals and therefore subject to deportation without trial. I should add that Harrison is a street corner orator who now works as a public lecturer for the New York Board of Education! This is deeply disturbing and raises questions of subversion in the schools. It is a matter for somebody in your New York office to follow up.

Regarding your questions about the African Blood Brotherhood's possible role in the violence in Tulsa I remain unconvinced. At the meeting, the chairman, Cyril Briggs (Nevis), spoke approvingly and at some length about armed resistance, but without any details or specifics beyond what a person could read in the New York newspapers. He knew nothing that would suggest he had contact with anybody involved. This reinforces my observation from the scene that the armed defense of the colored neighborhoods was conducted by local veterans with no ties to any national organization, subversive or otherwise.

Before closing this report I wish to raise with you a question regarding my final report on my investigation in Tulsa. I have as yet heard nothing about any agents looking into the roles of Tate Brady, Caleb Ridley, or the Ku Klux Klan in creating an insurrection in that city. I remind you that they were responsible for untold deaths and massive destruction of property. They also threatened the life of a Federal agent, namely myself. Thank you for your attention to this matter.

I will continue to look into the activities of both Cyril Briggs and Marcus Garvey. Should Agent 800 wish to coordinate any activity with me, it is best that he communicate through you. Any direct contact between us is dangerous to us both.

McClellanville, South Carolina
1921

October 14

The new school year finds me in a new school. Charleston County Schools Superintendent McCarley called me in personally to his office and assigned me to Lincoln School in McClellanville. He informed me, in exactly these words, "Septima, this is a great step up in the world." "Septima" he called me, not "Miss Poinsette," because despite my status as an experienced teacher, he is a white man and incapable of using my last name or any courtesy title. Maybe this *is* a step up. Lincoln is a three-teacher school while Promise Land remains a two-teacher school. I can get to McClellanville by car instead of by boat, and the town seems to have recently entered the 20th century. John's Island, by contrast, often feels like a place stuck outside of time itself.

I believe this "promotion" was intended to shut me up about our campaign to get Negro teachers hired in the colored schools of the city. Most of my classmates from Avery stay quiet about the policy of only assigning us to schools out in the county. Their families are so concerned about propriety and appearances. Mother, of course, wanted me to stay out of it, too. She still cannot accept the fact that I will never be welcomed by those families, no matter how demure and well-behaved I am. We will, in any case, not give up our demand for jobs in the Charleston colored schools. If the white people of South Carolina are so determined that our schools must be separate, then we can get them to deal with the consequences, by getting *their* daughters out of *our* schools!

I am trying to assess what changes I may need to make in my teaching in this new place. One difference is that I shall not be left unsupervised. At Promise Land School we never received a visit from Superintendent McCarley. He apparently believes that Regulation 1719 (which requires annual superintendent's visits) only applies to white schools. Perhaps he is right. In any case it meant that I could try whatever I wanted in my efforts to get the children to learn, because nobody was coming to check on me! But Lincoln School has high school students and a higher profile and I am told that Superintendent McCarley visits every year. Also, at Promise Land School I was the principal, so I was answering to myself. Here at Lincoln School, the Reverend Samuel Howard will be my principal. He is also the full-time teacher of grades ten to twelve, so he won't be in my classroom all the time, but I will have to see just what manner of person and supervisor he is.

I was extremely disappointed to receive a letter from Mr. Osceola McKaine informing me that he is leaving the United States to seek a home in Europe. I confess that I still held out hope that he might return here to South Carolina and that he and I might be more than pen pals. It is so hard for me to acknowledge that Mother is right about anything, especially when she seems to take such pleasure in my defeats. When he remained in New York after his service in France she told me that he would never come back here. She also said, and I think she smiled, that if he had any interest in me he would have declared it. I was so excited about the work he was undertaking among the veterans for the uplift of our race that I argued the point with her. And, in truth, had he asked me to join him in New York? Well, I would have gone immediately, wedding proposal or no. But, alas, he saw our friendship in a different light than I. Now I am twenty-three. If I am not to become a spinster schoolteacher, I must carefully evaluate my prospects. Yet another truth that Mother has been insisting on for longer than I care to remember.

October 28

Today was Frances Willard Day. South Carolina school law requires us to conduct an entire day of instruction on the evils of alcoholic drink and narcotics. This is all a thinly-disguised attack on our race. Miss Willard was a leader in the movement for woman's suffrage. She was one of those who argued for women's right to vote, while demanding that it be taken from us! She claimed that our race is undeserving of the franchise because we are ignorant drunks and that our men are all rapists, obsessed with white women. She spoke out for years, not only against drink, but against card playing, dancing, and even athletics. Yet she was endlessly reluctant to condemn lynching. Even when she finally, after years of being asked, denounced what she politely termed "lawlessness," she couldn't stop herself from blaming the *victims* of lynching, repeating the oft-told lie that they were perpetrators of unspeakable outrages. Moreover, she insisted at the same time on verbally attacking the character of our great shining leader, Mrs. Ida Wells-Barnett, simply because Mrs. Wells-Barnett spoke the truth about Miss Willard's defense of lynch murder. Miss Willard's calumnies against Mrs. Wells-Barnett were carefully calculated to harm the campaign against lynching.

I informed Principal Howard of my objections to devoting a day in Miss Willard's honor. I informed him that at a time when the white press considers the phrase "dope fiend" to be a synonym for Negro, narcotics education is anti-Negro education. He did not contradict any word I said. He merely informed me that we are employees of Charleston County and bound by Section 1820 of the General School Law of South Carolina which requires that the fourth Friday in

360

October be observed as Frances Willard Day. I don't know why he is so afraid of his white masters. Perhaps he is more vulnerable to them than I was on John's Island. In any case, my children heard me read aloud from Mrs. Wells-Barnett's book condemning lynching, *The Red Record*. I shared the chapter on Miss Willard's defense of lynching and her disgusting personal attacks on Mrs. Wells-Barnett. And that is how we celebrated Frances Willard Day in the sixth, seventh, and eighth grades at the Lincoln School of McClellanville!

November 21

Compared with the Promise Land School we are relatively well-supplied with textbooks here at Lincoln School. Compared with the Promise Land School we have a nicer building, too. That other comparison, though! The white children here just got a brand-new, up-to-date building. I suppose that fifty years from now, when they're ready for something even newer, they will give that building to us, just like they give us their old textbooks. I saw Superintendent McCarley's budget this week. On average he is spending $30.69 a year for each white student and $8.68 per colored student.

I brought this disparity to the attention of Principal Howard. He suggested an alternative way of looking at it, an alternative which I find subservient and infuriating. He reminded me that our budget is four times the state average for colored schools. I wish he didn't feel the necessity to defend this barbaric Jim Crow system. I know that Principal Howard is much more exposed to the whims of white supervisors than I ever was on Johns Island. He tries very hard, and is personally very charming. But I find it hard to accept his justifications, especially when it is only we two talking. This state is so backward. They cry that the education budget had to be cut because of the two-thirds drop in cotton prices since the end of the War, and by the ravages of the boll weevil on the cotton crop. If that were the reason for cheating us, we should have been flush with school supplies and new construction during the wartime boom!

My real problem with Principal Howard is rather a byproduct of what we *have* than of what we do not. At Promise Land School my greatest successes came when I brought the children's own knowledge into the curriculum: their stories, their recipes, their observations of and, truthfully, their participation in adult work. Here in McClellanville I have pupils who help their mothers make sweetgrass baskets, who help their fathers make shrimp nets, who know all sorts of stories about *haints* and *boogers*. But Principal Howard insists that we use the textbooks we are given, these dusty, torn, hand-me-downs with their white Dicks and Janes, their colored mammies, their heroic tales of the War Against

Northern Aggression, and their dry recipes for tasteless food. For my part, I am tired of fighting with him about this.

December 12

I will be spending the Christmas holiday again this year at Mother and Father's house on Henrietta Street. I need the time to get away from McClellanville and think. My principal, Reverend Howard, has hinted that he would like a closer, more intimate relationship. He is a widower who recently took over the A.M.E. church that his daddy founded here some fifty years ago. He is exactly the type of suitor that Mother has been hoping will woo me; he is a professional man, and affiliated with a high-class church. Perhaps I am reluctant because Mother would like him, but he is 43-years old and has a little boy, Samuel the Third! His stodginess is barely hinted at by the way he broaches the subject of marriage with me: He tells me that his parishioners believe that a pastor should be married. He tells me that I would make an ideal preacher's wife. I cannot imagine anything less romantic.

Meanwhile, I have been receiving increasingly passionate letters from Nerie Clark. He is a sailor I met at a dance two years ago. I entertained this correspondence without much seriousness because I was still imagining a future with Captain McKaine and… how to compare the two? Nerie never writes about political or social questions. He never asks about my teaching or my students. But he is so handsome. And when he has been in port and we have time together, he is so much fun to be with. I would be less than honest if I did not admit that perhaps I enjoy how much Mother hates him and hates the idea of my being with him. He does not propose the thought of our marriage as if it will advance his career. He proposes it as a great adventure. I only worry that he will be the one having the adventure as he cruises the seas with the Navy while I constantly await his return. Still, I am already twenty-three years old. My chance to find a husband may be passing me by.

Already the great hopes we all had of a new and more democratic America seem drowned in the blood of the last few years. Even Captain McKaine, a hero of our struggle, fled in despair. In his last letter he informs me that he has opened a restaurant in Belgium where – or so he claims – we are treated as people. I am almost incredulous to read that the country of King Leopold, the butcher of the Congo, is better for us than America. Perhaps it is true. Perhaps it is a measure of just how badly off we are. I hope that someday I can contribute to our larger struggle. For now I can only do my best to educate the children I see every day. And perhaps find some measure of happiness for myself. Maybe someday my teaching and my happiness will contribute to our freedom.

Leavenworth, Kansas
1921

"13111!" shouted the guard.

"Here!" answered Joey Quintana.

It was freezing this morning – literally freezing, the puddles from last night's rain completely iced over – but the sky was clear, the sun was out, and once they broke formation he would warm up from the work. For now, Joey was shivering in his light, prison-issue jacket, but he was happy to be outdoors on this construction crew building a shop for the penitentiary's shoe manufacturing business. He could turn his back on the limestone and steel battlements, ignore the guards on the walls, and pretend that this was a job. He could breathe real air. This November morning he could hear the honking of a million *ánsaras* migrating down the Missouri River a mile and a half away. He might be incarcerated, but they were not.

Roll called, all present or accounted for, the hack turned the crew over to its inmate foreman, James McNamara, #9431. He was a union ironworker and better qualified for supervising construction than anybody, prisoner or guard. Mac assigned tasks for the day and Joey began setting the big limestone blocks from the prison quarry. He worked, as usual, with his cellmate, Gabriel Joyner, #12252. The other prisoners were always surprised to learn that Joey and Gabriel knew one another prior to their incarceration. They asked where a Negro soldier crossed paths with a Mexican-American union organizer. Neither ever elaborated. Joey would sometimes say they met over a card game, but nothing more. Both Gabriel and Joey found it too painful to think about the fate of the other players who had been at that table.

Mac set the pace for the crew with a song, "Oh, Where Is My Wandering Boy Tonight." Nobody on the crew joined in with the sentimental ballad. They didn't like the maudlin lyrics and they really didn't like the tempo. "Again with 'the child of my love and prayer'?" complained Gabriel. But the hacks liked to hear the convicts sing. It seemed to entertain them, and they believed it sped the work.

As soon as Mac finished, and before he could start with "Farewell to Skibbereen" or "Danny Boy," Ralph Chaplin, #13104, began to sing. Out in the world, Ralph and his cellmate, Harrison George, #13158, were writers and intellectuals, but here in Leavenworth they were hauling materials – limestone and mortar – to those inmates like Joey who were working as stonemasons. To the tune of "John Brown's Body" Ralph sang, "When the union's inspiration through the worker's blood shall run…" They were Ralph's own lyrics and everybody, including Mac, joined in singing "Solidarity Forever." Because Leavenworth Prison was not primarily a place for robbers and check kiters and pimps. No, most of the two-thousand-and-some inmates in Leavenworth were prisoners of what Joey thought of as the class war.

James McNamara had bombed the offices of the *Los Angeles Times* ten years earlier during a labor dispute. Ralph Chaplin and Harrison George were tried and convicted with a hundred other IWWs in Chicago on trumped-up charges of espionage for opposing the War. Gabriel Joyner and dozens of his fellow soldiers in the 24th US Infantry were sent up for defending themselves against racist police in Houston. Joey himself had been convicted in Sacramento of sedition and opposing the War. And that was just on this one work gang.

Ricardo Flores Magón, the great propagandist of the Mexican Revolution was here in Leavenworth, inmate #14596. Ben Fletcher, the Negro trade unionist and head of the Philadelphia longshoremen was here, too, #13126. George Andreytchine, an intellectual and follower of Tolstoy and Thoreau from Minnesota was here, #13101. Earl Browder, a conscientious objector from only 35 miles away in Olathe, Kansas was here, #13314. Price Street, #12196, and his friend Arie Hardy, #12032, were here, both Black Seminole Indians and tenant farmers from Oklahoma. All of these men were convicted of opposing the War. The War had ended over three years ago, but more than a thousand men were still locked up in this grim penitentiary for speaking against it.

Even the other inmates were turning into political prisoners. Inmate 13396, José Martinez, was here on federal murder charges, but he had attached himself to Magón, studied history and philosophy, and was now a revolutionary. Inmate 13984, Joseph Jones, had been imprisoned for an assault he committed when he was a Vermont National Guardsman in the Philippines. His cellmate was Ben Fletcher, so now Joe was a well-read activist for Negro liberation. Most famous of all was inmate 15461, the former heavyweight boxing champion of the world, Jack Johnson. He was locked up in Leavenworth on sexual assault charges. Since the "assault" in question was traveling across state lines with his own white wife, it was clear to everybody that his actual crime had been beating white men in the ring. To the other inmates, that made Johnson a political prisoner, too.

When Ralph's song was done, Jesse Sullivan picked up the lead. Sullivan had been a career soldier, a corporal in the 24th Infantry with Joey's cellmate, Gabriel. Nineteen of their barracks mates were executed in secret for the so-called "mutiny" in Houston against racist police violence. Jesse, like Gabriel, was spared that. Now he was inmate #12275, sentenced to life in prison. He led them in the army song, "Mama, Mama Can't You See?" The prisoners liked the soldier songs: they were new every day, with lyrics that made them laugh about where they were and what they were doing.

He began as usual, lining the first two verses and letting the rest of them repeat each of them back:

Mama, mama can't you see
What this camp has done to me?

And then he got right into the satirical commentary:

Bread and parsnips for my meal
Warden Morgan made a deal.

It was true. There had been precious little meat in the stew the last few days. But what was the deal Sullivan was talking about?

Inmates can you fancy that?
Sold our beef for his wife's new hat!

And everybody laughed. All the men had seen Mrs. Morgan go out Sunday morning with a fancy peach-basket style on her head, covered with ribbons and flowers. But it took Jesse Sullivan's sharp eye (and sharper tongue) to connect her church crown with their diet.

He wasn't done with the topical observations:

Captain Leonard can't you see?
Mennonites are going free.

And that was true. There were dozens of religious pacifists – Mennonites and others – in the prison, locked up for their conscientious objection to the draft. They refused to fight in the army and they refused to work here at Leavenworth because of their conviction that their prison work, too, contributed to the war. The head guard, "Bull" Leonard, had ordered that they be beaten and put in solitary for weeks at a time. Several had died of exposure after being mercilessly hosed with water in their cold cells. Now President Harding had issued pardons for those who remained alive. Most of the politicals were hoping that the president might consider pardons for them. But they were a little muted in calling back the words that Sullivan lined, because – truth be told – they were intimidated by the vicious hack, Captain Leonard.

Sullivan, though, was undeterred by their subdued response:

> We want pardons and we want them fast
> Captain Leonard can kiss my…

Silence. Joey looked up in time to see Jesse Sullivan collapse to the ground, unconscious. Standing over him was Captain Bull Leonard, holding his prized spring-loaded blackjack. When had he arrived? Maybe the *viejos* back home were right about the devil: *"Nombrando al ruin de Roma, por la puerta asoma."*

"Any of you other niggers got something to say?" Leonard demanded. "What about you fucking reds? You're so fucking smart and so fucking well-read; say something smart now!"

Nobody answered, which seemed to enrage him even more. "This is not a fucking Soviet!" he shouted. "*I* run this joint!" This was Leonard's latest bizarre obsession. Despite every evidence that he did, in fact, run this brutal hellhole, he had begun daily rants about a "Leavenworth Soviet," as if he secretly believed that an elected committee of prisoners was calling all the shots.

"You?" he asked Mac. The foreman looked at the ground. "You?" he menaced Morris Levine, a young IWW from Seattle. Levine, inmate #13162, was frozen. "What about you?"

He stood over inmate #13144. Vincent St. John was 45 years old and looked twenty years older than that. At one time he had been a prominent member of the IWW, Secretary-Treasurer in fact. It was St. John who sent Joey to Mexico as an organizer for the union fifteen years before. But the shootings and beatings took a toll on him, as did the ideological and personal disputes among the leadership. When the War started St. John was living alone, not far from Joey's home village in New Mexico, prospecting a claim in the hills behind Los Cerrillos. That didn't stop the Bureau of Investigation from arresting him. That didn't stop Judge Landis from convicting him of sedition and espionage in the Chicago mass trial. Now a rabid, reactionary hack was threatening St. John with a blackjack. He sighed, audibly.

"What did you say, you fucking red bastard?" Captain Leonard brought his blackjack swiftly down behind St. John's right ear. St. John fell like a bag of laundry. But Leonard wasn't done. He bent over the inmate's inert body and continued raining blows on him as if… as if… Joey could not finish the thought. He simply couldn't imagine what Leonard was thinking.

Next to Joey his cellmate, Gabriel Joyner, whispered, "Somebody needs to put a shiv in that ofay motherfucker."

¡Ojalá! thought Joey. They all stood silent. Joey heard the geese honking again, directly overhead now. Free. They couldn't fly away like the geese, but they, too, could sing. Joey lifted his voice and began singing the opening words of the old song that had become the Leavenworth inmates' unofficial anthem. "Arise, you prisoners of starvation!"

Gabriel joined in immediately, "Arise, you wretched of the earth!"

And then the whole gang was singing, "For justice thunders condemnation."

Captain Leonard was apoplectic, but he seemed to have temporarily exhausted himself for further beatings. He snarled, "Get back to work!"

And they did. But they all continued singing. In a minute, Leonard would move on to brutalize some other inmate on some other work gang. In a minute, they would seek medical attention for Vincent St. John and Jesse Sullivan. For now, their song reminded them that – as bad as things might appear – the struggle was not over.

"A better world's in birth!" they sang.

"Rector!" welcomed Nessa as the apartment door opened. She sounded as enthusiastic as if she hadn't seen him in a month.

"How do you know it's me?" laughed Rector Beauchamp. "Anybody could come walking in through this unlocked door."

"Were you able to get a day at P.S. 119?" Nessa asked. The school was diagonally across from their apartment on 134th Street and a sometime source of employment. But as she came out of the kitchen and saw him in his work clothes, she knew the answer.

"Miss Larson said she didn't need a substitute teacher today," he explained. "I changed real quick, hurried downtown with Jim Rosco, and was able to get a day loading the S.S. Lafayette on Pier 51." Rosco was a boarder with their upstairs neighbors, Tony and Ella Stevens. He worked as a longshoreman on the West Side, mostly handling passenger luggage for the French Line.

"When do you think you'll be able to get a regular teaching job?" wondered Nessa.

"My best guess?" asked Rector. "Never." He had been thinking about this for the better part of a year now, since not long after their arrival in New York City. "I don't think they want to hire any regular teachers at all, not to mention Negroes. They hang on to those Class 1 licenses like it's their grandma's engagement ring. They save so much money by hiring subs, it's no wonder they won't give out a regular license."

"Sadie got a job over there," objected Nessa.

"The cake lady? She taught for five years in North Carolina before she got here, and they still wouldn't hire her until she got a master's degree from Columbia. *And* hired a locution teacher so she could learn to talk like a white woman. *And* why do you think she sells all those cakes? She got that Class 1 license and she still can't live on what they pay her."

"It sounds to me like you're giving up," said Nessa. "Did you even go over there this morning?"

"Yes, I did, baby." He paused because he didn't like her challenging his word this way. He took a deep breath and then went on, "Yes, I did. But I am really thinking about signing on regular on the ships."

Nessa understood his pause; appreciated his restraint. She waited a moment before going on. "Baby, you have a college diploma."

"Yes, I do," Rector answered. "But not one that they recognize here in New York. Leastways not when it's held by a Negro."

This was something that Nessa understood very well. She had been going downtown with Ella Stevens everyday to clean rich white ladies' homes and she didn't like it. Maybe these South Carolina Negroes were used to taking care of white folks, but she was from Boley, Oklahoma and she was a high school graduate. For her it was like anthropological fieldwork, not a career. And she had something to say on this same subject that she hadn't told Rector about yet.

"I went to register at Hunter College today," she began.

"That is *great* news!" smiled Rector. "How did that go?"

"Not well," admitted Nessa. "They don't recognize my diploma."

"Don't recognize it?" He began shaking his head. *New York.* "Any options?"

"Actually, the lady there took some time asking about Boley High and the courses I took there. She listed the exact credits I still need to get a New York diploma. And she told me who to speak to at Wadleigh High School if I want to take them now."

Rector was thunderstruck. "With a bunch of young girls?" he asked. "You're a grown woman."

"Yes, I am," said Nessa. "But that is not what's making me hesitate." She smiled.

Rector shook his head again, this time in puzzlement. He shrugged and made a face as if to ask, "What?"

Ness smiled a little more broadly. "I'm three weeks late," she said.

The puzzled look stayed for another second or two. Then understanding dawned across his face, his jaw dropped, his eyes opened wide, and he rushed to take his wife in his arms. "Baby," he laughed. "That is the best news! You had to wait all this time to tell me that?"

"We won't know for awhile. I could just be late. But I couldn't wait any longer. I just had to let you know."

Rector just said, "That is the best news!" And then, again, "That is the best news!" He hugged her and hugged her.

Nessa finally pushed herself back a few inches from his tight embrace. "Baby, I have to ask. If it's a boy, can we name him Ezekiel?"

He pulled her close again. "Why would you even need to ask?" said Rector Beauchamp. "Of course we will. Of course our son will be Ezekiel."

Nessa blinked back her tears. "Ezekiel Owalv," she said, adding the Creek and Seminole word for "prophet." "Because our children can never forget that they're native, too."

Somewhere nearby a neighbor cranked up a Victrola. The trumpet and trombone notes of the opening bars were unmistakable, "There'll Be Some Changes Made." It was the most popular recording in Harlem that year. Already embracing, Nessa and Rector began to dance along. But the juxtaposition of sad and happy news gave the song a different meaning. Rector would give up teaching, Nessa college; but there would be a new baby. Nessa's Daddy was gone, but perhaps she would have a son. The world as it was had taken so much from them, but there was still promise of a world to be. They were still living. They were still standing. They could still continue the struggle. So Nessa began to sing along with Ethel Waters. And now the song had stopped being a story about a disappointed lover. Today it had turned into a story about entire peoples and about that promise, the promise of a world to be:

> There's a change in the weather, a change in the sea
> From now on there'll be a change in me
> My walk will be different, my talk and my name
> Nothing about me's going to be the same.

When the record ended, Nessa wanted to say something more about Ezekiel, her Daddy. But the elevated train was going up Eighth Avenue, just down the block, and it drowned out all conversation with its loud clatter. Today, though, even the rattle of the IRT had taken on a new meaning:

He said to me, "Son of man, can these bones live again?"
And I said, "Lord God, only You know."

There was a noise, a rattling sound, and the bones came together, bone to bone.

So the Lord God said to the bones, "Here! I bring breath into you and you will live!

The breath entered them and they came to life, a vast multitude.

And so it was.

Glossary

For monolingual English readers, here is some of the vocabulary from this book .

Abrazo (Spanish) Hug, embrace

Abuela/o (Spanish) Grandmother/grandfather

Acequia (Spanish) Irrigation ditch

Acezintle (Spanish) Box elder tree

Agringada(o) (Spanish) Like a gringo

Ajuyentao (Spanish) A person who avoids their home place

Álamo (Spanish) Poplar tree, aspen tree

Anciana/o (Spanish) Senior citizen

Añil del muerto (Spanish) Goldweed, a medicinal herb

Aŋpawí (Lakota)Sun

Baile (Spanish) Dance

Balen Gabidan (Yuchi) Chief

Bárbara/o (Spanish) Savage

Basto (Spanish) Card suit, clubs

Bigotali (Apache) Deer Dance

Bisabuela/o (Spanish) Great-grandparent

Bolsero de Altamira (Spanish) A bird, yellow Texas Oriole

Borracha/o (Spanish) Drunk

Buckra (English) White man

Bulto (Spanish) A carved image of a saint

Burro (Spanish) Donkey

Cafecito (Spanish) Small cup of coffee

Capilla (Spanish) Chapel

Campesino (Spanish) Farmer, peasant

Camposanto (Spanish) Cemetery

Capilla (Spanish) Chapel

Casquería (Spanish) Entrails, organ meats

Cehekares (Muskogee) Good Bye

Čhaŋkpé Ópi Wakpála (Lakota)Wounded Knee Creek

Chara (Spanish) A bird, jay

Chiltepines (Spanish) A variety of small, spicy peppers

Chipe (Spanish) A bird, warbler

Chupaflor (Spanish) Hummingbird

Cobarde (Spanish) Coward

Comai (Spanish) *Comadre*, godmother to one's child or mother to one's godchild

Compa (Spanish) Buddy, pal

Contrayerba (Spanish) Caltrop, a medicinal herb

Corrido (Spanish) Ballad

Cuate (Spanish) Friend, pal

Curandera/o (Spanish) Healer

Cvhahtv (Muskogee) Black locust tree

Damisela (Spanish) Damselfly

Demonio (Spanish) Demon, devil

Descanso (Spanish) Rest stop in a funeral procession, shrine where a person was killed

Doliente (Spanish) Mourner

Don Nadie (Spanish) Nobody

Encino (Spanish) Live oak

Epitaphios (Greek) A large cloth icon with an image of the dead body of Christ, his mother, and other Gospel figures

Escopeta (Spanish) Rifle

Estecate (Muskogee) Native American

Estelvste (Muskogee) Black person, usually a Black Creek Indian

Fulanita/o (Spanish) Whoever, Jane/John Doe

Gabacho (Spanish) An American

Golondrino (Spanish) Brown horse

Gringa/o (Spanish) White American

Grulla cenicienta (Spanish) Sandhill Crane

Güero (Spanish) Blonde

Haŋbléčheya (Lakota) Vision quest, to cry for a spiritual experience

Haŋwí (Lakota) Moon

Heliotropo (Spanish) A flower, sometimes called scorpion tail

Hierba dulce (Spanish) Oregano

Hierba Negra (Spanish) A flower, sometimes called lantana

Hokȟátȟo (Lakota) blue heron

Húŋkpapȟa (Lakota) One of the seven Lakota tribes.

Huphéstola (Lakota) Bear grass

Iktómi (Lakota) Trickster, spider

Juve (Spanish) Southwestern coreopsis flower

Kineño (Texas) Employee of the 825,000 acre King Ranch

Khiíŋyaŋka Očháŋku (Lakota) Great race track, Red Valley, a geological depression surrounding the Black Hills of South Dakota

Kvco (Muskogee) Berry

Laguna (Spanish) Small lake

Malcriada/o (Spanish) Poorly-raised person, without manners

Manofashica/o (Spanish) A ludicrous person

Mariposa (Spanish) Butterfly

Mastranzo (Spanish) Apple mint, a medicinal herb

Mastrique (Spanish) A medicinal herb

Matanza (Spanish) Slaughter, butchering

Mayordomo (Spanish) Superintendent, steward

Micco (Muskogee) Chief

Mojada/o (Spanish) Wet, border crosser

Moreno (Spanish) Black, African American

Mvskoke (Muskogee) The Muskogee or Creek language

Nieta/a (Spanish) Grandchild

Nopal (Spanish) The pad of a prickly pear cactus

Ofay (English) White man

Paisano (Spanish) Countryman, homie

Partera (Spanish) Midwife

Pȟeháŋǧila (Lakota)Sandbill Crane

Pȟeháŋ ská (Lakota) Egret

Pȟeží wakȟáŋ (Lakota) Panic grass

Pȟežísla Wakpá (Lakota) Greasy Grass Creek, Little Big Horn Creek

Pȟeží šašá ókhihe tȟaŋkíŋkiŋyaŋ (Lakota) Big bluestem

Pinche (Spanish) Vulgarity that emphasizes an insult

Pisanica (Croatian) Easter eggs

Plashchanitsa (Slavonic) A large cloth icon with an image of the dead body of Christ, his mother, and other Gospel figures

Posketv (Muskogee) A fast day, Green Corn Dance

Ptéȟčaka (Lakota) Buffalo

Ptesáŋwiŋ (Lakota) White Buffalo Woman

Quinceañera (Spanish) A girl's formal debut, fifteenth birthday party

Rancho (Spanish) Hamlet, cattle ranch

Regla (Spanish) Gift, euphemism for menstrual period

Resaca (Spanish) Oxbow lake, former river channel

Resolaniar (Spanish) Hang around

Retablo (Spanish) Altar piece, a sacred icon

Rinchada (Spanish) The 1915 pogrom against Mexican Americans, Ranger terror

Rinche (Spanish) Texas Ranger

Roble (Spanish) Oak tree

Romerillo del llano (Spanish) Silver sage, a medicinal herb

Safke (Muskogee) Hominy soup, the national dish of the Creek Indians

Šahíyela (Lakota) Cheyenne Indian

Sakkonepke (Muskogee) Hominy and meat stew

Sauce (Spanish) Weeping willow

Seditty (English) High class, stuck up

Sičháŋǧu (Lakota) One of the seven Lakota tribes, also known as Brulé

Sinvergüenza/o (Spanish) Shameless person

Sipȟáwičhakaše (Lakota) Buffalo grass

Súŋkawakȟáŋ (Lakota) Horse

Susto (Spanish) Shock, possession

Svtv Semvnole (Muskogee) Persimmon

Taffadal (Arabic) Please, an invitation to do something

Tȟatȟaŋka (Lakota) Buffalo bull

Tȟayámni pȟá (Lakota) A constellation, the Pleiades

Tejano (Spanish) Texan descended from the people who lived there before it was the United States

Tȟanáǧila (Lakota) Hummingbird

Thióšpaye (Lakota) An extended family

Tsisinstsistots (Cheyenne) The Cheyenne language

Vendido (Spanish) Sell-out

Vieja/o (Spanish) Old person

Viejita/o (Spanish) Old person

Wačhípi (Lakota) A dance

Wagmíza Wakpála (Lakota) Corn Creek

Wápaha kamnímnila pȟeží (Lakota) sideoats grama

Wakíŋyaŋ (Lakota) thunder, the thunderers

Wašíču (Lakota) Fat taker, white person

Wičháša wakȟáŋ (Lakota) Holy man, medicine man

Wiwáŋyaŋg Wačhípi (Lakota) Sun Dance

Wvcenv (Muskogee) White American

Yerba buena (Spanish) Spearmint, a medicinal herb

Yerba mosquera (Spanish) Woody fleabane, a medicinal herb

Yerbanis (Spanish) A medicinal herb

Thank You

Maya Frank-Levine spent countless hours away from her paying work to edit this book. She helped me with clarity, with keeping the voices distinct, and with holding to one point of view in each section. She called me out for problems of expression and repetition. I cannot find words to sufficiently express my gratitude. The remaining infelicities are, of course, all mine.

Jeff Brody and Jon Levine looked over early drafts, too, and I am grateful for their comments and for their support.

Maria Joyce-Vilorio went over my Spanish and Awa Gaye rewrote my French. Again, if you find errors now, they are most definitely mine.

Lots of archivists provided me with historical materials. I want to mention Tawa Ducheneaux, though, in particular. She is archivist at the Oglala Lakota College library in Kyle, South Dakota. In the midst of catastrophic flooding at Pine Ridge in late winter 2019 she somehow found time to send me the minutes of meetings about the Black Hills lawsuit from 1920.

Judith Scott lived with me through this. I inhabited some very dark corners of our nation's history during the years I researched this book and I was not easy to be with. She was unfailing in her support. I read large chunks of it aloud to her. She listened with a critical ear and helped me get the voices right. I also changed one voice completely when she made it clear that she did not want to hear one more word from that man's mouth. I love you and admire you! Thank you!

If you have read this far, thank you, too! I am so glad to be able to share this work. Don't be afraid to check out the historicity of the events in this novel. I moved a few, in space and in time. But I don't have the imagination to create the horrors I have related here.

Made in the USA
Las Vegas, NV
04 April 2021

20763909R00225